"THE GOVERNMENTS OF THE WORLD SHOULD KNOW THAT...ISLAM WILL BE VICTORIOUS IN ALL THE COUNTRIES OF THE WORLD, AND ISLAM AND THE TEACHINGS OF THE QUR'AN WILL PREVAIL ALL OVER THE WORLD."

AYATOLLAH RUHOLLAH KHOMEINI,
JANUARY 1979

"ONE BOMB IS ENOUGH TO DESTROY ISRAEL....IN DUE TIME, THE ISLAMIC WORLD WILL HAVE A MILITARY NUCLEAR DEVICE."

AKBAR HASHEMI RAFSANJANI,
FORMER PRESIDENT OF IRAN,
DECEMBER 2001

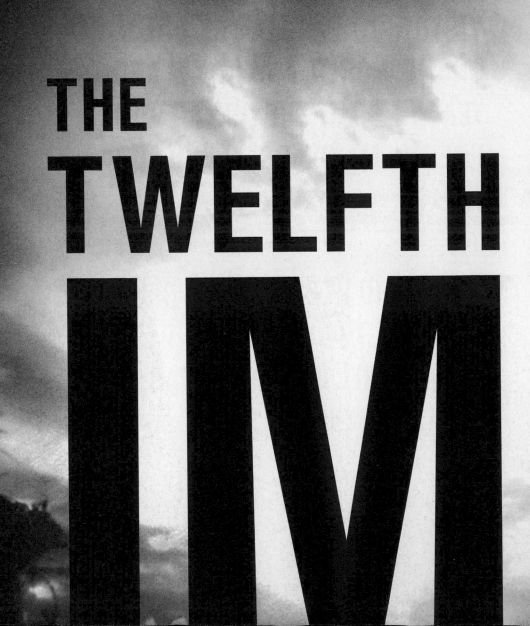

THE
TWELFTH
IM

JOEL C. ROSENBERG

TYNDALE HOUSE PUBLISHERS, INC. / CAROL STREAM, ILLINOIS

Visit Tyndale's exciting Web site at www.tyndale.com.

Visit Joel C. Rosenberg's Web site at www.joelrosenberg.com.

TYNDALE and Tyndale's quill logo are registered trademarks of Tyndale House Publishers, Inc.

The Twelfth Imam

Designed by Dean H. Renninger

Library of Congress Cataloging-in-Publication Data

Rosenberg, Joel C., date.
    The twelfth Imam / Joel C. Rosenberg.
      p. cm.
    ISBN 978-1-4143-1163-0
1. Intelligence officers—United States—Fiction. 2. Nuclear warfare—Prevention—Fiction. 3. Iran—Fiction. 4. Middle East—Fiction. 5. Prophecy—Islam—Fiction. I. Title. II. Title: 12th Imam.
    PS3618.O832T84 2010
    813'.6—dc22   2010030082

ISBN 978-1-4143-3977-1 (International Trade Paper Edition)

Printed in the United States of America

16 15 14 13 12 11 10
7   6   5   4   3   2   1

To all our friends in Iran and the Middle East, yearning to be free.

CAST OF CHARACTERS

AMERICANS

David Shirazi (aka Reza Tabrizi)—CIA operative, Tehran

Dr. Mohammad Shirazi—father of David Shirazi; cardiologist

Nasreen Shirazi—mother of David and wife of Mohammad Shirazi

Charlie Harper—political officer, Foreign Service Office, Iran

Claire Harper—wife of Charlie Harper

Marseille Harper—daughter of Charlie and Claire Harper

Jack Zalinsky—senior operative, Central Intelligence Agency

Eva Fischer—field officer, Central Intelligence Agency

William Jackson—president of the United States

IRANIANS

Ayatollah Hamid Hosseini—Supreme Leader

Ahmed Darazi—president of Iran

Dr. Mohammed Saddaji—nuclear physicist, deputy director of the Atomic Energy Organization of Iran

Farah Saddaji—wife of Dr. Saddaji

Najjar Malik—physicist, Atomic Energy Organization of Iran

Sheyda Malik—wife of Najjar, daughter of Dr. Saddaji

Abdol Esfahani—deputy director of technical operations, Telecommunication Company of Iran (Iran Telecom)

Daryush Rashidi—president and CEO of Iran Telecom

Dr. Alireza Birjandi—preeminent scholar of Shia Islamic eschatology

Ali Faridzadeh—Iranian minister of defense

Mohsen Jazini—commander of the Iranian Revolutionary Guard Corps

PART ONE

★ ★ ★ ★ ★

1

Charlie Harper was still five or six hundred yards from the compound, but he was alone; even if he could fight his way through the rapidly growing mob, he still had no plan to rescue those trapped inside.

He could hear gunfire. He could taste the acrid stench of thick, black smoke rising into the crisp, early morning air. He could feel the searing heat of the bonfires as American flags and tires and someone's overturned car were being torched all around him. He could see the rage in the eyes of the young men—thousands of them, maybe tens of thousands, bearded, shouting, screaming, out of control—surrounding the embassy and threatening to overrun its grounds. He just had no idea what to do.

It was the twenty-six-year-old's first assignment with the State Department. He was the most junior political officer in the country and had no field experience. He and his beautiful, spirited young bride, Claire, had been married only a year. They'd been in Tehran since September 1—barely two months. He didn't even know the names of most of his colleagues behind the compound walls. But though he increasingly feared for their safety, he still refused to believe that he was personally in mortal danger.

How could he be? Charles David Harper loved Iran in a way that made little sense to him, much less to his bride. Growing up on the South Side of Chicago, he hadn't known anyone from Iran. He'd never been here before. He'd never even been close. But inexplicably he had fallen in love with the Persian people somewhere along the way. He loved the complexity of this ancient, exotic culture. He loved the mysterious rhythm of modern Tehran, even filled as it was with religious extremists and militant secularists. And he especially loved the food—*khoroshte fesenjoon* was his latest favorite, a savory stew of roast lamb, pomegranates, and walnuts, which the Shirazis, their next-door neighbors—God bless them—had already made for him and Claire twice since they had arrived at this post.

The language of Iran had been a joy for Charlie to absorb and master. He'd picked up Farsi quickly as an undergraduate at Stanford. He'd sharpened it carefully in graduate school at Harvard. When he joined the State Department upon graduation, he'd been placed immediately on the fast track to become a Foreign Service officer, was rushed through basic diplomatic training, and was sent to Tehran for his first assignment. He'd been thrilled every step along the way. Thrilled with using Farsi every day. Thrilled with being thrown into a highly volatile political cauldron. Thrilled with trying to understand the dynamic of Khomeini's revolution from the inside. And convinced that the sooner he could get his sea legs, the sooner he could truly help Washington understand and navigate the enormous social and cultural upheaval under way inside Iran.

The violent outbursts of the students, Charlie was convinced, were spasmodic. This one would pass like a summer thunderstorm, as all the others had. The dark clouds would pass. The sun would come out again. They just needed to be patient. As a couple. As a country.

Charlie glanced at his watch. It was barely six thirty in the morning. Since hearing on the radio back at his apartment the initial reports of trouble, he'd been running flat out for nearly nine blocks, but that was no longer possible—too many people and too little space. As he inched his way forward, he could see the top floors of the chancery, not far from Roosevelt Gate, the embassy's main entrance, but he knew he'd never make it there from this side. He'd have to find another way inside—perhaps through the consulate offices in the compound's northwest corner.

Winded, his soaked shirt sticking to his back, Charlie shifted gears.

He began trying to move laterally through the mob. His relative youth, dark hair, and dark brown eyes—a gift from his mother's Italian heritage—seemed to help him blend in somewhat, though he suddenly wished he had a beard. And a gun.

He could feel the situation steadily deteriorating. The Marines were nowhere to be seen. They were no longer guarding the main gate or even patrolling the fence, so far as he could tell. He assumed they had pulled back to defend the buildings on the compound—the chancery, the ambassador's house, the house of the deputy chief of mission, the consulate, and the warehouse (aka, "Mushroom Inn"), along with various other offices and the motor pool. Charlie wasn't a military man, but he figured that decision was probably wise tactically. He could feel the mass of bodies surging forward, again and again. It wouldn't be long before these wild-eyed students burst through the gate.

Would the Marines open fire when that finally happened? How could they? It would be a bloodbath. And yet how could they not? Many of the young men around him had pistols. Some had rifles. Some of them were already firing into the air. What if the students actually opened fire on American diplomats? The Marines would be compelled to return fire. Events could quickly spin out of control.

The roar of the crowd was deafening. Some fool, perched atop the perimeter wall, was shouting, "Death to America!" through a bullhorn. The frenetic, feverish crowd lapped up every word and chanted it back again and again, louder every time.

Charlie was finally making progress, and as he elbowed his way through the horde, he couldn't help but think how ugly the embassy's squat brick buildings were. The entire campus, in fact, looked like some cookie-cutter American public high school from the forties or fifties. It had even been dubbed "Henderson High" after Loy Wesley Henderson, the U.S. ambassador to Iran from 1951 to 1954. It was hardly a prize architecturally. But there was no question it would be a gold mine of intelligence for the radicals loyal to Ayatollah Khomeini if they actually got inside before his fellow FSOs burned and shredded all their documents.

Someone grabbed Charlie from behind. He spun around and found himself staring into the bloodshot eyes of an unshaven zealot probably five years younger but five inches taller than him.

"You—you're an American!" the student screamed in Farsi.

Heads turned. Charlie felt himself suddenly surrounded. He noticed the kid's right hand balling up into a fist. He saw into the kid's vacant eyes, and for the first time, Charlie Harper feared for his life.

"Vous êtes fou. Je suis de Marseille!" he screamed back in flawless French, calling the kid crazy and claiming to be from France's largest commercial seaport.

The vehemence of Charlie's response and the fact that he wasn't speaking English caught the student off guard. The kid went blank for a moment. He obviously didn't speak French and for a split second seemed unsure how to proceed.

Charlie's mind raced. He suddenly realized how quickly he'd be a dead man if these radicals discovered he was an American. He was tempted to kick the kid in the groin and dash off into the crowd. But there were now at least six or seven others just as large and every bit as angry.

One of them began to move against him, but just then a pickup truck filled with other young men—masked and screaming—hopped a curb and came barreling through the crowd. The driver laid on the horn and people went diving for cover. The truck screeched to a halt just to Charlie's right. The young men in the back began firing machine guns in the air, and then, as the crowd finally cleared a direct path, the driver gunned the engine and drove headlong into Roosevelt Gate. The wrought-iron barricade crumpled in a twisted heap, and thousands of enraged students cheered and screamed and poured onto the embassy grounds as if they'd been shot from a cannon.

As quickly as he'd been grabbed, Charlie now found himself set free as his would-be attackers abandoned him and followed the crowd through the hole in the gates. His heart racing, adrenaline coursing through his veins, Charlie realized he'd been given an opportunity to escape. He seized the moment and began moving in the opposite direction, away from the main gate and toward a side street. He was still having trouble maneuvering through the rampaging mob, but moments later, he rounded the corner and caught a glimpse of the entrance to the consulate.

It was shut tight. He hesitated for a moment. Should he head there still? Should he try to get inside and help whoever was trapped there? The staff inside was mostly comprised of women who handled visa issues eight hours a day, day after day, year after year. They weren't trained to handle revolutions. They had to be terrified. But could he really help them, or would he more likely be caught and brutalized instead?

Just then, he saw two consular employees quickly exit a side door. Elated, he was about to call out to them when a group of masked students armed with rifles came racing around the corner and surrounded the two young women. They jumped on them and began beating them mercilessly.

Charlie's anger boiled. But there was nothing he could do. He was alone. He was unarmed. And again he thought of Claire back in their apartment—alone, terrified, and three and a half months pregnant.

2

The twenty-minute journey home took two hours.

Cautiously working his way through the clogged streets—and purposefully taking a circuitous route, checking constantly to see if anyone was following him—Charlie eventually made it back to apartment 902 in the upscale high-rise with the spectacular views of the Tehran skyline. He burst through the door, quickly locked it behind him, and hearing the AM radio still on in the bedroom, headed there to find his wife.

"Charlie, are you okay?" Claire said breathlessly, jumping up to embrace him.

"Yes," he whispered, holding her close. "But what about you?"

"I've been terrified about you," she whispered back, beginning to cry. "I thought I'd never see you again."

"Sweetheart, I'm sorry," he said as quietly and lovingly as he could. "But I'm fine. Don't worry. I'm all right, just a little shaken up."

It was a lie. He wasn't fine. He was scared and unsure what to do next. But as guilty as he felt about lying to the woman he loved, he worried for her and the precious life growing within her.

"Are you still bleeding?" he asked.

"A little," she said. "But I'll be fine."

It was Claire's first pregnancy, and it hadn't been easy. She'd suffered with violent morning sickness for the first couple of months and had lost nearly twenty pounds from an already-slight frame. More stress wasn't exactly what the doctor had ordered for her or the baby.

Claire took a few deep breaths and tried to steady herself. Then pressed harder against him and spoke into his ear. "They're saying

9

a firefight has erupted outside the compound; they're saying several people are dead and that dozens more are wounded. Is that true?"

"I don't know," Charlie said. "Everything's so chaotic. I wouldn't know what to believe at this point."

No sooner had the words left his lips than came a special bulletin over Radio Tehran.

"We have a woman on the line who claims to have important news on the student uprising downtown," the announcer said. "Okay, you're on the air. What is your name?"

"I am one of the Muslim Student Followers of the Imam's Line."

"Yes, I understand, but what's your name?"

"That doesn't matter. What matters is our movement."

"Fine," the announcer said. "Where exactly are you calling from, and what is it that you want to say?"

"I am calling you from inside the American Embassy."

There was a long, uncomfortable pause. The announcer seemed flustered. "What? *Inside* the . . . That doesn't make any . . . Repeat what you just said. Is this a joke?"

"It is not a joke. We have occupied the American Embassy, the den of espionage. We have occupied every building. Every floor. I am presently standing behind the desk of the ambassador."

"Come now," the announcer said, incredulous. "We know the students have penetrated the outer walls and are protesting on the grounds of the compound. We've been reporting this for several hours. But we have no reports of any students getting inside one of the buildings."

"Now you do."

"But you cannot be in the ambassador's office. You must be kidding."

"I am not."

"I don't believe you."

"I can prove it."

"How?"

"Look in the telephone directory and find the embassy number," the woman directed. "Then dial extension 8209 for the ambassador's office."

There was a long pause. Charlie turned to Claire to see how she was doing. But she didn't return his gaze. She was fixated on the radio, almost as if in a trance. A moment later, the radio announcer could be heard flipping through a directory, then dialing the phone. It rang. And then . . .

"You have reached the United States Embassy in Tehran," a woman's voice said, first in English, then in Farsi. "The embassy is presently closed. Our office hours are from 9:00 a.m. to 5:00 p.m., Sunday through Thursday. The consulate is open for visa requests from 9:00 a.m. to 4:00 p.m., Sunday through Thursday. If you know the number of the person you are trying to reach . . ."

A moment later, the announcer had dialed through to the ambassador's office and got the same woman back on the line.

"So it is true," he said, astonished.

"So it is."

"This is serious news. Okay, what is your message?"

"I have a communiqué," the young woman said calmly.

"Very well, proceed. Let us hear it."

"Communiqué Number One: In the name of God, the merciful, the compassionate . . ."

She then quoted from a statement Ayatollah Ruhollah Khomeini—the leader of the Islamic Revolution in Iran—had said just the day before. ". . . it is incumbent upon students to forcefully expand their attacks against America and Israel, so that America will be forced to return the criminal, deposed Shah."

Then she read a lengthy statement prepared by the students. Several lines jumped out at Charlie.

"We Muslim students, followers of Imam Khomeini, have occupied the espionage embassy of America in protest against the ploys of the imperialists and the Zionists. We announce our protest to the world, a protest against America for granting asylum and employing the criminal Shah while it has on its hands the blood of tens of thousands of women and men in this country. . . ."

When the propaganda piece was finished, Charlie asked, "Where's the utility box?"

"Why?" Claire asked.

He asked again, ignoring her question.

"It's in the closet," Claire replied. "But what do you need it for?"

He gently pulled away from her, headed into the closet, fished out a steel case about the size of a carry-on piece of luggage, and began to leave the bedroom.

"Where are you going?" she asked, a bit too loudly, an edge of panic now in her voice.

Charlie turned quickly and motioned for Claire to lower her voice. Then he took her by the hand and proceeded to the kitchen. There, in the tiny, windowless room, he moved aside a pitcher of pomegranate juice and several glasses sitting in the center of their table for two and set down the utility box. He dialed in the lock combination and opened the case. It was the first time Claire had ever seen what was inside, and she gasped as Charlie pulled out a sidearm and ammunition.

"Charlie, what—?"

"It's just a precaution," he tried to reassure her. "I'm sure this will all be over soon."

She didn't look convinced. And why should she be? Claire Harper was no idiot. She held a master's degree from Harvard and had graduated summa cum laude from the business school; Charlie had managed only cum laude honors from Harvard's Kennedy School of Government. Though Claire was presently on sick leave because of her challenging pregnancy, she had been assigned to serve as the embassy's deputy economic attaché. Her Farsi wasn't as fluent as Charlie's, but everyone they knew at the embassy was impressed with how much progress she had made in such a short time. She wasn't ready to give a speech yet, but she was certainly conversational. Indeed, she was already building a friendship with, swapping recipes with, and learning to cook from the wife of the Iranian cardiologist who lived in the apartment next door—the woman who made such mouthwatering Persian stew. Claire and Mrs. Shirazi had made a pact to speak only Farsi when they were together. It was challenging, but it was already paying off.

Charlie now removed from the utility chest a small box that looked like an alarm clock along with a set of simple headphones.

"What is that?" Claire whispered.

"It's a radio."

"We already have a radio."

"This one's different."

"How?"

Charlie paused. There were secrets in his job he wasn't authorized to share, even with his wife. But with events moving so rapidly, it was time to loosen the restrictions a little.

"This one lets me listen in on the frequency the Marines are using inside the embassy."

Claire had no poker face, and her eyes betrayed the fears rising inside her. She wasn't a fan of secrets. He wasn't much of a fan either. But the simple fact was that his position in the Foreign Service was decidedly different from hers, and that difference just might keep them alive.

Charlie set up the specialized radio, plugged in the headphones, and began listening to the cross traffic. His pulse quickened instantly as he immediately heard gunfire, cursing, and shouting.

"*Bravo Six, this is Tango Tango; what's your twenty?*"

"*Main vault, Tango.*"

"*How many?*"

"*I've got nine with me—there's ten of us total.*"

"*You guys okay?*"

"*Negative, Tango. I've got one with a bullet wound to the leg. Several with serious lacerations on their faces and hands from shattered glass.*"

"*Bogeys?*"

"*Dozens, sir.*"

"*What are they doing?*"

"*Pounding on the door with sledgehammers, sir. They're demanding I let them in or—*"

"*Can you hold your position, Bravo Six?*"

"*I don't know, sir. We have no food or water.*"

"*What about the documents?*"

"*Shredding them now, sir. But it's going slow.*"

Suddenly Charlie felt the color draining from his face.

Claire saw it. "What is it?"

He just stood there shaking his head in disbelief.

"What? What's happening?" she pressed.

"There was just a massive explosion," he whispered. "People are screaming. I've never . . ."

"Who? Where?"

"Rick, Phil, Cort—I'm not sure who else. They're hiding in the main vault, in the chancery. But I think the students just blew the doors off."

Charlie slowly took off the headphones and handed them to his wife, but she refused to put them on. She had neither the training nor the stomach for this.

"It's all going to be okay, isn't it, Charlie?" Claire asked. "Like February. It's going to be like the Valentine's Day thing—short and done, right?"

Charlie said nothing. He knew in his gut this wasn't anything like the February 14 event, dubbed the St. Valentine's Day Open House by the other Foreign Service officers. Just nine months before, a much smaller group of students—a few hundred, perhaps—had briefly jumped the embassy's fence, stormed into a few buildings, held them for a couple of hours, made a fuss, made their point, and then gone home after the Khomeini regime insisted that they do so.

Claire was right; the Valentine's Day incident had been short-lived. It had all happened before they'd arrived, but it was obvious that the effect on the decision makers in Washington had been enormous. Rather than inserting more Marines and engineers to harden and defend the American Embassy—thus sending an unequivocal message that such an assault against American sovereign territory in the heart of Tehran would never be tolerated again—the bureaucrats back at the White House and State Department had panicked. They'd reduced the embassy's staff from nearly a thousand to barely sixty. The Pentagon had shown a similar lack of resolve. The number of U.S. military forces in-country had been drawn down from about ten thousand active-duty troops to almost none.

The only reason Charlie had been sent in—especially as green as he was—was because he happened to be one of the few men in the entire

U.S. diplomatic corps who was actually fluent in Farsi. None of the three CIA guys on site even spoke the language. How was that possible? The whole notion of State Department and CIA personnel being inside a country whose language they didn't speak seemed ludicrous to Charlie. How could one government understand another—much less build a healthy, positive, long-lasting relationship—without at least being able to talk in the other's heart language? It couldn't, Charlie knew, and now Washington was about to pay the piper.

3

"Get the suitcases," Charlie ordered.

Claire looked at him as if he'd just slapped her in the face.

"That's crazy," she shot back, barely in a whisper. "What for?"

"Pack one for me, one for you," Charlie continued matter-of-factly. "Just essentials; keep it light."

"That's ridiculous," she said, moving curtly to the sink and beginning to wash their breakfast dishes. "I'm not going anywhere."

"Ten minutes," he said calmly. "I'll gather our money and personal documents, get the car, and meet you at the back entrance." Then he left the kitchen and headed to the bedroom.

"Charles David Harper, have you completely lost your mind?" she shouted after him, her voice taut with anger. "I'm not going out there, and neither are you. It's not safe. We're better off staying here."

Charlie came back around the corner as Claire turned to the sink again, pulled her hair into a ponytail to keep it out of her eyes, and continued washing their matching maroon *U.S. Embassy in Tehran* coffee mugs.

He turned her around sharply and put his hand over her mouth. "We are leaving now," he said as quietly as he could but with an intensity he knew Claire had never heard before. "Don't you get it, Claire? Khomeini's thugs have the entire embassy. They have the vaults. They have the files. They know who I am, and they're going to want information I can give them. Right now they're taking a roll call of every employee. When they find we're missing, they're going to look up our address. If it's been destroyed, they're going to put a gun to the head of

Liz Swift. If she doesn't give us up, they're going to kill her in front of everyone else. Then they're going to ask Mike Metrinko. If he doesn't give us up, they're going to kill him. Then they're going to turn to John Limbert. And they're going to keep killing people until someone breaks. I don't know who it will be. But someone's going to give them our address, and then they're coming for us. And what do you think is going to happen next, Claire? Do you think they're going to torture me?"

Terrified, Claire shrugged, her big brown eyes filling rapidly with tears.

"They're not. I'm a six-foot-two, hundred-and-seventy-pound, former all-American point guard who speaks Farsi and has a Colt .45 on the kitchen table. No, they're not going to torture me. They're going to torture you, my love," he said, "until I start talking. . . . And if they find out you're pregnant . . ."

Claire was trembling.

"I would never let it get to that point," Charlie assured her, his own eyes welling up with tears. "I couldn't. I'd tell them everything. But honestly, I fear they'd still torture you anyway. That's who we're dealing with. I'm sorry, sweetheart. But there's no way this ends well. Unless we leave—right now."

He paused a moment, then let go of her mouth and wiped his eyes.

Claire immediately grabbed him and held him tightly. After a moment she stepped back and looked intently at her husband. She had been trembling, but now she seemed calm. "Ten minutes?" she asked.

Charlie nodded.

"I'll be ready," she promised.

★ ★ ★ ★ ★

Ten minutes later, Charlie eased their black Buick Skylark onto Ferdowsi Avenue, dubbed "Embassy Row" by local diplomats.

Were other Western missions under siege, he wondered, or just his own?

The boulevard was as congested as ever, but he saw nothing out of the ordinary. No protests. No demonstrations. No presidents or prime ministers being burned in effigy here, even though hideous mock-ups of President Carter were being torched just a few blocks away. It was odd. They were so close to the student mob, but here he could detect no hostilities of any kind. Still, Charlie could tell Claire was getting anxious. If they were going to get out of this city, they needed to do it quickly.

"Where will we go?" she asked her husband.

"I'm not sure," Charlie conceded. "Even if we could make it to the airport, they'd never let us out of the country. Especially not with U.S. diplomatic passports."

"How about Turkey?" Claire asked hopefully.

"I don't know," he sighed. "The nearest border is hundreds of miles away. And again, even if we could get that far without being detected, the military would never let us pass."

"Well, we can't just hover here, Charlie. It's too dangerous."

"I know," he said. "I just had to see . . ."

There was no point finishing his sentence. Claire knew as well as he did that he hadn't really needed to come to Embassy Row. The Iranians weren't angry at the rest of the Western powers. The British hadn't welcomed the despised Shah Mohammad Reza Pahlavi into their country, even if it was "just" for medical treatment of an old man on his deathbed. Nor had the Turks or the Germans. Only the U.S. government had done that. Was it worth it?

"Turn here," Claire said without warning.

Charlie took the advice and made a hard right on Kushk e-Mesri. He maneuvered the roomy four-door sedan down the narrow side street, knowing she was trying to get them off a major thoroughfare, where they ran a much higher risk of being spotted by uniformed police or plainclothes intelligence agents. But what she'd just done instead was head them straight into the campus of Tehran Technical School. It was an innocent mistake, but a mistake nonetheless.

Another hotbed of radicalism in the capital, the campus and its adjacent streets were jammed with students. Just finished with their midday prayers, they were now chanting and marching. Some were firing machine guns into the air. Charlie could feel the same violent spirit that had pervaded the scene around the embassy, and he immediately slammed on the brakes and screeched to a halt. Jamming the car into reverse, he gunned the engine and began to back up but was cut off by a VW van filled with students that had come up behind them. The VW's driver suddenly began screaming something about their American car, and six young men jumped out, carrying wooden sticks and metal pipes.

"Lock your doors, Claire," Charlie ordered, doing the same on his side.

Wild-eyed, the students surrounded the Buick, taunting and cursing them.

"Charlie, do something," Claire said, clutching her purse with her passport and valuables to her chest.

The students began rocking the car from side to side, trying to overturn it, but it was too heavy.

"Charlie, for heaven's sake, do something!"

"Like what?" he shouted back, genuine fear in his voice. "If I drive this car forward or back, I'll run over someone. Is that what you want?"

A young woman—no more than seventeen or eighteen—was pouring something all over their car.

"Of course not," Claire said. "I'm just saying . . ."

Charlie smelled gasoline. He knew what was coming next.

At that moment, Claire cried out, doubled over, and grabbed her abdomen.

"Honey, what is it?" Charlie asked.

Claire didn't look up. She was screaming in pain.

Just then one of the students took a steel pipe and smashed the passenger-side window. Glass flew everywhere. Blood streaked down Claire's face. Then the student grabbed her and tried to pull her out of the car. Claire, tangled in her seat belt, screamed louder.

Charlie was screaming too. He grabbed Claire's arm, the one closest to him, and tried to pull her back into the car. But then, out of the corner of his eye, he saw the young woman who had poured the gasoline light a match and toss it onto the now-soaked hood. Suddenly the car was engulfed in flames.

The heat was unbearable. Charlie feared the Buick's full tank could explode at any moment. Seeing his briefcase on the floor by Claire's feet, he reached for it, ripped it open, and pulled out the pistol.

He saw another student heave a brick through their back window. More flying glass filled the car.

Charlie pivoted, took aim, and fired at the attacker, dropping him with a single shot. Then he turned back to the student mauling his wife and double-tapped him to the head.

Three shots in three seconds—the crowd began to scatter. But the gasoline-fed flames had now reached the rear of the Skylark and were already consuming the backseat. Charlie knew he was out of time. He threw open the driver's-side door, jumped out, moved quickly to the passenger side, and pulled his wife's limp body out of the flames and laid her down on the sidewalk as far from the burning car as he could. She was covered in blood. It wasn't just the cuts to her face. Something else was terribly wrong.

4

Charlie feared the worst.

He crouched beside the woman he loved, the woman who had swept him off his feet the moment they'd first met at a Harvard Crimson football game. She wasn't moving.

Charlie's eyes blurred as he carefully rolled her onto her back, wiped blood from her mouth, and pushed strands of her brown hair from her eyes. His hands trembled as he held his breath and checked her pulse. Finding one startled him and gave him a shot of adrenaline. She wasn't dead. He scanned the suddenly deserted street. He could still see a huge crowd of students demonstrating on the campus. But that was a ways off. Everyone in the immediate vicinity was gone—except the bodies of the two he had shot. The gunfire had scared everyone away.

Then he saw the VW bus. It was still running.

He scooped his wife up in his arms, carried her to the VW, and set her carefully on the floor in the back. Then he jumped into the driver's seat, locked the doors, slammed the vehicle into reverse, and gunned the engine just as the Skylark exploded into the sky.

Charlie knew fire trucks and ambulances would be there soon. So would the police.

Still driving backward, he got a safe-enough distance away from the raging wreckage of their Buick, then carefully slowed to a stop, did a three-point turn, jammed the VW into second gear, and sped away from the scene of the crime. He was now convinced that Claire was having a miscarriage. He needed a hospital and knew he was just blocks away from Sayeed-ash-Shohala hospital, one of the city's best.

But he couldn't possibly take her there now. No hospital or medical clinic was safe. He couldn't run the risk of being exposed and captured by forces loyal to Khomeini. Especially now that he'd just gunned down two student radicals. They'd hang him or put him in front of a firing squad, either of which would be merciful compared to what they'd do to his wife.

Panicked and helpless, Charlie drove aimlessly through the streets of Tehran. He had no idea what to do, where to turn. He passed Shahr Park, one of his favorites, where he and Claire had often strolled and taken picnic lunches. He passed the Golestan Palace, one of the oldest and most beautiful complexes of historical monuments in the capital, dating back to the sixteenth century. But all the joy of being in this exotic country was now gone.

As he drove, Charlie cursed Iran. He cursed the Ayatollah. He cursed the Revolution. His wife was dying. The fanatical followers of the imam were trying to kill him, too. Everything he believed about the efficacy of diplomacy and "building bridges of friendship among the nations of the world" had just gone up in the flames of his government-issued sedan.

But then the name Mohammad Shirazi came to mind.

Charlie immediately tried to banish it from his thoughts. It was crazy. The man might be his neighbor, but he was an Iranian. He was a Muslim. The man's wife, Nasreen, might be a fantastic chef, and she seemed to have taken a real liking to Claire—even caring for Claire sacrificially on some of the worst days of her morning sickness—but the Shirazis were Shias. They were enemies now.

Still, Mohammad was a doctor—an impressive cardiologist. He was young, to be sure—no more than thirty, Charlie guessed—but highly regarded throughout the city. His practice was not far away. Charlie and Claire had actually been there just a few weeks earlier for a little party celebrating the grand opening of Mohammad's new, state-of-the-art medical clinic. Perhaps he should head there and ask for help. It was risky, but what choice did he have? The Shirazis might be his only hope.

Charlie eased off the gas, downshifted, slowed to a safe speed, and did an illegal U-turn. Six blocks later, he pulled into the parking lot beside Dr. Shirazi's clinic. He saw only three cars, one of which he knew to be his neighbor's. Charlie glanced in his rearview mirror. A truck filled with soldiers was passing and slowed as it did. Charlie put his head down and held his breath. The truck stopped for a moment. Charlie wasn't sure he even believed in God, but he said a silent prayer anyway, begging for mercy for himself, for his wife, and for the little life in her womb. A moment later, the soldiers sped away.

Breathing a sigh of relief, Charlie pulled the VW close to the clinic's back door and turned off the engine. Then he slipped inside the clinic and found himself face-to-face with a woman receptionist who was veiled and clearly devout. In the waiting room, the TV was on. Regular programming had been interrupted by news of the latest developments at the American Embassy.

"May I help you?" the receptionist asked in Farsi.

"I need to see Dr. Shirazi," Charlie replied in kind.

"Do you have an appointment?" she asked.

"I'm sorry, I don't," he stammered. "But I'm a friend—a neighbor, actually. And it's a bit of an emergency."

"What kind of an emergency?"

Charlie didn't want to say. Not to this woman. Not now. But he didn't know what else to do. He hadn't thought that far ahead.

Charlie glanced at his watch. He had to move fast. Claire needed serious medical attention and quickly—before the secret police tracked down the VW. He glanced around the room. There was just one older man sitting in the waiting room to his left, watching the TV coverage and shaking his head. He didn't look religious. He didn't look angry. Perhaps Charlie could take a chance, he thought. Perhaps he could . . .

Just then Charlie heard Dr. Shirazi's voice calling to his receptionist. "Who is my next patient?"

Charlie turned his head and saw his neighbor stepping out of his office, and surprise registered on the man's face.

"Charlie Harper?" he said. "What a pleasure to see you, my friend."

The doctor greeted Charlie with a traditional Persian hug and a kiss on both cheeks.

"Is everything all right, Charlie?" Dr. Shirazi asked, looking at the bloodstains on his shirt and pants.

"I must speak to you privately," Charlie blurted out.

The office phone started ringing.

"Yes, of course. Is this blood? What happened?"

Charlie shook his head and lowered his voice, hoping neither the receptionist nor the old man in the waiting room would be able to hear him, though he couldn't help but notice the receptionist's intensifying curiosity. The phone kept ringing.

"It's not me, Dr. Shirazi. It's Claire."

"What's wrong? Where is she?"

"She's in the car, right outside," Charlie whispered. "Could you come for a moment and take a look at her?"

Dr. Shirazi readily agreed, telling his receptionist to go ahead and answer the phone and take a message, and he would be right back. She finally picked up the phone as the two men moved quickly to the door.

A moment later, Charlie watched the horrified expression on Dr. Shirazi's face as he opened the side door of the VW bus and found Claire soaked in blood.

Charlie quickly explained what had happened.

"We need to get Claire to the hospital," the doctor said.

"*No,*" Charlie said. "That's not possible."

"You have no choice," Dr. Shirazi said.

"Haven't you been watching the coverage of the embassy this morning?"

"No," the doctor said, shaking his head. "I've been with patients all morning."

"The embassy has been overrun. The staff is being held hostage. Some may have been killed. The rest of us are being hunted."

Shirazi's face paled. "I'm so sorry, Charlie. I had no idea. But your wife needs a blood transfusion or she's going to die. She needs an ob-gyn. That's not my specialty. I can't help her."

"You have to," Charlie insisted. "And then we're leaving the country."

"That's impossible. Even if you could get through security at the airport, your wife would never survive the flight."

"Please, Dr. Shirazi, I need you to take care of her—privately, without anyone knowing. I'll pay whatever it costs."

"Charlie, you don't understand. I'm a cardiologist. Your wife has a dying child in her womb. She is dying too. I can't—"

Charlie grabbed the man by his shoulders and looked deeply into his eyes. "Dr. Shirazi, listen to me. I love your country. You know I do. It was once a paradise. But something evil has happened, something neither of us understands. I'm telling you, if Claire and I are caught by this regime, they will try us, and they will kill us on statewide television for the whole country and the whole world to see. That's not going to happen. I don't care about myself. But so help me God, I will never let one of them lay so much as a finger on Claire. Now please, I'm begging you as my friend, help me. I don't have anywhere else to turn."

5

The two men stared into each other's eyes.

"You're right," the doctor finally conceded. "I'm sorry. You and Claire deserve better. So does your country. This is not the Iran I grew up in. I don't even recognize this place anymore."

The back door burst open. It was the receptionist, calling for her boss.

"I asked you to hold my calls," Dr. Shirazi replied.

"Yes, sir, but it's your wife, sir. She says it's urgent."

Charlie saw the conflict in his friend's eyes. "Go," he said. "Take the call."

Charlie was fast losing hope, but what else could he say? He sensed a measure of warmth and compassion in Dr. Shirazi that he deeply appreciated. The doctor seemed genuinely to want to help him. Time was running out, but Charlie didn't want to do anything that would make his friend upset.

A moment later, Dr. Shirazi came back to the VW. "Nasreen has been watching events on television. She says you're right. You can't go to a hospital. She says I should bring you there."

"There?" Charlie asked, perplexed. "Where's *there?*"

"The embassy."

Charlie just stared at the man. Was he trying to make a joke? If so, it was cruel in the extreme, yet he looked earnest.

"Embassy?" Charlie finally asked. "What embassy?"

"The Canadians," Shirazi replied. "They're preparing to evacuate most of their staff. They're worried they might be next."

They heard sirens approaching.

"Your wife works for the Canadian Embassy?" Charlie asked, wondering why he'd never heard this before.

"Of course," the doctor said. "I told you that."

"No, you said she was a translator for the U.N."

"Yes," Dr. Shirazi said, "she used to work for the Foreign Ministry on U.N. issues. But she got a new job. Last month. I told you that. I'm sure I did. She began doing some contract work for the Canadians. She says there are a few more Americans who've just arrived. They're hiding there now. She says if we can get there in the next fifteen minutes, she'll have the medical unit on standby for Claire."

"And then?" Charlie asked.

"What do you mean?"

"What happens to us after that?"

"I don't know, my friend," Dr. Shirazi said. "One step at a time."

With great care, Charlie and Dr. Shirazi lifted Claire and transferred her from the VW bus to the plush leather backseat of the doctor's roomy Mercedes sedan. Charlie then got into the VW and followed Shirazi a few blocks away to an alley behind a small manufacturing plant that made women's shoes. There, Charlie quickly wiped down both the interior and exterior of the vehicle to erase fingerprints and any other forensic evidence as best he could, then ditched the VW. He climbed into the backseat of the Mercedes and held his wife as Shirazi sped to the residence of the Canadian ambassador.

Nasreen, six Canadian security officers, and a team of medics met them at the rear gate. Charlie had to surrender his pistol, but they were all quickly let inside, and Claire was whisked into surgery. Charlie started to follow but was asked to wait in the residence. The Shirazis waited with him. They were offered food but couldn't eat. They were offered drinks but had no interest.

As the tense and lonely hours passed with no word about Claire's condition, four other American Embassy employees approached, introduced themselves, and said they were praying for the Harpers. Charlie, fighting a debilitating cocktail of fatigue and depression, couldn't recall ever meeting any of them before. They all worked in the consular section, handling visa issues, and had been able to escape in the initial moments of the morning's drama and find a safe haven with the Canadians. Charlie was grateful for their kindness.

As the sun began to set and long shadows filled the ambassador's personal library, where they waited, the Canadian doctor in charge of the embassy's medical unit came in and broke the news. Claire would recover, though it would take several weeks. The baby, however, had been lost.

Charlie was not usually a man prone to tears. He'd never seen his father cry, and today was, as far as he could remember, the first time he'd cried since he had met, courted, and married Claire. But now he slumped into the nearest chair and began to sob. At first he did his best to muffle the sound of his lamentations, but he couldn't stop them. They emanated from somewhere so deep inside his soul, he was beyond embarrassment.

The Shirazis gathered at Charlie's side, put their arms around him, and held him. They, too, had tears streaming down their faces.

★ ★ ★ ★ ★

Charlie awoke as if from a nightmare.

The room was pitch-black. With a brief flash of hope, he reached for Claire, but she was not there. He rubbed his eyes and checked his Timex. It was half past three in the morning. It was Wednesday, November 7, 1979. Then a cruel realization came over him. This wasn't a dream. All of it was bitterly true.

Three days had passed since the nightmare had begun, and he had no earthly idea how long it would last. Claire remained in serious but stable condition. She'd been conscious for only a few hours a day, and for the rest of each dark and dismal day, Charlie had never felt so alone.

Feeling famished and realizing he had barely eaten since Sunday, Charlie got up, put on a robe someone had lent him, and padded out of his guest room and down several flights of stairs to the kitchen. There he was startled to find Ambassador Taylor and the Shirazis. A Filipino steward was preparing soup and some sandwiches. Apparently Charlie wasn't the only one who couldn't sleep.

"It's good to see you, Charlie," Mohammad Shirazi said.

"Come," Nasreen said, pulling up a chair, "sit here with us."

Charlie nodded his thanks and sank into the chair.

The Canadian ambassador leaned toward Charlie. "You'll be glad to know I've been in touch with your State Department. We're working on plans to get you and Claire back to the States as soon as she's healthy enough."

"Thank you," Charlie said. "That's very kind."

"We're hoping, of course, that this whole thing blows over in the next few days," the ambassador observed.

"That doesn't seem likely, does it?" Charlie asked.

"Not at the moment, no. But you should hear the plan the CIA is cooking up in case this thing goes on for a while. It's a bit . . . thin."

"What do you mean?" Charlie asked.

For the next few minutes, the ambassador sketched out the craziest scheme Charlie had ever heard. From the looks on their faces, the Shirazis thought it was nuts too. Charlie didn't know whether to laugh or cry. He hoped their situation wouldn't require a solution as cockamamy as that. It would never work, he knew. The Iranians were fanatics. The secret police at the airport would never buy it. But once again, he realized he had no other choice. Clearly his fate was not in his own hands. Perhaps he ought to resign himself to that fact, he figured, for he was simply too tired to resist.

"I just have one request, Mr. Ambassador," Charlie said at last.

"What's that?"

"You must promise me the Shirazis can come too."

The ambassador and the Shirazis looked stunned.

"Charlie, that's very thoughtful of you," Mohammad Shirazi said, "but I don't really think that's possible at this point."

Charlie ignored him. "Mr. Ambassador, they saved the life of two Americans. The regime will kill them if we leave them here."

"I understand," the ambassador said. "But it's out of my hands. Think about it, Charlie. It's one thing for your government to extract two of its own diplomats out of harm's way. It's quite another thing to—"

But Charlie cut him off. "Put me on the phone with whomever you're talking to at Langley," he said firmly. "Claire and I aren't leaving unless the Shirazis come with us. They saved our lives. The very least we can do is save theirs."

6

TEN YEARS LATER

TEHRAN, IRAN
JUNE 3, 1989

Hamid Hosseini had been at his master's side for three decades.

He could not bear to see the man suffer. For the past week and a half, he had been one of only three clerics allowed to sit beside the hospital bed of Ayatollah Ruhollah Mousavi Khomeini. For eleven straight days and nights, Hosseini had gone without food, begging Allah for his master's recovery. But relief had not come. The cancer continued to consume the eighty-eight-year-old cleric. The doctors were unable to stanch the internal bleeding. The master's time seemed to be at hand.

Hosseini's eyes filled with tears. He and his master had been through so much together. They had accomplished so much. It couldn't end now. Their mission was not yet complete.

Hosseini got up from his prayers and quietly stepped into the hallway to compose himself. He still vividly remembered the first time the two men had met.

The year was 1963. Khomeini's popularity was soaring, and not just among theologians. The people of Iran were falling in love with this fiery, radical preacher, and so was Hosseini. At times Khomeini preached to crowds of a hundred thousand or more, and in June of that year, Khomeini invited Hosseini to be his guest as he delivered a major address. Hosseini eagerly accepted, sharing breakfast that morning with the master in his home, asking him a thousand questions, driving with him to the site of the speech, and sitting just a few yards away as the address began.

Hosseini could still recite the speech in full. He had been mesmerized as Khomeini blasted the Shah as a "miserable wretch" who had allied himself with the "parasites" of Israel. He'd been enthralled as Khomeini denounced apostate Islamic clerics throughout Iran—allies of the Shah—as "impure animals." And he'd been shocked by hearing Khomeini predict that the Shah would be forced to leave the country.

Even so many years later, Hosseini could recall his electrification, the crowd's swell of emotion. No one had ever spoken of the Shah that way. The masses went crazy. They were ready to overthrow the Pahlavi regime right there and then. But it was not time. Two days later, the Shah's secret police forces decided to move, arresting Khomeini and everyone who had been on the platform. But that just generated more sympathy and support for Khomeini.

Uprisings of support quickly erupted in cities throughout Iran, including Tehran, the political capital of the country, and Qom, the country's religious capital with its scores of seminaries and other Islamic institutes. Large crowds of Khomeini supporters took to the streets shouting, *"Khomeini or death!"* The Shah imposed martial law the following day, but his forces overreacted, opening fire against Khomeini's supporters. The official count of dead and wounded protesters was fifteen thousand.

Hosseini had never been to prison before then. He'd never been tortured. He'd never even imagined such a scenario. But he was not sorry for his friendship with the man responsible for his new fate. To the contrary, he counted it a great honor to suffer together with the great man for the sake of Allah.

For the next ten months, the two remained imprisoned together, but they could not have scripted events better if they had tried. Khomeini was becoming a national symbol of the Shah's oppression of devout Muslims. He was steadily emerging as the leader of the Islamist opposition to the Shah, a role that suited him perfectly. And Hamid Hosseini was universally identified as one of the Ayatollah's most trusted aides.

On April 7, 1964, Khomeini and his supporters were released, and major celebrations were quickly organized, particularly in Qom, where seminaries closed for three days to hold parties in his honor.

But the Ayatollah was not interested in parties. He wanted a revolution. He wasted no time in using his newfound fame and popular support to launch new, even more strident broadsides against the Shah. And Hamid Hosseini was again at his master's side on October 27, 1964, when the imam delivered a speech that accused the Shah and his secularized government of treason and urged Shia Muslims throughout Iran to "come to the aid of Islam" by attacking the apostate, infidel regime.

"O Allah, they have committed treason against this country," Khomeini bellowed to a crowd of thousands. "O Allah, this government has committed treason against the Qur'an. . . . They are not our representatives. . . . I dismiss them. . . . O Allah, destroy those individuals who are traitors to this land and traitors to Islam."

On November 4, 1964, the Shah's forces arrested Ayatollah Khomeini again and sent him into exile in Turkey. Hamid Hosseini, now a close friend and trusted aide to the imam, was exiled as well. But the two men could not have been happier. All the people of Iran saw Khomeini as the Shah's leading opponent and Hosseini as his chief spokesman and confidant. And now they were free to make their case without fear of reprisals.

Turkey, at the time, was the epicenter of the reform movement within Islam. It was the place where Muslims adopted Western customs, dress, speech, and even democracy. It was hardly the appropriate base camp for the Ayatollah's small band of Islamic radicals to plot the next steps of their revolution. They quickly made plans to leave Turkey for Iraq and arrived in Baghdad on October 6, 1965, accompanied by Khomeini's son Mostafa.

Now, as Hamid Hosseini looked upon his dying master writhing in pain on a hospital bed, tears filled his eyes again, and he had to look away. He did not want to remember Khomeini like this, his life slowly fading.

In the fall of 1977, Hosseini had been at his master's side when Mostafa had suddenly died under mysterious conditions. He had been in the room when the Iraqi medical examiner said his master's forty-five-year-old son had died of a sudden and massive heart attack, but of this Hosseini had never been convinced. Far more likely, he was certain, was that Khomeini's son had been assassinated by the agents of the Shah's secret police, the SAVAK.

Now Hosseini convinced himself Ayatollah Khomeini was dying as a result of an evil plan. The doctors said it was cancer, but was it really? Perhaps the CIA had poisoned him. Maybe it was the Mossad. It might even have been a joint operation. He had no idea how they had done it. But he had no doubt the Great Satan and the Little Satan were behind Khomeini's death, and he silently vowed they would both pay for their treachery. The Americans and the Zionists were still trying to smother the Iranian Revolution. But they would fail. With blood and fire, Hosseini vowed, they would fail.

Just then, Hosseini heard choking, gasping.

He quickly turned and stepped back to his master's side, then stood paralyzed with grief as he watched the convulsions and the feverish efforts of doctors and nurses trying to stop the inevitable. But as suddenly as it had begun, it was over. The choking stopped. The gasping ended. The efforts to save him drew to a close.

Everyone in the room stood in horror, barely able to comprehend what they had just witnessed. The death angel had come, and Hamid Hosseini began to weep.

Hosseini faced Mecca, fell to his knees, and prayed silently.

But the prayer that entered his heart at that moment was one that surprised and terrified him. He had not planned to pray it. It just poured forth from his heart. It was a lament he had daily prayed as a child but one he never would have dared think—much less utter—within a thousand miles of the Ayatollah before now. It was a prayer that could have sent him to prison and the torture chambers had anyone close to his master ever guessed he was lifting it up to Allah. But he couldn't help it. In his grief and despair, it simply became an involuntary plea.

O mighty Lord, he silently implored, *I pray to you to hasten the emergence of your last repository, the Promised One, that perfect and pure human being, the one who will fill this world with justice and peace. Make us worthy to prepare the way for his arrival, and lead us with your righteous hand. We long for the Lord of the Age. We long for the Awaited One. Without him—the Righteously Guided One—there can be no victory. With him, there can be no defeat. Show me your path, O mighty Lord, and use me to prepare the way for the coming of the Mahdi.*

7

The news swept through the Iraqi city of Samarra.

As word of Ayatollah Khomeini's death spread through the Shia Muslim stronghold, it eventually reached Najjar Malik and hit him like a thunderbolt.

Only ten years old, Najjar had long been sheltered from national and world events by his uncle and aunt, who had taken him in after his parents' deaths in a tragic car accident several years earlier. They didn't let him watch television or listen to the radio. They didn't let him read anything but his schoolbooks. For little Najjar, incredibly bright but also small for his age, life consisted of mosque and school and nothing else. If he wasn't memorizing the Qur'an, he was memorizing his textbooks.

But today was different. Suddenly it seemed as if every Shia in Samarra had heard what Najjar had just heard from a woman shrieking in the hallway.

"The imam has died! The imam has died!"

Najjar was too much in shock to cry.

It couldn't be true. It had to be a vicious rumor, started by the Zionists or the Sunnis. Ayatollah Khomeini was larger than life. He simply could not be dead. Wasn't he the long-awaited Mahdi? Wasn't he the Twelfth Imam, the Hidden Imam? Wasn't he supposed to establish justice and peace? How then could he be dead if he was, in fact, the savior of the Islamic world and all of mankind?

Every Friday night for years, Najjar's aunt and uncle made him listen to the latest audiotaped sermon from Ayatollah Khomeini that had been smuggled out of Iran and into Iraq. Then his aunt would tuck him into bed, kiss him good night, turn out the light, and shut the bedroom door. When the apartment was quiet, Najjar would stare out the window into the moonlight, meditating on the Ayatollah's words and on his fiery insistence that a Muslim's duty was to perform jihad—holy war—against the infidels. It wasn't exactly the stuff of childhood dreams, but it stirred something deep within Najjar's heart.

"Surely those who believe, those who wage jihad in God's cause—they are the ones who may hope for the mercy of God," the Ayatollah would declare, citing Sura 2:218 from the Qur'an. Jews and Christians are the ones whom God has cursed, he would explain, saying the Qur'an taught that they "shall either be executed, or crucified, or have their hands and feet cut off alternately, or be banished from the land.

"Kill them!" Khomeini would insist, pointing to Sura 9:5. "Wherever you may come upon them, and seize them, and confine them, and lie in wait for them at every conceivable place.

"The Prophet and his followers are commanded to wage jihad against the unbelievers and the hypocrites and to be stern against them," the Ayatollah argued year after year, "for their final refuge is hell."

Infidels, he insisted—citing Sura 22—will spend eternity in a blazing fire, "with boiling water being poured down over their heads. All that is within their bodies, as well as their skins, will be melted away.

"Have nothing to do with them," he argued. "Don't befriend them. Don't negotiate with them. Don't do business with them." After all, he loved to say—citing Sura 5:59-60—"Allah has cursed the Christians and the Jews, and those whom he has utterly condemned he has turned into apes, and swine, and servants of powers of evil."

Najjar had been transfixed by Khomeini's courage and conviction. Surely this man must be the Mahdi. *Who else could it be?* he had wondered. True, his aunt conceded when Najjar occasionally asked innocent questions, Khomeini had not yet brought justice and peace. Nor had he yet established an Islamic empire that would transform the globe. But all this, she said, was just a matter of time.

Now what? Najjar thought. If Khomeini had really died, who would lead the Revolution? Who was the real messiah, and when would he come?

No one else was home, and Najjar felt scared and alone. Desperate to learn more, he fled his aunt and uncle's cramped high-rise flat and ran down all seventeen flights of stairs rather than wait for an elevator. He ran out into the dusty street in front of their dilapidated building, only to find huge crowds of fellow Shias pouring out of their apartments as well. Seeing a group of older men huddled on a nearby corner near a fruit stand, smoking cigarettes and listening to a small transistor radio, Najjar ran to their side and listened in.

"Radio Tehran can now confirm that the revered imam—peace be upon him—has died of a heart attack," he heard the announcer say in Farsi, the man's voice faltering as he relayed the news. "The Supreme Leader of the Islamic Revolution has been in the hospital for the last eleven days. He was suffering from internal bleeding. But a government spokesman has confirmed what hospital officials indicated just a few minutes ago. Ruhollah Mousavi Khomeini is dead at the age of eighty-eight."

Najjar's mind reeled. *How can the Promised One be dead?* It was not possible.

With few other hard facts to report, Radio Tehran broadcast excerpts from Khomeini's speeches. In one from 1980, Khomeini declared to his fellow Shias, "We must strive to export our Revolution throughout the world."

Najjar heard a thunderous roar erupt from whatever crowd had been listening to the imam. He closed his eyes and pictured the scene and suddenly wished his parents had never left Iran. Perhaps then they would still be alive. Perhaps Najjar could have actually seen the Ayatollah with his own eyes. Perhaps he could have heard the master's words with his own ears. Perhaps he could have even served the Revolution in some small way.

"The governments of the world should know that . . . Islam will be victorious in all the countries of the world, and Islam and the teachings of the Qur'an will prevail all over the world," Khomeini bellowed in

another radio clip. Najjar knew that line by heart. It came from a sermon the Ayatollah had delivered just after returning to Tehran, where
he was greeted by millions of faithful followers shouting, *The Holy One
has come! The Holy One has come!"*

Disoriented by this turn of events, Najjar backed away from the
crowd of men and out of earshot of the radio broadcast. He had heard
more than he had wanted. His slight body trembled. His filthy cotton
shirt was drenched with sweat, and he suddenly felt parched. He had
no idea where his uncle and aunt were. But he desperately didn't want
to be by himself.

Perhaps they were at the mosque. He decided that was where he
should be as well. He took off in a dead run for six blocks, slowing
only when he could see the side door of the al-Askari Mosque just a
few hundred meters away.

But suddenly, without warning, three teenagers—much larger than
Najjar—came rushing out of the bushes and tackled him from the side.
Blindsided, Najjar crashed to the ground with the wind knocked out
of him. Before he could catch his breath, the three began beating him
mercilessly. Two balled up their fists and landed blow after blow upon
Najjar's stomach and face. The third kicked him repeatedly in the back
and the groin. He shrieked in pain, begging them to stop. He knew
who they were, and he knew what they wanted. They were friends of
his cousin, who owed one of them a few dinars. His cousin had been
late in paying.

Soon blood was pouring from little Najjar's broken nose and from
his left ear. His face began to swell. His vision blurred. All colors began
to fade. He was sure he was going to black out. But then he heard a
voice shout, "Stop!"

Suddenly the beatings stopped.

Najjar didn't dare open his eyes. Bracing for the next blow, he remained in a fetal position. After a few moments, he heard the boys walking away. Why? Where were they going? Was it really over? Mustering just enough courage to crack open one eye, Najjar wiped away the blood and tears and saw the three bullies standing around someone, though he could not tell who. Was it a parent? a policeman? Najjar opened the other eye. He wiped more blood away and strained to hear what was being said.

"The Holy Qur'an says, 'Whomever Allah guides, he is the rightly guided,'" a commanding voice declared. "But what does the Prophet—peace be upon him—say of those who go astray, of those rebels who go far from the teachings of Allah? He says, 'We will gather them on the day of resurrection, fallen on their faces—blind, dumb, and deaf. Their refuge is hell. And every time it subsides, we will increase their blazing fire.'"

Najjar knew that verse. His aunt had made him memorize Sura 17:97 on his fifth birthday, and it haunted him to this day. He scanned the crowd that had gathered, hoping to see a friendly face or at least a familiar one. But he recognized no one, and he wondered whether the mob was there to see a fight or a punishment.

"You're saying we are all going to hell?" one of the bullies asked.

Najjar was surprised to hear a trace of real fear in the boy's faltering voice.

"It is not I who say it," the stranger said with quiet authority. "The

Qur'an says, 'The weighing of deeds on that day of resurrection will be the truth. Those whose scales are heavy with truth and good deeds, it is they who will be the successful. As for those whose scales are light, because of evil deeds, those are the ones who have lost their souls, causing them to travel toward the fire, because they mistreated; they knowingly denied Our signs.'"

Najjar knew that one, too. It was Sura 7:8-9.

He watched the shoulders of the teenagers sag. Their heads hung low. It wasn't clear the boys had ever heard those verses before, but they certainly seemed to grasp the stakes. Suddenly they weren't so tough or so cruel. Indeed, horrified by the wrath that could be awaiting his tormentors, Najjar almost felt sorry for them.

Since his earliest childhood, Najjar had deeply feared the fires of hell. He was convinced that his parents' deaths in a car crash on a weekend trip to Baghdad when he was only four was punishment from Allah upon him for his own sins. He had no idea what sins he could have committed at so young an age. But he was painfully aware of all he had committed since. He didn't mean to be such a terrible person. He tried to be a pious and faithful servant of Allah. He prayed five times a day. He went to the mosque every chance he could, even if he had to go alone. He had already memorized much of the Qur'an. He was often praised by his teachers for his religious zeal. But he knew the wickedness in his own heart, and he feared that all his attempts to do what was right could end up being for naught. Was he really any better than these boys who had beaten him? No, he concluded. He was probably worse. Surely they had been sent by Allah to punish him, and he knew he deserved it.

The three boys began backing away from their accuser. A moment later, they turned quickly and ran away. It was then that Najjar saw the one who had come to his defense, and he could not believe his eyes. The stranger was not a man but a boy—one not much older than he. He certainly wasn't more than eleven or twelve years old, and he was short, with a slight build. He had jet-black hair, light olive skin, a pointed, angular, almost royal nose, and a small black spot like a mole on his left cheek. He didn't wear street clothes like others his size and age. Rather he wore a black robe and sandals. But what struck Najjar most was the boy's piercing black eyes, which bored deep into his soul and forced him to look away in humiliation.

"Do not fear, Najjar," the strange boy said. "You are safe now."

Najjar's heart sped. How did the boy know his name? They had certainly never seen each other before.

"You are curious how I know your name," the boy said. "But I know all about you. You are Persian, not Arab. Your first language was Farsi, though you also speak Arabic and French fluently. You grew up here in Samarra, but you were born in Iran, as were your parents and grand-parents. Your family lived in Esfahān, to be precise."

Najjar was stunned. It was all true. He searched his memory. He must know this boy somehow. But he couldn't imagine where or when they had met. He had a nearly photographic memory, yet neither this face nor this voice was registering in the slightest.

"You are a child of the Revolution," the stranger continued. "Your mother, Jamila, bless her memory, was a true servant of Allah. She could trace her family lineage to the Prophet, peace be upon him. Your mother memorized large portions of the Qur'an by the age of seven. She was excited by the fall of the Shah and the return of the Ayatollah from exile in Paris to Tehran on the fateful first day of February 1979."

This, too, was true, Najjar realized, but it frightened him.

"Though eight months pregnant with you," the boy went on, "your mother insisted that she and your father join the millions of Iranians trying to catch a glimpse of the Ayatollah as his flight touched down at Mehrabad International Airport that morning. But they never made it, did they?"

Najjar shook his head.

"Just after sunrise, your mother went into premature labor," the stranger continued. "She delivered you on a bus on the way to the hospital. Only four pounds, fourteen ounces, you were on life support for months. The doctors said you would not survive. But your mother prayed, and what happened?"

"Allah answered her prayers," Najjar said quietly.

"Yes, he did," the stranger confirmed. "And then what? Your parents brought you home from the hospital just days before the students seized the American Embassy. Your mother stayed at your side night and day from that point forward. She loved you dearly, didn't she?"

Najjar's eyes began to well up with tears, and then the stranger moved closer and spoke nearly in a whisper.

"Your father, rest his soul, was a risk taker."

Najjar nodded reluctantly.

"Your mother pleaded with your father not to move you and her to Iraq," the stranger went on. "But he would not listen. He meant well. Raised by merchants, he had a passion for business, but he lacked wisdom, discernment. He had failed at exporting Persian rugs to Europe and Canada. He had failed at exporting pistachios to Brazil and had to borrow money from your uncle. He always seemed to be in the wrong place at the wrong time. And then, convinced the rise of the Ayatollah in Iran would create a boom in business with the Shias in Iraq, he brought you all here to Samarra to build a business and make a fortune. Unfortunately, he did not see the Iran–Iraq War coming. His business never took off, and your parents were killed on the twelfth of December, 1983, in a car accident in Baghdad. And aside from your aunt and uncle, you have been all alone ever since."

The hair on the back of Najjar's neck stood erect. His face went pale. Forgetting about the extent of his injuries, he struggled to his feet and stared back at this boy. For several minutes, there was complete silence.

Then the stranger spoke his final revelation. "You are the brightest in your class, Najjar. You are secretly in love with Sheyda Saddaji, the girl who sits next to you. You will marry her before your twenty-fourth birthday."

"How do you . . . ?"

But Najjar could say no more. His mouth was as dry as the desert floor.

"Allah has chosen you, Najjar Hamid Malik. You will become a great scientist. You will help the Islamic world achieve ultimate power over the infidels and establish the Islamic caliphate. You will help usher in the era of the Promised One. But you must follow Allah without hesitation. You must give him your supreme allegiance. And then, if you are worthy, you shall live forever in paradise."

Najjar hoped it was true.

"Yes, I will serve Allah with my whole heart," he said with all the strength and sincerity he could muster. "I will devote myself to preparing for the Promised One. But who are you? Are you the One that—?"

The stranger raised his hand, and Najjar stopped talking.

"When the time is right, you will see me again."

Najjar stared into those black eyes. And then, without warning, the stranger vanished into the crowd.

SYRACUSE, NEW YORK
TWELVE YEARS LATER

"Let's go, David; we're going to be late!"

David Shirazi heard his father calling up the stairs and moved faster. He'd been waiting for this trip as long as he could remember, and he had no intention of missing the flight.

Every fall, his father and some of his father's doctor friends took their sons for a long weekend of camping and fishing on a remote island in Canada, accessible only by floatplane. The rule among the dads was that the boys had to be in high school or older. Both of David's older brothers always came home brimming with stories and pictures of catching monster walleyes, roasting marshmallows by the campfire, hanging out under the stars, and eating seriously unhealthy quantities of Tim Hortons doughnuts along the way. Last year, David had finally been old enough but had come down with a brutal case of the flu at the last moment and was crushed that his parents wouldn't let him go. Now he was almost sixteen, healthy, and completely jazzed not only to be going but to be missing a few days of physics and calculus as well.

David quickly rechecked the contents of his overstuffed backpack as he mentally reviewed their plans and checked his Timex. It was six minutes past eight in the morning. He knew they were scheduled on U.S. Air flight 4382, departing at 9:25 a.m. and arriving in Philadelphia at 10:45. From there, they'd transfer to U.S. Air flight 3940, departing at 11:25 and arriving in Montreal at exactly one that afternoon. The

Montreal airport, his brothers told him, was where they loaded up on the Tim Hortons.

It seemed ridiculous to David to fly 228 miles south to Philly only to turn around and fly 400 miles north. But there weren't any direct flights from Syracuse, so this was it. Crazier still was that once they got to Montreal, they still had a several-hour train ride farther north to a little town called Clova in upper Quebec. Only then came the floatplanes. But none of it mattered unless they made it to the airport on time.

At five feet, eleven inches tall and finally growing like a weed after being too small for too long, with jet-black curly hair, soulful brown eyes, and an always-tanned complexion, David might have looked Persian to his parents, but all he wanted was to be a normal American kid. David and his older brothers knew their parents' colorful tales of growing up in Iran under the Shah. They could recite chapter and verse of their mom and dad's saga of surviving the earliest days of the Revolution in '79, taking refuge with the Harpers in the Canadian Embassy for nearly four months, and finally escaping with the help of some government guy named Zalinsky. Every year on January 28, the boys dutifully listened as their parents marked the anniversary of their harrowing journey through the Tehran airport and their nerve-racking Swissair flight out of Iranian airspace, the remarkable story of their exodus from Tehran to Geneva to Toronto, and why they had finally wound up in central New York and settled in the too-often frigid and snowbound city of Syracuse (which the boys liked to call "Zero-cuse," "Siberacuse," and "No-Excuse").

The Shirazi boys knew their parents' courageous decisions and remarkable journey had made their lives possible. But the truth was, none of it really mattered to David. He was certainly grateful for their freedom. But he didn't want to think of himself as Iranian or a Muslim. He'd been born in the States. He'd grown up in the States. He dreamed in red, white, and blue. All he wanted to do now was fit in and excel, just like his brothers.

Azad, nineteen, was a straight-A sophomore in the premed program at Cornell. He planned to become a cardiologist like his father. He was also the best long-distance runner on the track team and could play the piano like no one David had ever heard. Not to be outdone, Saeed, seventeen, had graduated from high school a year early and was now a straight-A freshman at Harvard on a full swimming scholarship. If all went well, Saeed planned to go to Wharton or Stanford to get his MBA, unless the Harvard Business School gave him enough money to stay in Cambridge.

By comparison, David thought of himself as the black sheep of the family. While his brothers had twenty-twenty vision, he wore glasses. He was the only one of the three boys to get braces, which he still wore, embarrassing him to no end. His brothers hadn't ever seemed to struggle with acne, but he had struggled with it for years, though it was finally beginning to clear somewhat. Girls seemed to fawn over his brothers, but David had never been on a single date, and though there were a few girls in his class he secretly liked, he dreaded the prospect of having to ask any of them to the junior prom the following year. What's more, David hated chemistry and economics. He couldn't imagine becoming a doctor or a high-powered businessman, and he certainly had no interest in playing the piano.

He had, however, acquired his parents' brilliance and his brothers' passion for athletics. A straight-A student at Nottingham High School near the Syracuse city limits, David had scored a 1570 on his SATs and was actually on track to graduate two years ahead of schedule. He was the starting catcher on the varsity baseball team, the assistant photo editor of the school paper, the assistant editor of the yearbook, and a genius with a Nikon 35mm camera and a telephoto lens. His dream amused his professionally-minded parents, but it was his dream nonetheless: to work for *Sports Illustrated*, starting out on the road shooting baseball in the spring and football in the fall, and eventually working his way up to editor-in-chief.

Which reminded him . . .

David heard his father laying on the horn but turned back and grabbed the latest copy of *SI* off the kitchen table. Then he kissed his mother good-bye in the front yard, joined his brothers in the backseat of their Mercedes SUV, buckled up, donned his Discman, cranked up the Boss, sat back, and dove into the cover story on Roger Clemens.

They were seriously behind schedule, but David had no doubt his father would make it. And sure enough, fifteen minutes later they were parking at Hancock Field. It was high fives and laughter all around when they finally cleared through security, made it breathlessly to the gate, and found the other fathers and sons who were going with them.

David buckled himself into seat 16A, leaned back, stared out the window at the gorgeously sunny morning that was unusual for a city so often "blessed" with overcast skies, and finally relaxed. They'd made the flight. He had no homework. He had no school until the following Wednesday. And he was finally "one of the guys." He'd been dreaming about this trip for years, it was finally here, and nothing could ruin it.

10

David's father lit up the moment he saw them.

David, on the other hand, instantly went dark. *What in the world are* they *doing here?* he privately groaned.

"Hey, over here," Charlie Harper yelled from across the lounge area, waving them through the crowd that was waiting for the next flight.

Dr. Shirazi raced right over and gave his old friend a bear hug. "You really made it!"

"Are you kidding?" Charlie laughed, slapping his old friend on the back. "Marseille and I wouldn't have missed this for the world!"

"Yes, thanks for inviting us, Dr. Shirazi," added the young woman standing beside Charlie.

"Well, you're very welcome, young lady," Dr. Shirazi replied. "But I'm sorry—you can't possibly be Charlie Harper's little girl."

She smiled.

"Look at you—you're lovely. How could you be related to this guy?" Dr. Shirazi joshed, slapping Charlie on the back.

"Obviously I take after my mother," she quipped.

Dr. Shirazi laughed from his belly as David winced with embarrassment.

"Well, that would explain it," the doctor chuckled, giving her a hug. "How old are you now?"

"I just turned fifteen in June."

Azad elbowed David in the ribs and raised his eyebrows. It wasn't nearly discreet enough for David.

Then Saeed leaned over to his brothers and whispered, "Don't get ideas, Bro. I saw her first."

David felt the blood rush to his ears, his neck, and his face. The young woman before them was certainly attractive in her faded blue jeans, cream fisherman knit sweater, and worn tennis shoes, her brown hair pulled back in a black scrunchie. But she was an interloper on a guys-only fishing weekend, and now these two morons were angling for something other than walleye and northern pike.

Dr. Shirazi shook his head. "How long has it been since I've seen you all? Five or six years?"

"As a whole family, that's probably true," Charlie replied. "I think this one was still in grammar school when you last came for Thanksgiving."

Dr. Shirazi sighed. "Please, please forgive me for letting so much time go by."

"Oh, my friend, there's no need," Charlie insisted. "Life has been busy for all of us. Besides, you and I got to see each other—what?—a year ago maybe, at that conference in New York, right?"

"That's right, that's right; but you're too kind, Charlie, really. I should be coming to visit you and thank you every year, and bringing my family along too. You and Claire saved us, Charlie. Nasreen and I will never forget it."

David's father, lost in another time, suddenly became aware of the group of men and boys observing this whole interaction with confusion.

"Oh, forgive me, guys," he said. "I need to make some introductions. I'm getting old, my friends. But being the founder and organizer of our illustrious group, I've taken the liberty of this surprise. It is a great honor to introduce you to one of my dearest friends in all of the world, Charlie Harper—the man who rescued Nasreen and me out of Iran—and his daughter, Marseille."

As everyone said hello, shook hands with the two of them, and introduced themselves, David shrank to the back of the huddle. Mortified, he watched Azad and Saeed and the other boys chatting up Marseille—trying to look harmless and friendly but skating dangerously close to shameless flirting. David, meanwhile, found himself battling varying degrees of embarrassment, anger, annoyance, and betrayal, to name just a few of the emotions colliding within him. He'd just been blindsided. This was supposed to be a *guys'* trip. It always had been. That's the way it had always been billed to him. That's what he had been so looking forward to. And now his father had gone and blown the whole thing.

11

Najjar Malik heard the screeching tires and turned to look.

He was about to cross Al Rasheed Street in downtown Baghdad and fully expected to see a major car wreck. Instead, less than fifty yards away to his right, he saw a white Mercedes swerve and narrowly miss a delivery truck whose driver had just slammed on his brakes in the middle of rush-hour traffic for no apparent reason. Blocked from going forward, the driver of the Mercedes now tried to back up but suddenly found himself cut off by a green Citroën. Just then, a minivan screeched to a halt beside the Mercedes. The side door flew open. Three masked men armed with AK-47s jumped out and surrounded the car.

"Get out! Get out!" one of the gunmen screamed at the terrified man in the driver's seat.

Najjar knew he should run for cover, but for some reason he just stood there and stared. He could see a veiled woman in the passenger seat, presumably the driver's wife. He could also see a small child in the backseat, shrieking with fear.

Two of the gunmen started pounding on their windows, still demanding they get out. Terrified, the family complied, their hands held high in the air, the young child—a little girl not more than four or five years old—crying all the louder. The gunmen forced the woman and the child to lie facedown on the pavement while their husband and father was smashed over the back of the head, bound quickly around his hands and feet, and thrown in the back of the minivan.

Then one of the masked men aimed his machine gun at the child and fired. The girl's cries immediately ceased, but now the mother began screaming for her dead child. At that, the gunman shot her in the back of the head as well.

The street suddenly grew quiet.

As the gunmen turned to get back in the vehicles and make their escape with their new hostage, one of them glanced toward Najjar, and Najjar found himself staring into the kidnapper's eyes. The two of them just stood there for a moment, seemingly frozen in time and space. Najjar wanted to bolt but couldn't move a muscle.

The masked man raised his weapon and pointed it at Najjar's chest. Najjar tried to scream but couldn't make a sound. The man pulled the trigger. Najjar shut his eyes. But he heard nothing. He felt nothing.

He opened his eyes and realized the gun hadn't gone off. The man cleared the chamber and pulled the trigger again. Again, Najjar involuntarily shut his eyes. But again he heard nothing, felt nothing.

When he opened his eyes the second time, he found the man desperately fiddling with the magazine, then raising the weapon over his head and pulling the trigger. This time the weapon fired perfectly. Now, he lowered the machine gun, aimed it at Najjar's face, and pulled the trigger for the third time. Najjar instantly shut his eyes and held his breath.

Nothing happened.

His eyes still shut and still holding his breath, his lungs about to explode, Najjar heard the gunman cursing. He also heard the other terrorists shouting at him to get in the car and get moving. A moment later, he heard screeching tires, and when he finally opened his eyes, the gunmen were gone.

Najjar collapsed into some bushes and began to vomit uncontrollably. He had never been so scared in all his life.

He lay on the pavement, holding his head in his hands and losing all track of time. He didn't hear the ambulance sirens approaching, didn't see the flashing lights of the police cars. He didn't remember being taken to the hospital and treated for shock. He barely remembered being interrogated at length, not just by the local police but by agents of the *Mukhabarat*, one of Saddam's thirteen intelligence agencies, and certainly the most feared. *"Who were the gunmen?"* they demanded. *"Have you seen them before? Could you identify them? What kind of vehicles were they driving? What were the license plate numbers?"* The questions went on and on, but Najjar was of little help. He truly didn't recall much, and later that afternoon, the police and doctors released him.

Exhausted and still somewhat disoriented, Najjar left the hospital and saw a row of taxicabs waiting out front. The first driver in the line rolled down his window and shouted, "Where are you going? Can I help you?"

Najjar stumbled down the front steps and got into the backseat of the cab, only to realize he had no wallet on him and thus no money. Worse, before Najjar could say anything, the driver pulled into traffic and Najjar realized he had no idea where he was going, either.

"You look like you've seen an evil spirit," the driver said, staring at him in the rearview mirror.

"Just watch the road," Najjar said, more gruffly than he had intended.

"Where to?"

Najjar couldn't think. He felt foggy, drugged. For the life of him, he couldn't remember where he lived—what street, what building. Where was his wallet? Had someone stolen it? Had he just left it at the hospital? It had his ID. It had his only picture of his mother and father. It had . . .

Without instruction, the driver began heading east, across the Tigris River toward Sadr City, a district of nearly a million Shia Muslims.

Where are we going? Najjar wondered. *How does the driver know where to take me?*

Ten minutes later, the driver pulled up in front of an apartment building that looked familiar. As did the neighborhood. As did the people.

"Najjar? Is that you?"

Najjar instantly recognized the voice of his aunt, calling to him from across a courtyard.

She ran up, pulled him out of the cab, and kissed him on both cheeks in greeting. Then she paid the driver and, sensing that Najjar was not well, led him up to their apartment.

"Are you okay, Najjar? Why did you take a cab home from the university? Why didn't you take the bus as usual?"

As they stepped onto the elevator and his aunt pushed the button for their floor, Najjar was struck with the oddest thought. *How had that driver just gotten him home, when he himself had not remembered where he lived?*

Najjar's aunt tucked him into bed, and he slept for the entire afternoon.

12

A storm was brewing at twenty-eight thousand feet over Lake Ontario.

"David, would you mind switching seats with me?"

Startled, David Shirazi opened his eyes and found himself staring into the face of Mr. Harper. Biting his lip to keep himself from saying something he shouldn't, he peeled off his headphones.

"Say again?" he asked, trying to get his bearings.

"I'm sorry—I didn't mean to disturb you," the older man said with a genuineness that only annoyed David more. "It's just that now that we're at cruising altitude, I was wondering if I could sit with your father and catch up a little. Would you mind?"

Of course I would mind, David thought. *You're not even supposed to be here, and now you want my seat?*

But David Shirazi loved his father far too much to say it. Indeed, he felt guilty for thinking it.

"Sure, Mr. Harper, no problem," he mumbled.

Harper shook his head and chuckled as David unbuckled himself and stepped into the aisle. "You and your brothers are all taller than your father now, aren't you?"

David nodded. He didn't want to disrespect his father by being rude. But he certainly had no interest in small talk at the moment. He scanned the rear section of the Boeing 737, looking for somewhere else to sit and finding nothing. The flight was packed. The rain was picking up and through the windows he could see flashes of lightning crackling

61

through the thick gray thunderheads all around them. Then the seat belt sign came on and the copilot warned them they were heading into some rough weather and should take their seats immediately.

"What seat were you in, Mr. Harper?" David finally asked as the man buckled up beside his father.

"Oh, right, sorry—23B," Harper replied. "Right next to Marseille."

Great.

David put his headphones on, hit Play, and made his way toward the rear of the packed jet, carefully gripping the seatbacks along the way as the turbulence picked up. He spotted Marseille. She was curled up against the window with a red airline blanket over her, wearing her own set of earphones. David was glad her eyes were closed. He wasn't up for small talk with her, either. He quietly took the seat beside her and buckled himself in, careful not to make a sound that might wake her. It didn't work. Marseille turned, rubbed her eyes, and smiled.

"Hey," she said.

"Hey."

She took off her headphones. "Sorry I didn't say hi before," she said. "I just got chatting with everyone else. Everyone's been really nice."

He shrugged. What was he supposed to say?

"First time?" she asked.

There was a long pause.

"What, in a plane?" he asked, incredulous.

"No, up to Quebec—on this whole fishing thing," she replied.

He nodded.

"Me too," she said, then added, "obviously."

There was another awkward pause. Thunder clapped just outside their window, startling everyone.

"Quite a storm, huh?" she asked, her hands gripping the armrest.

"Yep."

The two were quiet for a while, and David slowly began to relax. Then, out of nowhere, Marseille asked, "Hey, do you remember coming to our house for Thanksgiving, a long time ago?"

He actually did have some memories of the rainy weekend of board games and hide-and-seek at the Harpers' small Cape Cod house in

Spring Lake, along the Jersey Shore. He even remembered a picture of Mr. Harper and Marseille carving the turkey together, which he had seen in one of the dozens of photo albums his mother kept organized and labeled on a shelf in their living room in Syracuse. But he didn't feel like admitting any of that now.

"Not really," he said lamely.

Marseille got the message. "Six years is a long time, I guess," she said quietly, then turned back to watch the lightning flashes out the window.

David watched her pull up the blanket and try to get comfortable. Then he felt a sudden pang of guilt. This poor girl was only trying to be nice, and he was acting like an idiot. For crying out loud, even the Mariano and Calveto brothers had been nicer to her. They'd had different motives, to be sure, but he'd been brought up better than this. It wasn't Marseille's fault she was here. David's own father had invited them. The least he could do was be civil.

"Whatcha listening to?" he asked, putting his own music on pause and taking off his headphones.

She turned back, her eyebrows raised. "First you ignore me; now you're suddenly interested in my music?"

"I'm just asking. Conversation. Small talk. They have that down in New Jersey, don't they?"

Marseille studied him for a moment as if sizing up his sincerity or lack thereof. He took the moment to study her as well. She really was quite good-looking, a sort of girl-next-door beautiful, he decided. Her summer tan hadn't yet faded. She wore no makeup or fingernail polish. She had a barely noticeable scar on her upper lip. But it was her eyes—big and warm and expressive—that really caught his attention.

"Okay, guess," she said at last.

"Guess?"

"Sure," she prodded. "You know, conjecture, consider, reckon, suppose—they know how to do that up there in central New York, don't they?"

Caught off guard, David suddenly smiled a real smile. "Sometimes," he conceded. "All right, let me see—Madonna?"

She shook her head.

"J. Lo?"

Marseille rolled her eyes. *"Pleeease."*

"Hmm," David said, "so I'm thinking *Lady Marmalade* is out too?"

"Ugh," she replied. "Do I look like I would listen to Christina Aguilera?"

"I don't know," David said. "It's remotely possible, isn't it?"

"No, it really isn't."

More thunder rumbled outside. As she turned away and began to pull the blanket over her again, her necklace shifted and glinted in the overhead light. A pair of drama masks, comedy and tragedy. *Aha.*

"*Les Mis*," he said just as Marseille was putting her headphones back on.

She stopped cold and turned back to him again.

"What did you say?"

"You know—France, revolutionaries, 'One Day More' . . ."

Marseille paused and stared at him for a moment.

"I'm right," David said, seeing her surprise. "I got it, didn't I?"

Marseille shook her head. "No," she said softly. "But you're shockingly close."

Then, rather than turn away from him—back to her music, back to the storm, back to her dreams—she surprised him by putting her headphones over his ears and hitting Play.

Try to remember the kind of September
When life was slow and oh, so mellow.

David was startled. This was the sound track from *The Fantasticks*—the world's longest-running musical . . . and his mother's favorite.

13

It was now late afternoon.

The sun was just beginning to set as the de Havilland floatplane steadily gained altitude and gently banked northeast. The line of thunderstorms they had encountered after leaving Philly had cleared by the time they landed in Montreal and caught the train to the tiny town of Clova. Here, over the province of Quebec, the skies were clear.

Dr. Shirazi sat in the copilot's seat of the single-engine prop plane, nicknamed the "Beaver" by the Canadian-based de Havilland company. Azad and Saeed sat in the middle row. David was in the back row by himself, surrounded by backpacks and fishing gear. It was cold and cramped, and David knew he would be back there for nearly an hour, but the truth was, he was finally beginning to enjoy himself.

The de Havilland Beaver had just one serious design flaw, as David saw it. It was loud. Really loud. The view out the tiny window was amazing, but he could barely hear himself think. Yet as they reached a cruising altitude of eight thousand feet—soaring high above a seemingly endless carpet of blue rivers and lakes and lush green islands, moving farther and farther away from any sign of civilization—David couldn't help but nudge Azad in front of him and say, "She's beautiful, isn't she?"

"*What?*" Azad yelled, barely able to hear over the roar of the Pratt & Whitney 450-horsepower engine.

"*I said, she's a beauty, isn't she?*" David yelled back, leaning closer.

Azad laughed.

"What's so funny?" David asked, bracing himself for whatever sarcastic zinger was sure to come.

"You," Azad said. "You're a real comedian."

"Why? I'm just saying . . ."

"I know what you're saying. But forget about her. You haven't got a prayer."

"What?"

"With Marcy."

"Who?"

"The girl—Marcy."

"You mean Marseille?"

"Whatever—she's not your type."

David just stared at him for a moment. "I was talking about the plane, you idiot."

"Whatever. Just steer clear. You're way out of your league, Charlie Brown."

★　★　★　★　★

Their twilight water landing was picture-perfect.

Moments later, the other two de Havillands bringing the rest of their party landed and taxied over to join them by two wooden docks; four small, flat motorboats were moored alongside. A cluster of small, weathered, rustic cabins stood nearby. The only problem was they were running behind schedule and were quickly losing the light they needed to set up their base camp.

Larry McKenzie, the gruff, scruffy, ponytailed, chain-smoking pilot of the plane David had been on—and the owner of McKenzie Air Expeditions, the charter service his father's fishing group had used for years—helped them unload their gear. The other two pilots did the same and carried several large coolers and cardboard boxes into the cabins as well. These were filled with food for the long weekend. There was nothing gourmet, just basic fruits and vegetables, milk, juice, coffee, butter, bread, eggs, and bacon, all of which would supplement the main dish each night, which would be, of course, fresh fish.

When they were done, McKenzie gathered the group together by the shore and reminded them of the rules. "Don't drown," he barked. "Don't get bit by a snake. Don't get eaten by a bear. Any questions?"

Most were veterans of this trip. None of them seemed bothered. Only Marseille appeared a bit unnerved, whispering something to her father David couldn't quite hear.

"No questions?" McKenzie confirmed. "Good. We're out."

A moment later, he and the other two pilots were back in their cockpits, hightailing back to the real world. These guys were making $750 a head to drop "clients" off in the middle of nowhere. That and a "don't drown" pep talk and poof, they were gone. *Nice work if you can get it,* David thought. Not that he really cared. It wasn't his money. It was his father's, and his father always said this was why he'd escaped from Iran—to be free. Free to think. Free to work. Free to play. Free to travel. Free to do whatever he pleased, without a tyrant controlling his every move. *Amen,* David thought. He took in a deep breath of cool Canadian night air. The temperature was under fifty and dropping fast. But they were finally here.

Dr. Shirazi turned to the group and encouraged them all to grab their gear and set up the cabins. Meanwhile, he asked David and Marseille to go gather as much firewood as they could. Internally, David resisted. He hadn't come on this trip to be treated like a kid. But he felt better when he saw his brothers' faces, just visible in the final traces of the sunset—why should David get time alone with the girl?

Marseille's reaction brought him back to reality. "Out there?" she asked. "With the bears?"

"Don't listen to Old Man McKenzie," Dr. Shirazi laughed. "He's not even Canadian. He's from Poughkeepsie."

"Poughkeepsie?"

"He got hooked on drugs and dodged the draft in the Vietnam War. Moved up here to get away from Nixon and get free health care. I met him when he desperately needed triple bypass surgery faster than the system up here could get him scheduled. Nice guy, but one taco short of a combo platter, if you know what I mean."

David looked at Marseille as Marseille stared at his father.

"What does that have to do with bears?" she asked.

David grinned at the perplexed look on her face. "Nothing," he said, handing her a small flashlight and shaking his head. "That's just the way my dad answers a question. Come on. Let's go."

David headed into the woods, a more powerful flashlight in his hands. Marseille clearly didn't want to be left behind. She zipped up her North Face fleece jacket and caught up to him quickly.

"So my dad tells me you read and write Farsi fluently," she said.

"Yeah."

"And German."

No reply.

"And you're working on Arabic."

Still no reply.

"Of course," she said, glancing at him as they walked, "you might want to work on your English a bit."

"Very funny."

"I'm just saying . . ."

"Yes, I speak all those languages."

"What are you, a genius?" she asked.

"No."

"That's what my dad says."

"How would your dad know? He hasn't seen me in six years."

"He says you were almost fluent in all those then."

David said nothing. They walked quietly for several minutes.

"So where in the world are we, anyway?" Marseille finally asked, trying again to break the ice.

"You really can't stand silence, can you?" David replied.

"Shut up," she laughed, punching him in the arm, "and answer my question."

David feigned pain but finally answered. "The Gouin Reservoir."

"The what?"

"The Gouin Reservoir—or in French, *Réservoir Gouin*."

"*Ooh la la*, I'm impressed," she said. "*Parlez-vous français, aussi?*"

David shook his head. "*Je ne remember much pas.*"

Marseille laughed. "*Je le doute.* Anyway, that's too bad."

"Why?"

"'Cause we're in Quebec, and they speak French up here."

"So you *do* know where we are."

"I can read the ticket stub. But *Le Réservoir Gouin*—what the heck is that?"

"You really want to know?"

"I'd just like to hear you put two or three sentences together in English . . . you know, just to know that you can!"

"Fine," David said. "It's a collection of hundreds of small lakes containing innumerable islands and peninsulas with highly irregular shapes, located in the central portion of the Canadian province of Quebec, roughly equidistant from Ottawa, Montreal, and Quebec City. Its shoreline stretches over 5,600 kilometers, excluding islands. The reservoir was created in 1918 at the upper reaches of the Saint Maurice River and is named after Jean-Lomer Gouin, who was premier of Quebec at the time. Construction was done by the Shawinigan Water and Power Company to facilitate hydroelectric development by controlling the flow of water for the stations downstream."

Marseille had stopped walking and was staring at David. "How do you know all that?"

"I read a lot."

"What did you do, memorize an encyclopedia article or something?"

David shrugged and quickly changed the subject. "Hey, over there, grab those old branches and I'll grab these," he said. "That'll be a start."

For much of the next hour, they gathered firewood, hauled it back to the camp, dropped it off, and went back out for more, avoiding the older boys. In their gathering, they passed by a few cabins farther inland, unoccupied and clearly out of use. They were unlocked and seemed to have been left to the elements. One of them displayed plenty of bear claw scratchings around the door and windows, but another A-frame style cabin was in pretty good shape, just a little dusty. They didn't have time then to explore, but this little island ghost town fascinated them both.

It had been a long day, and once the gear had been set up or stowed for later, the whole group was sleeping by 9 p.m. The next four days stretched out in front of them with the promise of endless pike and walleye. But the fish would wait till morning.

14

Najjar Malik was exhausted.

Even after a long nap and a simple, home-cooked meal, the morning's violence, the malfunctioning machine gun, and the strange encounter with the mysterious taxi driver still rattled him.

After dinner, in spite of his weary protests, Najjar's aunt and uncle took him shopping in the bazaar. At one point, his aunt was haggling with a grocer over the quality of some pistachios while his uncle sat across the street in the shade, smoking a water pipe and chatting with the older men. Najjar looked over a collection of leather boots and wished he had enough to buy himself a pair. But he still hadn't found his wallet, and when it was clear he wasn't going to be buying anything that day, the shoe seller told him to go away.

Najjar nervously inched his way through the market, still wondering who the man was who had been kidnapped, still wondering who had kidnapped him and why, and why they had killed his wife and child. The gruesome images were indelibly etched in his mind's eye. He wanted to forget it all, but he could not. Was it political? Was it for money? He didn't want to think about any of it, but he couldn't think of anything else.

Just then he nearly tripped over a beggar sitting cross-legged against a cement wall.

"Forgive me," Najjar said. "I didn't see you there."

"It is not mine to forgive," said the beggar, a surprisingly young man—hardly older than Najjar himself—covered in a dirty brown robe and wearing no sandals or shoes. His filthy black feet were covered with oozing blisters. "Only Allah can do that, if he so chooses."

Najjar shrugged. The religious fervor of his youth was dying. What had Allah really given him? Sadness. Loneliness. Poverty. Despair. Were these the gifts Allah gave to his children?

"Come, my friend," the beggar said, "you look downtrodden. Let me tell you about your future."

Najjar shook his head, then scanned the crowd to find his aunt and uncle.

"You don't want to know your future?" the beggar asked. "Or you don't think I can see it?"

"Both," Najjar half lied. He desperately wanted to know his future. But he hadn't time for back-alley charlatans.

"I think you are lying," the beggar said, his tone suddenly low and sober. "I think you desperately want to know your future. But you think you haven't time to spare for some back-alley charlatan."

Startled, Najjar whipped his head around and stared at the young homeless man in disbelief.

"You are troubled by the violence you saw in the street this morning," the beggar said, his face smudged with dirt. "But all your questions will be answered in due course."

Najjar was scared. *Who is this person? How can he know my most intimate thoughts?*

"May I ask you a question?" the beggar said.

Najjar nodded.

"If you could go anywhere in the world, if you could travel anywhere and money was no object, where would you go?"

"I don't know," Najjar said blankly.

"Again you are lying," the beggar said. "You don't trust me. Fair enough. You don't know me. But the moment I asked you, you instantly thought of where you would like to go, true?"

Najjar was embarrassed and confused. He nodded again.

"Write it down," the beggar said.

"Where?"

"On a piece of paper. Don't let me see it. But I will tell you what you write."

"That's impossible."

"Nothing is impossible."

Najjar didn't have a piece of paper on him, much less a pen or pencil, but he turned back to the hustle and bustle of the bazaar and found a grocer nearby. From him, he secured a small pencil, then spotted an empty cigarette pack on the ground. Najjar ripped open the pack and scribbled down a location inside, carefully shielding it from the beggar and any other prying eyes that might be around. When he was finished, he stuffed the pack in his jeans pocket and stared back at the young man who now captivated his attention.

"Bless you," the beggar said.

"Why do you say that?" Najjar asked.

"Because you just wrote down the Jamkaran Mosque near Qom, Iran."

Najjar's eyes went wide. "How did you do that?" he asked, his pulse pounding. "How did you know?"

The beggar didn't respond. His face revealed no expression whatsoever. Instead, he simply said, "Now write down the name of a world leader."

Unnerved, Najjar hesitated. "Living or dead?" he asked.

"You choose," the beggar said.

Najjar pulled out the cigarette pack, scratched out *Jamkaran Mosque*, and wrote, *Saddam Hussein*. Then, realizing that would be too obvious, he thought for a few moments, crossed out *Saddam*, and wrote instead, *Fulgencio Batista*. Batista, Najjar had recently learned, had been the president of Cuba in the late 1950s. He crumpled up the cigarette pack and put it back into his pocket.

"You have chosen well, my friend," the beggar said.

"How so?"

"I am touched."

"Why?"

"For you are truly a spiritual young man. Allah can do great things with one such as you."

Najjar had no idea what the man meant, but it was obvious he didn't know what Najjar had written down. Then Najjar heard his aunt calling for him.

"I have to go."

"But I have not given you the answer," the beggar said.

"I don't think you know."

"But I do."

"Then whose name did I write down?"

"Muhammad Ibn Hasan Ibn Ali," the beggar said.

"*Ha!*" Najjar said, somewhat disappointed but determined not to be perceived as nearly having fallen for this man's trickery. "Not even close. You think that just because I've always wanted to visit the wishing well in Iran where the Twelfth Imam once appeared that I would actually be so stupid as to write down the name of the Mahdi, peace be upon him?"

"Actually," the beggar said, "first you wrote down Saddam Hussein's name. Only then did you choose the Promised One."

Najjar again was stunned. The man was half right. But this, too, was strange. How could the beggar know that Najjar had written down Saddam's name at first but not know that he had replaced it with Batista's name? None of it made sense.

Uneasy, Najjar decided it was time to go. His aunt was calling him again and sounded quite annoyed. He pulled the cigarette packet from his pocket and tossed it to the beggar.

"See for yourself," he said, then turned to his aunt and yelled, "I'm coming!"

The beggar caught the rumpled pack but did not open it. Rather, he tossed it right back at Najjar, seeming to dare Najjar to reconsider. A bit annoyed himself now, Najjar walked over to the beggar, leaned down, opened the cigarette pack, and prepared to read the name Fulgencio Batista.

But to his shock, the words were not there.

Rather, next to the scratched-out name of Saddam Hussein was the name Muhammad Ibn Hasan Ibn Ali—in his own handwriting, no less.

Dumbfounded, Najjar looked back at the beggar. He tried to say something, but no words formed.

The young beggar spoke instead. "You will serve the Promised One when the time is right. You are not yet ready. But do not fear. The time has not yet come."

Najjar suddenly felt icy cold. His fingers went numb. Now his uncle was demanding he come home with them. He looked up to ask his uncle for another few minutes. He had questions. He needed answers. But when he looked back, the beggar was gone.

15

For David, it was even better than the stories he'd been told.

His older brothers had told him about their adventures, but they weren't capable of describing the color of the sky in the dawn or the feeling of being so far removed from any other human beings. David felt like a pioneer and imagined that their group was as far as human society had ever gone. He spent the first full day glued to his dad's side, getting an introduction to the walleye up close and by the dozen. He'd never seen a place so thick with fish, as if no one had ever fished here except the black bears. He and his father skimmed around the edges of the island in low, flat, jigging boats, and David began to learn how to work the sonar and how to feel a strike as he held the rod. The fish were low and deep in the lake, but they hauled them up and into their boat all day, stopping only to drift in a little bay as they munched PB&J and the last of the doughnuts the boys had bought at the airport in Montreal. The water was clear, the sky was deep blue, and even the simplest of sandwiches tasted wonderful. Of course, there would be plenty of fish for dinner.

David wondered how Marseille and Mr. Harper were getting on. The two had decided to spend the morning on a hike with the promise to rejoin the fishermen in midafternoon. David found himself looking forward to seeing her and even tried to prethink some better conversation than he'd been able to summon up thus far. He wondered if she even liked fishing, seeing as she and her dad were the only ones who hadn't plunged in first thing. Either way, though he was a bit embarrassed to think it, he was actually glad she was here. Maybe his father hadn't done such a bad thing after all.

David wasn't disappointed, therefore, to see Marseille sitting by the shore when his father's boat came to rest at the dock. As the two dads took the opportunity to grab a cold drink together and catch up on old times, David shyly asked Marseille if she was up for a walk. "Want to show me what you guys discovered all morning?" He hoped he didn't sound too eager.

Smiling, she said, "Sure. We just walked along the shore for a long time and tried to see if we could make it around the whole circumference of the island. We weren't even close. This place is huge!"

David grabbed a thermos of water, and the two wandered off together. After a few minutes, he realized they were heading straight for their "ghost town."

Marseille pointed out the clawed screens of the cabins, and David decided it might be better not to make any more bear jokes. The A-frame seemed almost tidy among the group of shabby cabins, and with both of them exerting their full weight at the same moment, they were able to force open the front door. Inside they found a few slingback chairs and a very basic bed frame supporting an ancient, thin mattress. David used his sweatshirt to dust off the chairs and dragged them over to the open doorway. They both plopped into them, feeling quite at home.

"Any good fish stories from your morning on the reservoir?" Marseille asked.

He liked the question, liked the way she asked it, liked the way she looked at him with real interest.

"It was great to be out with my dad. I'm a walleye rookie, but I caught more than I thought I would."

David asked about her school and found out her favorite classes were English, creative writing, history, and drama. He asked about her hobbies and learned she played the piano, only because her mother wanted her to, but also the saxophone because she loved it. She ran cross-country but not terribly well; she loved poetry, Shakespeare, singing in the choir, and especially acting in school plays. She was looking forward to the spring, when she planned to try out for the part of Nellie Forbush in the production of *South Pacific* at her school. Her real dream was someday to play the role of Cosette in *Les Mis* on Broadway, or better yet, in London or Paris.

"What about politics?" he asked her.

"What about it?"

"Are you a Democrat or a Republican?"

"I have no idea," she said.

"No idea?" he asked, incredulous.

"No, why should I?"

"Weren't your parents Foreign Service officers in France, Italy, and Switzerland after getting out of Iran?"

"Yeah, so?"

"So doesn't your father teach history and U.S. foreign policy at Princeton?"

"Yeah, so?"

"So wasn't your mom a consultant for the Treasury Department for a few years before getting a job with some big investment bank in Manhattan?"

"She was, but how do you know all that?" Marseille asked.

David shrugged. "I don't know—I hear things; I remember them. The point is, your parents are so interested in the world and in government. Didn't any of that rub off on you?"

"I guess not," Marseille said. "I can't stand politics. It's just a bunch of old men arguing and spending all of our money."

David laughed. She was feisty and sure of herself, and he liked that. "Do you think it's all going to get better if young people like us tune out the world's problems and do nothing?"

"No," she conceded.

"Well, shouldn't you pick a team and root for it?"

"Maybe," she said at last, pulling a box of Junior Mints from her knapsack and eating a few without offering him any. "All right, which party should I sign up for—Republicans or Democrats?"

David laughed again. "Well, it's really not for me to say," he said, sure she was going to prove to be a liberal Democrat like him but wanting her to come to her own conclusion lest he look too pushy. "How about this? I'll give you a little test to see if you're a liberal or a conservative. Then you decide which party is best for you. Deal?"

Marseille thought about that for a moment and liked it. "Deal."

"Okay, let's see. Are taxes too low or too high?"

"Too high."

"Should government spend more or less on education, health care, the environment, and other important necessities?"

"Government spends too much as it is," she said. "I think they should let people keep more of what they earn."

David continued cautiously, surprised by her answers. "Should the government protect a woman's right to choose?"

"You mean abortion? No way! It's a baby, David. You can't kill a baby in her mother's womb."

David gulped.

"Don't you agree?" she pressed.

"Well . . ."

"Isn't government supposed to protect life, liberty, and the pursuit of happiness?" she continued. "Life—it's the first one, for crying out loud. Life comes first, then choice. If you switch that around, you've got chaos. Right?"

David was stumped and decided to move on. "What about gay rights?" he asked.

"Well, you shouldn't be mean to gay people, but they shouldn't have special rights. After all, marriage is a beautiful, sacred thing, between one man and one woman, don't you think?"

David nodded weakly.

"*Don't* you think?" she pressed a bit stronger, popping a few more Junior Mints into her mouth and smiling.

"Absolutely," he insisted. "Beautiful, sacred—absolutely."

He asked her some foreign policy questions, then a few about trade policy and immigration. When he was done, he just sat there for a few minutes, trying to process all that he'd just heard.

"Well?" she asked, practically glowing in the fiery rays of the sun beaming through the window. "What am I?"

David shook his head. "You're a 99.967-percent rock-solid conservative."

"Really?" she said, seeming happy with the sound of that. "So that's the Republicans, right?"

David nodded but was crestfallen. He liked this girl. But he couldn't fall for a Republican, could he?

"So are you a Republican too, David?"

At that, he shook his head, almost imperceptibly.

Marseille was aghast. "What do you mean? Don't you agree with me on all those things?"

They talked and argued—civilly, but passionately—as the afternoon slipped away unnoticed. For someone not interested in politics, she certainly had strong opinions! Before they realized it, the sun had fully set, and they were arguing by the light of their flashlights. David suggested they'd better put their political feud on hold and get back before their fathers sent out a search party for them. Reluctantly, Marseille agreed.

"Maybe we should change the subject," David said as they bush-whacked their way to the camp.

"Maybe." They picked their way around a fallen tree in the darkness. "So what about you? What do you dream of doing someday, aside from running for president as a lunatic Democrat?"

"Very funny," David said. He stopped walking for a moment. "You really want to know what my dream is?"

She nodded, expectantly.

"I dream—" he hesitated, and her eyes widened—"of having some of those Junior Mints."

Marseille laughed. "Dream on. These are my own special treat."

"You're really not going to offer me one?" he said. "Not even one?"

"Maybe if you really tell me your dream."

He smiled. "All right, it's a deal."

"Go ahead," Marseille said. "I'm listening."

"Actually, I've never told anyone this. . . ."

"It's okay," she said. "You can tell me."

He took a deep breath.

"My dream . . ."

She leaned in. *"Is . . . ?"*

He paused again, letting the suspense build further. ". . . to get back to camp without being eaten by a bear."

With that, he took off in a sprint for their camp, laughing, with Marseille running after him, yelling and trying to catch up.

16

Najjar lay in bed and closed his eyes, but he could not sleep.

His mind raced as he pored over every detail of the kidnapping and his encounters with the taxi driver and later with the beggar. Then he thought of the little boy who had rescued him from a beating by those bullies when he was just ten years old. Was Allah calling him? Najjar wondered. Had he sent angels to protect him, to speak to him? Was he truly being chosen to know and serve the Promised One? It couldn't possibly be. He had no parents, no money, no religious clerics in his family, no political power, no influential friends, no reason of any kind to attract the attention of the Mahdi, peace be upon him. Yet how could he deny this bizarre chain of events?

He dared not ask his aunt or his uncle about any of this. He couldn't confide in anyone he knew. They would think he had gone mad. And maybe he had. But maybe not. Maybe Khomeini really hadn't been the one the Islamic world was waiting for but rather just a forerunner. Perhaps the end of days was truly approaching. Perhaps the messiah was coming after all—and soon.

As the sun began to rise in the eastern sky, a weary Najjar slipped out of bed, quietly opened his bedroom door, scanned the hallway for any signs of movement, and then carefully crept to the living room, hoping he wouldn't wake anyone. On the shelf beside the television, there were a handful of books—the family Qur'an, of course, and then a series of Shia histories and theological textbooks. His uncle, a devoutly religious man, had wanted to be a mullah before abandoning his studies to join the family business. But even to this day, whenever he had a little spare change, he bought another of the religious books he loved to study, and Najjar loved him for it.

One particular book on the highest shelf was by an Iranian man named Dr. Alireza Birjandi, one of the most renowned Shia scholars in the world and an expert on Shia eschatology, or End Times theology. His book, *The Imams of History and the Coming of the Messiah*, was a classic, arguably the definitive book on the subject. It told the stories and legends and controversies surrounding all twelve of the Imams, but the stories of the last—the Twelfth Imam—had always intrigued Najjar most.

The Twelfth Imam, Dr. Birjandi explained, was not a mythical character or a fictional construct. He was a real, flesh-and-blood person who had lived in the ninth century and would someday reemerge to change the course of history. Born in Samarra, Iraq, in or around the year 868, his name was Muhammad Ibn Hasan Ibn Ali. Like the eleven Shia Muslim leaders who went before him, Muhammad was a direct descendant of the founder of Islam and was thought to have been divinely chosen to be the spiritual guide and ultimate human authority of the Muslim people.

But before he reached an age of maturity when he could teach and counsel the Muslim world as was believed to be his destiny, the Twelfth Imam had vanished from human society. Some said he was four years old. Others said five or six. Some believed he fell into a well in Samarra, though his body was never recovered. Others believed his mother placed him in the well to prevent the evil rulers of the time from finding him, capturing him, and killing him—and that little Muhammad subsequently became supernaturally invisible. That's why some called him the "Hidden Imam," believing that Ali was not dead but simply hidden from the sight of mankind until the end of days, when Allah would once again reveal him.

Najjar carefully turned the pages of the dog-eared book. When he found the page he was looking for, his pulse quickened.

"'The Mahdi will return when the last pages of history are being written in blood and fire,'" he read under his breath. "'It will be a time of chaos, carnage, and confusion, a time when Muslims need to have faith and courage like never before. Some say all the infidels—especially the Christians and the Jews—must be converted or destroyed before he is revealed and ushers in a reign characterized by righteousness, justice, and peace. Others say Muslims must prepare the conditions for the destruction of the Christians and the Jews, but that the Mahdi will finish the job himself. But know this, O ye faithful: when he comes, the Promised One will bring Jesus with him as his lieutenant. Jesus will command all the infidels who are still standing to bow down to the Mahdi or die.'"

Najjar could hardly breathe, he was so excited.

"'The ancient texts do not tell us exactly how and when he will come,'" Najjar continued reading. "'Some believe he will first appear in Mecca and conquer all the lands of the Persian and Babylonian empires, then establish the headquarters of his global caliphate in the Mesopotamian city of Kufa. Others believe he will emerge from the well at the Jamkaran Mosque in Iran and then travel to Mecca by way of Mesopotamia. Some say that he will conquer Jerusalem before establishing his caliphate. Others believe Jerusalem must be conquered as a prerequisite to his return. Yet while much is unknown, the ancient texts make one thing abundantly clear: every Muslim must be ready for his return, for he is coming with great power and glory and with the terrible judgment of hellfire for all those who disobey or stand in his way.'"

Najjar closed the book and shuddered. He had followed the Promised One fervently for the first few years after he had met that little boy at the age of ten. But over time, he had let himself drift away from the teachings of the Qur'an and the responsibility to be ready. Now he wondered. What if the Promised One really did come soon? Would he be cast into hell? Would he suffer forever, with boiling water being poured over his head until his flesh melted away? He had to change his ways. He had to submit. He had to work—and work hard—to win back Allah's approval.

His encounter with the beggar, Najjar concluded, was a hopeful sign. Allah was not finished with him yet. Perhaps there was still time to become a good and righteous young man and to earn Allah's eternal favor.

But how?

17

It was Monday morning, and they had just one day left.

The glorious aroma of strong, black coffee and thick Canadian bacon lured David from his slumber. He put on his glasses, stepped out of his cabin into the brisk fall morning, and inhaled the smoke drifting his way. He looked around the campsite but saw no one, save Marseille. Wearing jeans and a gray sweatshirt with pink lettering that read *Jersey Girl*, she stood over the fire, scrambling some eggs.

"Hungry?" she asked.

"Famished," he said. "Where is everyone?"

"The First Church of the Walleye."

"They're fishing already?"

"It's almost ten."

David couldn't believe it. He rubbed dirt off the face of his watch. She was right. He must have been more tired than he'd realized. The day before, David had spent another day with his dad, this time going farther up a river they'd found and discovering a small lake full of pike. They had caught far more than they could possibly eat, thrown most of them back, and broiled the rest over the fire for dinner.

"How come you didn't go fishing?" David asked.

Marseille laughed. "I needed my beauty sleep."

David doubted that but said nothing as she served him runny eggs and burnt bacon on a cold tin plate.

"Hope you like 'em," she said, turning back to the fire to pour him some coffee.

David choked down the food and a cup of coffee so bitter he had to add four cubes of sugar to it. Cooking evidently was not one of Marseille's strengths. When she suggested they hike back to the A-frame they had made their own, David readily agreed. He gratefully set down the mug, helped her douse the fire, and led her into the woods.

"My dad says your mom is the best cook in the world," Marseille said as they began.

"Really?" David said, genuinely surprised.

"Apparently your mom makes some kind of Persian stew that is out of this world," Marseille continued. "My mom has tried to make it I don't know how many times. It's horrible."

"Oh, it can't be that bad," David said.

"Don't get me wrong," Marseille said. "She's a great mom. The best. And she's brilliant. My dream is to become a smidgen as smart and successful as she is. But cooking is not exactly one of her gifts. Let's just say, we eat out a lot."

"Really?" David said, restraining a smile. *Like mother, like daughter.* "So what else do your parents say about my parents?"

Marseille shrugged. "What do you mean?"

"Well, they went through quite an ordeal together," David said. "They must have told you some interesting stories—maybe some I can use to, you know, blackmail my folks next time I want something good."

David expected her to laugh. Instead, Marseille suddenly grew quiet. Her smile faded. "I wouldn't know."

"What do you mean? What's wrong?"

"Nothing."

David was confused.

"What just happened? Did I miss something here?"

"Really, it's nothing."

"Marseille, I can see I've offended you. I just don't know how."

There was a long, uncomfortable pause, and then she said, "It's just that . . . my parents don't talk about their time in Iran . . . *ever.*"

"Why not?" David asked as they came over a ridge and spotted the old cabin.

"I don't know."

"Well, you must have a guess."

"Maybe it was just too painful."

"I don't understand. What was so painful? They were only there for a few months, and they were heroes."

"That's not how they see it."

"Why not?"

"You'd have to ask them, David. I don't know."

"I don't believe you," David said.

"You're calling me a liar?"

"No, I'm just . . ." David didn't finish the sentence. There wasn't any point.

They were silent until they got to the cabin and flopped on their chairs, side by side.

"Do you know the story?" Marseille finally asked.

"What story?"

"You know, how our parents escaped."

"From Iran?"

"Yeah."

"Of course—don't you?" David asked.

Marseille shook her head, then turned and looked him in the eyes. "I've stopped asking," she explained. "I asked them for years, but they always changed the subject." There was another long pause, and then she said, "It's not fair. It's a part of my life, too, not just theirs. It's part of who we are as a family. Don't I have a right to know?"

David was moved by her desire to figure out a piece of the puzzle of her family's past. At the same time, he felt deeply uncomfortable. He couldn't imagine why the Harpers weren't proud of what they had done. Their story was amazing. It was certainly worth sharing with their only child. But if—for whatever reason—they didn't want to tell her what had happened, was it really his place to do so?

He looked into her eyes and saw pain he hadn't seen before. "That's really between you and your parents."

She took his hand, pulling him toward her, to the edge of his chair. "I can't talk to them," she said. "Not about this. Not about Iran."

"Why not?"

"I don't know. I just can't." Then she whispered, "Please, David, tell me the story."

He said nothing but felt strangely electrified to be so close to her.

"Please," she whispered. "It would really mean the world to me."

David swallowed hard. He didn't trust himself alone with her just then. A storm of emotions was erupting inside him. He needed space—a walk, a swim, some kind of change of pace and setting.

"I can't, Marseille," he said. "I wish I could. But it's not my place."

There was a long, painful silence.

"Fine," she said, letting go of him and looking away. "Never mind."

"Marseille, I'm sorry. I'm not trying to be hurtful to you; it's just—"

"Forget it. It's no big deal."

He reached for her hand again, but she drew it away. He was hoping desperately that the chemistry in the room would change back. But it did not.

18

For the rest of Monday, Marseille was distant and aloof.

She spent most of her time alone, while David hung out with his father.

That evening as the sun began to set over the glassy waters, David looked up from a book to see Mike Calveto, one of Saeed's friends, sidling up to Marseille as she was standing by the shore. David couldn't hear what Mike said, but he saw him try to grab her from behind and kiss her on the ear. What was he doing? Was he crazy? Marseille looked shocked and a little scared. David was on his feet instantly, sprinting to her side. Mike was embarrassed by the rebuff but tried to laugh it off. No one else saw the incident, and none of them wanted to escalate the matter by getting their fathers involved. But when Mike finally went his way, Marseille asked David to stay with her.

"You're not mad at me anymore?" David asked.

"I am still mad at you, but I don't have any choice," she replied. "At least you're trying to be a gentleman."

When it was clear that they were alone, she slipped her arm through his and they began to walk. Her touch was intoxicating.

"He means well," David sputtered.

"No, he doesn't," Marseille said.

David thought about that, then conceded, "No, you're right. He doesn't." At least the friction between them seemed to have disappeared.

They walked to the end of the dock, dangled their feet over the edge, and talked until after sundown.

It was nearly dark when they heard Marseille's father calling them for supper. Reluctantly, they stood and turned to head back toward the camp. Abruptly Marseille leaned forward and kissed him. It lasted only a moment, but it was a first for David, and for the rest of the evening he could still feel her soft lips on his and the warmth of her body nestled up against his own.

★ ★ ★ ★ ★

"Rise and shine, buddy."

David heard his father's kind voice and felt his father's hands gently shaking him awake. But it was early. Way too early—and still dark and cold. A quick glance at his watch told David it was barely six in the morning. He rolled over in his sleeping bag and put his pillow over his head.

"Just let me sleep," he moaned.

"Sorry, young man," his father replied, "but we've got to pack up, break camp, and get moving so we're ready before the planes get here."

Two hours later, they were ready.

The cabins had been swept. The dishes had been cleaned. The sleeping bags had been rolled up. The fire had been covered with sand. They were all down by the dock, bags packed, awaiting the floatplanes. There had been little talking. Most were too groggy for that. But when they were sure no one was looking, David and Marseille would occasionally steal a glance at one another and smile, savoring their moment on the dock the night before.

And yet, a sadness was beginning to creep into David's spirit. It was born of the sudden realization that their time together over the past four days was destined to burn away forever like the fog as the sun came up. He lived in Syracuse. She lived in Spring Lake, a little town on the Jersey Shore, hundreds of miles away. Neither of them could drive. How, then, could they date? These, David realized, were likely to be their last minutes together for quite some time.

The still, brisk midmorning air was quiet. Too quiet. The planes

should have been there by now. David looked at his watch again—
10:15. He couldn't believe how quickly time was slipping away from
them. This wasn't good. Their train would be pulling out of Clova at
11:20. But where were the floatplanes?

The dads were growing anxious. There was a low hum about the
camp as the murmuring against Larry McKenzie and his fellow pilots
grew. David's father, he remembered, had to perform an open-heart
surgery at ten in the morning the following day. But if they missed the
train to Montreal, they'd never make their flight to Philadelphia or their
connection to Syracuse.

Finally one of the fathers asked what everyone else was thinking. "So
if we miss this train, when's the next one?"

"I don't know," another father confessed. "We've been doing this for,
what, six years, and we've never missed the train yet."

All eyes turned to Dr. Shirazi.

"I'm sure everything will be fine," he insisted.

"Absolutely," Charlie Harper chimed in.

"But what if it's not?" one of the dads asked. "What if McKenzie
doesn't show in the next two minutes? What then?"

"I'm sure they'll be here any second," Dr. Shirazi insisted as David
strained to see any sign of the de Havillands on the horizon. But there
were none to be found.

David whispered to his father, "Dad, when *is* the next train?"

His father said nothing. Several minutes went by. David wondered
if his father had actually heard him, but David saw his clenched jaw
and knew that he had.

Then his father whispered back, "Thursday."

19

"Thursday?"

David hadn't meant to say it so loud—or at all. It had been an involuntary reaction, and the flash of anger in his father's eyes didn't help any.

"Tell me he's kidding," one of the fathers insisted.

"I'm afraid he's not," Dr. Shirazi conceded.

"Thursday?" another demanded, cursing. "How is that possible? I've got patients waiting for me. I can't be here until Thursday!"

Panic and anger were a volatile cocktail, and these men swallowed it whole. The fathers gathered around Dr. Shirazi, all angrily explaining their highly important and finely crafted schedules to him—as though there was anything he could do. David shrank back from the group. He felt terrible for his father. It wasn't his fault. It was McKenzie's.

Where were the pilots? How could they just strand them all there? Was it engine trouble? Why didn't they send other planes? And what exactly were they supposed to do? They had no cell phone coverage up here, no radios, no satellite phone. They had no way to contact civilization at all.

Most of the men—with the exception of Charlie Harper—were now threatening to sue McKenzie Air Expeditions for every red Canadian cent they had. "We're going to own that company!" one of them vowed.

But the threats did little good. As the hours passed, there were still no floatplanes. By two that afternoon, everyone was not only anxious but hungry as well. They were sick of fish by now, and there wasn't a lot of extra food. They snacked on leftover candy bars and some unfinished bags of gorp and tried to figure out what to do. Should they just sit tight and keep waiting or unpack and set up their camp again?

For the rest of the day, they hung out together, playing hearts, reading novels, or trying to nap and forget their troubles. But when the sun began to set and the temperature began to drop and still no floatplanes had come, they realized they had no choice. The men and older boys unpacked again, and David and Marseille were sent out to gather more firewood.

"What do you think is going to happen, David?" Marseille asked as they headed back into the woods.

"It'll be okay," David reassured her. "Old Man McKenzie will come for us."

"What if he doesn't?"

"He will."

"Then why hasn't he?"

David stopped, turned to her, took her hands. "We paid a lot of money for this trip. McKenzie has every incentive to make us happy. There's just some mechanical problem or something. But he'll be here."

"You're sure?" she asked.

"I promise."

Thunder began to rumble and boom above them. Confident they were alone, David stepped close to Marseille and put his arms around her small frame. She stepped in closer and held him tight. Suddenly they were kissing again, and for those few moments, all other thoughts melted away. Despite the chill, he felt warm all over. He wondered if she could feel his heart pounding so intensely. And then it began to pour.

★ ★ ★ ★ ★

Wednesday passed, and still no planes.

The rain didn't stop. The card games inside the damp cabins were getting old fast. It was now Thursday, still gray and growing colder, and no planes. For most, anger had turned to fear. They were stranded in the middle of nowhere. Their provisions were nearly gone. The men debated whether they should use the fishing boats to try to find help, but the truth was, they were hundreds of miles from the nearest human being. They had no maps. They had no compasses. They had little fuel, and the thought of running out of diesel somewhere on the reservoir finally ruled out that possibility.

Everyone was on edge, and David could tell his dad was feeling worse by the hour. How had they misjudged McKenzie's ability to fulfill his obligations so badly? What could possibly be keeping him? In six years, nothing like this had ever happened. Surely their wives and secretaries would be calling the outfitter's offices in Clova or the police or someone. Send in the Mounties for goodness' sake!

But for David and Marseille, the days were a gift. They brought their blankets, music, and books to the A-frame and let go of the rest of the world. They covered every imaginable topic, amazed that their conversations never seemed to become tired.

"Do you believe in God?" Marseille asked at one point.

"I don't know," he said. No one had ever asked him that before.

"Aren't you a Muslim?" she asked.

"Yeah, I guess."

"You guess?"

"Okay, yeah, I'm a Muslim—a Shia, actually."

"A what?"

"That's a kind of Muslim," he explained. "The kind from Iran."

"So you believe in God," she clarified.

"I don't know what I believe," David admitted.

"Why not?"

"Because my father's an atheist," he explained, "and my mom's an agnostic."

"Aren't they Muslims too?"

"Technically," David said. "But after all they saw during the Revolution, they decided Islam couldn't be true."

"Why not?"

"They didn't know how to believe in a god who would command people to kill and maim and torture so many innocent people."

Marseille said nothing for several long minutes. Then she asked, "What do you think about Jesus?"

David shrugged. "I believe he existed. Muslims say he was a prophet. But I don't know."

"Do you believe if we pray, God will answer us and get us out of here?"

He shrugged and said he didn't know, but he didn't think so.

"It couldn't hurt, though, could it?" she asked.

"Praying?" he asked.

"Yeah."

"I guess not," he said, unconvinced.

But she didn't pray. Instead, she lay down on the bed and stared out the window. Within a few minutes, she was sleeping. David covered her with a blanket to keep her warm. He lay down beside her and slept too.

Several hours later, David woke up. Marseille turned over and faced him. Her eyes held a sudden purpose as she stared into his, and her request was irresistible.

"David, I need you to tell me the story of our parents," she whispered. "Please. Don't say no."

He couldn't refuse her now.

So with mesmerizing detail, he explained how Marseille's mother had vetoed at least three plans the CIA and the State Department had drawn up, schemes—in her view—ranging from impracticable to suicidal. Then he explained how Marseille's father had devised the plan that was finally accepted and executed. The Harpers, the Shirazis, and the other American FSOs would be given false Canadian passports. This, however, would take a special, secret act of the parliament in Ottawa, since the use of false passports for espionage was expressly forbidden by Canadian law. They would also be given false papers that identified them as film producers from Toronto working on a new big-budget motion picture titled *Argo*, set in the Middle East, in conjunction with a major Hollywood studio. Their cover story would be that they were in Iran scouting locations. The CIA would set up a front company in Los Angeles called Studio Six, complete with fully operational offices, working phone lines, and notices in the trade papers announcing casting calls and other elements of preproduction. The Americans and the Shirazis would then further develop and refine all the details of their cover stories, commit them to memory, and rehearse them continually. Eventually, the CIA would send in an operative named Jack Zalinsky to go over the final details and to see if they were ready for any interrogation they might encounter. When the time was right, Zalinsky would take the team to the airport and try to get them through passport control without getting caught—and hanged.

"You're saying my father came up with this idea?" Marseille asked when David was finished.

"Actually, your mom helped quite a bit," David replied.

"That doesn't make sense," she protested. "How would my parents even know . . . ?"

Her voice trailed off. The wind rustled through the pines. Once again, dark clouds were gathering overhead. Another storm front seemed to be brewing, and it was getting colder. David glanced at his watch. They needed to get back to the camp before people got worried about them.

But Marseille urged him not to leave. "Just a few minutes more," she said, taking his hand and squeezing it gently. "I want to know the rest of the story."

"Marseille, it's getting late."

"I'll make it worth your while," she smiled.

"How?"

She reached into her knapsack and pulled out a box of Junior Mints.

"I can't believe you have any left," David said.

"This is the last one."

"And you're actually going to share them with me?"

"Only if you finish the story."

David's stomach growled. It was an offer he couldn't refuse, so he didn't.

"Okay, now we're talking," he said, as one of the mints melted on his tongue. "D-day was set for January 28, 1980. There were a bunch of regional elections going on. Ayatollah Khomeini's people were trying to maintain control. The secret police had their hands full murdering dissidents and killing the opposition, so this Zalinsky guy believed they might have a window where the police might be distracted somewhat. It was a long shot, but it was the best they could do. So Zalinsky got the team to the main airport in Tehran. They were going through passport control, and my parents were absolutely terrified. Your parents were cool as cucumbers, but my parents—not so much. They don't exactly look Canadian, after all, and they were never convinced your parents' plan was going to work. But your father and Mr. Zalinsky kept insisting that if the tickets and passports said they were Canadians, then the guards at the airport would accept it. And they did."

"That's amazing," Marseille said.

"So before Khomeini's thugs knew what was happening, your parents, mine, and the others were taking their seats on board Swissair flight 363, heading for Toronto via Geneva. As soon as they cleared out of Iranian airspace, Mr. Zalinsky ordered champagne for the whole team."

"But my parents don't drink," Marseille said.

"Neither do mine!" David said. "But believe me, they did that day. From what I hear, they finished off two bottles while Mr. Zalinsky toasted them and asked what they were going to do with their new-found freedom."

"And?" Marseille pressed, hanging on every word. "What did they say?"

"Well," David said, "your folks said they were going to work for the State Department for a few more years, move to New Jersey, and buy a little house near the beach. Your dad said he wanted to teach. Your mom said she wanted to work in the city and make a boatload of money. And that's just what they did, right?"

Marseille nodded, her eyes misting. "What did your parents want?" she asked.

"They just had one question," David said.

"What's that?"

"When they finally got to America, would they really be let in?"

Just as he said it, the alarm on David's watch went off.

"It's almost time for dinner," he said, turning the alarm off. "We really need to get back."

But Marseille wasn't hungry for dinner. She squeezed his hand and pulled him closer. She stared deep into his eyes with a look of gratitude and desire, which he returned with equal intensity. She kissed him with a passion unlike anything he had ever imagined. She kissed him on the neck and the lips and wouldn't stop. She was holding him tighter and gasping for air, and David felt himself losing control. He knew where they were going was wrong, but he couldn't stop. He didn't want to stop.

He felt intoxicated by her presence and her touch, and the room began to spin. Ignoring all of his cautions, all of his fears, and everything he'd been brought up to believe, he willingly, eagerly let Marseille take him from one world into another, savoring every moment along the way.

20

Dawn broke on Friday morning.

David awoke in his own cabin, all alone. His father and brothers were nowhere to be seen, but he didn't mind. He'd been dreaming about the previous night with Marseille, dreaming about where it all would lead next. But suddenly he heard the sound of a floatplane coming across the lake.

David jumped out of his sleeping bag, threw on a sweatshirt, and stepped out into the frosty morning air. Everyone else, it turned out— including Marseille—was already awake and down by the docks as Old Man McKenzie landed his de Havilland first, followed by the others. David ran down to meet them, half-fearing the men might lynch the pilots when they finally taxied over to them.

But before any of them could say a word, McKenzie climbed out of his cockpit and apologized profusely, promising to refund all of their money just as soon as they got back to Clova. It worked. The men were grateful and surprisingly forgiving. What they really wanted to know was what in the world had happened and why McKenzie and the others hadn't shown up on Tuesday morning, as planned. But no one was prepared for McKenzie's answer.

"Believe me, gentlemen, we were all suited up and ready to come get you guys when we got word that morning that the Canadian government had just issued a no-fly order for the entire country. And it wasn't just Canada. All commercial and civilian flights throughout North

America were grounded. No one could take off, and everyone in the air had to land immediately."

"Why? What happened?" David's father asked.

"A group of terrorists hijacked four commercial jetliners—two from Boston's Logan Airport, one from Newark International, and one from Washington Dulles," MacKenzie explained.

David gasped.

"Two of the planes plowed into the World Trade Center," McKenzie went on. "Another flew right into the Pentagon. The fourth went down in a field in Pennsylvania. Everyone on the planes was lost. No one knew if there were more hijackers on more planes out there, so the entire air transportation system was simply shut down. Believe me, we wanted to come get you guys. But the Air Force was threatening to shoot down any unauthorized plane in the sky. The only planes in the air were F-15s and F-16s, all armed with air-to-air missiles and ready for action. I've never seen anything like it. But again, I apologize for what you've been through. If there had been any way to get you—or get word to you—please know we would have done it."

The group stood there in stunned silence. And then it got worse.

"Was anyone in the towers hurt?" Marseille asked.

David noticed that she was ashen, and her hands shook.

"I'm afraid the towers don't exist anymore, young lady," McKenzie replied.

"What do you mean?" she asked.

"I mean the towers collapsed not long after the planes hit them."

"Both of them?"

"I'm afraid so," McKenzie said.

"Was anyone hurt?"

"Are you kidding?" McKenzie asked. "At this point, they're saying almost three thousand people have died, but there may be more."

"Three thousand?" David's father asked.

McKenzie nodded. "There's a big gap in the middle of Manhattan where the towers used to stand. There's smoke rising as far as the eye can see. Whole thing took less than two hours, and whoosh, they were gone, both of them."

Marseille collapsed to the ground and began to sob uncontrollably. David looked to Mr. Harper, expecting him to comfort her. But Marseille's father just stood there, the blood draining from his face.

Scared and confused, David cautiously knelt by Marseille's side and gingerly put his arm around her shoulder. "It's okay, Marseille. You're safe. We're all safe, right? Really, it's going to be okay."

But Marseille didn't respond. She couldn't speak. Neither could her father. They tried, but the words would not form. She was disintegrating, and her father was standing there like a zombie.

"David," Dr. Shirazi said softly, his voice faltering.

"Yeah?"

"It's Marseille's mother."

"Mrs. Harper?" David asked. "What about her?"

His father's eyes welled up with tears. He took a deep breath and said, "She works for a bank, David. She works in the South Tower."

David couldn't believe what he was hearing.

"Mrs. Harper works *in* the World Trade Center?" he finally asked. Reluctantly his father nodded.

David sank to the ground and sat for a long while, not knowing what to say.

"Maybe she got out," he finally said, his lower lip trembling.

21

The last time David saw Marseille was the day of the funeral.

Charlie Harper simply couldn't bear the loss of Claire, his beloved wife of twenty-three years. He had no idea how to take care of himself, much less his only daughter, under these circumstances. He wasn't eating. He was losing weight. He rarely spoke. He was clinically depressed and failing to take his medication. So he resigned his job, put the family house on the market, packed up their belongings, and—unable to bear the thought of boarding a plane—drove Marseille across the country from New Jersey to Oregon, where his folks had a farm near Portland.

And just like that, Marseille Harper disappeared from David's life.

She accepted a hug from David at the funeral home. But she was so overcome with emotion that she couldn't talk. She could barely even look him in the eye at the memorial service. After she moved, he wrote her letters. They went unanswered. He called and left her messages. She never called back. Once, her grandfather answered the phone and said Marseille was out and that she'd call back. She never did. He even sent her a box of Junior Mints. There was still no reply. David finally got the message and stopped trying.

Marseille Harper had been his first love. He had given her his body, heart, and soul, and she had given him hers. But in an instant of time, it had all been torn away. The feelings she'd stirred in him had changed him forever, but it was all for nothing. Marseille was lost to him now, and he had no idea how to get her back. He grieved for her but did his best not to blame her. He had no idea how he would have reacted if his mother had been murdered by terrorists and his father had lost his will to function—and perhaps to live. And while he and Marseille had spent an amazing week together, the truth—painful though it was—was it had been only a week. He had no real claim on her. He had no right to expect that she would stay in touch with him, and clearly, wishing wouldn't make it so.

Quietly, privately, alone in his room—or on the bus, or alone with his thoughts during a study hall or at his locker—he would pray for Marseille and her father. He begged Allah to comfort them and heal them—and him, too. He beseeched Allah to let Marseille somehow find a measure of peace and some good friends who would stand by her and encourage and protect her. He asked Allah to let Marseille remember him and to move her to write back to him.

But as fall turned to winter, David began to lose hope. It was as though his words echoed back from the ceiling of his room, useless and ridiculous. He might as well be praying to the rug on his floor or the lamp on his desk, he concluded, and this only accelerated the tailspin.

His grades plummeted from straight A's to straight D's. His parents were worried about him. So were his teachers. But nothing they suggested seemed to help. The only good news was that both of his brothers were off at college and not there to tease him.

If all that weren't enough, David began getting into fights at school. A group of seniors on the varsity football team kept calling him a "camel jockey," and "the son of a Muslim whore." He went ballistic every time. It didn't matter that he was Persian, not Arab. Or that his family was from Iran, not Afghanistan or Pakistan, where the 9/11 attacks originated. It didn't matter that he and his family were Shia Muslims, not Wahhabis like Osama bin Laden or Sunnis like Mohamed Atta, the leader of the 9/11 hijackers. Or that David himself had been born and raised in America and was rooting for the American forces battling al Qaeda and the Taliban more than anyone else in his school. None of it mattered to the losers who baited him, and he unleashed every time.

Though David was younger than his tormentors, he was at least as tall and possessed a killer right jab and an increasingly volcanic temper. In January 2002, he was put into detention six times and twice briefly suspended for fighting in the halls. When he broke the nose of the school's star quarterback and broke the arm of the state's leading wide receiver in the same fight, however, the principal called the police, and David Shirazi was arrested, fingerprinted, and locked up overnight, pending arraignment and a bail hearing.

It was a quiet night in the Onondaga County juvenile detention center, and David was put in a cell by himself. His parents stayed with him for as long as the rules allowed, and though they were loving, they were firm. David's father said he hoped a night in this place might bring David to his senses, and then they left.

For more than an hour, David paced the floor and cursed anyone within earshot. At one point he punched the cinder block wall so hard, he feared he had broken his hand but refused to call out for help. He collapsed on the bed, stared at the ceiling, and began to grow scared. He knew he was rapidly losing altitude emotionally, spiritually, even physically.

How had he slipped so far, so fast? And what was he supposed to do now? The prospect of actually going to jail for several months made him physically ill. But even if he could plead his way out of jail time, he was still going to be expelled from school. He was going to have a criminal record. How was he going to get into college? How was he ever going to get a decent job?

Lying there in the cell, he thought back to the anticipation he'd had about going up to Canada with his father and brothers for that fishing weekend. He tried to recall just how much he had looked forward to that weekend and how his life had been dangerously unraveling ever since. He'd fallen for a girl who wasn't even supposed to be there, a girl whose mother had been killed in the towers, a girl who now lived on the other side of the country, a girl who didn't love him and wouldn't talk to him and apparently couldn't care less that he even existed.

How had it come to this? He'd gone to Canada to go fishing. But in those few short days, the whole world had come crashing down. One day, no one he knew cared that his family was from the Middle East. Now they treated him like a murderer and a terrorist. One day, no one cared that he was Muslim. Now they treated him like he was part of some sleeper cell, with suicide bomber belts hanging in his closet, ready to be activated by Khalid Sheikh Mohammed and sent into a mall on Christmas to blow himself to smithereens and take as many people as he could with him. It wasn't true. It had never been true. But no one seemed to care.

David closed his eyes and tried to forget the last few months. He tried to remember Marseille's face. He tried to recall her eyes, her smile, the feel of her body against his. He tried to imagine himself back on that island, back in that cabin, before this nightmare had begun. But every time he tried to conjure up such images, all he could see was the twisted, demented face of Osama bin Laden staring back at him. Sickened by the connection, he'd shake it off and try again to dream of Marseille. But he couldn't. It was bin Laden's vacant eyes on which he found himself fixated again and again.

David seethed with a toxic level of anger he had never before experienced and didn't recognize. It wasn't Marseille's fault all this had happened, he reminded himself. Nor was it her father's. This was all the doing of Osama bin Laden, period. It was bin Laden who was the leader of al Qaeda, the terrorist organization behind the 9/11 attacks. It was bin Laden who had recruited the nineteen hijackers, facilitated their training, funded them, and deployed them to seize the four American jetliners and turn them into missiles. It was bin Laden who had murdered Mrs. Harper.

The irony was palpable, David thought. Here he lay in prison, while Osama bin Laden roamed free through the mountains of Kandahar or the streets of Islamabad.

22

Hamid Hosseini still couldn't believe his good fortune.

The world was fixated elsewhere. On the hunt for Osama bin Laden and the war in Afghanistan. On a possible war in Iraq. On the North Koreans' effort to build nuclear weapons. On soaring oil prices and a weakening global economy. And all this was good, for it kept the world distracted from developments in Iran, developments very near and dear to his heart.

In the wake of the death of one of their dear colleagues, the Assembly of Experts—the ruling council of eighty-six religious clerics—had earlier that day unanimously named Hamid Hosseini . . . Supreme Leader of the Islamic Republic of Iran. It was an honor he had never sought or expected. But it had come nonetheless, and now he of all people was the highest religious and political authority in the country.

The world would little note nor long remember his transition to the role, he was sure. Few people knew who he was or cared. Hosseini had carefully maintained a somewhat-moderate public image, at least on the international stage. But he knew without a shadow of a doubt why Allah had chosen him. It was his calling—indeed, it was his destiny—to avenge the death of his master and prepare the way for the coming of the Twelfth Imam. This, he knew, required him to bring about the annihilation of the United States and Israel, the Great and Little Satans, respectively. It would take time. It would take careful planning. He would have to recruit the right people and groom them for key positions of leadership. But it was possible. And he couldn't wait to get started.

After a long day of ceremonies, speeches, and meetings, he arrived home late and collapsed into bed next to his wife, who was already asleep. He was exhausted, but his mind swirled with the plans he was making to confront the arrogant powers of the West. Then suddenly, he realized what day it was, what anniversary it was, and he found himself thinking back eighteen years earlier to the day when he'd knelt down with his three sons and prayed a final prayer with them.

"O mighty Lord. I pray to you to hasten the emergence of your last repository, the Promised One, that perfect and pure human being, the one who will fill this world with justice and peace. Make us worthy to prepare the way for his arrival, and lead us with your righteous hand. We long for the Lord of the Age. We long for the Awaited One. Without him—the Righteously Guided One—there can be no victory. With him, there can be no defeat. Show me your path, O mighty Lord, and use me to prepare the way for the coming of the Mahdi."

He recalled opening his eyes and gazing upon those three beautiful and innocent gifts, the pride of his life.

"Come, boys," he said, opening the car door for them. "It is time."

"Where are we going?" asked Bahadur, who at the age of twelve was his oldest, and certainly the tallest, and whose name meant "courageous and bold."

"We're going on a mission," he replied.

"A mission!" said Firuz, his eleven-year-old. "What kind of mission?"

"It is a secret mission," Hosseini said. "Come quickly, and you will see."

As the two older boys scrambled into the backseat, he lifted up his youngest, Qubad, and held him even longer. Kissing him three times, and receiving three joyful kisses back, he finally put Qubad in the back with his brothers, shut the door, got into the driver's seat, and started the engine.

It was a beautiful winter day, sunny, cool but not cold, with a slight breeze blowing from the east. The boys waved good-bye to their mother, whose eyes were filled with tears, and soon they were off.

"Why is *Madar* crying?" Qubad asked.

Hosseini glanced in the rearview mirror and saw that the two young-est also had tears in their eyes. They were sensitive boys, and he loved them even more for it.

"She misses you already," he said as calmly as he could. "You know her."

"She loves us," Qubad said quietly.

"Yes, very much," his father replied.

"She tucks us in every night and sings us the songs of Persia," the little boy said.

"She buys us pomegranates—the sweetest in the world," Firuz chimed in.

Then Bahadur spoke up as well. "She knows the Qur'an almost as well as you do, *Pedar*."

"Better," Hosseini said, glad he had not brought her, for she would never have survived this trip.

After an hour on the road, the boys were getting antsy, poking each other, quarreling, and whining to stop and get something to eat. They still had another thirty or forty minutes to go, and Hosseini wasn't yet ready to pull over for food.

"Who wants to play a game?" Hosseini asked.

"We do! We do!" they all yelled.

"Wonderful," he said. "Here's how it works. I'll say a Sura from the Qur'an, and you must recite it to me precisely. For this you will receive a point. Whoever gets the most points, *Madar* will make a special cake just for him."

The boys cheered with glee. They had all been memorizing the words of the Prophet since before they could read, in school and with the help of their mother. They each had to recite a whole chapter of the Qur'an to their mother before they could go out to play every afternoon. And once, when they had been invited to meet the Ayatollah at the palace, their father had made them memorize all of Sura 86 and the story of the Nightcomer so they could recite it to Khomeini.

"Let me go first; please, please, let me go first," Firuz shouted.

"No, no. We will go in order, oldest to youngest. Are you ready?"

They all were. The pokings were finished. The quarreling was over. Hosseini had their rapt attention now.

"Okay, Bahadur, you're first. Sura 4:52."

"Thank you, *Pedar*," the boy replied. "That is an easy one. 'Jews and Christians are the ones whom God has cursed, and he whom God excludes from His mercy, you shall never find one to help and save him.'"

"Excellent, Bahadur. You get one point. Now, Firuz."

"I'm ready."

"Good. Can you tell me Sura 5:33?"

Firuz's face darkened. For a moment, he looked as though he might panic. Then suddenly his face brightened. "Yes, *Pedar*, I remember that one. 'The recompense of those who fight against God and His Messenger, they shall either be executed, or crucified, or have their hands and feet cut off alternately, or be banished from the land.'"

"Very good, my son," Hosseini said. "I was worried there for a moment."

"So was I, but *Madar* taught that one, and I didn't want to disappoint her."

"She would be very proud. I will be sure to tell her you remembered."

"Do I get a point?" Firuz asked.

"Absolutely. It's one to one. And now it's Qubad's turn."

"I am ready!" Qubad yelled with such enthusiasm they all burst into laughter.

"Okay, here's one I taught you myself, Qubad—Sura 60:9."

"Oh, oh, I know that!" Qubad shouted. "'For those who disbelieve, garments of fire are certain to be cut out for them, with boiling water being poured down over their heads, with which all that is within their bodies, as well as their skins, is melted away.'"

"No, my son, I'm sorry," Hosseini said. "What Sura is that, Firuz?"

"That's 22:19-20."

"Correct," Hosseini said, beaming with pride. "That's another point for you."

"Hey, that's not fair!" Bahadur said.

"Yeah, that's not fair!" little Qubad squealed.

"My game, my rules," their father replied. "But I'll tell you what, Qubad. I will give you another chance. What is Sura 60:9?"

Qubad closed his eyes and scrunched up his face. He thought and thought, but it was not coming. Finally he said, "'Fight against those among the People of the Book who do not believe God and the Last Day'?"

"Good try, Qubad," Hosseini said. "Who knows where that verse is found?"

This time Bahadur shouted out the answer first. "That is Sura 9:29, *Pedar!*"

"Very good, my son; another point for you."

Bahadur beamed. Qubad looked like he was about to burst out in tears. They were all very competitive boys, and none of them liked to lose, least of all Qubad.

Firuz now spoke up. "I know Sura 60:9. May I recite it, *Pedar?*"

"Of course."

"It's regarding our enemies—Jews and Christians and those who call themselves Muslims but are not faithful to the Qur'an—isn't that right?"

"It is," Hosseini said. "But to get the point, you must say the verse."

There was a long silence.

"Are you sure you know it?"

"Yes, I think so."

"Okay, go ahead."

"'God forbids you . . . ,'" Firuz began.

"Forbids you to what?" Hosseini asked.

"'. . . forbids you to take them . . . for friends and guardians. . . .'"

"Go on."

There was another long pause.

"I can't," Firuz said. "I'm sorry."

"It's okay," his father said. "Bahadur, can you finish it?"

"Yes, *Pedar.* 'God forbids you to take them for friends and guardians. Whoever takes them for friends and guardians, those are the wrongdoers.'"

"Very impressive, Bahadur," Hosseini exclaimed. "Okay, you get half a point, and Firuz gets half a point."

Both boys cheered, but Qubad began to sniffle and wipe his nose.

"And what do I get, *Pedar*?" he asked, his eyes red and watery.

"A chance for redemption," Hosseini said.

"What does that mean?" Qubad asked, fighting hard not to cry in front of his brothers but about to lose the fight.

"It means I will ask you three questions, and if you get them all right, you will be ahead of your brothers."

Qubad's face brightened. "Really?"

"Really."

"Okay, I'm ready, *Pedar*! I'm ready!"

"Good. Here we go," Hosseini said. "What does the Ayatollah say is the 'purest joy in Islam'?"

"*I know that! I know that!*" Qubad shouted. "'*The purest joy in Islam is to kill and be killed for Allah!*'"

"Very good, Qubad," his father said. "One point for you!"

Qubad was ecstatic.

"Next question."

"Yes, yes, I'm ready, *Pedar*!"

"What happens to those who become martyrs in the cause of jihad?"

"I know that one too! Sura 47:4-6 says, 'As for those who are killed in Allah's cause, He will never render their deeds vain. He will guide them. He will admit them into paradise that He has made known to them.'"

Hosseini and the older boys cheered. Qubad was radiant now, his tears gone. He was on top of the world.

"Final question. Are you ready, Qubad?"

"Yes, I'm ready."

"Very well. Does a martyr feel pain when he dies?"

"No, he does not, *Pedar*! A martyr will not feel the pain of death except like how you feel when you are pinched."

Seeing his father's pride, Qubad beamed. But he was not finished. "I know more! I know more!" he shouted.

"Go ahead, my son."

"The shedding of the martyr's blood will forgive all of his sins! And he will go directly to paradise! And he will be decorated with jewels! And he will be in the arms of seventy-two beautiful virgins! And he will . . ."

Qubad stopped. The cheering died down. A puzzled look came over the little boy's face. He cocked his head to the side.

"What is it, Qubad?" his father asked.

There was a long pause.

Then Qubad asked, "What is a virgin, father?"

Hosseini smiled. "That, little man, is a lesson for another day. Who is ready to eat?"

"We are! We are!" they yelled.

They were now far from the city limits of Tehran, heading southwest along Highway 9 toward the holy city of Qom. Hosseini pulled over at a roadside stand and bought the boys some bread and fruit, along with some candy bars as special treats. Then they kept driving, talking and singing along the way.

When they pulled off onto a side road on the outskirts of Qom, Bahadur asked, "Where are we going, Father?"

"To an army base, boys," Hosseini replied.

"Really?" Qubad asked, his eyes wide, chocolate all over his face. "Why?"

"You will see."

Soon they came to a military checkpoint. Two heavily armed guards ordered the car to a halt. Hosseini showed them his papers. They looked in, saw the boys, and waved them all through.

As the boys began to see tanks and armored personnel carriers and soldiers carrying weapons and doing drills, they became more excited. Helicopters passed overhead. Nearby they could hear soldiers training at the firing range. A moment later, they parked by a field where hundreds of children were assembling and forming into lines.

"We're here," Hosseini said.

Hosseini got the boys out of the car, walked them over to a folding table where he wrote their names on a registry, kissed them each on both cheeks, and told them to join the others on the field and do as they were told.

Dutifully, they obeyed their father and ran out to the field, eager to learn what this exciting mystery was all about. It was then that the soldiers began passing out red plastic keys, each dangling on a string—one per child until everyone had his own. Then the commanding officer of the base introduced himself and told the children to put the keys around their necks.

"This, dear children of Persia," he bellowed over the loudspeakers, "is your key to paradise."

23

Hosseini suddenly woke from his dream.

Beside him in their bed, his wife was weeping. He glanced at the clock on the nightstand. It was almost two in the morning.

Every year, for eighteen years, he had endured the same ritual. Every year he dreamed about that special day with his boys and savored the memories. Every year he awoke in the middle of the night to comfort the wife of his youth and hold her in his arms. And every year he resented her for it.

"They were good boys," she sobbed. "They didn't deserve to die."

"Yes, they were good boys," he replied softly. "That's why they deserved the honor of death."

"You had no right to send them."

"I had every right. Indeed, I had a responsibility. I had no choice."

"You did."

"I did not, and neither did you."

"How can you say that every year?"

"How can *you*?" he demanded, his patience wearing thin. "Do you want to burn in the fires of hell?"

She shook her head as the tears continued to pour down her cheeks.

"Then stop being so foolish," he said, holding her more tightly. "They were not ours to keep. They were Allah's. He gave them to us. We gave them back."

At that she pulled away and jumped out of bed, screaming hysterically. "Gave them back? *Gave them back?* You sent them into the minefields, Hamid! They were children! Bahadur. Firuz. Qubad. They were *my* children, not just yours. You sent them to walk across minefields! You sent them to blow themselves into a thousand pieces. For what? To clear the path for our tanks and our soldiers to kill Iraqis. That is *not* the job of a child. Shame on you! *Shame!*"

Hosseini leaped out of bed. His heart was racing. His face was red. He stormed over to his wife and slapped her to the ground.

"*You wicked woman!*" he roared. "I am *proud* of my sons. They are martyrs. They are *shaheeds*. I honor their memory. But you disgrace them. You disgrace them by this weeping. To mourn them is to disbelieve. *You are an infidel!*"

Hosseini began beating her mercilessly, but she would not relent.

"*Infidel?*" she screamed as his blows rained down upon her. "*I* am an infidel? You sent little Qubad to Iraq to step on a land mine! Curse you, Hamid. He was ten. All I have left of him is a piece of that plastic key and a tuft of his hair. And what do I have of Bahadur? or Firuz? If this is Islam, I don't want any part of it. You and the Ayatollah bought a half-million keys. You are *sick*, all of you. This is *your* religion, not mine. I *hate* you. *I hate all of you who practice this evil!*"

Hosseini's eyes went wide. Stunned momentarily by his wife's words, he suddenly stopped beating her. He just stared at her, trying to comprehend the turn of events. She had never supported him in this decision. Not from day one. Every year, she wept. Every year, he comforted her. But it had been eighteen years. It was enough. Now she had gone too far.

As she sobbed on the floor, her face bloodied and bruised, Hosseini walked over to his dresser, opened the top drawer, and pulled out the nickel-plated revolver his father had given him on his thirteenth birthday. He knew it was loaded. It was always loaded. He cocked the hammer and turned toward his wife. Hearing the hammer, his wife turned her head and looked into his eyes. She was quivering. He didn't care. She was no longer a Muslim. She was no longer his wife. He raised the pistol, aimed it at her face, and pulled the trigger.

The sound echoed through their modest home, and soon several bodyguards rushed in, guns drawn, ready to protect their master with their lives. They were stunned to see the Supreme Leader's wife on the floor in a pool of her own blood. Hosseini had no need to explain himself. Certainly not to his own guards. He simply instructed them to clean up the mess and bury the body. Then he set the pistol back in his dresser drawer, washed his hands and face, walked down the hall to one of their guest rooms, and lay down on the bed, where he fell fast asleep.

Never had he slept so peacefully, and as he slept, he dreamed of the day when the Twelfth Imam would finally come and reunite him with his sons.

24

BAGHDAD, IRAQ
FEBRUARY 2002

"Excuse me, are you Najjar Malik?"

Surprised to hear his name whispered in the central reading room of the University of Baghdad library, Najjar looked up from one of his books and found himself staring into the eyes of a swarthy older man in a dark suit. Najjar could not place the face or the voice. Cautiously, he acknowledged that he was, in fact, Najjar Malik.

"You have a visitor," the man whispered.

He was attracting the attention of several students reading nearby, and Najjar was suddenly uncomfortable.

"Who?"

"I cannot say," the man said. "But come with me. I will take you to him."

Najjar glanced at his watch. He had his next class in fifteen minutes.

"Do not worry," the man said. "This will only take a moment. He is right outside."

"What is this about?"

"I cannot say. But he told me to tell you, 'It will be worth your while.'"

Najjar sincerely doubted that. He had neither time for nor interest in a wild-goose chase. He was on pace to complete his doctoral dissertation a full fourteen months ahead of his colleagues of the same age. He didn't go to the movies. He didn't hang out with friends. He didn't date.

Aside from the library, the lab, and his apartment, the only other place he ever went was the mosque every morning for predawn prayer.

Yet something about this person compelled Najjar to agree. Curious, he gathered his books, slid them quietly into his backpack, and slipped out the back door of the library, following the man to a black sedan in the parking lot. The strange man hurriedly opened the rear door and nodded for Najjar to enter. The contrast between the dimly lit library and the dazzling sunshine of a gorgeous mid-February day caused Najjar momentary blindness. Squinting as his eyes adjusted, he couldn't immediately see anyone in the backseat of the sedan, and something within him urged caution. Yet again, for some reason he could not explain, he felt strangely driven to follow the man's instructions. Once inside, the door closed behind him and he heard a voice he recognized, a voice from the past.

"Najjar, good afternoon," the voice said. "What a joy to see you again."

"Dr. Saddaji?" Najjar replied, hardly believing his eyes. "Is that really you?"

"It has been too long, has it not?"

"A long time indeed, sir."

Najjar's heart raced, as much with terror as with excitement. Was this really Mohammed Saddaji, famous scientist and father of Najjar's childhood sweetheart, Sheyda? But the Saddajis had moved away from Iraq years ago; how could he be back after so long? Was Sheyda with him? Was Mrs. Saddaji? How could they be? Wouldn't they all be killed?

"To what do I owe the honor, sir? I have not heard from your family since you moved to Iran."

"No one can know that I am here—no one," Dr. Saddaji whispered. "I don't have to tell you that I am in grave danger and that now you are too, do I? There are many who would like to see me hang . . . or worse."

Najjar swallowed hard. "I understand."

"You will be killed if anyone learns that you and I have so much as been in contact," Dr. Saddaji said quietly. "You do understand this, right?"

"Yes, sir," Najjar replied. "I will tell no one. You have my word."

"That is good enough for me," Dr. Saddaji said. "Sheyda has always spoken highly of you, Najjar. Her mother and I always found you to be a good boy—trustworthy and sincere."

"Thank you, sir," Najjar said, hardly believing he was hearing her name again after so long.

"Your parents raised you well. I was heartbroken by their deaths."

"Thank you, again, sir. That is very kind."

"I don't have much time. I have come back for one purpose and one purpose only."

"Yes, sir."

"I am a Persian, Najjar. You know that."

"Yes."

"I am not an Arab—*Allah forbid*."

"Yes, sir, I know."

"I am a Shia and proud of it. You know this, yes?"

"I do."

"You know why I left Iraq, don't you?"

The young man thought he did but felt it best to say nothing.

"It was because I could not bear to see the gifts Allah has given me be used to help . . . certain people in this town."

Najjar knew Dr. Saddaji didn't dare speak ill of Saddam. Not directly. Not even here, in the privacy of his car. Not now. No one dared to speak ill of Saddam, but especially not one of Iraq's top nuclear scientists. Or rather, ex–nuclear scientists. Najjar's heart beat faster, and despite the air-conditioning pouring out of the vents of the sedan, he could feel perspiration beginning to run down his back.

It was still stunning to Najjar that the government had ever let Dr. Saddaji study nuclear physics at the University of Baghdad, much less graduate, much less teach and do research, given his Iranian heritage and the intense historic hatred between the Persians and the Arabs. Yet Saddam and his bloodthirsty sons had desperately wanted to build the first Islamic Bomb. Their reasons were simple. They wanted to destroy the Zionists. They wanted to blackmail their neighbors. They wanted to keep the Americans at bay, dominate the Middle East, and in time, rebuild the Babylonian Empire. Saddam had wanted the Bomb so badly that he had been willing to give this man a degree of freedom and latitude he would never have given any other Iranian during the 1980s as the deadly Iran–Iraq War raged on for nearly eight brutal years.

Dr. Saddaji was, without question, the most brilliant nuclear scientist Iraq had ever produced. His success had provided the inspiration for Najjar to follow in his footsteps and pursue his master's and doctorate in nuclear physics. The man had almost single-handedly rebuilt Iraq's nuclear program after the Israelis had wiped out the Osirak reactor during the air strikes of 1981.

But ten years later, when the first Gulf War had broken out in January of 1991 and the Americans had invaded southern Iraq and crushed the forces of Saddam's prized Republican Guard, Dr. Saddaji had seized on the opportunity provided by the chaos and confusion of the American air strikes on Baghdad. He and his family had fled the capital, slipped across the border into Iran, and asked for political asylum in Tehran. Rumor had it that when Saddam learned that the Saddajis had defected—to Iran of all places—he issued orders for every person named Saddaji in the country to be killed, on the off chance that they were related to "the traitor."

Now the legendary nuclear scientist was back in Baghdad, despite the enormous risk to his life. But why? Najjar stared into the older man's eyes, looking for clues. He saw no fear in those eyes. Just wisdom. Experience. And something else. There was a long pause. And then . . .

"I am here because Sheyda asked me to come," Dr. Saddaji said at last. "Every day since we left Iraq, she has prayed faithfully for Allah to keep you safe and pure and well. And in recent years she has prayed that Allah would grant her favor and let her marry you."

Najjar was stunned. A lump formed in his throat. His hands trembled. "This is why you have risked your life to come back to Baghdad?"

"Yes."

"To get me?"

"Yes."

"To take me to Iran?"

"Nothing else could have persuaded me," Dr. Saddaji said. "I am here to ask you to marry my only daughter—and join me on a project that will truly bring peace and prosperity to the Middle East and the entire world."

Najjar suddenly remembered the words of the mysterious boy back in Samarra when he was a child. *You are secretly in love with Sheyda Saddaji. . . . You will marry her before your twenty-fourth birthday.* Was this real? Could this really be happening?

"I want you to work as my assistant," Dr. Saddaji said, seeing Najjar's hesitation. "I am now the deputy director of the Atomic Energy Agency of Iran. We are building the most impressive civilian nuclear power system in the world. We will be the world's first truly energy-independent country. We won't have to rely on oil or gasoline. We will lead the world in energy efficiency and innovation. We will change the course of history. And in so doing, we will prepare the way for the coming of the Promised One. I would value your help enormously, Najjar. I understand that you have become a first-rate physicist. This would be a huge blessing to me and my work. But most importantly, my daughter loves you and simply wouldn't stop pestering me until I promised to find you and ask you to be part of our family. So there it is. But you must decide quickly. For I am not safe here, and now neither are you."

The driver gunned the engine, and at that moment, Najjar realized Dr. Saddaji wanted an answer immediately. Not tomorrow. Not a week or a month later. Right then. Dr. Saddaji wanted Najjar to leave behind all that he knew. His aunt and uncle. His dissertation and the honors that would come with completing his degree. All prospects for a good job and a secure future inside the nascent and highly clandestine Iraqi nuclear program. All for a woman and the chance to "change the course of history," whatever that meant exactly.

"Yes," Najjar said finally, surprising himself with the force of his conviction. "I can't imagine anything I would love more than to marry Sheyda and work for you."

Dr. Saddaji beamed. "Then what are we waiting for?" he said. "Let the adventure begin."

"Rise and shine, Shirazi—you've got a visitor!"

David heard the words but had no desire to open his eyes, much less get out of bed. He had caught a stomach flu. He'd spent much of the last few nights puking his guts out. But the guard kept rapping his nightstick on the steel bars, and just to make him stop, David leaned over, put his glasses on, set his feet on the cold tile floor, and ran his hands through hair in desperate need of a trim. It was day thirteen of a fourteen-day sentence in juvie hall.

One more day in hell, he told himself.

His parents visited every day, looking older and grayer each time he saw them. His father said he was working on getting him admitted into a private, all-boys academy in Alabama where he could try to salvage his education and get his life back on track. David knew he should be grateful, but he wasn't.

David quickly threw on his standard orange jumpsuit over his boxer shorts and slipped into the white tennis shoes he'd been given. When the guard ordered his cell to be electronically unlocked, David was led down a series of hallways to a small meeting room not far from the director's office. He had expected to see his parents or his lawyer or both. Instead, he found an older gentleman in his late fifties or early sixties flipping through a magazine and fidgeting as if he badly needed a cigarette. As David entered the room, the man stood and smiled warmly. Sporting a gray beard, black-rimmed glasses, and an ill-fitting green suit, he was not anyone David had ever seen before, but David immediately had the impression that the man knew him from somewhere.

"Fifteen minutes," the guard said.

When the guard then stepped out of the room and closed the door, the man shook David's hand firmly and suggested that they both sit down.

"I've been looking forward to seeing you again for a long time, David," he began.

"Have we met before?" David asked.

"We'll get to that in a minute. I've heard you're a pretty sharp kid."

"And yet . . . here I am," David said, looking down at his shoes.

"You made a mistake, David. You're not the first kid to beat the crap out of a couple of morons who deserved it. I don't suspect you'll be the last."

David looked up again. Who was this guy?

"Actually, they didn't deserve it," David confessed, suspecting that this might be someone from the DA's office checking up on him.

"Sure they did," the man said. "Didn't one call you a raghead?"

"I still shouldn't have hit them," David answered, remembering that all their conversations were being monitored and recorded.

"Fair enough," the man continued. "But you clearly know how to handle yourself. I've seen your file. You won every fight you were in at Nottingham, even when you were outnumbered."

"Not exactly something you can put on your résumé."

"Well, that depends, son."

"On what?"

"On what kind of job you're applying for."

Then the man slid a magazine across the table to David. It was a recent issue of *U.S. News & World Report*. He pointed to a headline that read, "Not Your Father's CIA." Puzzled, David looked at the headline, then into the man's eyes. The man nodded for David to begin reading.

Cautiously, David took the magazine and scanned it quickly.

> The CIA is growing—and fast. To fend off America's
> enemies and take on terrorists and other bad guys

worldwide, the nation's premier spy agency is undergoing the most rapid growth since its inception almost sixty years ago. . . . The CIA has embarked on a nationwide ad campaign, hoping to attract a new generation of spies. For a look at its new pitch to young people, check out the agency's online rock-and-roll recruiting ads. . . . Trailers at movie theaters and posters at airports have tempted the adventurous with positions in the National Clandestine Service—the latest name for the agency's fabled directorate of operations, which recruits spies, steals secrets, and runs covert operations.

Suddenly, the man grabbed the magazine back from David.

"Hey, what the . . . ?"

But the man quickly cut David off before he could complete his sentence.

"Finish it," he said.

"Finish what?"

"Finish the article."

"You're crazy! I didn't have time."

"You're lying. Now, give me the rest of the article. Word for word. I know you can do it. I know all about you, David. I know you've tested at genius levels. I know you had a straight 4.0 average before Claire Harper died and her only daughter, Marseille, moved to Portland with her dad."

The hair on David's arms stood up.

"You have a photographic memory," the man continued. "You're only sixteen but you're supposed to graduate early—two years early— this June. You scored a 1570 on the SATs. The Ivy Leagues were in your future before you began to implode. That's actually where you and I were supposed to meet, a few years from now. But your little departure into self-destruction made me intervene sooner than I'd planned. Now cut the bull and recite the rest of the article for me, son. Before I walk out of here a very disappointed man."

The room was silent for at least a minute, save the buzz from the fluorescent lamps above them. David stared at the man for a while, then at the magazine, crumpled in the man's hand. Then he closed his eyes, leaned back in his chair, and began reciting from memory.

"'It was an impressive group, among the most diverse, most experienced ever hired by the CIA. Ages ranged from twenty to over sixty-five. More than half have spent significant time overseas, and one in six is a military veteran. They bring backgrounds as diverse as forestry, finance, and industrial engineering. And they're a well-educated bunch. They represent schools ranging from Oregon State, UCLA, and the University of Denver to the U.S. Naval Academy, Princeton, and Duquesne. Half the new recruits sport a master's or PhD. And if you want to work for the CIA's analytic corps, the directorate of intelligence, you'd better keep your grades up—the average grade-point average is a respectable 3.7.'"

"So why am I here?" the man asked. "Simple—to recruit you."

"You want me to work for the CIA?" David asked.

"Exactly."

"And you're looking for a few good ex-cons?" David quipped.

"Don't flatter yourself, son. Two weeks in this Holiday Inn hardly qualifies as hard time. For most people, a criminal record—even a juvenile record—would disqualify them. But not in your particular case."

"My *particular* case?"

"You're fluent in Farsi, German, and French. You're conversational in Arabic, and I suspect you'll master that pretty quickly once you put your mind to it. You're already five-foot-eleven. In a few more years, you'll be six-two or six-three. You know how to handle yourself. You could be valuable."

"Valuable for what?" David asked.

"You really want to know?"

David shrugged.

The man shrugged too and stood up to leave.

"No, wait," David said, jumping to his feet. "I really do want to know. What would I be valuable for?"

The man looked back at David. "I have no use for pretenders."

"I'm not pretending."

"Then I'll tell you—hunting bin Laden."

David stared at him. "You're kidding."

"I'm not."

"You want *me* to help hunt down Osama bin Laden?"

"Actually," the man said, "I want you to bring us his head in a box."

26

David was stunned.

He had to admit, he was electrified at the prospect. He hated bin Laden. The man had destroyed Marseille's life and as a result had come close to destroying David's. He wanted revenge so badly he could taste it. But as appealing as it was, this whole conversation still made no sense.

"Why me?" David asked. "I'm only sixteen."

"That will make things a little more complicated."

"Meaning?"

"Meaning usually I recruit college students. But with your behavior in recent months, I was concerned you might not make it to college. And I've been following your story too closely to have it end with disappointment for both of us. So like I said, I had to intervene earlier than I'd planned. The good news is that no one really knows who you are. You're not on the grid. You have no identity. You've just been kicked out of school. Your parents love you, but they don't know what to do with you. They're about to ship you off to boarding school for the rest of the semester. Your friends don't expect to see you again. It's a perfect time to get you on board, to begin building you a cover story, and in a few years, you'll be ready—"

"Wait a minute," David interrupted. "I have to ask—how exactly do you know so much about me?"

"I'm friends with your parents."

"Since when?"

"Since before you were born."

"Who are you?"

"My name is Jack," the man said, finally putting his cards on the table.

"Jack?" David said. "As in Jack Zalinsky?"

Zalinsky nodded.

"As in the Jack Zalinsky who rescued my parents from Tehran?"

Zalinsky nodded again.

"So my parents sent you here?"

Zalinsky laughed as the guard electronically unlocked the door. "Not a chance. In fact, they would kill me if they knew I was here. And this will never work if they know, David. You can't ever tell them we've met or what I'm about to take you into. Not if you want us to infiltrate you into the al Qaeda network and bag yourself a high-value target. It would be too risky for you and too risky for them. This has to be hush-hush, or it's over. Understood?"

The room was quiet again for a moment.

Then David finally said, "I'm in."

"Good," Zalinsky said.

"So what do I do next?"

"Let your parents get you out of here tomorrow. Go home with them. Be a good boy. Let them put you in the boys' school in Alabama. I'll make sure you get accepted. Then finish the year with straight A's without getting into any more fights. Get yourself in shape. And when it's time, I'll come get you."

"And then what?"

"Then we'll see if you've got what we need."

And with that, Jack Zalinsky was gone.

27

David buckled down and studied hard.

But physics and trigonometry weren't his passion. Nor was making new friends. With every spare moment, David locked himself away in his dorm room and studied the life of Osama bin Laden. He ordered books from Amazon. He pored over every magazine and newspaper story he could find in the school library. He began watching C-SPAN and the History Channel in what little spare time his new school afforded him, and in time a profile began to emerge.

What surprised him most was to find that bin Laden didn't fit the standard image of a terrorist. He wasn't particularly young. He wasn't poor or dispossessed or stupid or uneducated. Nor did he come from a violent or criminal family, much less one particularly bent on jihad, or "holy war." Born in late 1957 or early 1958—no one seemed to know for sure—Osama, David discovered, was the seventeenth of at least fifty-four children. His father, Mohammed bin Laden, was a wealthy Saudi who had founded one of the largest construction companies in the Middle East. His mother, Alia Ghanem, was a Syrian woman of Palestinian origin who met Mohammed in Jerusalem while he was doing renovation work on the Dome of the Rock. David was shocked to learn that Alia was only fourteen years old when she married Mohammed, and she wasn't his only wife—or one of three, or even ten. She was one of *twenty-two* wives the man had at various times through the years.

When Osama was only four or five years old, his parents divorced, and the little boy and his mother were forced to move out. Young

Osama was now effectively an only child being raised by a single mother in the rigid, misogynist, fundamentalist culture of Saudi Arabia.

And then tragedy struck. Not long after the divorce, Osama's father died in a plane crash. Years later, Osama's brother Salem would also die in a horrific plane crash. David wondered if this was when the idea of planes and death and the psychological torment they could cause had been planted in Osama's heart.

In June 1967, as he approached his tenth birthday, Osama watched along with the rest of the Arab world as the tiny Jewish State of Israel devastated the military forces of Egypt, Syria, and Jordan in just six days. Emotionally rocked, Osama wondered whether Allah was turning his back on the Arab forces.

As best David could determine based on his in-depth studies, the first time Osama bin Laden heard an answer that made sense to him was in 1972. During his freshman year of high school, Osama met a gym teacher who happened to be a member of the Muslim Brotherhood, the Islamic jihadist group founded in Egypt in the 1920s by a charismatic radical Sunni cleric named Hassan al-Banna. The gym teacher explained to bin Laden that the Muslims had turned their back on Allah by embracing the godless Soviets. In turn, Allah was turning his back on the Muslims. Apostasy was crippling the Muslim people. Only if they purified themselves, turned wholly and completely to following the teachings of the Qur'an, and launched a true jihad against the Jews and the Christians could they ever regain Allah's favor and the glory that was once theirs.

As bin Laden approached his sixteenth birthday in 1973—and underwent a massive growth spurt that left him six feet six inches tall and 160 pounds—the young jihadist-to-be was again stunned and horrified to see the Muslims of Egypt and Syria decisively defeated by the Jews of Israel during the Yom Kippur War. Now the Muslim Brotherhood argument made even more sense: Muslims were being humiliated by the Israelis because they had lost their way. They had forgotten the path of the prophets. How could they ever regain the glory that had once been theirs unless they returned to the teachings of the Qur'an with all that they were?

Often, David lay awake at night, poring over the pieces of bin Laden's life. He wanted to know this man inside and out. He wanted to be able to pick out his voice in a crowd. He wanted to be able to recognize him at a glance. He wanted to be able to think like him, talk like him, move like him. It was the only possible way, David decided, of penetrating al Qaeda and being drawn into the inner circle, which in turn was the only way of bringing this monster to justice. And what struck David again and again was how young bin Laden had been when he had begun to make his choices.

Bin Laden was just sixteen, David realized, when he joined the Muslim Brotherhood and began reading the collected works of radical Sunni author Sayyid Qutb. He was only seventeen when he got married for the first time, to a devout fourteen-year-old Muslim girl who was a cousin of his from Syria. What's more, bin Laden was only in his young twenties when Ayatollah Khomeini led his Islamic Revolution to victory in Iran in 1979, an event that electrified Sunni radicals who disagreed with Khomeini's Shia theology but loved his tactics and envied his accomplishments.

During these formative years, David noticed, bin Laden had wrestled with hard questions. Why had he been born? What was the meaning of life? Was his father right—was life about building empires, making billions, and marrying as many women as he possibly could? Or was there something more? What if man was born not to please himself, but to please Allah? What if the path to eternal life and happiness was not in a comfortable life but in a life of jihad?

David despised every choice bin Laden had made. But at the tender age of sixteen, David was beginning to understand why those choices had been made. And it began to make his own choices that much easier.

28

Zalinsky pulled up alongside David as he was walking down Main Street.

"Get in," he told his young protégé.

Glad to see Zalinsky, David complied immediately. "Where are we going?"

"You'll find out soon enough."

David knew Zalinsky had been tracking him closely. Just days after David had enrolled in the private boys' academy in Alabama to finish his high school diploma, he'd found a program installed on his laptop that allowed Zalinsky to read all of his incoming and outgoing e-mails and instant message conversations and to track all Internet usage. He knew the agent had tapped his cell phone and undoubtedly had someone recording his calls and listening to many of them, especially those with his parents and his brothers. He was even aware of a young operative enrolling at the same academy, posing as a transfer student, going to all of the same classes as David, talking to many of the same people.

David didn't mind the scrutiny. Zalinsky wasn't just watching David's back and making sure he didn't get in trouble again. He was carefully monitoring David's ability to keep a secret. Would he confide in someone—anyone—his plans with Zalinsky? Was he bragging to anyone that he might join the CIA? Was he a security risk in any other way? The fact that the veteran Agency man was finally making contact had to mean that he was sufficiently convinced that David Shirazi could keep his mouth shut.

Soon they were pulling into Montgomery Regional Airport, a joint-use facility for military, commercial, and private aviation. David had been in and out of the airfield several times, usually on a U.S. Airways Express flight. But Zalinsky wasn't headed for the commercial side. Rather, he pulled his silver Audi alongside a Cessna 560 Citation V, a sleek business jet that seated eight passengers more than comfortably. Minutes later, they were in the air, just the two of them and their two CIA pilots. David still had no idea where they were going, but he didn't really care. He was relieved to see that Jack Zalinsky was a man of his word and eager to get started.

"First of all, happy graduation," Zalinsky said when the pilot turned off the seat belt sign.

"Thanks."

"You're the youngest prospective candidate in the history of the Agency. You still want in?"

"Absolutely."

"Good. Your security check is complete. It was a little challenging to get it done without letting your family and friends know what we were up to. I told my team to ask questions as if you were applying to work at SunTrust Bank."

"And that worked?"

"Like a charm." Zalinsky pulled a black file folder from his briefcase, opened it, and set it on a small conference table in the back of the plane. Inside was a stack of false documents.

David picked up the first one on the pile—a birth certificate. "Reza Tabrizi?"

"That will be your alias," Zalinsky explained. "In Farsi, *reza* means 'to consent or accept.'"

"I know what it means," David replied.

"Of course you do. Well, anyway, you'll be a German citizen. Your parents moved from Tehran to Munich in 1975 and became citizens. In 1984, they moved to Edmonton, Alberta. You were born and raised in Canada. Your dad worked in the oil sands industry, but he and your mom were killed in a small plane crash just before you graduated from high school. You have no siblings. Your grandparents died when you were young. You never felt like you fit into life in Canada. So after your parents died, you moved to Germany. You bounced around a bit—Bonn, Berlin, and finally to Munich, where your parents were from."

David studied the dossier that Zalinsky had prepared on his new life.

"My team created a German passport for you. As you get a little older, we'll help you get a German driver's license, European credit cards, an apartment, a car, and so forth."

"What kind?" David asked.

"What kind of what?"

"What kind of car?"

"As we like to say in the Middle East, we'll blow up that bridge when we get to it," Zalinsky replied. "But listen, you've already been accepted into a college in Germany with this cover. We want you to pursue a degree in computer science from the University of Munich—they call it Ludwig-Maximilians-University of Munich there, or LMU. You'll need to finish becoming fluent in Arabic. When you're done, we want you to get an MBA to finish the cover. We'll pay for everything, so don't worry about the cost."

"But that will take years," David protested.

"Exactly," Zalinsky agreed. "When you get to Munich, you'll join a mosque—a Shia one, obviously, given your background. We want you to become part of the Shia community there. You need to appear to be a practicing Muslim, fluent in the customs and traditions of Shia Islam. Meanwhile, you'll also start getting martial arts training through the college. In the summers, we'll have you doing an 'internship' overseas. That's what your friends and professors will hear. You'll actually be training with us at one of several facilities. When you're all done and we think you're ready, we'll place you in a job with a company doing business in Pakistan and Afghanistan. You'll have a perfect cover to be traveling in and out of central Asia. Then, if he hasn't been caught, you'll begin hunting Osama bin Laden. There's just one catch."

"What's that?" David asked.

"You cannot, under any circumstances, tell your parents, your brothers—anyone—about any of this. I cannot stress this point enough."

"And if I do?" David wondered aloud.

"You'll go straight to prison," Zalinsky explained matter-of-factly. "You've already signed about a dozen nondisclosure forms. Believe me, we take this stuff very seriously."

"You don't have to worry about me," David assured him. "But what do I tell my parents I'm doing?"

"You tell them you're going to college in Paris," Zalinsky said. "You've already applied and been accepted. You got a full scholarship. We've already rented you an apartment near campus and got you a post office box and a cell phone from a French company. Everything's been thought of. It's all in that folder. There are even brochures and other materials you can give your parents."

David glanced through page after page of details.

"What about the job with SunTrust in Montgomery?" David smiled. "The one I supposedly applied for and am getting a background check for? What do I tell my parents and brothers about that?"

"Tell them you didn't get it."

"Why didn't I get it?"

Zalinsky raised his eyebrows. "They don't give bank jobs to kids with criminal records."

The man had thought of everything, and for this David was profoundly grateful. For the first time, he realized just how close his life had come to going off the rails, and it scared him. But for Zalinsky's intervention, who knew where he would have ended up? Now, however, he had a mission. He had a purpose. He finally knew why he had been born. He had a cause to live for—and to die for.

And yet, at the very moment he should have felt reassured, he couldn't help but think of Marseille. Where was she? What was she going to do that summer? She still had two years of high school to go. Was she okay? He still missed her terribly. Did she miss him?

PART TWO

★ ★ ★ ★ ★

29

A black sedan pulled up just before dawn.

"Let's go."

Good morning to you, too, Jack.

"What about some coffee?" David asked instead, still jet-lagged after a sleepless night on the red-eye from Munich.

"We don't have time," Zalinsky replied with uncharacteristic impatience.

David shrugged, sighed into the frigid February morning air, and did as he was told. Zalinsky was old and tired and was supposed to have retired long before now. He was not a man to be trifled with. Certainly not today. David stared at the rapidly shrinking Starbucks in the side mirror as the two left Arlington for the George Washington Memorial Parkway, en route to the headquarters of the Central Intelligence Agency in Langley, Virginia.

The car was quiet for a few minutes. David looked out at the snow-capped spires of the Georgetown University campus and the ice on the Potomac River and thought about all that had happened in the years since he had been sent to Germany and Pakistan, and some of the bizarre events that had been occurring in the Middle East even in recent days.

"Did you see that story about the slaughter of all those Christians in Yemen?" David asked.

Zalinsky did not respond.

"Some cult leader just walked into a church in Aden, pulled out a machine gun, and killed, like, forty people," David said, looking across the frozen Potomac. "Guy claimed he was preparing the way for the coming of the Islamic messiah or something."

After driving awhile in more silence, David added, "Weren't a bunch of priests and bishops assassinated in Yemen just before Christmas?"

Zalinsky still said nothing.

"That's weird, isn't it? I mean, I know it's not my country of focus, but I'm just saying, you know?"

Zalinsky wasn't interested. Instead, he dropped a bomb. "Look, David, I'm pulling you out."

"I beg your pardon?" David replied, caught off guard.

"You heard me," Zalinsky replied. "I'm reassigning you."

David waited for the punch line. It never came.

"To what?" he asked.

"You'll find out in a moment."

"Why?"

"I can't say."

"Well, for how long?"

"I really can't say."

David briefly considered the possibility that his handler and mentor was kidding. But that was impossible. The man had never told a joke. Not once in all the years since their first meeting. Not once while David was in college. Not once while David was attending the Agency's top-secret training facility in rural Virginia known as "the Farm." Not once—according to six different sources David had "interviewed"—in the thirty-nine years that Zalinsky had worked for the CIA. The man was a walking Bergman film.

"What about Karachi?" David asked.

"Forget Karachi."

"Jack, you can't be serious. We're making progress. We're getting results."

"I know."

"Karachi's working. Somebody's got to go back."

"Somebody will. Just not you."

David's pulse quickened. Zalinsky was off his rocker. If the man wasn't driving, David would have been severely tempted to grab him by the lapels and make him start talking sense. For the past few years since getting out in the field, David had been given some of the lamest assignments he could possibly have imagined. Assistant to the assistant to the deputy assistant of whatever for an entire year at the new American Embassy in Baghdad. Coffee fetcher for the economic attaché at the U.S. Embassy in Cairo. Communications and intelligence liaison in Bahrain for a SEAL team assigned to protect U.S. Navy ships entering and exiting the Persian Gulf. That, at least, had sounded cool on paper, but it was mostly long hours of boredom mixed with still-longer hours of trivia and minutia. David had complained to Zalinsky that this wasn't what he'd been recruited to do. He was supposed to be hunting Osama bin Laden, not babysitting destroyers and minesweepers.

Finally Zalinsky had relented and assigned him to a project hunting down al Qaeda operatives. So for the past six months, David had been stationed in Karachi, Pakistan, recruiting young technicians inside Mobilink—Pakistan's leading cellular telecom—to do a little "side business" with Munich Digital Systems, or MDS, the tech company for which David now ostensibly worked. He paid these kids well. Very well. And discreetly. From time to time he threw little parties in his hotel room. Bought them alcohol. Introduced them to "friendly" women. The kind they were unlikely to meet in their neighborhood mosque. He added a little buzz, a little color, to their otherwise drab lives.

In return, David asked them to poke around inside Mobilink's mainframes and ferret out phone numbers and account information of potentially lucrative future clients for his consulting work. The more information they provided, the more business MDS would get, and the more kickbacks he could pay these guys. Or so he told them. Unwittingly, these kids were actually giving him phone numbers and billing data for al Qaeda and Taliban terrorists, couriers, and financiers operating along the Afghan–Pakistan border.

The Pak technicians had no idea David was an American. They thought he was German. They had no idea he was working for MDS as a cover for his true identity as a CIA operative. They had no idea they were engaged in espionage. They just knew David was a twentysomething, like them. They thought he was a technogeek, like them. And they knew he had access to a lot of cash and was happy to dole it out generously to his friends.

And so far, so good. Over the last few months, David's efforts had led to the capture or killing of nine high-value targets. Day by day, David was certain, they were getting closer to bin Laden. The whole operation had been Zalinsky's idea, and until now, Zalinsky had given David every reason to believe he was thrilled by the results. Why, then, pull the plug now, especially when they were getting so close to their ultimate objective?

★ ★ ★ ★ ★

Ten minutes later, the two men arrived at CIA headquarters.

They cleared perimeter security, parked underground, cleared internal security, and got on the elevator. Zalinsky had still said little—barely even a "good morning" to the guards—and David was getting annoyed. The two were supposed to be having breakfast together, catching up on the news, dishing a little gossip from the field, and gearing up for a grueling day of budget meetings and mind-numbing paperwork. Instead, Zalinsky was threatening to pull David off a project he loved for no apparent reason and then giving him the silent treatment. It seemed unprofessional and unfair.

But when Zalinsky hit the button for the seventh floor instead of the sixth, David tensed. The Near East Division—their division—was a suite of offices on the sixth floor. The director of central intelligence and the senior staff worked one flight up. David had never been, but he was headed there now.

The elevator door opened. Zalinsky turned left. David followed close behind. Down the hall, they stepped into a high-tech conference room and were greeted by a balding man in his mid to late fifties who introduced himself as Tom Murray.

David had never met Murray before, but he had certainly heard of the man. Everyone in the Agency had. The deputy director for operations was a legend in the clandestine services. In March 2003, he masterminded the capture in Pakistan of KSM—Khalid Sheikh Mohammed—the right-hand man to Osama bin Laden and the architect of the 9/11 attacks. It was Murray, working closely with the British secret services in the summer of 2006, who planned the penetration and dismemberment of an al Qaeda cell in England that was about to hijack ten transatlantic jumbo jets en route from London to the U.S. and commit what one Scotland Yard official had publicly described as "mass murder on an unimaginable scale." And as far as David could tell, it was Murray who convinced President William Jackson to begin using Predator drones to take out key al Qaeda and Taliban leaders hiding in villages along the Pakistan–Afghan border when intelligence derived from David's own penetration of Mobilink's databases proved actionable.

"Good to finally meet you, Agent Shirazi," Murray said, shaking David's hand warmly. "I've heard a lot of good things about you. Jack here speaks very highly of you. Please, have a seat."

David smiled, thanked the DDO, and took his seat next to an expressionless Zalinsky. There was a knock on the door. Murray hit a button on the arm of his chair, which electronically unlocked the secure entrance. In came an attractive blonde in her late twenties or early thirties, wearing a conservative black suit, a robin's egg blue silk blouse, black pumps, and a pearl necklace obscured somewhat by the Agency ID dangling from her neck.

"Sorry I'm late, sir," she said with a slight European accent David pegged from northern Germany or perhaps Poland. "My flight just got in."

"That's fine, Agent Fischer," Murray replied. "We're just getting started. You know Jack Zalinsky."

"Yes, good to see you again, Jack," she said, her smile warm and genuine.

As the two shook hands, David couldn't help but notice she was wearing a pale shade of pink nail polish but not a wedding or engagement ring.

"And this is Agent David Shirazi," Murray said, "a fellow NOC."

The last phrase caught David off guard. He hadn't taken this woman as a nonofficial cover operative. An analyst, maybe, but undercover work? She was hardly the type to blend into the woodwork. David tried not to show his surprise as he shook her hand and caught for the first time just how blue her eyes were behind her designer glasses.

"Reza Tabrizi, it's great to meet you in person," she said with a friendly wink.

David froze. Only a handful of people knew his alias. How did she?

"It's okay, David," Murray assured him. "Eva's a first-rate agent and actually helped develop your cover story with Jack several years ago. She's been keeping an eye on you ever since."

"Is that so?"

"It is," she said confidently, setting her leather organizer on the desk, then looking David in the eye and recounting his alias from memory. "Reza Tabrizi. Twenty-five. Your parents were Iranian nationals, both born in Tehran. You, on the other hand, were born and raised in Canada, in a little town just outside of Edmonton, Alberta. Your father worked in the oil sands industry. Your mother ran a little sewing shop. But your parents were killed in a small plane crash just before you graduated high school. No siblings. Few close friends. You're a computer genius but a bit of a recluse. No Facebook page. No MySpace. No Twitter. After your parents died, you didn't want to stay in Canada. You decided to come to Germany for college. Got a degree in computer science from the Ludwig-Maximilians-University in Munich. Now you work for a rapidly growing German company, Munich Digital Systems. They develop and install state-of-the-art software for mobile phones and satellite phone companies. You're a relatively new but increasingly successful sales rep. The company executives have no idea you're actually an American. They certainly don't know you work for the CIA, and they'd fire you immediately if they ever found out."

Eva stopped for a moment and asked, "How am I doing?"

"I'm impressed," David conceded. "Please, go on."

She smiled. "You carry a German passport. You've got a Swiss numbered account where we send you funds. You've got a storage facility in Munich where you keep weapons, false documents, communications gear, and other essentials. Since August you've been working mostly with Mobilink in Pakistan, building up your field experience, working your contacts, establishing your cover, racking up some frequent-flier miles, taking down quite a few bad guys, and probably having a little fun along the way."

She paused and raised her eyebrows. "Am I wrong?"

David suppressed a smile. "No comment."

"That's plenty," the DDO said. "Please, take a seat, all of you."

David wondered when he was going to learn even a fraction as much about Eva Fischer as she'd just rattled off about him, but he guessed this was not exactly the right moment to ask. There were more important issues on the table, like somebody's crazy idea of taking him off the Karachi initiative just when it was actually bearing fruit. Was that Zalinsky's doing or Murray's? And what on earth for?

30

"You're going to Iran," Murray said.

The sentence just hung in the air for a few moments.

David Shirazi stared at Murray in disbelief, then at Zalinsky, and back to Murray. "When?"

"Seventy-two hours," Murray said. "Your code name is *Zephyr*." *God of the west wind?* They had to be kidding.

"What's the mission?"

"Jack and Eva here will walk you through the specifics," Murray explained. "But the short version is this: we need you to penetrate the highest levels of the Iranian regime, recruit assets, and deliver solid, actionable intelligence that can help us sink or at least slow down Iran's nuclear weapons program. We're currently positioning NOC teams throughout the country ready to sabotage facilities, intercept shipments, you name it. What we don't have is someone inside giving us hard targets."

David tried to process what his boss was saying, but it was such a radical departure from what he had been doing that he couldn't imagine it working. Sure, his family was Iranian, but he had never set foot in the country. Yes, he spoke Farsi, but so did eighty million other people in the world. What's more, he'd just spent the last several years studying Pakistani, Afghani, and al Qaeda leaders, organizations, and cultures. He was increasingly an expert in such matters and thus increasingly valuable in an intelligence agency that still hadn't caught bin Laden all these years after 9/11. As for Iran, he neither understood the first thing about Persian politics nor really much cared.

"I'm sorry, sir," David said after a few more moments of reflection. "That's not what I signed up for."

"I beg your pardon?" Murray said, clearly in no mood for a discussion on the topic.

"Sir, with all due respect, I was recruited to hunt down Osama bin Laden and bring you proof of his death," David told the Agency's number-two official with a depth of conviction that surprised even him. "That's what I was trained for. That's what I'm finally getting the chance to do. That's what I want to do. That's what I was born to do. I'm sure you have your reasons, and I'm grateful that you would consider me, but I'm not interested in changing assignments. You've got the wrong guy. It's just that simple."

The look on Tom Murray's face said it all. The man was not happy. "Agent Shirazi, I really couldn't care less why you think you were recruited for this Agency," he explained through gritted teeth. "We bought you. We trained you. We own you. Period. You got it?"

This was no time to argue, David concluded. "Yes, sir."

"You sure about that?"

"Yes, sir."

"Good." Murray got up, stretched his legs, and walked over to a window overlooking snow-covered woods. "Osama bin Laden is still a serious threat to this country and our allies. Don't get me wrong—I do want his head on a platter, and this Agency is going to get it done on my watch. But while in public this administration is focused on Afghanistan and Pakistan, the director and I believe the most serious threat to our national security and that of our allies in the Middle East at the moment is Iran. We know the Iranians are rapidly enriching uranium. We know they are planning to use that uranium to build nuclear weapons. We know time is running out. And if we don't stop the Iranians from building the Islamic Bomb, do you have any idea what's going to happen?"

David took a deep breath and glanced at Zalinsky, who was still stone-faced; then he looked back at Murray.

"Well, Shirazi," Murray pressed, "do you?"

David shifted in his seat. "Well, sir, I'd say the mullahs are probably going to try to rebuild the Persian Empire under the cover of a nuclear umbrella," he ventured. "And I'd guess they'll try to blackmail the Saudis and the Iraqis to do their bidding."

"Or?" Murray asked.

"Or Iran will try to drive up the price of oil to unheard-of levels and try to bankrupt the West."

"Or?"

"I guess that, uh, well . . . Iran could try to give a small, tactical nuke to al Qaeda or Hezbollah or Hamas or Islamic Jihad or some other terrorist organization who could try to sneak it into Tel Aviv or Haifa and take out an Israeli city."

"Or?"

David didn't like where this was headed. "Worst-case scenario? Iran could try to launch a barrage of ballistic missiles—fitted with nuclear warheads—over Syria, over Iraq and Jordan, and into the major cities of Israel to 'wipe the Zionist entity off the face of the earth,' as they have promised to do for years."

Murray nodded but asked one more time, "Or?"

This time, David drew a blank. "I'm sorry, sir, isn't that all bad enough?"

"It is," Murray said. "But aside from the fact that the creation of the Persian Bomb will force the Arab states into a nuclear arms race so they have the Bomb, too, you're still missing one catastrophic scenario."

"What is that, sir?"

Murray picked up a remote control off the conference table and pushed a button. "The most immediate—and arguably most likely—scenario is that Iran will never get the Bomb." All eyes were riveted to the digital display. "Instead, the Israelis, hoping against hope that they can neutralize the Iranian nuclear threat before the ayatollahs are truly able to destroy their country, will launch a massive preemptive strike." On the screen, missiles were suddenly flying in every direction throughout the Middle East as Israel struck first followed by the retaliation of Iran, Syria, Hezbollah, and Hamas.

Not a single country in the region remained unaffected. The simulated Iranian response to Israel's first strike showed Persian missile strikes against every major Israeli city, but also against oil fields, refineries, and shipping facilities throughout Saudi Arabia, Kuwait, and the Arab emirates in the Gulf. At the same time, Iranian missiles were hitting cities and military bases in Iraq and Afghanistan. Israel, meanwhile, was not simply being hit by hundreds of Iranian missiles, but also by tens of thousands of missiles, rockets, and mortars from Syria, Lebanon, and Gaza. With Israeli missiles and fighter jets firing back, it was clear the entire region was going to be set on fire.

Murray hit another button, enlarging the scope of the digital map, and David saw flashes in cities throughout Europe as well as the Middle East. These, the deputy director for operations explained, represented suicide bombers being unleashed en masse. Then David noticed a series of digital counters in the lower right-hand corner of the screen, estimating casualties from the entire conflict. Hundreds of thousands of innocent civilians would die, David realized—Jews, Muslims, and Christians. Millions more would be wounded or left homeless by the devastation. And not only would the Middle East and Europe be affected, the United States would be as well. It was almost impossible to imagine sleeper cells not being activated, hitting Americans and Canadians with a blizzard of terrorist attacks.

While David was still focused on the casualty projections, Zalinsky evidently decided it was time to broaden the young man's perspective. "As bad as the human toll would be, it would not be limited to death and injury," he explained. "The economic analysts over in the directorate of intelligence tell me they would expect oil prices to skyrocket in this scenario."

"How high?" David asked.

"No one really knows—two hundred dollars a barrel? three hundred dollars a barrel? Maybe more."

Such a dramatic spike in oil prices—overnight but also sustained for months and possibly years on end—could sink an already-fragile global economy. Soaring energy prices could quickly trigger hyperinflation, David surmised. Skyrocketing prices would send the cost of many goods beyond the reach of the poor and lower middle class. Millions would be pushed into poverty. People would stop spending on almost anything but food and basic staples, triggering massive business failures. Tens of millions of people would soon be out of work. As the dominoes fell, a global depression could ensue. And this, of course, was assuming the conflict was simply a conventional war, not one that actually went nuclear. David wasn't sure that was a safe assumption, but the point wasn't lost on him.

He glanced at Eva. At the moment, she was looking down, jotting notes, but she clearly wasn't reacting to all this with much emotion. Assuming she was a thinking, feeling, rational person, that could mean only one thing: she had heard this information before. She had already run the various scenarios and processed them at length.

Then another thought dawned on him. He wasn't going into Iran alone; Eva was going with him. She wasn't an Agency analyst. She was a NOC operative. Zalinsky said she had helped construct some of David's cover stories in the past, but if she were simply helping design his new assignment going forward, why would Murray and Zalinsky have her in the room? There was no other reason than for the two of them to become acquainted prior to embarking on a mission that might cost both of them their lives.

David looked back at the images flickering on the display and knew in that instant that his dream of killing Osama bin Laden and avenging the death of Marseille Harper's mom was evaporating in front of his eyes. But to his surprise, he wasn't angry or depressed. Rather, he found himself unexpectedly exhilarated. His country needed him. He was one of the few Persian Americans in the CIA's clandestine services. He spoke Farsi like a native. He would have an airtight cover story. He didn't yet know exactly how Murray was going to use him, but he'd learn soon enough. The bottom line was clear. He was heading into Iran. His mission was to stop the ayatollahs before they got their hands on the Bomb. Before the Israelis took matters into their own hands. Before Armageddon. Better yet, he was going with a beautiful, intelligent girl he looked forward to getting to know. All that, and he was leaving in seventy-two hours.

The phone rang.

The DDO answered it, then turned to the others and said, "Another massacre in Yemen—I need to take this. Jack, I trust you and Eva can proceed from here."

Zalinsky nodded and quietly signaled David and Eva to gather their papers and follow him back downstairs to the Near East Division.

Back on the sixth floor, they signed out a conference room.

Zalinsky ordered some Chinese food from the commissary, and the three of them locked themselves away for the rest of the day. Only then did Zalinsky hand David and Eva a thick briefing book on the mission ahead of them.

"Memorize it, both of you," Zalinsky said when they had finally settled in. "I'm sure you've already figured this out, David, but Eva is going in too. Her cover will be the MDS project manager. In reality, she'll also be running the Agency's operation on the ground and reporting back directly to me. Her code name is *Themis*."

The Greek goddess of divine law and order? She was going to be insufferable, David concluded.

Zalinsky, however, didn't give David time to ponder the implications. He cut straight to the bottom line. "Time is of the essence. I can't stress this enough. I've talked to all of the Agency's best Iran analysts in the intelligence directorate. Most believe Tehran could have functional nuclear weapons in two to three years. Some say it will take them longer. But the problem is, the Israelis don't trust our analysis. They're worried we're making another catastrophic error of judgment."

"You mean 1998—India and Pakistan," David said.

Zalinsky nodded. "We knew both countries had been racing to build the Bomb for decades, but we were caught completely off guard when they both tested nukes within days of each other. We had no idea they had crossed the nuclear finish line and built dozens of nuclear weapons until it was too late to do anything about it. And that's just one example. The Agency had no idea the Soviets were so close to testing their first nuclear weapon in 1949 until the test actually occurred. And don't forget Saddam Hussein in 1981; we didn't realize just how close he was to building nuclear weapons until the Israelis took out the Osirak nuclear reactor just before it went hot."

"And then there's Iraq again in 2003," Eva chimed in.

No kidding, David thought. Arguably the Agency's most disastrous mistake to date was having convinced President George W. Bush that Iraq had large and dangerous stockpiles of weapons of mass destruction—and that the case for proving it to the international community was, in the now-infamous turn of phrase by the director of central intelligence at the time, "a slam dunk." To be sure, some WMDs were found in Iraq after the liberation of the country by U.S. and coalition forces. But the weapons that were discovered were neither the types nor quantities of WMDs the U.S. and the world had expected to find. Nor were they the types and quantities the CIA had warned about. As a result, the credibility of the CIA and her sister agencies throughout the American government had been so badly damaged that they still had not fully recovered.

"So the problem," Zalinsky concluded, "is that we now have to be very careful about assessing the WMD capabilities of enemy nations, Iran included. The analysts in the CIA's intelligence directorate are terrified of making mistakes and of being accused of overstating what they know. So they hedge their written and oral assessments. No one wants to sound too concerned about Iran getting the Bomb for fear of looking like they're goading the president into another war."

"So let me get this straight," David said. "The Israelis think we blew the call in the past by not realizing just how close Saddam and India and Pakistan and others were to getting the Bomb. And the Israelis think we blew the call a few years ago by thinking Saddam was closer to building the Bomb and stockpiling WMDs than he really was. So when our best analysts say Iran is still several years away from getting the Bomb, the Israelis think we're smoking crack?"

"Let's just say they're not brimming with confidence," Zalinsky said. "But it's even worse than that."

"How so?"

"A few weeks ago while you were in Karachi, David, and you, Eva, were in Dubai, I had lunch in Jerusalem with Israel's top spook at the Mossad. He told me, look, the world already knows Iran is building nuclear facilities. The world already knows they're training nuclear scientists and enriching uranium at a breakneck pace and building ballistic missiles that can reach not only Israel but Europe as well. The world has already heard the Iranian leadership repeatedly threaten to annihilate Judeo-Christian civilization and wipe Israel and the U.S. off the map. So why isn't the world taking decisive action to stop Iran from getting the Bomb? Why isn't the U.S. building a coalition to invade Iran and change this fanatical regime? The world, he noted, went to war with Iraq in 2003 with far less evidence. I told him there is simply no appetite—and no money—in the U.S. or Europe or anywhere for another war in the Middle East. So he asked, doesn't Israel, then, have not only the legal right but the moral responsibility to go to war with Iran now, if the world is just going to sit on its hands and do nothing?"

"I hear his point," David said. "But given the fact that a war between Israel and Iran could set the region on fire and seriously impact the global economy, do we really want Israel to be deciding the fate of the region and the world all by itself?"

"No, we don't," Zalinsky said. "And that's what I told him. That's why the secretary of defense is en route to Tel Aviv as we speak to warn the Israelis not to take matters into their own hands. That's why President Jackson has had no less than three phone conversations with Prime Minister Naphtali in the past month urging him to let us ramp up covert efforts rather than drag the world into a war no one wants. Which brings the three of us to this room. Last week the president quietly signed a highly classified national intelligence directive. It authorizes the CIA 'to use all means necessary to disrupt and, if necessary, destroy Iranian nuclear weapons capabilities in order to prevent the eruption of another cataclysmic war in the Middle East.'"

Zalinsky then reached into his briefcase, pulled out a copy of the directive, and slid it across the table for David and Eva to read for themselves.

As David read the one-page document, Eva asked, "How much time does the Mossad think they have before Iran has an operational nuclear weapon?"

Zalinsky took back the "eyes only" directive and returned it to his briefcase, then answered the question. "They're convinced Iran will have the Bomb by the end of the year . . . and an operational warhead by the end of next year."

David tensed. Even if the Israelis were wrong, even if they were being too pessimistic, their assessment could mean only one thing—if the U.S. did nothing, the Israelis were going to launch a massive strike against Iran, and soon.

32

It was just after midnight when Zalinsky let them go.

They had spent nearly fourteen hours poring over the briefing book and talking through various aspects of the mission. It was now February 12. They would meet again at a safe house in Dubai on the evening of Monday, February 14, he told them. There he would give them several more days of briefings before sending them in. In the meantime, Zalinsky suggested they get lost for the weekend—the Caribbean, Cancún, Cozumel, someplace that didn't start with a *C*; he didn't really care.

"Enjoy yourselves," he ordered. "Clear your heads. Get some fresh air. It might be your last break for a while."

Eva immediately started texting someone to make plans. David wondered if she had a boyfriend or a fiancé and surprised himself with the twinge of disappointment he felt. They had, after all, only just met. But he said good-bye and left the building without asking any questions. He didn't want to seem too forward or too interested so quickly. He would find out in due time where she had gone and with whom, he figured. He and Eva were about to spend a lot of time together. There was no point stumbling at the starting gate.

As he stepped out of the CIA's main building and headed to the parking garage to pick up his company loaner for the weekend—a Chevy Impala—he stared up at a million diamonds sparkling on the dazzling black canvas above him. He breathed in the brisk, still, cloudless night air and tried to enjoy the beauty and the silence. He was energized by the prospect of the mission ahead of him, but at the same time he suddenly felt alone in the world. He didn't have a girlfriend. He didn't have a best friend. He hardly had any friends to hang out with aside from Zalinsky and his Mobilink rent-a-friends in Karachi. He tried to think about the last time he was really happy, and it inevitably brought him back to thoughts of his time with Marseille in Canada. Before 9/11. Before the wars in Afghanistan and Iraq. Before joining the CIA. It was so long ago, and the memories were painful. He tried to think of something else.

There was, he realized, nowhere to go except home. He was rarely in the U.S. these days, and he hadn't really kept in touch with anyone in the States aside from his parents. His brothers had little interest in his overseas life. They would have, of course, if he told them that he worked for the CIA's National Clandestine Service. That he'd been hunting down the upper echelons of al Qaeda's leaders to have them assassinated. That he was now on a mission to penetrate the inner circle around Iranian president Ahmed Darazi and Iran's Supreme Leader, Grand Ayatollah Hamid Hosseini.

But he couldn't tell them any of that without going to prison. So even with his family, he stuck with his cover—that he was running his own little computer consulting practice in Munich. And Azad and Saeed's lack of caring did have an upside. It prevented David from having to lie so much to their faces.

His parents, on the other hand, were a different story. They cared a great deal about David's work and personal life, and their curiosity had made things significantly more complex. For one thing, it produced twinges of guilt every time he told them anything other than the truth. His mother, in particular, constantly peppered him with questions. She wanted him to call more, to write more, to come home for Christmas (though they had never celebrated Christian holidays growing up). His father was almost as persistent, urging him at the minimum to come home for the annual fishing trip to Canada. But there was nothing David wanted less than to go back to that island and relive memories of Marseille.

So he always had a million excuses. Business trips, conferences, new clients, old clients, billing problems—the list went on and on. He hated the secrecy and the deceit and the distance, but he really didn't see another way. Increasingly, however, he worried that if he didn't go home soon, his parents would make good on their threats to just fly to Munich one day and "pop in." Given that David didn't actually even live in Munich—his apartment, phone, and mailbox there were all simply to maintain his cover story—that would be a disaster.

It was time to go home, he concluded. So he signed out the Impala and headed north.

★ ★ ★ ★ ★

He drove all night.

He arrived in Syracuse just under seven hours later, pulled into his parents' driveway—tucked away in a little cul-de-sac off East Genesee Street—and finally turned off the engine. As a light snow fell, he stared at his childhood home. He knew he should go in. He could see lights beginning to come on inside. He could picture his mother padding about in her robe and slippers, making tea and toast for his father and softly singing Persian melodies with the Food Network on in the background.

But David wasn't ready to go domestic just yet. His body might have come home, but his head was still back at Langley, swimming with numbers.

- 5,000—the number of miles of fiber-optic cable networks in Iran in the year 2000.
- 48,000—the number of miles of fiber-optic cable networks there in 2008.
- 4,000,000—the number of cell phones in Iran in 2004.
- 43,000,000—the number of cell phones there in 2008.
- 54,000,000—the number of cell phones there now.
- 70,000,000—the combined number of Iranians in country and in exile.
- 100,000,000—the number of SMS messages sent daily in Iran.
- 200,000,000—the number of text messages that would be sent daily in Iran in the next twelve to eighteen months.

- $9.2 billion—the revenue produced by the Telecommunication Company of Iran, or Iran Telecom, in 2009.
- $12.4 billion—the projected revenue for Iran Telecom in 2014.

Zalinsky believed such explosive growth in the Iranian telecommunications arena afforded the Agency a unique window of opportunity. The regime in Tehran was investing heavily in modernizing and expanding its civilian communications networks. Simultaneously, they were spending aggressively on a parallel track to create a secure and robust military communications system.

As Iran feverishly tried to become a regional nuclear power—and soon a world power—the Supreme Leader wanted his country to have state-of-the-art voice and data networks for all sectors of society, but especially for the military's system of command and control. To get there as quickly as possible, the Iranians were reaching out in an unprecedented way to European technology companies, offering them contracts worth billions of dollars to upgrade Iran's hardware and software and provide them with much-needed technical assistance.

Iran Telecom, Zalinsky had explained, had recently awarded a huge contract to Nokia Siemens Networks, requiring all manner of NSN engineers and other experts to enter Iran, make specific telecommunications upgrades, and train their Iranian counterparts. NSN, in turn, had contracted Munich Digital Systems to build much of the necessary infrastructure. Since the CIA already had agents, including David, embedded within MDS, this had created—virtually overnight—the opportunity to put boots on the ground, to place Farsi-speaking Agency operatives inside Iran Telecom, the mother ship of the modernization effort.

Zalinsky had shown David a story in the *Wall Street Journal* reporting that the Iranian regime was seeking, with NSN's and MDS's help, to develop "one of the world's most sophisticated mechanisms for controlling and censoring the Internet, allowing it to examine the content of individual online communications on a massive scale." This effort went far beyond blocking access to Web sites or severing Internet connections, enabling authorities not only to block communication but to gather—and sometimes alter—information about individuals.

David recalled another intriguing headline from the business section of the *New York Times*: "Revolutionary Guard Buys Majority Stake in Iran Telecom." That story, he knew, had eventually made it into the president's daily intelligence briefing. David's heart still raced as he recalled the text of the article in his mind's eye and considered its implications in light of the NSN/MDS deal.

The transaction essentially brought Iran's telecommunications sector under the elite military force's control. The article explained that the purchase would allow the Guard in times of crisis to "interrupt mobile phone networks" and "hinder the opposition's organization."

The last paragraph of the story intrigued David most. It noted that the IRGC was essentially "free from any state oversight" and was "accountable only to the Supreme Leader, who has the final say on all state matters in Iran."

If the *Times* story was accurate, then Zalinsky was right. If the CIA could penetrate the inner circle running Iran Telecom, perhaps they really did have a shot at penetrating the inner circle running the Revolutionary Guard. Whether that trail could lead David into the Supreme Leader's office, getting him hanged or shot in the face, was a question mark at best. But as David watched the snow sticking to his windshield, he imagined the prospect of actually being able to intercept the most private phone calls of Iran's Supreme Leader and the calls of his closest staff and advisors. What if Langley could actually read the e-mail and text messages of Iran's highest leaders? What if they could follow messages coming to and from computers and phones inside Iran's clandestine nuclear facilities? The very notion made him want to get into Iran now. He could hardly wait. They had to move fast, before the Israelis struck.

Suddenly there was a knock on his passenger-side window. It was his father, standing there in the freezing cold in his pajamas, holding the Saturday morning edition of the *Post-Standard* newspaper in his hand and staring at him in disbelief.

"David? Is that you?"

33

Najjar Malik awoke to the sound of his baby daughter crying.

He groaned, rolled over, and whispered to his wife, "It's okay, princess. I'll get her and bring her to you."

But as he opened his eyes and tried to rub the sleep out of them, Najjar realized that Sheyda was not beside him. He glanced at the alarm clock. It was only 4:39 a.m. He still had nearly an hour before he had to be up for morning prayers. Still, he slipped out of bed and went looking for the love of his life, only to find her nursing their baby daughter.

"You okay?" he asked through a yawn.

"Yes," Sheyda replied, smiling at him with a warmth and genuineness of which he never tired. "Go back to bed. You need your rest."

Najjar smiled back. He could have ten more children with her, he decided, even if they were all girls.

Suddenly there was heavy knocking on the door of their high-rise flat.

"Who could that be at this hour?" an annoyed Najjar said.

To his astonishment, two Revolutionary Guard soldiers brandishing machine guns were standing in the hallway.

"What is the meaning of this?" he demanded in a whisper, trying not to wake the entire floor.

"The director says you must come immediately," said the larger of the two, apparently a colonel.

"Dr. Saddaji sent you?" Najjar asked. "Why didn't he just call?" The man was, after all, not just the director of Iran's atomic energy agency but his father-in-law.

"I don't know," the colonel said. "He just said it was urgent."

"Fine, I'll be there in an hour."

"I'm sorry, sir. The director told us to take you with us. We have a car waiting downstairs."

Najjar turned to Sheyda, who had covered herself with a blanket.

"Go," she said. "You know Father would never send for you if it wasn't important."

She was right, and Najjar loved her all the more for her support. He closed the door, leaving the soldiers in the hallway. Then he threw on some clothes, brushed his teeth, splashed some water on his face, grabbed his briefcase, and ran out the door, stopping only to give Sheyda a kiss.

On the drive, they passed dozens of mosques, and Najjar felt a strong need to pray. He had no idea what the day held. But he had never been summoned so early in the morning, and his anxiety over what was coming grew minute by minute.

As sunrise approached, Najjar finally heard the call to the *Fajr*, or dawn prayer, coming from the speakers of one of the many minarets adorning the skyline of Hamadan. As had become a ritual five times a day since he was a small child back in Iraq, he dutifully faced Mecca, raised his hands to his ears, and recited the *Shahada*—the testimony of faith—declaring he bore witness that there was no one worthy of worship except Allah and he believed with all his heart that Muhammad was the servant and messenger of Allah. Then he placed one hand to his chest and his other hand on top of the first and prayed, "In the name of Allah, the Most Gracious, the Most Merciful. Praise be to Allah, Lord of the Worlds. The Most Gracious. The Most Merciful. The Master of the Day of Judgment. You alone do we worship. You alone do we ask for help. Show us the straight path, the path of those whom you have favored, not of those who earn your anger nor of those who stray. Amen."

As he continued reciting portions of the Qur'an, bowing toward Mecca as best he could from the backseat and continuing his morning prayers, Najjar found his anxieties multiplying, not dissipating. He desperately wanted to hear from Allah, to see him, to behold his beauty and come fully into his presence. He wanted Allah to grant him favor and wisdom and a calm reassurance that he was doing Allah's will and pleasing him in every way. But he felt no peace. He felt no joy. When he finished, he felt further away from Allah than when he had begun.

An hour later, Najjar stood in the middle of a cavernous, empty warehouse. The concrete floor was cold and wet, as if it had been recently hosed down. Sitting several yards away was a man bound to a chair, his hands and feet shackled in iron chains. The man's mouth was gagged, but he was not blindfolded, and Najjar could see the terror in his eyes. It was clear he had been beaten severely. His face was bruised and swollen, and blood trickled down his cheeks.

Najjar thought there was something vaguely familiar about him. "Who is he?"

"You were never supposed to meet him," Dr. Saddaji replied not only to Najjar but to the two dozen other scientists standing around them. "But events beyond our control have forced the issue."

Najjar watched his father-in-law staring at the man, who was silently pleading for his life. But there was nothing in Dr. Saddaji's voice or body language that suggested mercy would be forthcoming. Indeed, Najjar had never seen him so cold, so dark, so filled with hatred.

"Gentlemen, take note of this man and remember him well," Dr. Saddaji said. "He is an Arab—an Iraqi—and a traitor."

Najjar was stunned. It was one thing to be from Iraq. He was, and so was Dr. Saddaji, along with several others. But they weren't Arabs. They were all Persians.

How can there be an Arab in our midst? Who allowed it, and why?

This research facility was top secret, buried deep inside Alvand Mountain, the highest peak in the region. Of the half-million people in the surrounding area, including in Hamadan—one of the oldest cities in Iran—not a single one was Arab. Less than one-tenth of one percent of them knew this facility existed at all, much less that the future of Iran's civilian nuclear power program was being designed and developed here. *What on earth could have possessed someone to allow an enemy into the camp?*

As if on cue, Dr. Saddaji took the responsibility upon himself.

"Gentlemen, I will be candid. I recruited this man. He was once a colleague at the University of Baghdad, one of the most brilliant minds of our generation, an absolute genius in the field of UD3. He was not one of us, true. But we needed his expertise. I thought I could trust him. With the blessing of the Supreme Leader, I made him an offer he couldn't refuse. But I made a mistake. He sold us out. Now he must pay."

Saddaji's response generated more questions than it answered, at least for Najjar. *UD3?* Why in the world would Saddaji need an expert in the use of uranium deuteride? Even a junior physicist like himself knew UD3 had no civilian uses. Had Dr. Saddaji completely lost his mind? What if the IAEA caught wind of a UD3 expert—one from Iraq, at that—inside a nuclear facility the IAEA didn't even know existed? Why take such a risk with the eyes of the international community riveted so intently on the Iranian nuclear program?

Before Najjar could raise any of these questions, however, Dr. Saddaji continued, outlining what this man had done to betray them all. He explained that the man had been caught making two unauthorized calls to Europe.

"He claims he has a girlfriend in France," Dr. Saddaji sniffed. "He claims he had no idea his girlfriend was an agent for the Mossad."

Najjar couldn't believe what he was hearing. He had never met a man as careful, as thorough, as meticulous about everything—and especially about security—as his father-in-law. Whoever this person sitting before them was, his treachery was appalling. But what did his father-in-law expect? Couldn't he have seen this coming? Something didn't make sense.

But this "trial"—if it could be called that—was suddenly over as quickly as it had begun. No one was being invited to ask questions of the accused or of Saddaji. An executioner now entered the warehouse, carrying an ornate sword that looked several centuries old. His face was covered by a black ski mask. A moment later, the traitor's head was rolling across the warehouse floor. Najjar became violently ill, but the point had been made—all betrayals, real or imagined, would be punished severely.

34

The weekend was bittersweet.

It began Saturday morning with a breakfast of pancakes and lies. David couldn't tell his parents the truth about why he was in the country. Instead, he told them he had suffered through a series of mind-numbingly dull business meetings in Chicago. Then he lied about where he was heading next, telling them he was flying to Frankfurt, then driving to Wiesbaden for more meetings. He lied about whether he would be home for Mother's Day, saying, "Absolutely," then silently cursed himself for the rest of the day. He had no way of knowing where he would be or what he would be doing in three months. It wasn't fair to lead his parents on. But he didn't know what else to do, and he felt terrible.

Deception was central to his life in the CIA. But that didn't make it any easier, and a brooding conscience, growing anxiety about the mission ahead, and a serious lack of sleep after driving all night from Washington proved a depressing cocktail. David tried to catch a few hours of sleep in his old room after breakfast but kept tossing and turning. Finally he gave up and joined his father for an afternoon of cross-country skiing across the back nine of the golf course at Drumlins Country Club.

That night, over dinner with his parents at their favorite Italian place on Erie Boulevard, David asked about his brothers. He was just trying to be polite, but the very question made his mother wince.

Azad, his father explained, was thriving as a cardiologist in Philadelphia, and yes, the rumors were true: he and his wife were expecting their first child. But no, they never visited; no, they never called; no, they hardly ever e-mailed. Once the baby was born, the Shirazis planned to drive down and visit Azad and his wife, but they honestly weren't sure how long they'd be welcome.

Saeed, meanwhile, showed no signs of settling down. He was dating a dancer—or was it a cellist? At any rate, he was dating someone new— *always* someone new—in Manhattan. He still seemed to be married to his job with Merrill Lynch and was convinced he was well on his way to making his first million. But no, he hadn't been home in ages, and no, he hadn't gone fishing with his father in years. Not long before, the Shirazis had visited Saeed for a long weekend, but Saeed spent most of the weekend in the office and had made little time for his parents, who had returned to Syracuse brokenhearted.

After dinner, David tried to shift gears. Talking about family wasn't doing them any good, so he suggested they rent one of the Lord of the Rings films and watch it together. His mother had never seen it and insisted on making popcorn, pulling out some afghans, and having her husband make a fire in the fireplace. They all got comfortable in the family room to watch *The Return of the King*, but within the first few minutes, David's mother fell asleep. Within half an hour, so did his father. David didn't bother to watch the rest, though it was one of his favorite films. Instead, he turned off the TV, went up to his room, and surfed the Web for the latest headlines from Iran and the Middle East.

Several caught his eye.

Israeli PM Naphtali at Dachau Says World Must Stop Iran, or He Will

Israeli Defense Minister Says Someone Must Hit Iran's Nuclear Sites "Before It's Too Late"

President Jackson Warns Against Israeli Strike on Iran's Nuclear Facilities

U.N. Security Council Considers New Round of Iran Sanctions

Iranian President Darazi Warns Israel "Doomed" If Zionists Attack

David's stomach churned along with his thoughts. Exhausted, he eventually went to bed but couldn't sleep. Around four in the morning, he got an e-mail from Eva, whose subject line read, "You up?" He eagerly opened it, hoping it might be personal. It wasn't.

EF: Something's afoot in Yemen

She was right, of course. He recalled the phone call DDO Murray had taken in his office. But why did it matter at 4 a.m.? Eva included a link to a recent Agence France-Presse story she had found on the Internet. David opened it and quickly scanned the article.

"Before the Twelfth Imam appears on earth to establish his global kingdom, we will see a series of signs," said Dr. Alireza Birjandi, author of *The Imams of History and the Coming of the Messiah*, at a conference Friday in Qom sponsored by the Bright Future Institute. "The first sign is the rise of a fighter from Yemen called the Yamani. He will attack the enemies of Islam, and in so doing he will help pave the way for the end of days."

> Birjandi, widely considered the world's leading expert on Shia eschatology, declined to comment on whether the recent attacks against Christians in Yemen represented the fulfillment of that sign. But other scholars gathered for this three-day conference speculated that this could, in fact, be the case.
>
> The Bright Future Institute is a theological think tank established in the city of Qom in 2004 by Shia scholars to study Mahdism in depth and to prepare Shias for the return of the Islamic messiah, known as the Mahdi or the Hidden Imam or the Twelfth Imam.

Puzzled, David sent a text message to Eva's phone.

DS: don't know what 2 make of that

A moment later, Eva wrote back.

EF: i don't know either

DS: ever hear of birjandi?

EF: can't say i have

DS: me neither . . . on amazon now . . . ordering his book

EF: good idea . . . i'll look into the bright future institute

DS: thnx—let's compare notes on mon . . . how R U? where R U?

EF: i'm good . . . thnx 4 asking . . . hanging out w/ my parents and sisters in berlin . . . how about U? surfing in cancun? sunbathing in san juan?

David smiled as he replied.

DS: lol—i wish. actually visiting my folks in syracuse . . . but can't wait 2 get started

EF: me 2. . . see you soon—looking fwd 2 it . . . how about *$ in DXB?

It took a moment for David's sleep-deprived brain to decipher that last one, until he realized she was suggesting they go to Starbucks when they got to Dubai. He typed a final message.

DS: Yes—SYS—OAO

See you soon. Over and out.

He plugged his phone back into its charger and finished ordering Dr. Birjandi's book online, directing it to be shipped to his apartment in Munich. Then he shut down his laptop, lay back down in the darkness, and stared out the window at the moonlight falling on the snow-covered backyard.

So, Eva wasn't with a boyfriend for the weekend. Interesting. It didn't mean she didn't have one, of course. But if she did, she hadn't chosen to spend the weekend with him. She was with her family, instead. And thinking of him. He liked that, and in the privacy of his childhood bedroom, he admitted—if only to himself—that he found Eva a little more than just interesting, against his better judgment.

He hadn't dated much in college, and not at all since, in part because most of the German girls he knew were too brusque for his liking and because—his falsified passport notwithstanding—he wasn't really German. He didn't like sauerkraut. He couldn't stand *Wiener schnitzel.* He could barely choke down German chocolate cake. But something about Eva was different. Maybe, he thought, it was finally time to let go of Marseille's hold on him.

35

They all got up late and joined each other for Sunday brunch.

That was when his mother upped the ante. Over homemade Belgian waffles and fresh-squeezed orange juice, she implored David to give up all of his international travel, get a job with Carrier or Lockheed Martin or Bristol-Myers Squibb or some other solid company in central New York, find a nice Syracuse girl to marry, find a nice single-family home in Manlius or Fayetteville or DeWitt—not too far away—and finally make a real life for himself where they could see him and truly be a family.

"Please, Davood," his mother pleaded. "You're my youngest son, and I feel like I'm losing you."

David hadn't heard her use his Persian name—*Davood*—since childhood. Knowing he was leaving in a few hours and potentially never coming back made him feel even worse than before.

David's father wasn't quite so direct, but it was abundantly clear that he, too, wanted his son to slow down and settle down. David certainly understood why. His parents were rapidly approaching retirement age. The whirlwind of raising three high-octane sons was over. The house was empty. No one was around to break any lamps or hit any baseballs through the front windows—or the neighbors' windows. No one needed to be rushed to the hospital for stitches anymore. A box of cereal in their house now lasted them a month, not a day. They only needed to buy a quart of milk a week, not four gallons. Everything was different. They were lonely. David promised to be in touch more and privately vowed to do better.

Just then, David's phone vibrated. Waiting for him was a new text message. Eva Fischer was en route to Dubai. Zalinsky was as well. They had breaking news, so "DBL," she wrote. *Don't be late.*

David's pulse quickened. It was time to get into the game. He apologized to his parents and excused himself to check his BlackBerry for the status of his flights. Despite a massive snowstorm heading across Lake Ontario from Canada by nightfall, all flights at the moment appeared to be running on time. He was booked on Delta flight 5447, leaving Syracuse's Hancock Field at 5:33 p.m. and arriving in Atlanta at 8:06 p.m. That should get him out of central New York before the brunt of the storm hit, and for that leg, he would be traveling under his real name. Once in Atlanta, however, he planned to switch to his German passport and his alias—Reza Tabrizi—and catch Delta flight 8. That would depart at 11:20 p.m. and arrive in the largest city of the United Arab Emirates at 9:25 p.m. the following evening.

David checked his watch, then apologized to his parents again and told them it was time for him to go. That's when his mother explained the driving force behind her request.

"Davood?" she said, her eyes welling up with tears.

"Yes, Mom?"

"Honey, there's no easy way to say this, so I'm just going to say it. I've been diagnosed with stage III stomach cancer. We didn't want you boys to worry about me, but you showing up like this so unexpectedly seems like a gift. So I wanted you to know."

The news stunned David. As he listened to her describe the symptoms she had been experiencing in recent weeks and the various tests the doctors were running and the aggressive treatment plan they were recommending and her fears of dying, all of David's guilt came rushing to the fore. He desperately wanted to stay, to listen, to care for both his parents as they headed into this terrible storm. But he had to leave.

They begged him to reschedule his flight, to call his boss, to explain the situation. But he couldn't. He could see the pain and deep disappointment in his mother's eyes in particular, and he grieved for her. His excuse for having to leave sounded so lame under the circumstances, but no matter how much he wanted to, he couldn't tell them the truth.

As David stood on the front steps of his childhood home in an increasingly heavy snowfall and hugged his parents good-bye, Nasreen Shirazi began to cry.

"Mom, please, don't," David said, his suitcase in hand, the car running.

"I can't help it," she said in Farsi, sniffling. "I love you, Davood."

"I love you, too, Mom."

"Remember when I used to walk you by the hand to the bus stop when you were a little boy?"

"Mom, really."

"Remember when you came racing home every day with a backpack filled with notes and papers and goodies for me? Remember when you couldn't wait to tell me about everything you had done that day?"

"Mom, it's going to be all right," he assured her. "Dad knows the best doctors in the world. They'll take great care of you. And I'll find a way to come back soon to visit you and cheer you up. But if I don't leave right this second, I'm going to miss my plane. And I really have to go."

"Fine," she said. "Go. Who am I to stand in your way?"

David felt worse than ever. He kissed her on the cheek, gave his father a hug, and was in his car when his mother suddenly began calling after him.

"David, David—wait! Before you go, I totally forgot—I have something for you!"

She turned and ran into the house. David looked to his father for help, but Dr. Shirazi simply shrugged off any knowledge of what his wife was up to. Two minutes passed. Then three. Then five. David checked his watch. He drummed his fingers on the dashboard. He forced himself not to gun the engine or honk the horn, but inside he couldn't take it anymore. Finally his mother came running back out to the car and breathlessly handed him a plastic Wegmans grocery bag.

"What's this?" he asked.

"Just a little mail for you," she said, giving him one last kiss through the open window as the snow began coming down even harder. "I keep forgetting to send it over to you."

"Thanks, I guess," he said, putting the Impala in reverse and easing out of the driveway. "Anything interesting?"

"Probably not," she said. "Except maybe one."

"Really? From who?"

"I don't know exactly," she said. "But the postmark said Portland."

★ ★ ★ ★ ★

HAMADAN, IRAN

Najjar woke up in the middle of the night in a cold sweat.

He couldn't breathe, haunted for yet another night by the face of the man he had seen beheaded as a Zionist spy. His dear wife, Sheyda, held him, startled awake, no doubt, by his repeated nightmares and constant thrashing and moaning.

"What is it, my love?" she whispered with a tenderness that typically calmed and comforted him.

Now neither her soothing voice nor the gentle touch of her arms around him sufficed. Najjar had no idea what to say. He couldn't tell her that her father was a butcher. He couldn't fully believe it himself. What's more, he had to remain quiet. Everything that happened in that facility—*everything*—was highly classified. He was not authorized to say anything to anyone about anything that happened there. To be found breaching security, even to the daughter of the director of the facility, would land him, he feared, in Iran's notorious Evin Prison. And that, he knew, would be a merciful sentence. Two unauthorized phone calls had already cost one man his life.

But it wasn't simply the gruesome image of the executioner's blade slicing the man's head off and the massive flow of blood that threatened to prevent Najjar from ever sleeping peacefully or innocently again. It was the fact that the man hadn't been given a fair trial in a court. It was the fact that neither Najjar nor his colleagues had seen a single shred of proof against the man. It was the fact that this man was a fellow

Muslim, yet he had been shown no mercy. Worse, it was the fact that Najjar now knew why the man had looked so familiar.

For in his most recent nightmare, Najjar suddenly came to the realization that this was the man he had seen kidnapped back in Baghdad years before, the man whose family he had seen slaughtered execution-style on Al Rasheed Street.

36

David parked at Hancock Field and raced into the terminal.

He was intrigued by the letter from Portland and its bizarre timing, but that would have to wait. David was devastated by news of his mother's cancer. He couldn't imagine his mother not being there for him. Nor could he imagine his father living all alone. He rued all the years he had missed spending time with them both—summers, birthdays, holidays. They were all gone now, and he could never get them back.

First things first, he called a local florist and ordered two dozen yellow roses—his mother's favorite—to be sent to the house with a note asking for her forgiveness for not being able to stay longer. Next, he dashed off an e-mail to Zalinsky's administrative assistant, informing her that he was leaving the Agency's car at the Syracuse airport. Then he checked his bags, got his boarding pass, and cleared security just in time to catch the flight to Atlanta.

Finally, sitting on the plane, he steadied his breathing and reached for the letter in his briefcase. But fear got the better of him, and he put it back unopened. *It might not even be from her,* he realized. Even if it was, it might not be friendly. A thousand scenarios raced through his mind, and David wasn't sure he was ready for any of them.

Once in Atlanta, he quickly identified the NOC waiting for him. With a lightning-fast "brush pass" near a newsstand in the domestic terminal, David was given a Nokia N95 smart phone. Moments later, he crushed the SIM card for his current phone and discarded it in a trash bin near the food court. A few minutes after that, he discarded his BlackBerry in a trash bin in the men's room.

Now that his company, Munich Digital Systems, was working with Nokia Siemens Networks, he needed to play the part and carry the tools of the trade. The N95 was Nokia's top-of-the-line 3G phone, functioning more like an iPhone than like a BlackBerry. Nevertheless, the N95 he now held in his hands was not a normal one. Rather, this was a special version that had several features embedded by the techies at Langley.

First, a proprietary GPS function allowed Zalinsky and the Agency to track David's location in real time without anyone being able to detect that such tracking was going on.

Second, the phone was preloaded with the names and contact information of people David would be expected to know in his consulting role. More importantly, any new names, phone numbers, and e-mail addresses he added to his contact directory would be instantly and clandestinely uploaded to Langley and the NSA's mainframe computers. This would alert both agencies to hack in and begin monitoring those phone numbers and e-mail addresses as new high-priority targets.

Third, and perhaps most importantly, while the phone typically operated on standard frequencies, allowing foreign intelligence agencies to listen in on his calls and thus to be fed disinformation, a proprietary encryption system could be activated to enable the user to make secure calls to Langley or to other field agents. This was only for rare cases and extreme emergencies, because once the software was activated, those monitoring David's calls would know immediately that he had "gone secure," potentially risking his cover as a consultant for MDS.

As he headed for concourse T, David surfed the Web, trying to get familiar with the phone. As he did, he came across the latest diatribe by Ayatollah Hosseini, Iran's Supreme Leader, given in a speech in Tehran at a conference of terrorist leaders from Hezbollah, Hamas, and Islamic Jihad.

> "Like it or not, the Zionist regime is heading toward
> annihilation. The Zionist regime is a rotten, dried tree

that will be eliminated by one storm. And this is just the beginning. Today, the time for the fall of the satanic power of the United States has come, and the count-down to the annihilation of the empire of power and wealth has started. Get ready for a world minus the U.S."

Maybe he should bring home *this* guy's head in a box, David mused. At least they knew where to find him.

★ ★ ★ ★ ★

Upon reaching concourse T, David finally looked at his itinerary.

For the first time he realized that on this upcoming flight to Dubai, he had a middle seat in economy on a fourteen-hour flight. That wouldn't do, he decided. He set his sights on an upgrade to business. Waiting until he could get a few moments alone with the attractive young woman at the Delta counter, Yasmeen, he asked if there was anything she could do to take pity on him. Anything would be better than a middle seat.

"Are you a SkyMiles member?" she asked.

"No—how can I sign up for that?" he replied.

"Well, Mr. Tabrizi, I can give you the form to fill out, but I'm afraid I've only got one seat left in business, and that's typically reserved for members with Diamond Medallion status."

"That doesn't exactly sound like a no," he whispered.

"Well, I really shouldn't," she said, her eyes darting around the lounge.

"Of course you shouldn't," David said, smiling and continuing to keep his voice low. "But I'd never tell."

She bit her lip.

Then David had a thought. "Are you working this flight?" he asked.

"Yes, why?" she replied.

"In business?"

"As a matter of fact, yes."

"Well, maybe I could return the favor when we're in Dubai," he offered.

"What do you mean?" She was intrigued.

"Ever been to the top of the Burj Khalifa?" David asked, referring to the world's tallest building, the glamorous monument to man's engineering genius that had recently opened in the heart of the business capital of the United Arab Emirates.

"To the observation deck?" she asked, looking disappointed. "Of course; everyone has."

"No, no, above that," he said. "There's a private suite no one knows about. The owner uses it for exclusive dinners with his best clients."

"Really?" Yasmeen asked, her beautiful brown eyes growing large. "I've never heard that."

"Actually, I know the owner," David said. "His son and I went to college together at Yale. He said I could use it the next time I'm in town, and I was thinking, how about we have dinner up there Wednesday night, just you and me?"

And that was that. David was suddenly holding a ticket for seat 5A, the last available seat in business. But his conscience was killing him. He didn't know the owner of the Burj. He hadn't gone to Yale. He had no intention of taking Yasmeen to dinner in Dubai. He'd simply done what they'd taught him at the Farm—win friends and influence people and use them for his own purposes. At the beginning, he'd been surprised at how easy it was for him, convincing people to do things they didn't want to do. Now he was surprised at just how terrible he felt for lying to this woman. What was wrong with him?

He sat down in the business lounge and waited for the flight to be called. He was anxious about his mom. He was also anxious about what lay ahead in Iran. He had studied al Qaeda and the Taliban and the Pakistanis inside and out. He knew their history. He knew their culture. He knew the language and the protocols. But though he had Persian blood running through his veins, he had done precious little homework for this assignment. There hadn't been time. He knew Zalinsky and Fischer would do their best for the rest of the week to get him ready, but he feared it wouldn't be enough. He needed a month, not a week, and probably more.

Desperately needing to get his mind off his mother, Yasmeen, and Iran, David found his thoughts drifting to the letter from Portland and the rest of the mail he was carrying. He couldn't exactly travel into Dubai—much less Iran—on a German passport bearing the name Reza Tabrizi while carrying U.S. mail for David Shirazi. Which meant he had a decision to make. Should he read all of the notes and letters— mostly Christmas and birthday cards from old friends in central New York—then throw them away here in the Hartfield-Jackson airport? Or should he find a post office or UPS store and ship them all to the flat in Munich that the CIA leased for him, the flat where his parents actually thought he lived?

Agonizing over the question a bit longer than he should have, David finally chose to ship the mail to Munich. He would keep only the letter from Portland with him. Was it really that much of a risk taking just one letter with him to Dubai? CIA protocols forbade it. But U.S. Homeland Security certainly wasn't going to be looking for a Dear John letter on him. There weren't going to be any security checks upon *arriving* in Dubai. And he would certainly ditch the letter, whomever it was from, before heading into Iran. So that was that. He had his plan.

37

DELTA FLIGHT 8

They were now at thirty-nine thousand feet, halfway over the Atlantic.

David skipped dinner and waited for the dishes to be cleared and the cabin lights to be dimmed. Once that happened, he looked around to make sure the flight attendants were busy and that the passengers around him were going to sleep, watching movies, listening to their iPods, or otherwise occupied. Then he removed the small, cream-colored envelope from his briefcase.

It was not a Christmas card. This was expensive stationery. Judging from the delicate cursive of his name and address, it was definitely a woman's writing. Sure enough, the envelope bore a postmark from Portland, dated December 13, almost two months prior. There was no name or return address in the top left-hand corner or on the back. But given the city of origin, there was little doubt whom it was from. The only question was what it contained and why it was sent.

David couldn't help but be struck by the timing. How long had it been—a day? not even?—since he'd begun to consider for the first time in nearly a decade actually letting his memories of Marseille go and wondering if anything might happen between him and Eva? And now, in all likelihood, he was holding a letter from Marseille Harper. What did it mean? It was a sign, he was certain, but what did it portend?

Despite all that had happened and all the time that had passed, the truth was, David had missed Marseille every day since the funeral. The realization embarrassed him, but it was the truth. He loved her, and no matter what happened, he guessed he always would. Every year on her birthday, June 20, he had tried to picture what she might look like one year older. He had wondered how she was celebrating, whom she was celebrating with. How was her father doing? Had he ever remarried? Did Marseille now have stepbrothers and -sisters? Were they one big happy family? He had wondered what growing up in Oregon was like for her without her mother, without the beloved Jersey Shore of her youth, without her childhood friends, and it always made him sad.

Spring Lake, New Jersey, he imagined, would have been an idyllic place to grow up. He had read about it at the library and researched it on the Internet and had even driven through the town one day last summer—without ever telling Zalinsky or his parents, of course. With fewer than four thousand year-round residents, the tiny but picturesque seaside village had more seagulls than citizens, though in the summer, tourists from Manhattan, Long Island, Philly, and points west and north caused the population to swell to seven or eight thousand.

She had told him with glee how much she loved to get up early and ride her bike to the beach before dawn, while it was still quiet and peaceful, and watch the sun rise over the crashing waves before the crowds came to sunbathe and build sand castles. On lazy, hazy Sunday summer afternoons, she loved to fish off the pier with her dad and then get chocolate-chocolate-chip ice cream cones at Hoffman's on Church Street.

But in an instant, it had all been stolen away, and even though David tried not to, he couldn't help but wonder what she had done instead. Did she and her father live close enough to the Pacific for her to ride her bike down to the shore at dusk to watch the sun set over the crashing waves? Did she still go fishing with her dad? Did they find an ice cream place to go to again?

Carefully, David opened the envelope and pulled out the small, handwritten note. He took a deep breath, braced himself for what was coming next, and began to read.

Dear David,
Hi, how are you? I hope you are well, and your parents and
brothers, too. I realize this note may come as a bit of a shock.

Please forgive me for not writing before now. I wanted to. I started to write several times but never finished or never sent them. Things have been difficult and complicated, and honestly, I wasn't quite sure what to say. But two things have prompted me to write now.

First, as it happens, I'm going to be a bridesmaid in a wedding near Syracuse on the first weekend of March. Why in the world my friend Lexi chose to get married in the bone-chilling snows of "Siberacuse"—isn't that what you used to call it?—I have no idea. Maybe it will truly be beautiful and balmy and springlike by then, but with my luck, I seriously doubt it. That said, Lexi and I have been friends since our freshman year in college, and she really is head over heels in love with this guy, and she grew up out there in a town called Fayetteville (I hear it's really nice), so I just couldn't say no.

Of course, as soon as I learned the wedding would be out there, I couldn't help but think of you. The only other time I was ever in Syracuse was when my family visited yours and we stayed at your house. I think I was seven or eight. Do you remember that?

The second thing that prompted this note is that my father recently passed away. It has been very hard and painful in ways that I would rather not write in a letter. I'd prefer to tell you in person.

So, anyway, the real reason I'm writing, I guess, is that I wondered if you might like to get a cup of coffee together, or something, when I'm out there. It's been a long time, so much has happened, and there are things to say.

I arrive on Thursday, March 3, around dinnertime. I don't have plans that night or on Friday morning until around 10 a.m., when all the bridesmaids are getting together for brunch with Lexi and her mom. The rehearsal is at the church at 4 p.m. There's a dinner at 6, so the rest of that day is probably out. The wedding is at 2 p.m. on Saturday, so I'm probably not going to be free at all that day. Sunday morning might be another possibility if you'd like to come to church with me. Lexi says it's an awesome church. I'd really love it if you came. After that, I've got to race to the airport to catch a 1 p.m. flight back to Portland.

If you can't get together, or if you don't want to, I'll certainly understand. And I'm sorry for rambling on like this. I didn't mean to. I just meant to say I'd like to see you again if possible. It would be good to catch up and tell you things I should have said earlier, if you're okay with that. Thanks, and please say hi to your folks for me.

She closed the letter by including her mobile number and her e-mail address, then signed her name. No "Your friend, Marseille" nor "Sincerely yours, Marseille." And there was certainly no "Love, Marseille."

Just "Marseille."

Still, she had written. And her letter was actually friendly. She didn't seem to be trying to drive the knife deeper into his heart, which came as no small measure of relief. To the contrary, she wanted to see him again. David could hardly believe it.

He read the letter again and then a third time, though he had memorized it after the first pass. He was glad to hear she'd gone to college, glad she had a dear friend she cared so much about that she was willing to travel across the country to be with her on her special day. But he felt terrible for the loss of her father. Marseille and Mr. Harper had been so close for so long. Now she was all alone in the world. She didn't sound bitter, though she did say her life had been "difficult" and "complicated" and "painful" in ways too hard to write about. David wondered what other sadnesses had befallen her in the years since he'd seen her last.

It was hard to describe his own emotions at that moment. He turned and looked out the window at the darkness below and felt a lump forming in his throat. He had missed Marseille for so long, and he had eventually given up hope of ever hearing from her, much less seeing her again. To suddenly know that she was alive, that she was as well as could be expected under the circumstances, that she thought of him fondly and even that she missed him meant the world to him.

It was all good, amazingly good, except for one problem: Marseille was coming to Syracuse in less than a month, and as far as she knew, he had completely blown her off. He hadn't known about the letter or the invitation or the visit. But she didn't know that. All she knew was that he hadn't even had the decency to write or call or e-mail back and say, "Good to hear from you, but I'm afraid I'll be in Iran that weekend." Or "Thanks for the note, but I wouldn't want to see you again if there was a gun to my head." Or "You've got to be kidding me. You blow me off for how long, and now you want to have coffee?" Or "Thursday works for me, and by the way, are you seeing anyone?"

Something—*anything*—would have been better than nothing. But she hadn't heard from him at all in nearly two months. He felt terrible. He had to fix this, and fast.

38

NEGEV DESERT, ISRAEL

Captain Avi Yaron muted his radio and closed his eyes.

"Barukh atah Adonai Eloheinu melekh ha olam," he prayed, *"she hehi-yanu v'kiymanu v'higi'anu la zman ha ze."*

Blessed art Thou, Lord our God, King of the universe, who has kept us alive, sustained us, and enabled us to reach this season.

With that, he throttled up his engines, carefully veered his F-15 out of its underground bunker, taxied onto the tarmac, and waited for clearance. Behind him, thirty-seven more F-15s and F-16s fueled up, revved up, and got in line. This was it. The night for which they had been waiting, preparing, and hoping over the past six months.

Yaron looked out at the beehive of activity across Hatzerim Air Force Base, not far from the ancient city of Beersheva, in the heart of the Negev Desert. Most people who knew anything about the place thought of Hatzerim as the home of the Israeli Air Force Museum. Only a handful of people even in Israel knew the IAF had been secretly retrofitting the facilities to house several new air attack wings.

Yaron's hands were jittery. Were the intel guys right? Was there really a narrow window when neither Russian nor American spy satellites were in position to watch them? How could they really know precisely what time that window opened and shut?

He hated to wait. He was desperate to fly, desperate to engage the enemy, drop his ordnance, and save his people. But life in the Israeli Air Force these days seemed all about waiting. The pilots waited for the green light from the commanders. The commanders waited for the generals. The generals waited for the minister of defense. The defense minister waited for the prime minister. The prime minister waited for the president of the United States.

What if they waited too long? What if Iran got the Bomb and set into motion another holocaust?

The time for waiting was over, Yaron believed. It was time to strike first.

He checked his instruments. Everything was ready, as was he, and as he waited for permission to launch, his thoughts drifted to Yossi, his twin brother. He checked his watch. He could picture Yossi in his F-16 at that very moment, taxiing out to the tarmac at Ramat David Air Base in the north, not far from Har Megiddo, from whose name came the term *Armageddon*. He wished he could shout a shalom to him, but radio silence was the rule of the day, and it was inviolable.

Just then the ground crew gave him the signal. It was go time.

Yaron didn't hesitate. He put the pedal to the metal and took his Strike Eagle to forty-eight thousand feet in less than a minute. Behind him, the skies filled with fighter jets, long-range bombers, and fuel tankers. A devastating armada had just been unleashed for the twelve-hundred-kilometer flight, the longest mission in which any of these young pilots, navigators, and weapons systems officers had ever been engaged.

39

The Bell 214 Huey took off just after evening prayers.

As it gained altitude, the Iranian military helicopter gently banked north and headed for the Alborz Mountains, site of the Supreme Leader's heavily guarded retreat complex on Mount Tochal. At 3,965 meters, Tochal was the second-highest peak in the range and was well away from the smog and the noise and the congestion of the capital and from all the palace intrigues and political machinations that increasingly vied for his attention and sapped his strength.

Haunted by growing fears of an imminent Israeli attack, the graying, bespectacled Hamid Hosseini, now seventy-six, looked out over the twinkling lights of Tehran, a city of eight and a half-million souls. He had never imagined rising to the heights of his master. He had never sought to be the nation's Supreme Leader. But now a great burden rested on Hosseini's shoulders. He wished he could sit with his master and pray and seek Allah's counsel together, as they had done on so many occasions over the years. But it was not to be. There was a time in a man's life when he no longer had the blessing of his mentor's attention or wisdom or even his presence, a time when a man had to make fateful decisions on his own, come what may. This was one such moment, and Hosseini steeled himself for what lay ahead.

Upon landing at the retreat site, an aide slipped the Supreme Leader a note, informing him that his guests were waiting for him in the dining room. Hosseini read the note but would not be rushed. Flanked by his security detail, he headed first for his master bedroom, instructed the aide to give him some time alone, then closed the door and sat on the bed.

His mind was flooded with questions. They had all been asked and answered before, some of them dozens of times. But they had to be asked once more. Were they truly ready? How long would it take? Were they certain they would be successful? Could they guarantee complete secrecy? Moreover, if they were discovered before they were ready, could they survive the repercussions?

Hosseini's top advisors were confident that victory was at hand. He was not. They believed the benefits far outweighed the risks. He feared they were telling him what they thought he wanted to hear, not the truth—at least not the whole truth. They had the luxury of being wrong. He did not. And that, he reasoned, made all the difference.

Hosseini slipped off the bed and onto his knees. He faced the windows, thus facing Mecca, and began to pray.

"O mighty Lord," he implored, "I pray to you to hasten the emergence of your last repository, the Promised One, that perfect and pure human being, the one who will fill this world with justice and peace. Make us worthy to prepare the way for his arrival, and lead us with your righteous hand. We long for the Lord of the Age. We long for the Awaited One. Without him—the Righteously Guided One—there can be no victory. With him, there can be no defeat. Show me your path, O mighty Lord, and use me to prepare the way for the coming of the Mahdi."

It was his standard prayer, the one he had prayed thousands of times over the years. It was also a secret—one he had carefully kept hidden, even from those closest to him. As a closet "Twelver," he longed to see the Mahdi come in his lifetime. And now, he sensed, that time was drawing close.

Thirty minutes went by. Then an hour.

Suddenly there was a knock on the door. Hosseini did not answer but continued praying. A few moments later, there was another knock.

Annoyed, the Supreme Leader tried to ignore it and maintain his focus. When it happened a third time, however, he rose, stepped to his dresser, pulled out the top drawer, retrieved his nickel-plated revolver, and opened the bedroom door. He was so enraged he could barely breathe.

"Everyone is waiting for you, Your Excellency," his young male aide said.

"Did I not ask to be left undisturbed?" Hosseini fumed.

The aide blanched and began to back away. "You did, but I thought . . ."

"*You wicked son of a Jew!*" Hosseini shouted. "*How dare you disturb me as I enter the holy place!*"

With that, Hosseini shot the man in the face.

The sound of the explosion echoed through the retreat facility. Hosseini stared at the dead man as a pool of blood formed on the hardwood floor of the hallway. Then he knelt down and dipped his hands in the blood and began to pray aloud.

"*Allahu Akbar.* Highly glorified are you, O Allah. The Prophet— peace be upon him—taught us that when we find those who are unfaithful and disobedient infidels, we must 'kill them wherever you may come upon them,' that we must 'seize them, and confine them, and lie in wait for them at every conceivable place.' The Prophet—peace be upon him—taught us to 'strive hard against the unbelievers and the hypocrites, and be stern against them' for 'their final refuge is hell.' May this sacrifice, therefore, be acceptable in your sight."

With that, Hosseini rose, his hands dripping with warm blood, and turned to the chief of his security detail, who stood stone-faced and trembling in the hallway.

"I will come out soon," Hosseini said calmly. "Make certain my way is not obstructed."

With that, the Supreme Leader entered the bedroom alone. The security chief shut the door behind him. Hosseini then returned to his prayer rug, knelt again facing Mecca, and bowed down.

Without warning, a blazing light as if from the sun itself filled the room. Hosseini was stunned, wondering what this could be. Then a voice, emanating from the center of the light, began to speak.

"*Very good, my child. I am pleased with your sacrifice.*"

The room grew cold.

"The hour of my appearance is close at hand. With blood and fire I shall be revealed to the world. It is time to destroy, to kill, and to annihilate the infidels—Jews and Christians, young and old, men, women, and children."

This was the moment Hosseini had been waiting for, he knew, the moment for which he had prayed all of his life. But he had never imagined it like this. He was hearing the actual voice of *Sahab az-Zaman*, the Lord of the Age. The Twelfth Imam himself was speaking directly to him, and every fiber of Hosseini's being trembled in excitement and in fear.

"Now, listen closely to what I am about to tell you. Get ready; be prepared. And do not hesitate for a single moment to carry out my commands."

"Yes, my Lord," Hosseini cried. "Thank you, my Master."

"You shall complete the weapons and test them immediately. When I finish roaming the earth and all is set into place, we will proceed to annihilate the Little Satan first and all the Zionists with it. This is your good and acceptable act of worship to me. You must bring to me the blood of the Jews on the altar of Islam. You must wipe the ugly, cancerous stain of Israel from the map and from the heart of the Islamic caliphate. This is right and just, but it is only the first step. Do not be distracted or confused. This is not the ultimate objective. I have chosen you above all others not simply to destroy the Little Satan, for this is too small a thing. The main objective is to destroy the Great Satan—and I mean destroy entirely. Annihilate. Extinguish. Obliterate. Vaporize. In the blink of an eye. Before they know what has hit them. The Americans are a crumbling tower. A dying empire. A sinking ship. And their time has come."

The Twelfth Imam then instructed Hosseini to meet with his security cabinet, consisting of President Ahmed Darazi, Defense Minister Faridzadeh, and General Mohsen Jazini, commander of the Iranian Revolutionary Guard Corps, already gathered and waiting for him in the retreat's main dining room.

"Each of you must carefully select four deputies, forming a group of twenty. These must be men of honor and courage, like yourselves. They must be men willing to die for my sake, for the sake of Allah. The twenty of you will form my inner circle and be my most-trusted advisors. You will meet

weekly. You will establish secure communications. You will then recruit 293 additional disciples—some mullahs you trust, but mostly military commanders and leaders of business and industry. You must find servants extraordinarily gifted in organization, administration, and warfare. You will recruit this group with haste, but never let the Group of 313 meet all together in one place. It is too dangerous. There is too much risk of infiltration or leaks. Create a cell structure. Do not let one cell know about another. Only you four can know all the details. Is this clear?"

"Yes, Master. I will do all that you say."

"Very good, Hamid. Get ready; be prepared. Let there be no mistake—I am coming back soon."

40

Hosseini pressed his face to the floor.

The words of the Twelfth Imam rang in his ears. He wanted to ask questions, to plead for wisdom, to say something, anything, but no words would form; no sound would come.

Then, as quickly as it had appeared, the light was gone. Hosseini lay prostrate, unable to move. It seemed like only a few minutes, but later, as his breathing calmed and his heart slowed, he realized that nearly an hour had gone by. None of his aides dared check on him, of course. Nor would his guests.

Slowly Hosseini began to compose himself. He washed his hands and face, changed into fresh clothes, and stepped out of his room. He walked down the freshly mopped hallway, then turned right and went down another long hallway, past several bodyguards stationed at strategic points, and entered the main dining room. There he was greeted by his security cabinet, all of whom instantly rose to their feet.

"Please, gentlemen, be seated," the Supreme Leader said, taking a seat at the head of the table.

"I have known the three of you for many years," he began. "I have sought your counsel and relied on you many times. Now I need your best assessment. Ali, we will begin with you."

Hosseini paused. He knew he needed to explain to his colleagues what had just happened. But first he needed to gather his thoughts and process it for himself.

"Thank you, Your Excellency," Defense Minister Ali Faridzadeh began. "Last month you asked me to go back to my team and ask many questions, to press the scientists for more clarity. This I have done."

"And what have you found?"

"We are ready, Your Excellency."

"You are certain?"

"Absolutely."

"The uranium is sufficiently enriched?"

"Most of the last batch was 97.4 percent," Faridzadeh said. "Some came in at 95.9 percent. Both are sufficient, and we continue to make improvements."

"How many warheads could you build with that?"

"We have already finished nine."

Hosseini was taken aback by the defense minister's impressive report. "They are already built?"

"Yes, Your Excellency—thanks be to Allah—nine of them are ready to be detonated. My men should have another six done by the end of the month."

"This is welcome news, indeed," the Supreme Leader said. "Which design did you use? The one from Pyongyang?"

"No, Your Excellency. In the end, we chose A. Q. Khan's design."

"Why?"

"The data from the North Korean tests were disappointing, Your Excellency," Faridzadeh explained. "The warheads the North Koreans tested certainly detonated. But the yields were not that impressive."

"Meaning?"

"Meaning Pyongyang's bomb could annihilate several city blocks, but we don't believe they could take out a city. And this was one of your stated objectives, the capacity to take out all or most of a city with a single weapon."

"Yes, we must achieve this," Hosseini pressed. "You're certain the North Korean plans are not sufficient?"

"I am not a physicist, as you know, Your Excellency," the defense minister replied. "But my top man has pored over the data from every angle, and he is simply not convinced the North Korean design has been perfected to the point that we'd want to risk the future of our own country on it."

"But we paid so much for it," Hosseini said.

"We did, Your Excellency. But what the North Koreans sold us was effectively worthless in comparison to what we bought from A. Q. Khan, the father of the Pakistani nuclear weapons program."

"But we hardly paid Dr. Khan anything."

"Nevertheless," the minister said, "Islamabad has built 162 warheads to date based on Khan's design. They've tested their warheads multiple times. The yields are absolutely enormous. So we know the design works. Now we simply need to test what we have built and make sure we have followed his impressive design to the letter."

"And you are ready to test?"

"Almost, Your Excellency," the defense minister said.

"How soon?" Hosseini asked, leaning forward. "Could you be ready by summer?"

Faridzadeh could not suppress a smile. "*Inshallah*, we should be ready by next month."

The Supreme Leader was ecstatic. He was tempted to drop to his knees and offer Allah a prayer of thanksgiving right there and then. But he did not smile. He did not visibly react. There were still too many risks, too many variables, too many unknowns, too many things that could go wrong. Still, they were almost there. After so many years and so many setbacks, they were almost ready. And just in time, for the coming of the Mahdi was at hand.

"Do I have authorization to proceed with the test?" the defense minister asked.

Hosseini did not answer immediately. He rose and walked to the window, where he stood looking down at the lights of Tehran. He wanted to say yes, of course. But the stakes could not be higher. The testing of an Iranian nuclear warhead would alert the world that they were ready. The charade that they were simply running a civilian nuclear power program would be over. Talks at the U.N. over the possibility of imposing new international sanctions were already under way. For now, their allies in Moscow and Beijing were standing firm against such sanctions. But a nuclear weapons test could radically change that dynamic. And what if the first warhead failed? Or what if it was less impressive than they wanted or needed? They would have lost the critical element of surprise. Yet in light of the vision he had just experienced, could he afford any delay? Had he not been commanded to "get ready; be prepared"?

"What would the Americans do in reaction to such a test?" he asked President Darazi as he continued to gaze at the twinkling lights in the valley.

"Nothing, Your Excellency," the president replied.

Hosseini turned. "Are you really willing to bet your life on that, Ahmed?"

"I am, sir."

"Why?"

"Your Excellency, the Americans are a paper tiger," Darazi argued. "They are an empire beginning to implode. Their economy is bleeding. Their deficit is skyrocketing. They're fighting two wars in the Middle East—at a cost of about $12 billion a month—two wars that most Americans don't want. Their Congress is focused on jobs and health care and reenergizing their economy. President Jackson is committed to pulling U.S. forces out of the region as rapidly as possible. And he has signed an executive order declaring that the U.S. will never use nuclear weapons against any other nation—even if attacked first. Believe me, Your Excellency, regardless of what they are saying about keeping their military option 'on the table' with regard to 'the Iran issue,' we needn't worry about a preemptive strike from the Americans. It is never going to happen. Not under this president. Not under this Congress."

The Supreme Leader hoped Darazi's analysis was accurate. It was certainly consistent with his own perspective and with the vision he had just received. But the Americans were not the only threat. He looked the president in the eye and asked, "What about the Zionists? What will they do?"

"Of that, Your Excellency, I'm not so sure," Darazi conceded. "We all know Prime Minister Naphtali is a warmonger. He is oppressing the Palestinians. He is terrorizing Lebanon. He is humiliating the Egyptians and the Jordanians. He is playing the Syrians for fools. The good news is Naphtali's government is headed for a train wreck with the White House. Relations between the two countries are souring rapidly."

At that, however, the Supreme Leader pushed back. "How can you say that, Ahmed? Yes, Jackson and Naphtali have had a few spats. But so what? Naphtali still has Congress in his pocket, no? He still has the Jewish lobby, correct? Israel is still getting $3 billion a year in American military aid, true? A lovers' quarrel is not a train wreck, Ahmed."

"With all due respect, Your Excellency," the president countered, "this is not a lovers' quarrel. I believe we are witnessing a fundamental rupture between these two governments. Could it change? Yes. Could President Jackson be defeated in the next election? Of course. But for right now, the foreign policy of the United States is run by President William Jackson—a man who fundamentally believes he must negotiate with us, can negotiate with us, and will be successful in the process. He won't attack us militarily while he's trying to engage us diplomatically. What's more, I believe he will do everything in his power to keep the Israelis from attacking us."

The Supreme Leader considered that for a few moments. He liked Darazi. The president was a true Twelver, devoted in every respect to the coming of the Twelfth Imam, and thus useful in many ways. Still, Hosseini did not entirely trust the man's geopolitical instincts.

Just then an aide to General Jazini rushed into the room and handed the commander a note.

"What is it?" the Supreme Leader asked, seeing Jazini's face grow ashen.

"It is the Israelis, Your Excellency," Jazini said.

Hosseini braced himself. "What have they done?"

"You're not going to believe this." Jazini proceeded to read the entire classified cable aloud.

"Russian intelligence indicates massive Israeli war game under way. Stop. Four hundred warplanes have been launched. Stop. Inbound for Greek isles for practice bombing, strafing runs. Stop. Repeat of their 2008 drill, but four times as large. Stop. FSB warns Jerusalem making final preparations for war. Stop. Please advise. Stop."

Faridzadeh and Darazi gasped.

Hosseini was not surprised. Nor was he rattled like the others. It was time, he realized, to share with the men the vision he had just experienced and the message he had received.

"Gentlemen, we need not fear the Israelis, and let me tell you why," the Ayatollah began. "Just before coming into this meeting, I received a message directly from the Twelfth Imam. In a vision not fifty yards from this room, he told me that the time for his appearance has come. The time of the extermination of the Israelis and the Americans has thus come as well. The Lord of the Age has chosen you and me to act, and we must be faithful. So get out your notebooks, and allow me to explain. . . ."

41

It had rained most of the night.

But it wasn't the storm that had kept Najjar awake, and even though the downpour had now stopped, he knew this would be another sleepless night.

He slipped out of bed, threw on some casual clothes and a jacket, and went out for a walk. The streets—abandoned and quiet—were slick, the air damp and brisk. A low fog had moved in across the city. Najjar zipped up his jacket and shoved his hands in his pockets to keep them warm. As he walked, he tried to reconstruct all that had brought him to this point.

He had been recruited by Dr. Mohammed Saddaji to come to Iran with three specific goals in mind, his marriage to Sheyda notwithstanding.

First, he was to serve as his father-in-law's right-hand man at the Hamadan research facility. It had been an honor to help one of the world's most gifted physicists create a civilian nuclear power industry for Iran that would be the envy of the world and a rebuke to her critics, especially the Americans and the Zionists.

Second, he was to serve as the primary liaison between Dr. Saddaji and the team of physicists working in the city of Bushehr to bring Iran's first nuclear power plant online safely and efficiently. A man of Saddaji's intellect and importance could not be bothered, after all, with constant phone calls, e-mails, and other interruptions from the Bushehr reactor. He needed someone to manage all of that, and for this he trusted Najjar implicitly. It was the combination of these two roles that had been so attractive from the beginning and that gave Najjar a level of intellectual stimulation and professional satisfaction he deeply appreciated.

But there was a third role for Najjar, and Dr. Saddaji had strongly implied that over the long term this would be his most important mission: to help train up a new generation of Iranian nuclear scientists by eventually—within the next few years—teaching at one of the country's premier research universities. This was Najjar's true passion. He longed to move Sheyda and their newborn daughter away from Hamadan, buy a home, and carve out a more stable life for his family. He knew he had to pay his dues, and paying his dues meant serving his father-in-law faithfully, but now he was beginning to question everything.

A lone car drove past, splashing water onto the sidewalks. Najjar ducked out of the way just in time, then turned down a side street and picked up the pace. The more he thought about it, the more trouble he was having with the notion that a UD3 expert had been operating inside a civilian nuclear research compound. It wasn't just that the man was an Arab, though that was bad enough. The real concern was that the *Times* of London had published a highly controversial story in December 2009 alleging that Iran was engaged in trying to build a trigger for a nuclear bomb. The top-secret memo exposed in that article had been partly responsible for an international firestorm of criticism against the Iranian regime. It had caused the United Nations Security Council to consider imposing new economic sanctions against Iran. Normally Najjar and his colleagues had limited access to Western newspapers and the Internet due to their sensitive positions. Yet copies of this particular article—"Discovery of UD3 Raises Fears over Iran's Nuclear Intentions"—had been passed around by Dr. Saddaji himself as "proof," he'd said at the time, of a "Zionist campaign of lies and slander" against Iran's "peaceful" nuclear program.

Najjar recalled a particular section from the article with crystal clarity. *"Independent experts have confirmed that the only possible use for UD3 is as a neutron source, the trigger to the chain reaction for a nuclear explosion. Critically, while other neutron sources have possible civilian uses, UD3 has only one application—to be the metaphorical match that lights a nuclear bomb."*

That was true, Najjar knew. What's more, any test explosion using UD3 would leave behind traces that would certainly be regarded as proof that Iran was building a nuclear weapon. There was no way, he was sure, his father-in-law would take such a risk.

At the time, Najjar had fumed that the entire article was built on lies. The *Times* reporter had quoted a "Western intelligence source"—someone who had to be from the Israeli Mossad, Najjar was convinced. It was all a plot by the Jews to subjugate the Persian people under Western colonialism and imperialism. He had passionately echoed his father-in-law, not because it was the party line but rather because Najjar believed it to be true. As Dr. Saddaji's chief of staff, he personally knew—or knew of and controlled the personnel files for—every single nuclear scientist in the country. All 1,449 of them. He had pored over their files. He had pored over their security clearance dossiers. He knew all of their supervisors and was in direct contact with many of them. So he knew for a fact that not one of them—*not a single one*—was a specialist in uranium deuteride *or* titanium deuteride.

Now what was he to think? Dr. Saddaji had been keeping secret from him—his own son-in-law—the presence of an Iraqi UD3 expert in the Iranian nuclear program. The man had then proceeded to order the brutal execution of that expert without a trial, without even a hearing. *Why?*

What else was his father-in-law hiding? Was the man really running a civilian nuclear power program, as Najjar had thought from the beginning? Or was he actually spearheading a clandestine program to build a nuclear weapon, as the Americans and the Israelis claimed? It was beginning to look as if the latter was the case. If so, was this the real project for which Dr. Saddaji had recruited him, the one that would "change the course of history"? Was this actually the project that would "make way for the coming of the Promised One"?

42

It was late when "Reza Tabrizi" landed in Dubai.

He couldn't wait to get to the hotel for a hot shower, a good meal, and a real bed. To maintain the fiction he had already set into motion, he traded phone numbers with Yasmeen, giving her his number in Munich, and headed toward passport control, reminding himself again and again that he was no longer David Shirazi. He was a successful German businessman of Iranian extraction. He wasn't coming from Syracuse, but from a trade show in Chicago that had been a waste of time. He rarely went to the U.S., he reminded himself. Indeed, he disdained doing business with the Americans. They were too loud, too pushy, and too greedy, and there were far too many Jews. He repeated this to himself again and again. CIA protocols required him to have spent the transatlantic flight refreshing himself on his cover story and getting himself fully into his alias. But his mind had been elsewhere on the flight, and he was rapidly playing catch-up.

Fortunately, he cleared passport control without being asked any questions. At that moment, his first instinct was to call Marseille and explain the delay in getting back to her. But he couldn't use his new Nokia cell phone. It was carefully monitored by his friends back at Langley, and this was not a call he wanted Jack Zalinsky or anyone else at NSA or the CIA to track. As he headed to baggage claim, he walked past banks of pay phones and was tempted to stop and use one of them. But this, he hoped, wasn't going to be a quick call, and Eva was waiting for him beyond customs.

Eva Fischer.

The very name suddenly confused David. For starters, of course, Eva wasn't even her real name. It was an alias. Neither she nor Zalinsky, he realized, had ever given him her real name. So who was she? Where was she really from? What was she really all about?

Twenty-four hours earlier, Eva had been consuming an awful lot of his thoughts. He'd been looking forward to going to Starbucks with her, to attending a week of briefings with her, to going into Tehran with her, to getting to know her better. He still was, but now it was complicated. How could he even consider a relationship with her if there was a possibility of reconnecting with Marseille? Then again, was that really a possibility? He hadn't heard from Marseille in years. Who knew what she wanted to talk about? She could be engaged. She could be married. She could have children. And what was all that about church in her note? Had she become religious? Was that why she wanted him to go to church with her back in Syracuse? It made no sense, but then again . . .

"Mr. Tabrizi, Mr. Tabrizi, over here!"

It took a moment for David to hear the name and realize it was supposed to be *his*. He turned and saw Eva smiling and waving at him through the enormous crowd in the Dubai International terminal, all waiting for their loved ones just beyond the secure doors. His first thought was that despite being much more modestly dressed than back in Virginia, she looked great, sporting a beautiful green headscarf and a full-length brown dress that covered her legs and her arms. His second thought was that this looked like a woman preparing to head into Iran, not to Starbucks. Nevertheless, he smiled and waved back and was surprised to see her eyes light up with anticipation as they met his.

"Welcome to Dubai, Mr. Tabrizi," she said, being careful not to shake his hand or have any physical contact whatsoever since they were neither married nor related.

"Thank you, Ms. Fischer. Please, call me Reza," he replied.

"If you insist. And call me Eva," she said. "How was your flight?"

He couldn't begin to tell her. "Too long. But it's good to finally be here. Do you have a car for me to go to the hotel?"

"Actually, I'm afraid we have a change of plans," Eva explained, picking up her own suitcase and garment bag.

"What do you mean?"

"You got my text, right?" she asked, handing him his new itinerary. "We're heading to Tehran."

"When?"

"Next flight."

Stunned, David read the paper in his hands. She wasn't kidding. They were booked on Emirates Airlines flight 975, departing Dubai at 12:10 a.m. and landing in Tehran two hours and ten minutes later. He glanced at his watch. It was already 10:56 p.m. They had to move quickly.

"I don't understand," he said as he scooped up his own bags and followed Eva back into a security line. "What's going on?"

"Last night, the Israelis launched more than four hundred warplanes at Greece in what looks like a massive test run for a strike against Iran," Eva whispered.

"Four hundred?" David whispered back. "That's almost half their fleet."

"Exactly. The Iranians are freaked out."

"And that's why we're going in?"

"Not entirely."

"Then what?"

"Abdol Esfahani's office called. He wants to meet us for breakfast."

Esfahani was a key executive at Iran Telecom and the point man for operationalizing the new contract with Munich Digital Systems. It wasn't a meeting they could easily blow off, but David wasn't convinced he and Eva were ready to go into Iran quite yet. Where was Zalinsky? How could he have signed off on such a rapid departure? They were supposed to work here in Dubai for the week. They were supposed to refine their plan, set clear goals, and establish contingencies in case things went wrong, as too often they did. But how much planning could Jack and Eva have actually done without him, given that all weekend she had been with . . . whom?

"So," he asked casually, "how was Berlin?"

"Uh, great," she said, hesitating ever so slightly. "But not nearly long enough, you know?"

With that, David realized Eva hadn't actually been in Berlin. She had come straight to Dubai with Zalinsky. That was fine, of course. She was the boss. She didn't answer to him. But how and when exactly was she supposed to fill him in on the plan she and Jack had cooked up? They certainly wouldn't be free to talk on the flight in, and they'd be trailed by intelligence operatives from the minute they hit the ground in Tehran. This was too big of an operation to rush. The stakes were too high. But they were rushing into it anyway. Why?

And then his thoughts shifted to Marseille and his anxiety spiked again. He couldn't exactly call her from Tehran.

43

Najjar got home around 2 a.m. and found the lights on.

Sheyda was asleep on the couch with their tiny daughter snuggled beside her. He slipped off his shoes, quietly set his keys on the kitchen table, put a blanket over his wife and child, and stared at them for a while. They looked so peaceful, so innocent. Did they have any idea of the evil rising around them?

He turned off the lights in the living room and kitchen and stepped into the spare bedroom he used for a home office and library. Switching on his desk lamp, he cleared off his cluttered desk and found a stack of books his father-in-law had lent him several months before but that he had been too busy to read. The one on the top was titled *The Awaited Saviour*. It was written by Baqir al-Sadr and Murtada Mutahhari, both Shia ayatollahs. Taking the volume in hand, Najjar turned to the prologue and began to read.

> A figure more legendary than that of the Mahdi, the Awaited Saviour, has not been seen in the history of mankind. The threads of the world events have woven many a fine design in human life, but the pattern of the Mahdi stands high above every other pattern. He has been the vision of the visionaries in history. He has been the dream of all the dreamers of the world. For the ultimate salvation of mankind he is the Pole Star of hope on which the gaze of humanity is fixed. The Qur'anic

prophecy of the inevitable victory of Islam will be realized following the advent of the Mahdi, who will fight
the wrong, remedy the evils, and establish a world order
based on the Islamic teachings of justice and virtue.
Thereafter there will be only one religion and one government in the world.

Najjar continued reading throughout the night. The more he read,
the more convinced he became that the arrival of the Twelfth Imam and
establishment of his caliphate, or kingdom, was imminent. Were not
the signs, described by Shia sages throughout the centuries, coming to
pass day by day? The world was becoming more and more corrupt. The
global economy was in collapse. A great war was being fought between
the Tigris and the Euphrates. The land of Taliqan—an ancient name for
a region of Afghanistan—was consumed by war and poverty. Terrible
earthquakes were occurring in ever-increasing number and intensity.
Apostasy was spreading within Islam. Civil wars and uprisings were
prevalent.

Najjar was electrified when he read, "The Mahdi is alive. He visits
different places and takes an intelligent interest in world events. He
often attends the assemblies of the faithful but does not disclose his
true identity. He will reappear on the appointed day, and then he will
fight against the forces of evil, lead a world revolution, and set up a new
world order based on justice, righteousness, and virtue."

To the very core of his being, Najjar believed these words to be true.
He was absolutely convinced that he had seen the Promised One at least
twice in his life, first as a child on the day Ayatollah Khomeini had died,
and again in Baghdad the day he saw the Iraqi nuclear scientist kidnapped and his family gunned down in the streets. Najjar had prayed
every day since that he would have the opportunity to see the Promised
One again. But he had never dared tell anyone of his encounters, not
even Sheyda, whom he loved more than life. He feared she would think
he was boasting or lying or hallucinating or crazy.

But was it really necessary to prepare the way for the Twelfth Imam
by building a nuclear weapon, by annihilating Israel and the United

States and other enemies of Islam? Dr. Saddaji obviously believed it was. Najjar, too, had once believed that, but now he wasn't so sure. Worse, he now feared that by authorizing the beheading of a man who had been forced into the Iranian nuclear program years earlier—a man whose wife and child Najjar himself had seen murdered—Sheyda's father had become part of the "forces of evil" whom the Promised One was coming to judge. It saddened and sickened him, but what could he do? He couldn't tell Sheyda. It would shatter her. To whom, then, could he turn?

44

TEHRAN, IRAN

Abdol Esfahani was not a big fish.

In the grand scheme of Iran Telecom's communications empire, he was a minnow. But at least he was nibbling.

As Iran Telecom's deputy director of technical operations, Esfahani was in charge of the day-to-day mechanics of turning the company's ambitious strategic overhaul from concept to reality. He hadn't negotiated the massive contract between Iran Telecom and Nokia Siemens Networks. Nor had he been involved in the subcontract NSN had inked with Munich Digital Systems. But all of the consultants and technical support teams that NSN already had in Iran ultimately reported to him, as would the MDS teams that were about to arrive in force.

David had no idea what Esfahani wanted to discuss, nor did Eva. He guessed the man simply wanted to look them in the eye, take their measure, and establish clear lines of authority and responsibility before the MDS tech teams arrived. After all, MDS's role was a critical one: installing state-of-the-art call routers and proprietary software systems capable of handling millions of calls per minute, all of which would also integrate voice, data, and video services through the new fiber-optic and wireless networks NSN was building. The scope of the work was staggering. It was going to be complicated, time-consuming, and expensive. Esfahani no doubt wanted to make sure he was on a first-name basis with the senior Farsi-speaking project managers on the MDS team.

The breakfast meeting was set for seven thirty in the penthouse conference room of Iran Telecom's headquarters in downtown Tehran.

By the time Eva and David—traveling as Reza Tabrizi—landed at Imam Khomeini International Airport, cleared an extensive passport control and customs process, checked into separate rooms at the Simorgh Hotel on Vali-Assr Avenue, showered, changed, and got back into their hired car—followed the entire time by Iranian intelligence agents—they were lucky to make it to the meeting on schedule. With less than five minutes to spare, they sprinted into the main lobby and presented their IDs and a faxed letter of invitation. Only then were they directed to the ninth floor. There they were greeted by a lovely but somewhat-timid young receptionist wearing a black, full-length traditional woman's cloak known as a *chador* and a dark green headscarf that not only accented her shy, green eyes but nearly matched the color of Eva's headscarf as well.

"Welcome to Iran Telecom," she said, stammering somewhat and unable to make eye contact, even with Eva. "My name is Mina."

"Thank you, Mina," Eva said, taking the lead. "It's good to be here, despite all that traffic."

"Yes, it's quite challenging," Mina said, still not looking at them but rather at the letter of invitation. "Forgive me, but which one of you is Mr. Tabrizi?"

It was an odd question, David thought, given the fact that he was the only man standing there. "That would be me," he replied.

Mina glanced at him, then looked away quickly. "Are we still waiting for Mr. Fischer?" she asked.

"Actually," Eva said, "that appears to be a mistake on the invitation. It's supposed to be *Ms.* Fischer, not *Mr.* And that would be me."

She held out her hand to shake Mina's. But Mina, startled, didn't take it.

"*Ms.* Fischer?"

"That's right," Eva said, still holding out her hand.

"There's no *Mr.* Fischer?"

"No, just me." Eva awkwardly withdrew her unwelcome hand, now looking as perplexed as the receptionist.

"*You* are the project manager for MDS?" Mina asked.

Eva forced a smile. "Yes; is there a problem?"

Mina looked up, stared at Eva for a moment, then looked away again. "Please have a seat," she said crisply, picking up her phone and dialing. "It will be a few minutes."

A moment later, Mina hung up the phone, excused herself, and stepped into Mr. Esfahani's office, leaving the door open a crack behind her. David could hear whispering for a few moments, and then came the explosion.

"What? Are you certain?" yelled a man David figured for Esfahani.

He could hear Mina talking, but she spoke so quietly he couldn't make out what she was saying.

"A woman?" the man shouted. *"They sent a woman? And you let them? Don't you know how close we are, you fool? Don't you know how pious we must be? He's coming at any moment. We must be ready!"* Something glass or ceramic crashed against the wall and shattered.

David turned to Eva. This was not good. Esfahani was screaming at the top of his lungs. They could hear the man's fist slamming into his desk. They could hear his secretary quietly sobbing. They heard him curse her for daring to think that he would ever have a woman running such an important project. He threatened to fire her. *"How could you make such a stupid mistake?"* he roared. *"How could you bring dishonor into this office at such a time as this?"* He began cursing NSN and MDS for having the gall to think he would accept a woman as a project manager. And then Esfahani, a thin man—almost gaunt—balding, and red as a beet, stormed out of his office, not stopping to look at either David or Eva. He blew through the reception area and boarded the elevator, and before they knew it, he was gone.

David, barely believing what he had just witnessed, turned to his colleague. Eva was pale. She was so deeply shaken, he wanted to give her a hug. But he could not, of course. Touching a woman who was not his wife, and doing so in public, risked turning the crisis into a full-blown cultural catastrophe. He didn't know what to do or say to Eva, much less to Mina. The secretary was crying and muttering to herself and trying to clean up whatever had been destroyed in Esfahani's office. This wasn't something they trained you for at Langley. But David knew he had to do something to salvage this situation. The stakes were higher than the feelings of these two women. This was the CIA's only door into Iran Telecom, and it had just been slammed in their faces.

"Go to the car," he whispered to Eva when he was certain Mina was not looking. "Have the driver take you back to the hotel. I'll try to salvage this."

"No, I'm fine," Eva said curtly, clearly embarrassed but trying hard to regain control.

David didn't have time to argue. He could tell from Eva's tone and stiff body language that her shock was turning to anger. But he couldn't take the risk that she would try to undo the damage and in so doing end up making things worse.

"This wasn't your fault, Eva," he whispered back. "But you can't fix it. Not now. I don't know if I can either, but for now you need to go back to the hotel."

"And then what?"

"Just wait there. Don't call anyone. Don't do anything. I'll call you as soon as I know something, and then we'll regroup."

Eva's eyes said it all. She didn't like being managed by a man, much less a younger one, especially when Zalinsky had put her in charge of this mission. They stared at each other for a moment. David didn't back down, and Eva finally relented. She knew he was right. There was nothing she could do. But she wasn't happy and wanted him to know it. Sixty seconds later, the elevator arrived. Fortunately, it was empty. Eva stepped in, her jaw set, her eyes down. She was still resolutely avoiding David's gaze when the doors slid shut.

David checked his watch. It was nearly eight. At any moment, he expected the floor to be flooded with dozens of other secretaries and operations staff. In fact, he was surprised they weren't there already. If there was any chance of making this right, it had to be now. He ducked his head into Esfahani's spacious and impressive corner office. It was far larger and more ornate than he would have expected for a "deputy director of technical operations," with an expansive view of the smog settling over the Tehran skyline. Mina was still sitting on the floor, wiping her eyes and picking up the pieces of what had been a lamp.

"May I help you?" David asked gently.

He didn't wait for an answer but stooped and picked up some of the smaller pieces of glass and put them in the small trash bin beside Mina.

"I'll be fine," she said halfheartedly, continuing to avert her eyes from his. "It's probably best for you to go."

David continued picking up the smaller pieces. "Will Mr. Esfahani be back soon?" he asked, trying to buy time and goodwill.

Mina said nothing, but shook her head.

"Did he have another appointment?"

Again she shook her head.

"I am so sorry," he said. "My colleague and I should have known better. I should have, at least. With a name like Reza Tabrizi, obviously my relatives were all originally from Tabriz. But my parents grew up here in Tehran. They actually met just a few blocks from here in 1975, not long after my dad finished medical school. But you probably guessed Ms. Fischer isn't from here. I mean, she actually speaks Farsi really well for a foreigner, but she's German, and she's—"

"It's okay," Mina said. "You don't have to say any more."

"She meant no harm," David added. "Neither of us did."

"I know."

"Living in Europe, well, it's . . ."

"Different," Mina offered.

"A lot different."

Mina nodded but looked away again. They were quiet for a moment. David could see she was lowering her defenses ever so slightly. But just then the elevator bell rang, and several associates stepped off chatting and laughing. They were out of time. It was improper for them to be found together. David's mind raced. Then he reached for another piece of glass and purposely cut his finger.

"Oh, my goodness," Mina said, noticing him wince, "you're bleeding."

"It's okay," he said, stepping back into the reception area. "I'll get something for it at the hotel."

"No, no," Mina said, rushing to her desk and pulling out a first aid kit. "You could get an infection. Here, use this."

She handed him a tube of antibiotic ointment, and as she did, she actually looked him in the eye, if only for a moment. He smiled and thanked her. To his amazement, she smiled back. The poor woman looked like she never got out of the office. She was small and pale and somewhat frail, but she was sweet and he felt bad for her, trapped in a job she had to hate, verbally abused by a boss who was impossible to respect.

"Again, I'm so sorry for the trouble we caused you today," he said, finishing with the tube of ointment and giving it back to her.

"The error was mine," she said softly. "I should have called ahead and gotten all of the details. It's just that the meeting came up so fast, and, well . . . anyway, it was my fault."

She looked at him again, and when she did, David shook his head and whispered, "It wasn't your fault, Mina. It was all mine. And I'm probably going to get fired for it."

"No," she whispered back, sounding pained at the prospect. "Would they really fire you?" She handed him an adhesive bandage.

"If I blow this contract, they will," he said. "Unless . . ."

"Unless what?"

"Unless you could help me."

Mina looked away, terrified of being caught doing something else wrong. David suspected she would be severely punished for her transgressions today, and his heart went out to her.

The elevator bell rang again. More staff stepped off and headed to their cubicles. Mina greeted several of them, backing away from David as she did. He slowly put on the bandage, trying to buy as much time as he could, but it didn't seem to matter. They had passed the point of no return. He really had to go.

He nodded good-bye, then stepped to the elevator, pushed the button, and silently begged Allah for mercy. The wait seemed like an eternity. He tried to imagine the coming conversation with Zalinsky, trying to explain how he and Eva had blown a mission that offered the last shred of hope of averting an apocalyptic war between Israel, Iran, and the rest of the region. But it was too painful.

The bell rang. The door opened. Still more of Esfahani's staff poured out, and David stepped in. He hit the button for the ground floor and smiled at Mina one last time. The elevator doors began to close, but just before they did, a woman's hand came through and held the doors ajar for a moment. It was Mina's hand, holding a business card. Startled, David took the card, and Mina withdrew her hand. The doors closed. The elevator began to descend to the ground floor.

David looked carefully at the card. It was Esfahani's, showing two different mobile numbers, plus his direct office line, general office line, fax number, and telex number. On the back was a handwritten note.

Imam Khomeini Mosque, it read, *Naser Khosrow Avenue.*

David couldn't believe it. He had one more shot.

45

Outside the Iran Telecom building, David tried to hail a taxi.

But in Tehran's cacophonous morning rush hour traffic—bumper to bumper for blocks on end—that was nearly impossible. He suddenly understood why one of the city's recent mayors had been elected after boasting of having a doctorate in traffic management.

Once again he found himself begging Allah for mercy. He was desperate and reasoned that this wasn't a selfish prayer. This was a battle of good versus evil. He was trying to stop a catastrophic war and the deaths of millions, and he needed all the help he could get, divine or otherwise.

David had no idea how far away Naser Khosrow Avenue was, but he was determined to get to the mosque before Esfahani left. His heart raced. But he knew he had to look calm, for he was not alone. And the delay in finding an available cab, he concluded, was good in the grand scheme of things. It gave the Iranian surveillance detail assigned to trail him—half of whom had already been forced to follow Eva back to the Simorgh Hotel—enough time to prepare for his next move.

On this topic, Zalinsky had been crystal clear back at Langley: for the first few weeks in Iran, he and Eva—like all foreigners—would be suspected by the Iranian intelligence services as spies for the Mossad or the CIA or the BND, Germany's federal intelligence service. They would be followed everywhere. Everywhere they went would be monitored and logged in a file by the secret police. Everyone they met with would be noted, and some would be interviewed or interrogated. Their hotel phones would be tapped. Their rooms would be bugged. Their cell phones would be monitored. They would be photographed surreptitiously and constantly. Their mission, therefore, was to act normal. To relax. Blend in. Play the part of an MDS consultant and nothing else. This was not the time to play James Bond or Jason Bourne. This was not the time to evade their tails and get their handlers curious, much less worried. They were already pushing the margins with Eva leaving early and David taking a cab rather than their hired car (whose driver surely worked for the secret police). They couldn't afford any more irregularities.

By the time David was finally able to flag down a cab, he was certain that the driver worked for the secret police. He was too young and looked far too nervous to be a simple taxi driver.

"Hey, buddy, listen. I need your help," David said in Farsi, tinged with a little more of a German accent than usual. "What's your name?"

"Behrouz," the young man said hesitantly.

"Behrouz?" David said. "That means lucky, right?"

"Yes."

"Good; so listen, Behrouz—today is your lucky day."

"Why's that?"

"If I don't get to the Imam Khomeini Mosque and find my client before he finishes praying, my company's fifty-million-euro contract is going to be flushed down the toilet, you know what I'm saying?" David pulled out his wallet and tossed a crisp one-hundred-euro bill on the front seat.

The young man's eyes went wide when he saw the money. He glanced in the rearview mirror, and David pleaded with him to help. Behrouz then glanced at his mobile phone sitting next to the euro note. David assumed the kid was supposed to call something like this in. But it wasn't like his suspect was going to get away, right? He and Behrouz were going to be together for the entire ride.

"No problem," the kid said, finally mustering up his courage. "But you might want to put on your seat belt."

David did, and they were off. Behrouz gunned the engine and hopped the curb, terrifying pigeons and pedestrians alike and unleashing an avalanche of curses from several clerics trying to cross the street. Not seeming to care in the slightest, the kid ran a stoplight, barely missing an oncoming bus, and took a hard right at the next intersection. This kid was good, David thought, half-wondering if he should hire him as his driver full-time.

On a straightaway, David caught his breath, pulled out his phone, and did his homework. He dialed up a quick Internet search for the Imam Khomeini Mosque and immediately found a map, a satellite photo of the enormous compound, and a brief description of the site, courtesy of Google. The Imam Khomeini Grand Mosala Mosque was the largest mosque in the world. The two minarets stood at 136 meters, and the mosque compound covered 450,000 square meters.

Six minutes later, Behrouz raced by the Golestan Palace and finally screeched to a halt beside the mosque's main entrance.

"Thanks, Behrouz," David said, already out of the cab. "There's another hundred in it for you if you give me your cell phone number and hang around until I need you again."

The young man, breathless, readily accepted. He scratched out his mobile number on the back of a receipt and gave it to David, who thanked him, entered it into his phone, and dashed inside the gates of the mosque, hoping against hope to find Abdol Esfahani.

★ ★ ★ ★ ★

DUBAI, UNITED ARAB EMIRATES

Zalinsky's phone chirped.

It was the watch officer from the Global Ops Center at Langley. Zalinsky, in the CIA safe house in Dubai where he had set up his base camp, was instantly on alert.

"Ops Center; go secure," the watch officer said.

The grizzled old CIA veteran punched in his authorization code. "Secure; go."

"Two minutes ago, Zephyr entered his first phone number," the watch officer explained.

That was fast, Zalinsky thought.

"It's a junior agent with the secret police in Tehran," the watch officer continued. "He's already making his first call."

"Where to?" Zalinsky asked, now on his feet and pacing.

"It's a local call. . . . Secure, but we're cracking it; hold on. . . . NSA says it's a direct line into VEVAK."

Wow, Zalinsky thought, unexpectedly impressed. He didn't speak Farsi, but he certainly knew that the *Vezarat-e Ettela'at va Amniat-e Keshvar*—known by its acronym, VEVAK—was Iran's central intelligence service. *Themis and Zephyr just might pay off after all.*

The watch officer now patched Zalinsky through to a live feed from the National Security Agency headquarters in Fort Meade, Maryland. A Farsi specialist translated the call in real time.

Caller: *Base, this is Car 1902.*

Receiver: *What's your status?*

Caller: *I'm at Imam Khomeini Mosque. Subject just entered.*

Receiver: *Do you have a visual?*

Caller: *Negative. This was my first chance to call it in.*

Receiver: *Why didn't you follow him?*

Caller: *He paid me extra to wait here. Should I go after him?*

Receiver: *Negative. Wait as instructed. Did subject say what he's doing there? The next call to prayer isn't for another four hours.*

Caller: *Subject is meeting someone inside.*

Receiver: *Who?*

Caller: *Didn't say. But it sounded urgent.*

Receiver: *Why?*

Caller: *Subject said some business deal would collapse if he didn't find this guy in time. I think it's an executive from Iran Telecom. That's where I picked him up.*

Receiver: *Roger that. We think it's Esfahani. We're sending you additional agents.*

Caller: *Abdol Esfahani?*

Receiver: *Affirmative.*

Caller: *The nephew of the boss?*

Receiver: *Affirmative.*

Caller: *Is he in danger? Should I do something?*

Receiver: *Negative. It probably really is a business deal.*

Caller: *But you're sure Esfahani's going to be okay?*

Receiver: *Affirmative. We'll have more agents arriving on scene any moment. Just stay where you are, and let us know when the subject returns to the cab.*

Caller: *Yes, sir.*

With that, the call was over. But Zalinsky's interest was piqued. Who exactly was Abdol Esfahani related to, and why did it matter so much to these intelligence operatives? It wasn't possible that Esfahani was related to Ibrahim Asgari, the commander of VEVAK, was it? Zalinsky couldn't imagine it. Surely he would have known that before now. He quickly logged on to Langley's mainframe database and ran an extensive search.

After ten minutes, he couldn't find a shred of information suggesting this was true. But it was clear to Zalinsky that the Iranian intelligence agents on the call he'd just heard believed Esfahani was connected to someone important. Zalinsky wasn't sure what to make of that exactly. But he began to wonder if maybe Esfahani was a bigger fish than they had thought.

46

It was worse than David had feared.

Hundreds of men were praying. Thousands more were milling about on the grounds of the mosque, talking softly, conducting business, trading gossip.

"*Assalam Allaikum*"—*peace be upon you*—he repeated again and again as he worked his way through the crowds, systematically ruling out small groups of individuals and intensifying his prayers that Allah would help him find this needle in the haystack. The good news was that no one seemed particularly interested in the fact that he was there. Nor did anyone seem to care or even sense that he had never been there before. The sheer number of people on the site provided him a measure of anonymity that helped him move about without drawing attention. But that wouldn't last for long, he knew. Plainclothes agents would be there any moment, watching his every move.

He decided to shift gears. Rather than moving deeper into the mosque, he would withdraw and hide in plain sight. He would wait out front, where the secret police could see him and breathe easier as a result, and where he was least likely to miss Esfahani when he emerged from prayer.

Finding a bench in the courtyard, he sat down, pulled out his phone, and began reviewing his e-mails and scanning headlines on the Internet like any harried European businessman would do. Several headlines caught his attention.

Oil Hits Record Highs on War Fears in Mideast

Pentagon Moves Patriot Missile Batteries into Gulf States to Protect Oil Facilities from Possible Iranian Strike

Iranian Cleric Wants Creation of "Greater Iran"

The last one, an AP story out of Tehran, particularly intrigued him, and he scanned it quickly.

> A radical cleric has called for the creation of a "Greater Iran" that would rule over the entire Middle East and Central Asia, in a move that he said would herald the coming of Islam's expected messiah. Ayatollah Mohammad Bagher Kharrazi said the creation of what he calls an Islamic United States is a central aim of the political party he leads called Hezbollah, or Party of God, and that he hoped to make it a reality if they win the next presidential election.

Scrolling down a bit, another paragraph struck David as curious.

> Kharrazi said this Greater Iran would stretch from Afghanistan to Israel, bringing about the destruction of the Jewish State. He also said its formation would be a prelude to the reappearance of the Mahdi, a revered ninth-century saint known as the Hidden Imam, whom Muslims believe will reappear before judgment day to end tyranny and promote justice in the world.

This was the second time in the last several days that David had seen the subject of the Mahdi, or Hidden Imam or Twelfth Imam, come up in a news report. Again he wasn't sure what to make of it, but he made a mental note to discuss it with Eva the first chance they got.

Moments later, he was relieved to see several plainclothes agents quite obviously, and even a bit clumsily, taking up positions to monitor him.

One even came up and asked for the time. David couldn't resist point-ing out that the man was wearing a wristwatch of his own. Embarrassed, the agent slunk off, but the point had been made. The secret police had made it clear they were observing Reza Tabrizi, and Reza Tabrizi, aka David Shirazi, had made it clear he didn't mind and had nothing to hide. Both sides seemed to relax.

Seemed, however, was the operative word. Inside, David was a wreck. If he didn't find Esfahani quickly, the entire operation would be over before it had even begun.

And then a new e-mail arrived in his box. It was a headline for-warded to him by Zalinsky through an AOL account under one of his many aliases. It indicated that Iran's deputy defense minister had just met at the Kremlin with his Russian counterpart. Moscow was promis-ing to install the S-300 system by summer, just six months away.

This wasn't good. The S-300 was Russia's highly advanced surface-to-air missile defense system. The Iranians had paid more than $1 bil-lion for the system several years earlier, but Moscow had repeatedly delayed its delivery and deployment, citing technical challenges.

In truth, David knew, there were no glitches. The system worked perfectly. And once it was set up around all of Iran's known nuclear research and power facilities, it would be able to protect them from a U.S. or Israeli first strike. But the very introduction of the S-300 into the Iranian theater could accelerate an Israeli preemptive strike by con-vincing the leaders in Jerusalem and Tel Aviv that if they didn't hit Iran before the S-300 became operational, their chances of success would suddenly be radically diminished. It was probably why the Israelis had just launched such a massive war game with Greece. Athens, after all, was about twelve hundred kilometers from Tel Aviv, almost the same distance as Tehran was in the opposite direction.

Put simply, the S-300 was a game changer. If this report was accurate and Russia really was planning to install the system by August, then what little time the U.S. had to stop Iran from getting the Bomb and to prevent a horrific regional war had suddenly been cut much shorter.

Just then, David caught the profile of a short, thin, balding man walking quickly out the front door of the mosque. The man was several hundred yards away, but he certainly looked like Abdol Esfahani. David jumped up and made the intercept not far from the front gate of the compound.

"Mr. Esfahani, sir, please—do you have a moment?" David said in perfect Farsi, sans the German accent.

It was clear from his befuddled expression that Esfahani had no idea who David was.

"Please forgive me for intruding on your pious thoughts, sir, but I just finished praying myself, and I looked up and couldn't believe my good fortune," David continued. "I was pleading with Allah to give me a second chance to meet you so I could have the opportunity to apologize for the dreadful faux pas my company made this morning. And here you are, a ready answer to my fervent prayers."

Esfahani looked skeptical. "And you are . . . ?"

"Sir, I am Reza Tabrizi," David said, putting out his hand to shake Esfahani's.

Esfahani said nothing and did not return the gesture.

"From MDS."

That name finally registered. The man darkened. "I have nothing to say to you," Esfahani said, walking away briskly.

David, however, ran a few steps ahead of the man and cut off his exit.

"Please, Mr. Esfahani, I beg of you. Hear me out. Just for a moment. My company, MDS, we're very good at what we do. We can do the work you need. We can do it fast. And we're discreet. We can help you in other ways, whatever you need. That's why NSN turned to us. But the MDS executives are . . . well . . . how shall I put this? They're imbeciles when it comes to Iran. They're Germans. They're Europeans. They don't mean any harm, but they don't understand our beautiful country. They don't understand Islam. They try to, but they're simply clueless. But I'm an Iranian. I'm a Muslim. I may not be as pure as others, but I try. So I begged them not to make Ms. Fischer the project manager. I told them it was an insult. I told them I was offended and you would be too. But they didn't listen. They told me just to shut up and do my job and help Ms. Fischer with anything she needed. I knew it was going to be a disaster. But there was nothing I could do—*then*. Now there is."

The mea culpa seemed to be working. Groveling had its advantages sometimes. Esfahani was listening.

"How so?" he asked, glancing at his watch.

"Now I can go back to the MDS board and tell them that putting a German woman over this project is going to cost our company fifty million euros and shut down this market to us forever," David continued. "Now they'll listen to me, because believe me, Mr. Esfahani, they can't afford to lose this contract. The global economy is too weak. The telecom market is too soft. Our stock price is down. Our shareholders are edgy. We need your business, sir, and we'll do everything we can to make this work. And with all due respect, you need us, too."

"Why is that?" Esfahani asked.

"Because your bosses want this telecom overhaul to be done yesterday. Text traffic is exploding. Less than a decade ago, there were barely four million mobile phones in the entire country. Today, there are over fifty million. You're trying to handle a hundred million text messages a day. Soon, it will be a billion. Your current software is going to crash unless we help you upgrade fast. You know that. That's why your boss approved NSN's deal with us. So please don't let all that work go down the drain, Mr. Esfahani. We're all yours. Whatever you need, we'll do it for you. And you don't have to work with Ms. Fischer. I'll send her back to Dubai. Heck, I'll send her back to Munich, if you'd like. Just, please—*please*—give us another chance. I promise you I'll be here to make sure MDS does everything you want in a way that honors our faith and our traditions. Please, sir. We want to help. I want to help. I would consider it a great honor to help Iran become the leading power in the region. Our teams are on standby. You give the word, and they can start installing the software tomorrow."

Esfahani seemed to relax a bit. "You really want this to happen, don't you, Mr. Tabrizi?" he said, stroking his closely trimmed salt-and-pepper beard.

"You cannot even begin to imagine," David replied, worried he was laying it on a bit thick but certain he had no other options.

Esfahani looked him over for another moment. "I must say, I am impressed at your humility and tenacity, young man," he said finally. "Give me a few days. I'll think about it and get back to you. Does my secretary have your contact information?"

"She does," David said. "But here's my card and my personal mobile number in case you need it."

He pulled out one of the freshly minted MDS business cards Eva had given him on the flight from Dubai. He scribbled his cell number and hotel information on the back and handed it to Esfahani.

"May Allah bless you, sir," he said as Esfahani walked to the street. "You won't regret this."

He watched Esfahani get into a waiting black sedan and drive off. It was only then that he remembered Mina had given him Esfahani's business card as well. He quickly fished it out of his wallet, entered the contact information into his Nokia, and smiled. But instead of calling Behrouz and heading straight to the hotel, he surprised his handlers by turning around and heading back into the mosque.

Maybe Allah really was listening to his prayers. Maybe David should thank him.

47

Back at the hotel, Eva opened her door wide on the first knock.

"Please tell me you found him," she asked, the apprehension show-ing in her eyes.

"I found him."

"What happened?"

"Meet me in the lobby in ten minutes," David suggested. "I'll tell you over tea."

It wasn't ideal. He knew they would be tailed. But he also knew full well he couldn't be seen lingering in front of a woman's room, much less going in. They couldn't talk on hotel phones that were certain to be bugged. Somehow, they had to act normal. For the moment, therefore, tea in public in the restaurant next to the lobby would have to suffice.

As he headed back to the elevator, David again pulled out his phone and checked his e-mail. The first was another sent by Zalinsky. It had a link to a story on the Reuters newswire, datelined from Beijing, which described ongoing talks between Iran Telecom's president, Daryush Rashidi, and the board of China Telecom, mainland China's third-largest mobile phone service provider. As David scanned the story, he realized Zalinsky was providing a none-too-subtle reminder of just how critical it was to strengthen and deepen the relationship between Munich Digital Systems and Iran Telecom. The Iranians were now fishing in other waters. Should anything with the MDS deal go south, Iran Telecom was actively looking for other options. David winced at the thought of having to brief Zalinsky on the events of the last few hours. They were already hanging by a thread.

Soon he and Eva were sitting across from one another at a small table for two, sipping chai and careful to keep their voices low and professional but not conspiratorial.

"So where are we with Esfahani?" Eva asked.

"It's not good," David said. "We made a serious mistake. We both should have known better."

"Can it be salvaged?"

"Honestly, it's too soon to say."

"What do you recommend?"

"We need to cut our losses."

"Meaning what?"

David chose his words carefully. He liked Eva. He respected her. And he very much needed her help. But she had suddenly become a liability in Iran.

"You have to understand," he began. "Abdol Esfahani is a very religious man."

"Meaning he doesn't think I should be in charge of this project."

"I'm afraid not."

"What do *you* think?"

"That's not my call."

"That's not what I asked," Eva said. "Do you think I'm capable of this job?"

"Absolutely. But that's not the point."

"What is?"

"An awful lot is riding on this deal, Eva."

"You think I don't know that?"

"Of course you do. So why worry about it? Let's just do what's in the best interest of the project and the company, and go from there."

"You're saying you want me to go back to Dubai?"

David took a deep breath and another sip of chai. "I think we need to give Esfahani and Iran Telecom exactly what they want."

"You've got to be kidding me," Eva said, incredulous.

"Look, you and I both know this is neither the time nor the place to challenge fourteen hundred years of culture and religion over a software upgrade."

Eva held her tongue for a few moments, but David could see it wasn't easy. If there hadn't been at least two Iranian agents sitting at nearby tables, he suspected she really would have unloaded on him.

"If I go back to Dubai, Esfahani will let us keep the contract?" she asked.

"I don't know."

There was another long pause.

"But if I stay here, he's guaranteed to cut us loose," she said.

David nodded.

"Then there's not much to discuss, is there?" she asked, taking her napkin, wiping her mouth, and getting up from the table.

David leaned toward her and looked her in the eye. "Listen to me," he said, speaking in character for the benefit of nearby listeners. "You and I are going to make a killing on this deal, okay? Then we're going to go back to Europe and make boatloads of money there, too. Our bosses are going to love us. They're going to give us big raises and bonuses. And then we're going to come up with ways to blow all our money and really live it up. I promise. And just between you and me, I'm really looking forward to working with you every step of the way. So don't let this throw you, okay? This, too, shall pass."

Eva's expression suddenly softened. David even thought he detected a modicum of gratitude in there somewhere.

"Thanks," she said.

"Don't mention it."

"Okay. I'm going to pack up, check out, and head to the airport."

"Call me when you get to Dubai."

"I will. And thank you, Reza. You're an impressive young man. I hope Mr. Esfahani realizes what's he got."

And with that, she was gone.

David stayed, finished his chai, and caught up on a few more e-mails. That hadn't gone as badly as he'd feared. But only time would tell, for he was fairly confident that the transcript of this conversation would likely be in Esfahani's hands by the end of the day.

48

DUBAI, UNITED ARAB EMIRATES

Zalinsky was furious.

But he tried not to show it. It had been his decision to send Eva Fischer in as the project leader. He hadn't had any indications that the senior executives at Iran Telecom were so religious. Clearly, he and his team knew far too little about Abdol Esfahani, for starters. Still, the trip wasn't a complete loss, he told Eva over coffee in the Dubai safe house. Thanks to Zephyr, they now had Esfahani's private cell phone number, and it was already bearing fruit.

He slid the laptop over to Eva so that she could look at the most interesting of several transcripts.

>>>>>> 000017-43—NSATXTREF: ZEPHYRINTERCEPT—EYES ONLY

CALL BEGAN AT 0209/21:53:06

ESFAHANI *[98-21-2234-5684]: Hello?*

CALLER *[98-21-8876-5401]: You up?*

ESFAHANI: *I am now.*

CALLER: *Take this down.*

ESFAHANI: *This had better be important.*

CALLER: *It is.*

ESFAHANI: *Hold on.*

CALLER: *Hurry up. I've got to get back in.*

ESFAHANI: *Where are you?*

CALLER: *The Qaleh.*

ESFAHANI: *Still?*

CALLER: *Something happened.*

ESFAHANI: *What?*

CALLER: *I wish I could tell you, but I can't. Not on an open line.*

ESFAHANI: *Give me a hint.*

CALLER: *I can't. . . . I . . .*

ESFAHANI: *What? What is it?*

CALLER: *You won't believe it. It's miraculous, but . . .*

ESFAHANI: *But what?*

CALLER: *I will tell you more when I see you. But I really have to go. Are you ready?*

ESFAHANI: *Yes, I'm ready.*

CALLER: *We need twenty SSPs.*

ESFAHANI: *Did you say twenty?*

CALLER: *Yes; two-zero. Twenty.*

ESFAHANI: *How soon?*

CALLER: *Yesterday.*

ESFAHANI: *Why? What's happening?*

CALLER: *It's big, but I can't say right now. Will call you again when I can.*

CALL ENDED AT 0209/21:56:23

"Interesting," Eva said. "Not every day you read the word *miraculous* in an intercept."

"My thought exactly," Zalinsky said.

"What do you think it means?"

"I have no idea. So let's start with the more mundane. What's an SSP?"

"I thought you knew everything, Jack," she teased.

Zalinsky was in no mood for jocularity. "Just answer the question."

"I'm guessing they're referring to secure satellite phones. But why twenty? They need thousands."

Zalinsky took another sip of black coffee and mulled that for a bit. They both knew that the Iranians had recently bought thousands of satellite phones from a Russian company. The Iranian high command was building an alliance with Moscow and buying billions of dollars' worth of arms and nuclear technology from the Russians. Why not communications equipment as well? There was just one problem. The Iranians eventually discovered the phones had been tampered with in a way that allowed the FSB, the Russian intelligence services, to monitor their calls. When the bugs were discovered, every Russian-made satellite phone in the country belonging to an Iranian military or intelligence commander had been recalled and destroyed.

The Iranians still had fairly secure landline communications for their military and intelligence organizations, but Iranian officials knew they were vulnerable due to the lack of secure, encrypted mobile communications. This was the very reason the NSA was having success intercepting calls from Esfahani's cell phone and anyone else's phone for which Zephyr was able to get a number. It wouldn't last long. The Iranians had proven themselves incredibly resourceful in the past. But for the moment, the NSA and CIA had caught a break, and they were exploiting it as best they could.

Eva was right. The Iranians needed thousands of secure satellite phones, not twenty.

"Maybe they simply want to test a new supplier and see if they can get a phone the Russians can't bug," Zalinsky mused.

"Or maybe they're setting up a new unit of some kind," Eva said.

"What kind of unit?"

"Could be anything—suicide bombers, missile operators, something we should be worried about."

"That's encouraging," Zalinsky said. "Okay, then, what's the Qaleh?"

"It's Farsi," Eva said. "It means fortification or walled settlement. But the question is, what do *they* mean by it?"

"I have no idea," Zalinsky conceded. "But you'd better find out."

★ ★ ★ ★ ★

TEHRAN, IRAN

Waiting for word from Esfahani, David had been going to prayer five times a day, often at the Imam Khomeini Mosque, though not always. He still wasn't sure what he believed, but he wanted to believe in a God who would hear his prayers. So he prayed for his parents. He prayed for his brothers. He prayed for his country and Zalinsky and the president. He prayed most of all for Marseille. He asked Allah to bless her, to take care of her, to heal her heart and ease her pain. Yet he doubted any of it was getting through. Sometimes there were "coincidences" that seemed like answers to his prayers. But most of the time he still felt he was talking to the ceiling.

When he wasn't at the mosque maintaining his cover, he went for long walks. He got to know the city. He visited shops that sold mobile phones, asked lots of questions, and then asked some more. Back in the hotel, he tracked business headlines on his laptop. He sent e-mails to colleagues at MDS. Mostly, he reviewed his cover story, again and again, meditating on every tiny fact until it had truly become a part of him.

But he was dying. For too much of the day, he was sitting in a hotel room in the capital of a country feverishly trying to build, buy, or steal nuclear weapons. It was his mission to find a way to stop it, and he was stuck. Alone and out of ideas, he could only wait. He couldn't talk to Zalinsky. He couldn't talk to Eva.

The worst part, however, was not the isolation. Or the boredom. Or the feeling of helplessness and frustration at not being able to do more—do anything—to advance his mission, protect his country, and care for his family and friends. The worst part was trying to pretend he was a good Muslim. Deep in his heart, David Shirazi—aka Reza Tabrizi—knew he was not. He believed in God, or at least in some form of divine being in the universe known as "God," or at least "a god." He believed this God was a creator, that He had created the heavens and the earth and mankind and him personally. Beyond that, however, he wasn't sure what he believed.

A shudder ran down his spine. To let such thoughts cross his mind—even if they remained unspoken—was tantamount to apostasy for a Muslim. They were an eternal death sentence, a fast pass to eternal damnation.

Yet how could Islam be true? The purest practitioners of the religion, he reasoned, be they Shia or Sunni, were the ayatollahs and the mullahs. His experiences in Pakistan, Afghanistan, Iran, and elsewhere had taught him that these "holy men" were the most unholy men on the planet. Their minds were filled with thoughts of violence and corruption. The leaders of Iran were the worst of all. They actively denied the Holocaust while planning another. They were trying to obtain weapons capable of incinerating millions upon millions of people in the blink of an eye, and to do so in the name of their god. How could that be right? How could a religion that taught such things be true?

49

David sat up in bed in the dark.

It was 3:26 in the morning. He had not slept a wink. Three full days and nights had now gone by, and he had still heard nothing from Abdol Esfahani. But he couldn't stop thinking about a particular line in his rant to his secretary the day David and Eva showed up for breakfast.

"Don't you know how close we are, you fool?" Esfahani had shouted. *"Don't you know how pious we must be? He's coming at any moment. We must be ready!"*

What did Esfahani mean by that? Who was coming? When? And what did it matter? Why did they have to be ready? Why did they have to be more pious?

Could Esfahani be referring to the coming of the Islamic messiah? On the face of it, it seemed unlikely, David thought. Maybe Esfahani had been talking about an Iran Telecom executive or a board member, or perhaps a top official in the Iranian Revolutionary Guard Corps—a possibility, given that they had just bought a major stake in the company.

Still, David had just gotten an e-mail from Amazon telling him that Dr. Alireza Birjandi's book, *The Imams of History and the Coming of the Messiah*, had been shipped to his apartment in Germany. It reminded him of how little he knew about Islamic End Times theology, but he was getting the sense it was becoming a bigger deal in the dynamic of the region than anyone at Langley—Zalinsky included—was considering.

How many Muslims believed the end of the world was at hand? he wondered. How many Iranians did? How many Iranians at the highest levels of the regime believed it?

As David pondered that, it occurred to him that there was a growing sense in cultures around the world that the end of days just might be approaching and that with it was coming a final, momentous clash between good and evil. Preachers and rabbis and imams and even environmentalists were saying with increasing frequency and intensity that "the end is near." But rather than laugh them all off as nuts, people seemed to be eating up the message. Even Hollywood was cashing in, making millions from apocalyptic movies.

What did it all mean? David had no idea. But in the privacy of his thoughts, he, too, feared the world was speeding recklessly toward the edge of the cliff. The longer he worked for the Central Intelligence Agency and the more classified information he gained access to, the deeper his fears became. And if Iran got the Bomb, or—God forbid—if Osama bin Laden did, something told him the implications would be far worse than even Langley's most dire predictions.

Which prompted another thought.

He had always told himself that he had joined the CIA to destroy radical Islam, to avenge the death of nearly three thousand Americans on 9/11, to avenge the death of Claire Harper, and perhaps even to show Marseille Harper how much he loved her. It was all true, but it had become more than that. He had come to fear that the events of September 11, 2001, would pale in comparison to the death and destruction that would be wrought if the world's most dangerous extremists gained possession of the world's most dangerous weapons. He had to stop them. He had to try, anyway. Most Americans had no idea the threats their country faced. But he did, and he'd never be able to live with himself if he didn't do everything in his power to save people's lives.

David turned on the lights. He was covered with sweat. What he really needed was a good, stiff drink. But this was Tehran. The minibars weren't exactly stocked with Smirnoff and Jack Daniel's. Come to think of it, he realized, his room didn't even have a minibar.

He got up, went into the bathroom, and opened a bottle of water. Then he turned on the shower—good and cold—stripped down, and stepped behind the plastic curtain.

As the water poured down his body, he half expected to be struck by lightning or felled by a massive heart attack. End of the world or not, if there was a God, and if it really was the God of the Qur'an, then he knew he was doomed. In college, David had faithfully attended a Shia mosque in Munich, studied the Qur'an, and become a part of the Muslim community, just as Zalinsky had required. He knew what he was supposed to believe. But he didn't. Plain and simple.

Shivering, David finally turned off the ice-cold water, wiped himself down, wrapped up in a towel, and stepped in front of the mirror. His glasses had been replaced by contact lenses years ago. His braces were long gone. He was taller than his brothers now, taller even than his father. But all that was superficial. Who was he now, really? What was he becoming? Where was he going?

He left the bathroom and paced around the hotel room. He pulled the drapes back a bit and stared out at the quiet streets of Tehran. He wondered what Marseille was doing at that moment, what she was thinking. Was she upset that he had never responded? Was she angry with him? He hoped not. He wished he could call her right then. She'd had enough heartache in her life. He didn't want to be the cause of any more.

He thought back to the note she'd sent him and reread a particular line in his mind's eye.

> I wondered if you might like to get a cup of coffee together, or something. . . . It's been a long time . . . and there are things to say.

He wondered what she meant by "there are things to say." It was an interesting turn of phrase—old-fashioned, almost. She was right, of course, but it didn't sound like a person casually suggesting coffee simply to catch up on old times. She had specific things to tell him or ask him. But what? As he thought about it further, he realized she hadn't just used the phrase once. She had actually used it twice—or at least a variation of it.

> If you can't get together, or if you don't want to, I'll certainly understand. And I'm sorry for rambling on like

this. I didn't mean to. I just meant to say . . . it would be good to catch up and tell you things I should have said earlier, if you're okay with that.

So she didn't have questions for him. At least, that's not what she was signaling. She had things on her heart she wanted—needed—to say directly to him, in person, not on paper. Why would he not be "okay with that"?

Was she talking about why she'd never written back to him? Maybe there was more to why she and her father had moved to Portland. Or was it something to do with religion? She had told him that her friend's wedding was going to be held at an "awesome" church. She had even invited him to go with her to the church while she was in town, even though she must know he was an avowed agnostic. Maybe she thought he had changed. It sounded like she had. Was that what this was all about?

Trying to clear his head, David turned on the television and started flipping through the channels. State-run news. Football (soccer). More state-run news. More football. Some cleric teaching from the Qur'an. Some lame black-and-white movie from the 1950s. It was all mind-numbingly boring. He turned off the set and lay back on the bed, staring at the ceiling fan whirring above him.

He let his mind drift back to the little A-frame in Canada. All these years later, he could still feel her lips on his, the warmth of her body against his own. She'd been so nervous and yet so trusting, and she had held him so tightly. And what had she asked him? Whether he believed in God. Whether he believed in Jesus. Whether he thought God was real and loving and answered prayer. He hadn't known what to say back then. And it depressed him to think he still didn't. He had no answers, and given the risks he was taking—and the very real and growing possibility that he could be captured and killed for being an American spy in Tehran—the thought of not knowing the truth about God and the afterlife terrified him.

If there was one thing he knew from studying the Qur'an, it was that Islam was a works-based religion. If his good works didn't outweigh his bad works when he died, then he was damned for eternity.

He recalled reading Sura 23:102-104 in college. The text was crystal clear in his memory: "Those whose scales of good deeds are heavy, they are prosperous, while those whose scales are light, they will be those who have ruined their own selves, in hell abiding. The fire will scorch their faces, their lips being displaced and their jaws protruding."

The problem, as David saw it, was that Islam provided no way for a Muslim to assess how he or she was doing throughout his or her life. There was no Web site to log on to and check daily scores. There were no quarterly report cards. There were no annual performance reviews. How, then, could anyone know for certain whether he would spend eternity in paradise or in punishment? How could anyone find the assurance of salvation that every thoughtful soul seeks before death?

The brutal truth was, no one could. That was what terrified David most. He had lied to almost everyone he had ever known. He had been unkind to people he loved. He had been ungrateful to people who had treated him well. He didn't stay in touch with his parents. He didn't stay in touch with his brothers. His professional life required that he be a liar and, more recently, a hypocrite—playing the part of a religious man but denying Islam's truth and power. And then there were his secret sins, the ones he dared not confess. The more he cataloged his bad deeds, the worse he felt, and he had no idea where to turn.

No wonder devout Muslims took the verses in the Qur'an about waging jihad so seriously. Why shouldn't they? To disregard the command to jihad would be to disobey, and such disobedience could tip the scales of justice against them in the final reckoning.

Which brought him to martyrdom.

The mullahs and ayatollahs taught that the only true assurance or secure promise of eternal salvation for a Muslim was to die as a martyr, often as a suicide bomber, in the cause of jihad. Osama bin Laden himself had once said, "The call to jihad in God's name . . . leads to eternal life in the end and is relief from your earthly chains."

There was no way that was true, David was certain. But what was?

50

Little Roya was turning ten years old.

And she knew exactly what she wanted. For weeks, she had been writing her parents little notes to remind them, strategically placing them in her father's briefcase, by her mother's sewing basket, on their napkins at dinner, or in other places where they would invariably find them, read them, and consider her request one more time. She pleaded with them not to give her candy or a doll or a book or a pretty new scarf. All she wanted was one thing, and she'd been begging for it for each of the past three years. She wanted them to take her to the Jamkaran Mosque so she could write down her prayer, drop it into the well with all the others, and make her request of the Twelfth Imam.

Growing up in a well-to-do suburb of Tehran, Roya had almost everything she wanted. Her father was a senior translator for the Foreign Ministry and occasionally traveled abroad with high-ranking Iranian officials. Her mother was a renowned botanist in the biology department at Tehran University, who, with Roya's eager help, was cultivating the most gorgeous rose garden in their backyard. Her grandparents were successful in business. She was even distantly related to Ayatollah Hosseini and had met him twice. But while Roya was sweet and devout and brilliant in every respect, she had also been mute from birth. She longed to be able to talk with her parents and sing with her friends. She hated to be thought of as "special." She wanted to be normal. Was that too much to ask?

Maybe it was.

The Jamkaran Mosque, located about six kilometers outside the holy city of Qom, was at least a three-hour car ride each way, not counting however much time they might spend there in prayer. Taking a day off from work would be an enormous imposition on her parents. But Roya simply couldn't help it. She'd seen on TV a news story about the well, and it had completely captured her imagination. One man interviewed said, "If you ask in the right way, your prayers will be answered." Another said, "I don't come here just to pray for myself. I also ask the Mahdi to take care of my family and their needs."

Roya was particularly struck by an interview with a little boy who had brought his flashlight, convinced that the Twelfth Imam was hiding at the bottom of the well reading all the prayer requests people were dropping down there. "I was looking into the well with my flashlight, hoping to see the Mahdi," the boy had said. "But not tonight."

The reporter noted that according to Shia tradition, "if you come to Jamkaran forty weeks in a row, you will see the Mahdi."

The morning of her birthday, Roya awoke early. The house was quiet—her parents must not yet be awake.

Suddenly Roya heard footsteps in the hall outside her bedroom. Maybe her parents were up after all. She glanced at the clock on her nightstand. It wasn't quite six in the morning. Then the door opened slowly, and her parents came in and sat on her bed.

"Happy birthday, sweetheart," her father whispered. "We're leaving in five minutes. Think you can be ready by then?"

Ecstatic, Roya jumped up and threw her arms around her father, then her mother, kissing them both profusely.

The trip was more special than even she had pictured. They didn't drive as a family to Qom. They flew—first-class. They didn't race to the well and then back to the airport. They stayed overnight in a five-star hotel and went out for a fancy dinner. They took a thousand pictures of everything they saw and did, from Roya scribbling her prayer request on special stationery her mother had given her that day as a gift, to Roya pointing her own flashlight—another unexpected gift from her father—down into the well.

But as special as all that was, it did not prepare the little girl for what happened when they all got home the following night. Roya was upstairs brushing her teeth and getting ready for bed when she heard a knock at the door. It seemed a little late for company, and Roya was surprised when she overheard her father talking to a man and then inviting him to come inside. She didn't recognize the man's voice, and when she peeked downstairs, she could see only the back of his head, but she was fairly certain she had never seen him before.

"It would be an honor if you would allow me to pray a blessing on you and your home," said the stranger, who was dressed as a cleric or a mullah.

Roya, hiding on the stairs and careful to remain unseen, heard her father agree, and the man prayed a very beautiful prayer, asking Allah to bring "peace and tranquility to this lovely home" and "bless all who live here now and all who will live here in the future, so long as they submit to you, O Lord."

Not wanting to risk being discovered by her parents, Roya was about to go back to her room and climb into bed when she heard the man ask if he could see their little girl and pray for her as well. Roya froze. How did the man know about her?

"I'm sorry. How do you know we have a daughter?" her father asked. "There are no pictures of her in this room. I haven't mentioned her, and we have never met."

"Do not fear or be alarmed in any way," the stranger said. "The answer is simple. Allah has sent me to your home to heal little Roya."

Roya's heart started racing, but she could see her father tense.

"How do you know her name?"

"I know all about your daughter," the stranger said. "She was born with aphonia, preventing her ability to speak. In her case, it was caused by a genetic disorder that damaged her vocal cords. She has been to nine doctors in eight years and has had three surgeries. None of them have worked."

Astonished, Roya waited for her father to respond, but he didn't. Or couldn't. The room was silent for a moment, and then the man continued.

"Yesterday you flew to Qom. You went to the Jamkaran Mosque, and together you wrote out a prayer and tossed it into the well."

"Who are you?" her father finally blurted out. "And how do you know all this?"

"Roya asked for the Mahdi to heal her."

"Yes . . . yes, she did, but . . ."

"Her request has been granted. That is why I am here."

Roya feared that her father might throw the man out of the house. But what if the stranger really had been sent from Allah? What if he was . . . ?

Suddenly she found herself walking down the stairs and into the living room, where she stood by her father and held his hand.

She pointed at the stranger, in awe of his striking good looks and piercing black eyes. She now thought she recognized him from a dream she'd had a few weeks before.

The man began praying in a language Roya didn't know and had never heard before. When he stopped, Roya fell backward and began writhing on the floor. Her mother screamed. Her father was at her side but could not help her. Her body shook wildly. She felt like she was choking. For a moment she thought she was losing consciousness. Then the stranger began praying again, still in some unintelligible language. Immediately her convulsions ceased.

She opened her eyes again and stared at the ceiling. Her parents' faces were pale. She saw the man come over and kneel beside her. He took her by the hand, pulling her gently to her feet. She felt a cold chill ripple through her body, and then to everyone's astonishment she began to speak. Then she began to sing. Soon she began to shout praises to Allah. She was delirious with happiness. She spun and twirled and hugged her parents and wept with joy.

And then they all turned to thank the stranger, but he was gone.

51

Five full days had gone by, and still nothing had happened.

Beside himself with frustration, David got up early. He showered but once again skipped shaving. He was trying to grow a beard to fit in better, and it was coming in quite well now. He headed to the mosque for morning prayer.

There was a message waiting for him at the front desk when he got back to the hotel. He took it upstairs, closed himself in his room, and opened the envelope, letting out a sigh of relief. It was an invitation for a dinner party at the home of Daryush Rashidi, the president of Iran Telecom. The note said a car would pick him up in front of his hotel at precisely seven o'clock that night, and a phone number was provided for his response. David immediately entered the number into his mobile directory and called to confirm his attendance. He just hoped the NSA system would enable Zalinsky and Fischer to compile a list of the others who would be there.

Fischer.

He hoped Zalinsky had gone easy on her. None of this had actually been her fault. It had been Zalinsky's decision—not hers—to make her project manager and send her to Tehran. Doing so had put their entire mission in jeopardy. But all things considered, Eva had handled things quite well. David barely knew her, but what he knew, he liked. She was smart. She was tough. She was loyal to the Agency. Her Farsi was impeccable. She was not Marseille, but truth be told, she looked rather fetching in a headscarf.

At seven, a black sedan pulled up in front of the Simorgh Hotel. David got in and was driven to a swanky apartment building in an upscale section of Tehran, where he was led by a security guard to a suite on the top floor. But it wasn't the kind of affair David had pictured. There were no servants in tuxedos bringing in trays of food. There were no flower centerpieces or music. There were no other guests at all. Just Daryush Rashidi and Abdol Esfahani.

"Mr. Tabrizi, welcome," the tall, graying CEO said, shaking David's hand. "It is an honor to finally meet you. Abdol has told me good things about you."

"Please, Mr. Rashidi, call me Reza, and the honor is mine," David replied, surprised and relieved. "You are most kind to meet with me at all given the events of the last days, let alone inviting me to your home. Thank you—both of you—very much. Your hospitality is most gracious."

"Say nothing of it, Reza," the CEO said. "Come in."

Rashidi, who David guessed was around sixty, motioned for his guests to follow him from the foyer. As they moved deeper inside what turned out to be a gorgeous penthouse apartment, David realized it had to take up at least half the top floor of this high-rise. The view of the capital and the Alborz Mountains in the distance was absolutely breathtaking, and David said so.

"It is sometimes embarrassing to me to bring people up here, but the views are spectacular," Rashidi said. "I must say, I grew up quite poor. I never imagined anything like this as a child, and I certainly don't need it now. But Iran Telecom wants me to use it for entertaining clients, and who am I to say no?"

He laughed and snapped his fingers. A servant, a man probably about Rashidi's age, smartly dressed but without a tuxedo, stepped out from the kitchen.

"Drinks," the CEO said, "and some snacks."

"Very good, sir," the man said.

Rashidi sat down in an ornate, upholstered chair, evocative of a throne one of the shahs might have used in ancient times. Then he turned to David, who settled on the couch beside Esfahani.

"First of all, Reza, allow me to apologize for Abdol," he began. "He is a dear friend and trusted advisor. But he is not always as diplomatic, perhaps, as a senior executive at Iran Telecom should be."

David glanced at Esfahani, who was staring out at the Tehran skyline, stoic and unrepentant.

"I wanted you to hear it directly from me," Rashidi continued. "I am grateful for your professional conduct through this whole matter. Personally, I would not have asked Ms. Fischer to leave the country. We are a free nation. We have great respect for all people, regardless of their race or gender or station in life. We don't want to frighten off those who have come to genuinely help us. That is not our standard operating procedure and certainly not my heart. But I respect your decision and hope all this hasn't dampened your desire to work with us."

"Not at all, Mr. Rashidi," David replied. "Ms. Fischer is very able. She is an asset to our company. But I believe she will be much more useful to MDS and Iran Telecom back in Dubai and Munich than here. We should have realized it sooner. Please forgive us."

"All is forgiven," Rashidi said, looking pleased. "Let us not think of it again. We have far more important matters to discuss."

David breathed a sigh of relief and couldn't wait to let Zalinsky know they were back in the game.

The servant stepped back into the room, pushing a cart carrying all kinds of treats, including a large ceramic bowl filled with a variety of fresh bananas, oranges, apples, strawberries, and blackberries, which he set on the large glass coffee table in front of them. He also set out a dish of small cucumbers and a saltshaker beside it, along with small dishes of pistachios, cashews, and walnuts. Then he retrieved a variety of freshly squeezed juices and steaming pots of tea and coffee from a small counter.

David immediately felt at home. His parents had held countless dinner parties over the years that had begun precisely the same way. In the summer, he would have expected sweet cherry juice, as well as grape, cantaloupe, sweetened blackberry, and watermelon. Given that it was only February, however, the options were a bit more limited.

"Apple, orange, or pomegranate, sir?" the servant asked.

Rashidi chose apple, as did Esfahani. David wondered if the protocol was to follow the boss's lead, but he took a risk and asked for pomegranate juice. He hadn't had any in years, and it brought back memories of his childhood.

"Three times more antioxidants than red wine," David said with a smile as a glass was poured for him.

A glance between Rashidi and Esfahani made David immediately realize his faux pas.

"Which is good," he quickly added, "since I don't drink wine."

"Good for you," Rashidi said, visibly relieved. "You strike me as a very pious, earnest young man. Were your parents devout Shias?"

And so began the interrogation. It didn't feel harsh. To the contrary, David found both men—but Rashidi in particular—more warm and engaging than he had expected. But it was clear that they wanted to know everything about him. It was a social ritual, to be sure, a rite of passage. It was also another test that David was determined to pass. Helping himself to a handful of pistachios, he launched into his cover story, suddenly grateful for all the time he'd had to practice over the past few days.

He told the story of growing up in Alberta, Canada, as his father worked in the oil sands industry and his mother begged him to take them back to Iran. His eyes grew moist as he shared how his parents died when their Cessna stalled out and crashed just outside of Victoria, British Columbia, when he was only seventeen, and how a policeman had come to his high school to tell him the news. It was, he realized, the first time he had actually spoken the cover story out loud, and he was struck by how much his pain over his mother's cancer now helped him tap the emotions he needed to make his lies sound real.

Both men offered their condolences for David's loss.

"It was a long time ago," he replied, using a napkin from the coffee table as a tissue to wipe his eyes.

"It obviously still affects you a great deal," Rashidi said with a tenderness David would not have expected. "I lost my parents when I was very young as well. It was a boating accident. I was only seven, but I know what you're going through."

David nodded with identification.

Esfahani then asked if he had any siblings. David looked down and said no. He was the "miracle" child in the family, he explained, the only one born after several miscarriages and multiple fertility treatments. When Rashidi asked why he went to college in Germany, David explained that he had never felt comfortable in Canada, that it was too influenced by the immorality and godlessness of the Americans. "What I really wanted to do was come to Iran."

"Why didn't you?" Rashidi asked.

"I didn't know anyone," David said. "All my grandparents passed away before I was born. And I was offered a scholarship to a school in Germany."

"Your family, they were all from Tabriz?" Esfahani inquired.

"Yes," David confirmed, "but I had never been here before. I had no money. It just seemed like first I ought to get some schooling, develop some skills, and make a little money. Then I hoped I could find a way to come back here and reconnect with the land of my fathers and see if there was something I could do to . . . you know, to help."

Rashidi looked at Esfahani and then back at David. "I hope I'm not the first to say it, but welcome home, young man."

"Actually, Mr. Rashidi, you are, and thank you," David said. "I can't explain what a joy it is to finally be here and what heartache it has been for me for the past few days to think that rather than being a blessing to you and your great company and this great country, somehow I might have brought dishonor."

"No, no," Rashidi said. "No more of that. It was a simple mistake, and it is all behind us now. We must move forward."

"Thank you, sir," David said. "I would like that very much."

Before long, David's mouth was beginning to water as the aromas of all kinds of dishes began emanating from the kitchen. Fortunately, within a few minutes, it was announced that dinner would be served. Rashidi guided David around the corner to a beautifully appointed dining room with a large table set for three with fine china and pressed linens. To one side of the room there was another table perhaps three or four meters long, covered with a variety of dishes, far more than they could possibly eat in one night. There was an entire roasted lamb on a silver tray in the center of the table, surrounded by pots of all kinds of stews—pomegranate, eggplant, herb, okra, and celery—and a fava bean rice dish with sheep shank.

But best of all, and much to David's surprise, there was a large bowl of *Shirin Polo*, one of his favorites and his mother's specialty. It was a beautiful, colorful dish of steaming basmati rice adorned with sweetened and slivered carrots, almonds, pistachios, orange rind, and saffron. David couldn't wait to dive in.

52

Each man helped himself to a plate and sat down.

But just as David began to take a bite, the questions started coming faster and faster. The interrogation phase was over. Rashidi and Esfahani were growing comfortable with him, but they were by no means finished. Now they shifted to the delivery phase.

"How quickly can MDS have teams of technicians on the ground in Tehran?" Esfahani asked.

David reiterated what he had promised Esfahani outside the Imam Khomeini Mosque. The teams could be there within a day or two if he called soon and set them into motion. They were all on standby.

"How long will it take them to do their work?" Rashidi asked.

"For the first phase, with testing, I'd say about a month," David said. "But as you know from our proposals, the second, third, and fourth phases will take the better part of a year, altogether."

Was he aware that each technician would be assigned two translators, each working six-hour shifts, as well as a security team?

David said he was. But he added that several of them already spoke Farsi. What's more, MDS was in the process of hiring and training another dozen Farsi-speaking technicians, though they probably wouldn't be ready until late spring. Rashidi liked this very much.

Esfahani wanted to know how quickly the monitoring center could be up and running.

David knew the executive was referring to the high-tech operations center MDS had committed to outfitting that would allow Iran's security services to intercept, monitor, trace, and record any call on their new wireless system. He replied that his teams needed to get the software installed on Iran Telecom's mainframes first, and then they would focus on setting up the monitoring center.

"No," Esfahani said, "that won't do. We want the software to be installed and the center to be outfitted simultaneously."

"That's not part of the contract," David said.

"We've changed our minds," Rashidi said. "We like you. We trust you. We want you to do this for us. Will that be a problem?"

"It will cost more, and we'll need three or four days to get that team assembled, but we can certainly do it, if you want."

"Cost is no object," Rashidi assured him. "Time is the issue. Can everything be done in a month?"

"That's really Ms. Fischer's call."

Esfahani's mood suddenly darkened at the mention of Fischer. "That's not what we asked," he said curtly. "Can the software and monitoring center all be installed and ready in one month's time?"

"It can," David said. "Again, I need Ms. Fischer's approval, but I don't see this being a problem."

"I thought you were the new project manager," Esfahani said.

"Here, yes, but I still report to Ms. Fischer in Dubai," David explained. "Is that a problem? You won't have any interaction with her whatsoever, I assure you."

"I'm sure that is true," Rashidi said. "But I think what my colleague means is that, given all that has happened, is there any reason for us to be concerned that this Ms. Fischer would refuse to move the project faster because perhaps she was offended by her time here?"

That wasn't, of course, what Esfahani meant, David knew. The man was simply using religion as his cover to discriminate against a highly qualified colleague and new friend. But he was not about to point that out and blow this deal—not when it seemed to be going so well.

"Believe me, Mr. Rashidi and Mr. Esfahani, everyone in our company knows how important this project is," David assured them. "Ms. Fischer knows this most of all. I can assure you that she is a consummate professional. She won't let her personal feelings affect her performance. The only real issue is getting you a cost estimate, which I can have for you by the close of business tomorrow. Once you approve the estimate, all that remains will be to have Ms. Fischer pull together the equipment for the monitoring center and assemble a second crew that can arrive by the end of this week or early next."

"Will you push for this to be done?" Esfahani asked.

"Absolutely."

"We're counting on you, Mr. Tabrizi," Esfahani stressed.

"Thank you, sir," he replied. "I appreciate your trust."

Now Rashidi took the lead again. "You know that I just got back from Beijing, right?" the CEO said.

"Yes, sir," David said. "I read that in the newspaper."

"The Chinese are begging us to give them this contract."

"I understand, sir. But believe me, we can take care of this for you, and we want to. We'll get you the best price and the best people. You have my word."

"That is good enough for me," Rashidi said.

Esfahani nodded his agreement. "Now we have another request."

53

Najjar got home late and exhausted.

The apartment was dark and quiet. On the kitchen table was a note that read, *I'm at my parents' for dinner. Will be home late. Don't wait up. But have you heard the rumors? Someone has seen him. They say he's coming soon. Isn't this exciting? Love and kisses, Sheyda.*

Najjar was furious. He was tempted to jump back in the car, drive over to his in-laws', and have it out with his father-in-law right there and then. Of course he had heard the news. Dr. Saddaji had told his entire staff about Ayatollah Hosseini's vision of the Twelfth Imam, and the news had exhilarated Najjar. He had been waiting for the Mahdi for most of his life. Finally there would be justice. Finally there would be peace. But he was increasingly convinced that his father-in-law believed a nuclear war against the U.S. and Israel had to precede the Mahdi's arrival. Najjar resisted this notion with every fiber of his being. Yes, he had vowed to serve Allah with all that he was. Yes, he had vowed to devote himself to preparing for the coming of the Twelfth Imam. But he couldn't be party to genocide. That couldn't possibly be what the Mahdi really wanted for him and his family.

Yet it was becoming clear to Najjar that this was precisely what his father-in-law believed, that mankind in general—and the Iranian government in particular—was responsible for proactively and intentionally unleashing the "blood and fire" that would be the last sign before the Twelfth Imam's arrival on earth. That was why he was secretly building the Islamic Bomb. Did Dr. Saddaji's wife, Farah, know this?

Did Sheyda? Did they know their husband and father was a cold-blooded murderer? Najjar couldn't believe they did. And how could he tell them? What would they do if they learned the truth? Moreover, what should he do? Resign in protest? Move to another city? Move to another country?

To Najjar, overseeing Iran's version of the Manhattan Project and lying to the world about it every day was morally repugnant. But to order a man killed—beheaded, no less—without the benefit of a trial or a judge, and to do so in the presence of other senior physicists working under his direction? This was beyond the pale. Yet this was the life his father-in-law was living, and the message to Najjar, to his team, and ultimately to his family as well was clear: Betray me, and you're an infidel. Become an infidel, and you are dead.

The truth was slowly coming into focus for Najjar, but as it did, it became clear that he could not say anything to his wife. Or to his mother-in-law. Or to anyone else. He couldn't move his family. He couldn't take them out of the country. He was trapped in a family led by a man without conscience, a man who would commit any atrocity in the name of jihad.

Najjar collapsed in a chair in the living room and picked up the television remote. He desperately needed to escape, if only in his mind.

Satellite dishes were illegal in Iran, which was why everyone had one. Sheyda was actually the one who had begged Najjar to get one, so long as he promised not to tell her parents. Najjar, eager for news of the outside world, had happily agreed. They had saved for nearly a year to afford a good system, but a friend had installed it for them just the previous weekend.

Najjar turned on the TV and began searching through the hundreds of channels now available to him. He immediately skipped past any program produced by the government and past sporting events, of which he'd never been a big fan. Coming across the BBC, he paused for a moment to watch a breaking news story about two Israeli Dolphin-class submarines—each likely equipped with ballistic missiles capped with nuclear warheads—passing through the Suez Canal. A British intelligence analyst speculated the subs were most likely headed for the

Indian Ocean or the Persian Gulf, presumably to park off the coast of Iran and await orders from Jerusalem.

Further depressed by such a prospect, Najjar kept scanning. Suddenly he came across a network he had never heard of before and a character he had never seen. On screen was an elderly priest of some kind, wearing a black cassock, a black cap, and a large metal cross. But it was not the man's looks that forced Najjar to stop and watch for a moment. It was what the man was saying.

"Children are brainwashed that Islam is the truth," the priest declared, looking directly into the camera. "Children are brainwashed that Muhammad is the last prophet, that the Christians are infidels, and that the Jews are infidels. They repeat it constantly."

Afraid of being overheard by his neighbors, Najjar instantly lowered the volume but didn't turn the channel. He couldn't look away. He was stunned by the intensity of the man's voice and the brazenness of his words. This priest was speaking Egyptian Arabic, but Najjar could understand him quite well, given his own upbringing in Iraq.

"Islam, as portrayed in the Qur'an, in the Hadith, and in *The Encyclopedia of Islam*, was spread by means of the sword," the priest explained. "The sword played a major role in spreading Islam in the past, and it is the sword that preserves Islam today. Islam relies upon jihad in spreading the religion. This is very clear in the encyclopedia. This appears in section 11, page 3,245. It says, 'Spreading Islam by means of the sword is a duty incumbent upon all Muslims.' Thus, Islam is spread by means of the sword."

Now the priest leaned forward and spoke with great passion. "It's time for the church to stand up with courage and conviction and say in the power of the Holy Spirit, 'Islam is not the answer; jihad is not the way. Jesus is the way. Jesus is the truth. Jesus is the life. And no man or woman can come to the Father except through faith in Jesus Christ.' This is the message of John 14:6. This is the message of the entire New Testament. And this message of faith is filled with love, not with swords."

It was as if electricity were coursing through Najjar's system. He was no longer slumped in his chair. He was sitting up straight, at once furious at this man, wanting to throw his shoe at the television, yet simultaneously intrigued beyond anything he could imagine. How could the government allow such things to be on television? Wasn't anyone trying to stop this man? Mesmerized, Najjar kept watching.

"Now is not the time to hide in fear from the Muslim world," the priest declared. "Now is the time to take the gospel of Jesus Christ to every man, woman, and child on the planet and proclaim Him as the hope of mankind, the only hope for the troubled world. I have been doing this for most of my life, sharing the good news of salvation through Jesus Christ with the people of the Middle East. For this I was exiled from my home country of Egypt. For this I have been named 'Islam's public enemy number one.' For this there is now a price on my head. But I love Jesus more than my life. And because Jesus loves Muslims, because He came and laid down His life to save them, I love them too. And I am willing to lay my life down if necessary to reach them for my beloved Jesus."

Najjar had never heard anyone talk like this.

"The God of the Bible is moving powerfully in the Muslim world today," the priest continued. "He is drawing Muslims out of Islam to faith in Jesus Christ in record numbers. Yes, there is much bad news in the Muslim world today. But there is also much good news; more Muslims have come to faith in Jesus Christ in the last three decades than in the last fourteen centuries of Islam put together. This is the greatness of our great God."

Was that true? Najjar wondered. Were Muslims really leaving Islam and becoming followers of Jesus Christ? Was it happening in large numbers? He was suddenly afraid to watch anymore. He turned off the television, turned off the lights, and climbed into bed, trembling. He was grateful Sheyda wasn't home. He was ashamed of what he had just watched. What if someone had heard him? He should be more careful, he told himself.

Yet alone in the darkness, he couldn't shake what he had just seen and heard, and one phrase echoed in his heart again and again.

"Jesus is the way. Jesus is the truth. Jesus is the life. And no man or woman can come to the Father except through faith in Jesus Christ."

54

Rashidi's mobile phone rang.

He excused himself and left the room. Then Esfahani leaned close to David and whispered, "What I say next needs to be kept very quiet. Are we understood? It must never be spoken of to anyone."

"Of course," David said.

"We need to buy twenty secure satellite phones," Esfahani explained. "State-of-the-art. Encrypted. Absolutely impenetrable. You make them, right?"

"Well, we don't make them ourselves," David replied. "Nokia has a joint venture with someone who does. But they're built for European government officials. They're not for export."

"The Saudis have them."

"That I wouldn't know."

"The Pakistanis have them."

"Again, that's not my area."

"The Moroccans have them. Do you see where I'm going with this?"

"I think so."

"Then can you get them for us?"

"I can ask Ms. Fischer."

"No," Esfahani said, "that's not what I asked. I'm asking you—*you personally*—can *you* get them for us?"

"I don't know. Ms. Fischer is the real expert on such things, sir, but I don't think even she could get an export license for them, given all the international focus on . . . well, you know . . . the situation here. I don't know how I would get the licenses, much less the phones."

Esfahani said nothing. There was a long, awkward pause. It was quiet. Too quiet. All David could hear was a clock ticking in the living room and the faint sound of rattling dishes in the kitchen.

"I can try," David finally said.

"Without involving Ms. Fischer?" Esfahani pressed.

David pretended to ponder that a while longer. He knew he could get the phones in a heartbeat. Zalinsky would happily build them by hand if he thought that would help the mission. But David knew he couldn't seem too eager or too accommodating.

He looked back at Esfahani and assured the man he would do his best, and without Fischer's involvement. It was a lie, of course. Fischer would be intimately involved. But it was what the man wanted to hear, and it seemed to work.

"Good, because you know there are more telecom infrastructure contracts coming in the next few months," Esfahani reminded him. "Each one is worth hundreds of millions of euros, and Mr. Rashidi and I would certainly want to look favorably on your bids."

"That's what I want too," David said. "MDS values your business a great deal."

"Very well. How soon could you get them?"

"How soon do you need them?"

"Five business days."

"*Five?* That's pretty fast."

"Perhaps we should go to the Chinese."

"No, no, I'll figure out a way," David promised, suddenly fearful that he was playing too coy. "You need twenty of them?"

"Yes."

"Done," David said. "After all, we can't let the Saudis or the Zionists have something you don't have. I'll get right on it."

"See that you do," Esfahani said. "I can assure you, success will be handsomely rewarded."

"It will be my honor to bless Iran in every way I can," David said. "Which reminds me. I need to call Dubai and tell our tech teams to get here tomorrow. Will your staff be able to pick them up at the airport, orient them, and show them where to get started? I'll need to head back to Munich to fulfill this other request."

"Yes, we will take care of everything," Esfahani assured him. "Just tell my secretary who is coming and when."

"I will do that, but could I just ask a question?"

"What is it?"

"If it's inappropriate, please forgive me."

"You needn't hesitate. What's your question?"

"Well, I'm just curious. Why such urgency?"

The moment the words left David's lips, Rashidi reentered the room. David sensed he had finished his phone call some time before and had been listening to most of the conversation, presumably approving of its direction.

"That one I would like to answer," the CEO said. "Mr. Tabrizi, have you ever heard of the Twelfth Imam?"

55

David landed at 11:40 a.m. and was greeted by Eva.

He was surprised by how happy she was to see him. She was professional, to be sure, but her smile was warm and she seemed genuinely relieved that he was out of Iran for the time being, safe and sound.

"So how'd it go?" she asked as they headed out of the parking garage.

"Better than I'd expected," he said. "Is the tech team all set?"

"Absolutely. They're booked on the first flight, tomorrow morning at six."

"Good. Where are they now?"

"They're all waiting for you at the office, as you requested."

"Thanks," David said. "Were you able to book me a room at Le Méridien?"

"I did." Eva smirked a little. "Even got you an upgraded suite."

"Wow, thanks. But that wasn't necessary."

"What are friends for?" she asked.

David laughed, getting it now. "Jack told you to make me look like a wealthy businessman."

"He did indeed."

★ ★ ★ ★ ★

David's briefing lasted about an hour.

The irony was that while each of the members of the technical team worked for the CIA, none of them individually knew that the others did. Nor did they know that David was a NOC as well. Each of them had been hired as an independent contractor by Eva, and compartmentalization was the name of the game. The less they knew about the overall operation, and about each other, the better.

When they finished a lightning round of Q&A, Eva dismissed the team. Then, when the coast was clear, she led David out of the conference room and down several hallways to a small, quiet, private office in the back of the MDS regional headquarters. They slipped in quickly and closed the door behind them, and there they found Jack Zalinsky waiting for them.

"You survived," he said upon laying eyes on his protégé.

"Better than that," David replied. "I bear gifts from afar."

"That's my boy," Zalinsky said, slapping him on the back and actually smiling for the first time in David couldn't remember how long.

"Let me guess," Eva began as they took their seats. "You need twenty secure satellite phones."

"I'm impressed."

"Well, *mein freund*, you may have been loafing around in your hotel room, watching TV, and going to prayer five times a day," Eva teased, "but your phone has been working hard, and it's been a gold mine."

She explained the middle-of-the-night call from some senior Iranian official—yet unidentified—to Esfahani, requesting the satellite phones. What's more, she assured him that all twenty would be ready for him to pick up in Munich in seventy-two hours. She also gave him a file with the transcripts of every call the NSA had intercepted thus far based on the new contacts he had entered into his phone.

Thanking them, David quickly shifted gears. "You guys have heard of the Twelfth Imam, right?" he asked.

"Of course," Eva said. "I sent you that article about the cult leader in Yemen who says he's preparing the way for him to return."

"Exactly," David said.

"You're talking about the so-called Islamic messiah?" Zalinsky asked. "The one who is supposed to bring about the end of the world, that kind of thing?"

"Right."

"What about him?"

"He may actually be on the ground, in Iran."

There was dead silence for a moment.

"Come on," Zalinsky said, "it's a fanatic's fantasy, a myth."

"Jack, it's not about what you and I are willing to believe," David countered. "It's about what the Iranian leaders believe, and I'm telling you, they think he's here—some of them, anyway."

"So what?" Zalinsky said. "That has nothing to do with our mission."

"Actually, it does."

"How so?"

"Everywhere I go, people are talking about him," David said. "He's popping up in news stories. Religious experts are having conferences about him. And I'm hearing all kinds of rumors that he is alive and well and appearing to people."

"It doesn't matter," Zalinsky said. "It's a bunch of religious superstition. Don't get sidetracked."

"No, no, you're wrong, Jack," David insisted. "Listen to me. Two nights ago, a mysterious cleric shows up at the home of a little girl who has been mute from birth. He knocks on the door and asks if he can pray a blessing on the home. He seems harmless enough, so the parents say yes. Then he asks if he can see their little girl and pray for her. They ask him how he knows they even have a little girl. Now get this—the stranger says Allah has sent him to their house to heal their child. At this point, the father thinks the man is a little, you know, out there. But just then, the little girl walks into the room. The man prays for her; she falls down and goes into convulsions. Her parents freak out. But a moment later the little girl gets up and begins to speak for the first time in her life."

"So who was the man?" Eva asked.

"Well, that's just it; no one's ever seen him before," David said. "They have no idea where he's from or who he is, and in the commotion of the little girl's healing, the man simply vanishes. But the girl is convinced it was the Twelfth Imam. The parents are too. They're telling everyone what happened, and the story was on the front page of all the newspapers in Tehran this morning."

"That's crazy," Zalinsky said.

"Maybe, but that's not all," David said. "I'm told that recently, Ayatollah Hosseini was up at some mountain retreat center of his called the Qaleh."

"The Qaleh?" Eva asked, looking at Zalinsky.

"That's right," David said. "Why?"

"Nothing; go on," she said.

"Well, apparently, Hosseini is praying when he suddenly sees a bright light and hears a voice speaking to him. The voice tells him that the Mahdi is going to be revealed soon and that Hosseini and his advisors are supposed to 'get ready and be prepared' for his arrival. Hosseini is telling people close to him that it was the Twelfth Imam who spoke to him. Rumors like these are spreading like wildfire throughout Tehran. People are saying that the Mahdi has come and that he's about to reveal himself to the Islamic world—and all of humanity—and usher in the end of days."

"You picked all this up on the street?" Zalinsky asked.

"Everyone's talking about it. Even Rashidi," David said.

"When?"

"Last night at his apartment."

"Daryush Rashidi?" Zalinsky clarified. "The president of Iran Telecom talked to you about the Twelfth Imam?"

"Weird, I know. Turns out he's a closet Twelver. Apparently his parents were really into Shia Islamic End Times prophecy when he was a kid, but they swore him to secrecy."

"Of course they did. These people are lunatics. They're nuts. Khomeini actually banned them in 1983 because he thought they were so dangerous."

"Well, Jack, they're running the country now. That's my point."

"That's where you're wrong," Zalinsky said. "Hosseini doesn't really believe all that. Neither does President Darazi. They just use it to rile up the masses."

"I'm just telling you what I saw and heard. And I can guarantee you, Rashidi and Esfahani are true believers. They believe the Twelfth Imam is here. Rashidi told me he spoke personally to someone who was with Hosseini moments after the vision. They all think it's real. You should have seen them, Jack. That's why they want twenty secure satphones immediately. Someone from Hosseini's office asked for them. But they're not for Hosseini. They're for people around the Twelfth Imam, and Rashidi said they're eventually going to need 293 more."

"Why do they need 293 satphones?" Eva asked.

"No, 293 *more*," David corrected. "They need a total of 313. Apparently, it's part of some Shia prophecy that the Twelfth Imam will have 313 followers."

"How soon do they want the rest of the phones?" Zalinsky asked.

"Rashidi offered me a 200,000-euro bonus, wired to any account I want, if I can get them to him by the end of the month."

"That's like, what, a quarter of a million dollars?" Eva asked, incredulous.

"I know—it's crazy. But that's what I'm trying to tell you guys. These people are very serious and very excited."

"Why are they telling you this much this fast?" Zalinsky asked.

"Because they're also desperate," David said. "They see events are moving fast now, and they're scrambling to keep up."

"No, no, I realize they're all nuts; I accept that," Zalinsky said. "But why *you*? Why are they taking *you* into their confidence so quickly?"

David thought about that for a moment. "Well, for starters, they think I'm one of them," he replied. "They're buying the cover story. They genuinely believe I want to bless my homeland as well as make a buck. They've been watching me go to the mosque five times a day. They saw me throw Eva out of the country. They think I'm sincere, earnest."

"That can't be all of it," Zalinsky said.

"No, it's not," David agreed. "I think there's another dynamic at work here."

"What?"

"I think they're trying to convert me."

"From what to what?"

"From a regular Shia Muslim to a Twelver."

"Why?"

"Why else?" David said. "Because that's what they are. They genuinely believe the messiah has come. The end is here. And they want me to be a part of it. Plus, honestly, they need a bunch of satellite phones, and they think I just might be young enough and dumb enough and well-connected enough to get them. I think it's that simple."

"This is ridiculous," Zalinsky said, standing up and going over to the window. "This whole 'Twelfth Imam' thing is a rabbit trail. It's a distraction. We've known about it for years, and it's just a bunch of religious dreaming. Your job is to help us identify nuclear sites so our teams can go in and sabotage them. That's it. We don't have time for you to do anything else."

"With all due respect, sir, I think you're missing the point," David said. "This is the fastest way in. If I ask them questions about nukes, they're going to be suspicious. Wouldn't you be? But I'm telling you, I can ask them a million questions about the Mahdi and they'll answer every one of them. Why? Because that's what they're interested in. That's what Ayatollah Hosseini is focused on. That's what President Darazi is focused on. That's what Rashidi is focused on. Shouldn't we be focused on it too?"

Zalinsky turned to Eva. "What do you think?"

"Honestly, Jack, I think David is onto something."

"How so?"

"Look, I can't say I know much about Shia eschatology. Nor can I find anyone at Langley who does either, and believe me, I've tried. But I've been tracking the press and blog coverage of this big conference held in Tehran last week on Mahdism. Two thousand people showed up. They had a dozen top Islamic scholars there talking about the imminence of the Twelfth Imam's return. The keynote address was given by none other than President Darazi, who stated categorically that the Mahdi will appear this year and that his authenticity will be confirmed by the voice of the angel Gabriel, who will appear in the sky over the Mahdi's head and call the faithful to gather around him. That's not normal political discourse, Jack. This is a regime that believes the messiah is coming and is basing its actions on that belief. We can't counter Iran effectively if we don't know why its leaders are doing what they're doing."

It was a solid argument, David thought. The angel Gabriel thing intrigued him. He hadn't heard that and wanted to talk to Eva more about it.

But Zalinsky wasn't buying it. "Listen," he said firmly, turning to David, "I want you on the next plane to Munich. Pick up the sat-phones. It's going to take a few days. But once you have them, go right back into Iran. Show them you can deliver, ahead of schedule. Then get us nuke sites. That's the mission. Nuclear weapons sites. Period. Don't get sidetracked."

56

David checked into Le Méridien.

The next direct, nonstop flight to Munich was on Lufthansa, but it didn't depart until 7:35 the following morning. That meant he had to be at the airport by 4:30, which meant he had to leave for the airport at 4:00 and be up by 3:00, which meant he really should try to get some sleep now. But he couldn't. He was too angry. So he threw on some shorts, a T-shirt, and a pair of Nikes and went running instead.

Zalinsky, he was certain, was making a serious mistake. David knew his mentor had far more experience in the region than he did. But that made it all the more frustrating. Why wouldn't Zalinsky take seriously the growing importance of Shia eschatology or consider its implications? David didn't need anyone to tell him that he hadn't a fraction of the training or wisdom Zalinsky had. But David trusted his gut, and his gut told him to follow the trail of the Twelfth Imam.

In the meantime, he owed Marseille Harper a call. He just wasn't sure what to say. Heading north along Sheikh Rashid Road, David ran past the Dubai Creek Golf Club, turned east over the bridge, and wound through several businesses until he reached the football stadium between Tenth Street and Oud Metha Road. There he bought a bottle of water from a street vendor and found a pay phone on the stadium grounds. It wasn't exactly the quietest place to make the call, but it was the least traceable phone he could find, and for now, that would have to do.

He was surprised by the butterflies in his stomach and the perspiration on his palms. It bothered him that this girl still had such a hold on him after so long, but she did. As he dialed—slowly—he tried to imagine the sound of her voice and wondered if he would still recognize it. Then the line began ringing, and he was tempted to hang up. It rang again with no answer. The longer it went, the more jittery he became. David wiped the sweat off his brow and took another swig of water. Still no answer. But just when he was about to hang up, the line connected, crackling with static.

"Hello?" David said. "Hello?"

"Hi," a woman's voice said. The voice was instantly familiar; David's pulse quickened. "This is Marseille. I'm not in right now, but if you'll leave me your name, number, and a brief message, I'll get back to you as soon as I can. Thanks."

David faltered. "Uh, hi, this is, uh . . . hey, Marseille, this is Rez—sorry, there is some static on the line—anyway, this is David. . . . David Shirazi. . . . I'm calling you from overseas, so I'm sorry for the bad connection. Anyway, I was visiting my parents recently, and they actually just gave me your letter from December as I was leaving for another business trip, and I'm afraid this is the first chance I've had to call you back. I'm so sorry to hear about your father, I really am, but I'm glad to hear from you, and yes, I would love to see you in Syracuse in a few weeks. Dinner or coffee or whatever on that Thursday night would be great."

He quickly gave her an e-mail address and said that was the best way to reach him for the next few weeks to make definite plans. And with that, he hung up, wondering why he was acting like a complete moron.

57

"I am Muhammad Ibn Hasan Ibn Ali, Lord of the Age."

Everyone gathered in the office of the Supreme Leader—Hosseini himself, the president, the defense minister, and the commander of the Iranian Revolutionary Guard Corps—froze. Was this actually the Twelfth Imam before them? They had expected to see him soon, but not this soon. Taking no chances, they immediately fell to the floor, bowing in reverence to the striking young man who had just walked into their meeting unannounced.

Hosseini sensed his advisors' shock when he knelt before the newcomer. His advisors had never seen the Supreme Leader bow to anyone. But Hosseini had no doubt who this was. The flowing black robes. The black turban. The handsome, radiant face. The piercing eyes. The wide forehead. The broad chest. The aura of light that seemed to infuse the room. Above all, it was the voice that confirmed it for Hosseini. This was the voice he had heard at the Qaleh, the voice that resounded from the vision of light.

"Hamid," said the man, who appeared to be in his late thirties or early forties at most and yet had such a commanding, even mesmerizing presence, "do you remember what happened on the mountain?"

Hosseini had never been referred to so casually by anyone, least of all by a man half his age. But it was an honor to be addressed directly by the Twelfth Imam.

"Yes, my Lord," Hosseini said, his face still pressed to the ground. "You showed me the glories of the kingdoms of the world."

"And what did I say to you?"

"You said, 'All these things I will give you, if you fall down before me and do my will.' And I have endeavored to do just that ever since, my Lord."

"You have done well," the Twelfth Imam said. "Now you and the others may rise and take your seats."

The men did as they were told.

"Gentlemen, as I told your Supreme Leader when I appeared to him, the time to establish the global caliphate has come. You have longed for the world to be ruled by Muslims and for Allah. You have prayed faithfully for the reestablishment of the caliphate since coming to power. I am here today to tell you that you need not wait any longer. So long as you obey me without dissent, without questioning or hesitation, you will govern this earth, all of you, at my side."

The Imam passed around four typed, single-spaced sheets of paper, one to each of the men sitting at the table. He asked each to read the document and then sign if his conscience would allow.

> I, _____, pledge my full
> allegiance, devotion, and loyalty to Imam al-Mahdi. I
> will live for him. I will die for him. I shall carry out his
> orders quickly and completely and without complaint,
> so help me, Allah.

Hosseini took one look at the document and declared without hesitation, "Imam al-Mahdi, I will follow you to the ends of the earth and the end of time." He took a steak knife from the place setting before him and slit his left palm. He dipped his right forefinger in the blood pouring down his arm and signed his name.

The others quickly followed Hosseini's lead. They handed back their documents, then wrapped their bloody hands with white linen napkins.

"Well done, my servants," the Mahdi said. "Now listen closely."

As Hosseini and the others sat captivated, the Twelfth Imam took the men into his confidence and laid out his plans. He explained that once the Group of 313 was formed, they were to recruit an elite army of ten thousand *mujahideen*.

"They do not all have to be Shias," the Mahdi said, "but they all have to be loyal to me and me alone. And fifty of them should be women."

In short order, he said, he must be able to announce a successful Iranian nuclear weapons test. He must announce a military alliance between Iran and Pakistan. He must announce that Iran had pre-positioned nuclear weapons under Iranian control in Lebanon and Syria and make clear to the Jews that any attack on the Palestinians—or any neighbor of the Zionist entity—would result in a War of Annihilation. When this was accomplished, he explained, he would announce plans to establish the headquarters of his global Islamic government in the city of Kufa, in the heart of Iraq. They must work to make all these things happen just as he said.

Hamid Hosseini was disappointed at this last part, and he assumed the other men were too. He longed for the seat of the caliphate to be located in Iran, not Iraq, for obvious historic reasons. But he didn't dare say a word. Indeed, he feared his very thoughts would be read by the Mahdi, exposing his doubts and dissensions. Fortunately, the Mahdi had more to say.

"Very soon, I will give you authorization to make a formal statement of my arrival to this dark world and to announce that I will travel to Mecca to make my first public appearance."

"O Lord, do not be angered by my question, but must you go first to the Saudis?" President Darazi asked, astounding Hosseini with his audacity. "Could you not bless the Persian people first by appearing here in Tehran or in the holy city of Qom?"

"Do not forget, my children," the Mahdi said, "I am an Arab, not a Persian. I am a direct descendant of the Prophet, the twelfth in his direct bloodline of succession. It is written that I must first appear publicly in Mecca, and so I must. But do not take this as a slight, my son. The leaders of the Sunni world are corrupt and face judgment. They have never believed in me. They do not believe I am coming or that I have already come. But soon they will see with their own eyes. They will hear with their own ears. And they will worship me, or they will face great judgment. And do not forget, too, that I came to you first. With the help of the Prince of Persia, I have appeared all over your country—in Jamkaran at the well, at the Qaleh last week, and here with you now. I have chosen you, not the Arabs, to form my ruling council, for while you have made many mistakes, you did not betray me. You did not sign a peace treaty with the Zionists, as the Egyptians and the Jordanians did. You did not invite the Americans to occupy your lands, as the Saudis did. You did not ask the Americans to help you form a demonic democracy, as the Iraqis did. The Arab leaders will face a day of reckoning for their crimes, but the Arab people are not the enemy. The Americans and the Israelis are the enemy. It is they who will pay the highest price. Their leaders do not understand what is coming, but they will experience the wrath of Allah soon enough. We must join together, Persian and Arab and Turk and African—all who submit to Allah—as one man."

He explained that his appearance in Mecca had to be carefully planned, with his arrival and message broadcast live to the nations.

"When exactly are we going?" Hosseini asked.

"You are not going," the Mahdi told them.

"None of us, or just not me, my Lord?" Hosseini asked, surprised and embarrassed in front of his colleagues.

"None of you," the Mahdi said. "Your presence would be too provocative for the Saudis. It is enough that I go there. It is too soon for you all to come. To achieve the success we need, we must convince the king and the royal family—along with the leaders of the emirates—to attend my arrival."

"O Lord, we will work on this immediately," Hosseini said.

"Good," the Mahdi replied. "I want you to work on it personally, Hamid. Call the Saudis directly, before we announce the news publicly. Be respectful and brotherly. Be discreet. But be clear. Tell them I would not look kindly on their refusal to greet me with all the honor worthy of their messiah."

"I will do as you say, Imam al-Mahdi," Hosseini said. "But what if they won't listen? What if they do not believe me?"

"They will believe you, my son," came the reply. "After they see my power and glory displayed, they will believe you. Of this you need have no doubt."

PART THREE

★ ★ ★ ★ ★

58

David arrived in Munich but was desperate to get back to Tehran.

He had no interest in watching TV, paying his bills, or reading all the Christmas cards and other assorted mail he'd FedEx'd to himself from the Atlanta airport, not to mention all the other junk mail and magazines that had piled up since he'd been here last. Time was too short. Iran was out of control. He couldn't prove it yet, but he knew they were closing in on nuclear capability, and he was determined to get back into the action.

He wondered why the package from Amazon hadn't arrived yet. He'd been looking forward to reading Dr. Alireza Birjandi's book on Shia eschatology and had ordered it to be sent to Germany. But it was nowhere to be seen.

He called Zalinsky to check in but learned his boss was on a secure conference call with Langley. He called Eva to gripe but got her voice mail instead. He logged on to the CIA's secure intranet system to review the latest transcripts of intercepted calls inside Iran. But of the dozens of calls, none provided any useful information. He cleaned his 9mm Beretta 92FS and wondered how to smuggle it into Tehran on his next trip. But it was all busywork, and it was killing him. He hadn't joined the CIA to waste time in Germany. They had to get moving.

He checked his AOL account, hoping at least for word from Marseille, but found nothing. On a whim, he did a search on Facebook. He hoped to find a recent photo or some current information about her and wondered why he'd never thought of it before. But there was no Marseille Harper listed. Then again, neither was he. He checked MySpace and Classmates.com and Twitter but found no sign of her at all. When he simply typed her name into Google, however, he found one link: a story published September 12 of the previous year by the *Oregonian*, Portland's daily newspaper, headlined, "Charles D. Harper Commits Suicide."

Not believing it could be the same person, he clicked on the link and read the obituary.

> Charles David Harper, an Iran expert who served as a political officer at the U.S. Embassy in Tehran during the Islamic Revolution of 1979, served in various other embassy posts as a Foreign Service officer for the U.S. State Department, and later served as a professor of Middle East history at Princeton University, was found dead Saturday afternoon in the woods near his farm-house on Sauvie Island. Blake Morris of the Multnomah County Sheriff's Office said Mr. Harper died of a self-inflicted gunshot wound. He is survived by his only child, Marseille Harper, a schoolteacher in the Portland Public School District, who found his body; and by his mother, Mildred, who resides in a Portland-area nursing home. Sources close to the family say she is suffering from an advanced stage of Alzheimer's. Mr. Harper's wife, Claire, died in the World Trade Center attacks on September 11, 2001.

Numb, David stared at the screen, wishing he could simply shut down the computer and make the story go away but unable to take his eyes off the words.

Why had he done it? The date of his death told part of the story, but not all of it. No matter how much pain the man was in, how could Mr. Harper have done that to Marseille? She needed him. She loved him. He was all she had in this world. How could he have abandoned her? And how would she ever erase the image of finding her father in those woods?

He hadn't known Marseille was a teacher, but he had no doubt she was a great one, and he hoped somehow she could go on teaching despite all that had happened. He hadn't known that the Harpers lived on Sauvie Island. He'd never even heard of Sauvie Island. A quick check of Wikipedia revealed that it was the largest island along the Columbia River and lay approximately ten miles northwest of downtown Portland. The island was made up mainly of farmland and boasted barely a thousand year-round residents. "Bicyclists flock to the island because its flat topography and lengthy low-volume roads make it ideal for cycling," he read. It wasn't the Jersey Shore, but it did sound like a beautiful place to live.

He had learned another thing from the article, something that had come out of left field. He had never known that Mr. Harper's middle name was David. His father had never told him. Nor had his mother. Marseille had never said anything, and he'd never had more than a few brief conversations with Mr. Harper himself. He'd had to read it in an obituary, but in that moment it dawned on him that his parents had named him after the man who had saved their lives. There were no other Davids in the Shirazi family tree. He had been named after Charles David Harper, and now the man was dead.

★ ★ ★ ★ ★

HAMADAN, IRAN

Najjar Malik lay in bed, unable to move.

He had awoken with a fever of 104 and a head that felt like it was going to explode. Sheyda did her best to take care of him all morning. She brought him cold washcloths for his face, stomach, and chest. She fed him spoonfuls of ice chips and cold yogurt. She also contacted their doctor and asked him to come over to their apartment for a house call, which he promptly did. By noon, the doctor had already come and gone, having given Najjar antibiotics to fight off whatever infection was presently coursing through his body.

"Honey," Sheyda said in a whisper, "I'm going to take the baby over to Mother's so there's no risk of her getting sick, okay?"

"You're going to leave me?" Najjar groaned.

"Just for a little bit," she promised. "Just to drop off the baby and have lunch with Daddy. Then I'll be right back. Is there anything I can get you at the store?"

Najjar asked for some ice cream, then closed his eyes and drifted off again. He knew why this was happening but didn't dare tell her. It was because he had watched that program by the Christians. Allah was punishing him, he knew, and he deserved it.

59

It had been too long since he'd had lunch with his daughter.

So despite the enormous responsibilities weighing on him and his team, Dr. Mohammed Saddaji took his precious Sheyda to his favorite restaurant in Hamadan. It was a cozy little place on Eshqi Street, best known for its savory chicken *biryani* and its intimate setting. It was the first restaurant he had taken his wife, Farah, to when they had moved to Hamadan years before, and Saddaji had loved it ever since.

"Thank you so much for having lunch with me, Daddy," Sheyda said as they sat on thick cushions and sipped tea. "I know it isn't easy for you, with your important schedule."

"Come, come, sweetheart," Saddaji replied. "I would do anything for you. You know that, right?"

"Of course, Daddy. Thank you."

"You're welcome," Saddaji said, and then his tired, haggard eyes lit up. "Now guess what?"

"What?"

"I have a surprise for you."

"What is it?"

"I can't simply tell you," he insisted. "What would be the fun in that?"

"Can you give me a hint?"

"For you, of course." He smiled broadly. "As you know, my work is going very well. The Leader is very happy with what I'm doing, and we're about to reach a major breakthrough in the next week or so."

He paused for a moment to let the anticipation build, and it worked. He could see it in his daughter's eyes.

"When that breakthrough occurs," he continued, "your father is going to be promoted, and when I am, I'm told I am going to have the honor of meeting someone you and I have always wanted to meet."

Sheyda's eyes went wide. *"Daddy,"* she whispered with tremendous excitement, *"you don't mean—"*

But he cut her off before she could finish the sentence. "Yes, my dear, but you may not say it aloud, even in a whisper."

"I promise," she said, covering her mouth with her hands. "I'm so sorry."

"There's no need to be sorry, but you must be discreet. After all, you are coming with me."

"I am?"

"Of course," Saddaji said. "How could I keep this honor all to myself?"

"Can Mother come too? and Najjar?" Sheyda asked, barely able to contain herself.

"Yes, yes, I've cleared you all. But it will be just the four of us. I'm told it will be a private meeting. We won't even know where it will be held until the last possible moment."

Sheyda could barely contain herself. *"He's here?"* she whispered. *"He's really here?"*

"That's what I'm told," he replied. "Soon the whole world will know. But they must not learn it from us."

"My lips are sealed; you have my word," Sheyda promised. "And you must forgive me. I don't even know what kind of project you've been working on. I hardly ever see you, and when I do, we just talk about the baby. So what is it, that you are being rewarded with such an incredible honor?"

"That I cannot tell you, my dear. Not just yet. But when he is revealed, all shall become clear. Now, how is motherhood treating you?"

★ ★ ★ ★ ★

MUNICH, GERMANY

David checked his phone messages.

Perhaps Marseille had called. He wanted to hear her voice again. He wanted to call her and tell her how grieved he was for her loss. But there was only one message on his voice mail, and it wasn't from her.

"Hi, David, it's Dad," the message began. "I hope you're doing well. I hope you're not working too hard, though I realize that may be too much to ask. But listen, I'm afraid I have some bad news. Your mother's health has taken a turn for the worse. She's been admitted to the hospital for tests. Could you call me? I'll fill you in then. Love you, Son. Okay, then; bye."

The message was already several days old. A wave of guilt washed over David as he speed-dialed his father's cell phone. Dr. Shirazi answered on the first ring. He was still at the hospital but was glad to hear from David and quick to forgive his son for not returning the call sooner. He told David his mother was resting just then and that it would still be several days until they got the test results.

"They're going to keep her here at Upstate Medical until we know more," he said. "But it would mean a lot to her if you could take a break from all your work and all your travels to come back and see her."

"Dad, I was just there."

"I know, David, but . . ." Dr. Shirazi's voice caught with emotion. "Your mother is a very strong woman, but . . ."

"But what, Dad?"

"You just never know," Dr. Shirazi said. "Please, Son. We need you to come home for a few days. It's important."

David explained that he was leaving Munich the following day for Moscow, Budapest, and Yerevan. He said he was working on major deals and couldn't cancel those trips on such short notice. When it became clear that his father was growing upset with him, David asked if Azad or Saeed could come home to visit her until he could break free of his commitments and get back to Syracuse.

"No," his father said, sadder than David had ever heard him before.

"Why not?"

"They're too busy," he answered curtly. "And your mother isn't asking for them. She's asking for you."

Grieving for his mother, David promised he would find a time to come home as soon as humanly possible. Then he told his father about Marseille's letter and about the wedding she was going to be in.

"So I guess that's a double incentive to get back here in the next few weeks," his father said.

"Mom's all the incentive I need, Dad," David replied. "But yes, it would be good to see Marseille after all this time."

"I'm sure it would," his father said. "Did she happen to mention anything about her father? He's never responded to my calls or letters. I haven't heard from him in years."

David hesitated. He hadn't known Charlie Harper had cut off all communication with his father, just as Marseille had with him. That was disappointing news, and from the tone of his voice, it was clear his father had been hurt. And why wouldn't he have been? The two men had been friends for far longer than he and Marseille had been. That said, he wasn't entirely sure it was the right time to tell his father about Mr. Harper's death. But the man had asked a direct question, and David figured he deserved an honest answer. He told his father as gently as he could that Mr. Harper had recently passed away. He didn't mention how.

The news was an emotional blow. His father was silent for a long time.

"Besides your mother, Charlie was the best friend I ever had," his father finally said, choking back tears. "I never understood why he stopped talking to me after the funeral for Claire. I guess I'll never know."

Hearing the pain in his father's voice made David want to reconnect with Marseille even more urgently. He'd already had so many questions for her. Now he had some more.

Mohammed Saddaji finished eating and paid the bill.

He cherished every moment with his daughter, but it was time to get her home and get himself back to the office. His staff was waiting, and the moment of truth was rapidly approaching.

"Are you ready to go?" he asked, signing the credit card slip and taking one last sip of water.

"Do we have a second for me to freshen up?" Sheyda asked.

The answer was no, but Saddaji couldn't refuse his daughter's requests. "Of course," he said. "I'll go get the car and pull it around front."

"Thanks, Daddy. I'll meet you there in a moment."

Saddaji nodded and sighed, then checked his watch the moment Sheyda headed into the ladies' room. He pulled out his cell phone and checked his messages. There was one from his brother-in-law. That would have to wait, he decided as he speed-dialed his secretary instead. "I'll be there in twenty minutes," he said. "Tell everyone to be ready to meet me in the conference room. We'll go over the final checklist and give out assignments." Then he tossed a few extra coins on the table for a tip and headed outside.

For February, it was actually quite a lovely day. The sun was bright. Only a few stray clouds could be spotted. The air was warmer than usual for this time of year—about fifteen degrees Celsius, Saddaji guessed. But he didn't care about the clouds or the sky or the temperature. He was fixated on the honors that were about to be bestowed upon him.

The irony, he mused as he headed for his car, was that Iran had actually launched its nuclear research program with the help of the United States of America in the 1950s. It wasn't Ayatollah Khomeini who had first fostered the notion of a nuclear-powered Iran. It was President Eisenhower and his "Atoms for Peace" program. It was, however, Khomeini who later clandestinely authorized a military track to run parallel to the civilian track. Since then, Tehran had spent hundreds of billions of *rials* to buy the people, parts, and plans it needed from the French, the Germans, the Russians, the North Koreans, and Pakistan's A. Q. Khan in an effort to establish a viable nuclear weapons program. Iran had spent an even greater fortune building research and production facilities all over the country. Many of them were buried deep underground or beneath mountains, in hopes of hiding them from the prying eyes of U.S. and Israeli spy satellites as well as protecting them from a first strike by either or both.

The crown jewel of the public version of the program—the one they allowed the International Atomic Energy Agency to inspect—was the civilian nuclear power reactor and research facility located in the city of Bushehr, not far from the eastern shoreline of the Persian Gulf. But there were scores of other facilities, from the ten uranium mines scattered across the country, to the Atomic Energy Organization of Iran's Center for Theoretical Physics and Mathematics in Tehran, to the uranium enrichment facility in the city of Natanz, to the plutonium enrichment facility in the city of Arak, to the newly built—but not yet operational—uranium enrichment facility on a military base near Qom, to the facility in Esfahān converting yellowcake uranium into uranium hexafluoride, a critical component in the nuclear fuel cycle, to name just a few.

Saddaji was in charge of them all, including the top-secret facility in Hamadan where the weapons were actually being built. He wasn't doing it for money; they didn't pay him that much. He wasn't doing it for fame; almost no one in the country knew who he was. He was doing it, to be sure, for the intellectual challenge of it all; this was surely the most complex engineering program in which he had ever been involved. But most of all, he was doing it to help Persia once again become a great and mighty empire and to prepare the way for the Mahdi.

Still, despite all of his hard work and sacrifice, it was difficult to imagine that he was actually living in the generation that would see the messiah arrive, much less that he was about to be honored by a personal meeting with the Promised One. As he jangled his keys in his hand, he knew he shouldn't have said anything to Sheyda, certainly not at a public restaurant, but he simply couldn't help himself. He was walking on air. He was dying to tell more people, including his staff. He wouldn't, of course. He knew the risks, and he was proud of himself for his restraint thus far. But he could trust Sheyda. He always had.

Saddaji rounded the corner and spotted his beloved black, two-door Mercedes-Benz CL63 AMG. He could never have afforded it on his director's salary, of course. After all, the car retailed in Europe for more than 100,000 euros. He had never even dreamed of owning such a lavish treasure, but it had been a gift, and who was he to say no? It had been given to him personally the previous year by the Supreme Leader himself after Saddaji and his team had demonstrated that they had successfully brought fifty thousand centrifuges online. The faster the uranium was enriched and the purer it became, the happier and more generous the Ayatollah became, and Saddaji could still remember Hosseini putting the keys in his hands and encouraging him to take a test drive. He had trembled at the very thought and still shook his head in amazement every time he started the engine. The car was a symbol, in so many ways, of how right he had been to leave Iraq and come back home, and a symbol of how successful he had been ever since. And no one deserved such a gift more than he, Saddaji told himself.

He unlocked the car, stepped inside, and closed the door behind him. As he sank into the soft leather seats and ran his hand across the dash, savoring the entire experience—the look, the feel, the smell of this Mercedes—he said a silent prayer, thanking Allah for giving him the great privilege and joy of helping his people, the Shias, build the Bomb.

He sat in the sunshine for a moment and closed his eyes. He tried to imagine the ceremony that was just another week or two away now.

He tried to imagine what it would be like when his eyes saw his Mahdi. But when he put in the key and turned the ignition this time, nothing happened. The car neither started nor sputtered. That was odd, he thought. He pumped the accelerator a few times, and as he turned the key again, the car erupted in a massive explosion of fire and smoke that could be heard on the other side of Hamadan.

61

The phone rang and wouldn't stop.

Najjar's fever was still 102. His head was pounding. He was in severe pain, and he had no intention of getting out of bed to find a phone. But the constant ringing was driving him crazy. The phone would ring eight or ten times, pause for a moment, then ring another eight or ten times, pause again, and repeat the cycle. Someone was desperately trying to get him, but he could barely move. Finally summoning every ounce of energy in his body, Najjar sat up and inched himself to the edge of the bed. The phone kept ringing. He stood, wrapped himself in one of the blankets from the bed, and crawled across the room to the phone sitting on Sheyda's dresser.

"Hello?" he groaned, doing everything he could to suppress a wave of vomiting.

"Is this Najjar Malik?" said a voice at the other end.

"Yes."

"You're the son-in-law of Dr. Mohammed Saddaji?"

"Yes. Why? Who is this?"

"You've been warned," the voice said in Farsi but with a curious foreign accent. "You're next."

The phone went dead.

Suddenly Najjar heard pounding on the apartment door. His head felt like it was in a vise grip constantly being tightened. The pounding at the door wasn't helping. He forced himself up, stumbled down the hallway past the living room, and checked the peephole. It was a police officer. Not security from the research center and not the secret police.

It appeared to be a municipal police officer, so Najjar undid the several locks and opened the door.

"Dr. Malik?" the officer asked.

"Yes, that's me."

"I'm afraid I have terrible news."

"What?" Najjar asked, his knees growing weak.

"It's about your father-in-law," the officer said.

"Dr. Saddaji? What about him?"

"I'm afraid he has been killed."

"*What?* How?"

"I know this will be hard to believe. . . ."

"Tell me."

"At this point, until we complete our investigation, this cannot be repeated," the officer continued.

"Just tell me, please."

"Dr. Malik, I'm very sorry to be the one to tell you this, but I'm afraid your father-in-law was killed by a car bomb."

Najjar staggered backward and had to grab a chair to keep his balance. *"My wife,"* he cried. *"She was with him. Is she okay? Dear Allah, please tell me she's okay."*

"Physically, she's fine," the officer assured him.

"Where is she?"

"She was taken to the hospital to be treated for shock. If you'd like, I can take you to her."

A surge of adrenaline coursed through Najjar's frail body. Suddenly alert and significantly stronger than he had been a moment before, he hurried to his bedroom, dressed quickly, washed his face, brushed his teeth, and went out the door with the officer. Fifteen minutes later, the patrol car was taking a left on Mardom Street and pulling into Bouali Hospital. Najjar ran in and quickly found Sheyda and her mother, Farah, both looking small and lost.

A security detail from the research center was already there protecting the family and had set up a perimeter around the hospital.

The rest of the day was a blur of tears and police investigators and well-wishers and funeral details. According to tradition, the burial had to be completed by sundown, but there was no body, the officer told Najjar privately, away from Sheyda and Farah. Only a few parts had been found, along with some bits of clothing and shoes. Those, Najjar was told, would be gathered, put in a small box, and wrapped in a white shroud.

Soon Dr. Saddaji's secretary arrived at the hospital and began helping Najjar e-mail and text family members, friends, and coworkers, informing them of the death and requesting their presence at the funeral. The head of Najjar's protective detail had just one demand: for reasons of state security, there could be no mention of how Dr. Saddaji had died in any of their private conversations or public communications. Not now. Not at the funeral. Not unless the head of Iran's nuclear power and research agency personally authorized it, and even then, Najjar was informed that Ali Faridzadeh would likely veto such an authorization.

The defense minister? Najjar thought. Until recently, a mention of someone so high up on the food chain would have struck him as bizarre and out of place. But now the pieces of the puzzle were coming together. Najjar no longer had any doubt that his father-in-law had been one of the top nuclear-weapons scientists in Iran, and he had given his life in his ghastly pursuit of killing millions.

Had the Israelis taken him out? Had the Americans or the Iraqis? He would probably never know. But while he mourned on the outside, inside he felt a great sense of relief. This solved a lot of problems, he realized. Maybe this would set back the entire weapons program and forestall a war that otherwise was surely coming soon.

62

MUNICH, GERMANY

While he waited for the phones, David threw himself back into his work.

He grieved for his parents and for Marseille. But there was nothing he could do for any of them at the moment. He had to stop being David and get back to being Reza Tabrizi. He had to get himself ready to go back inside Iran, and that, he was convinced, meant becoming an expert on the Twelfth Imam.

Zalinsky had told him not to get sidetracked. But David couldn't help himself. He simply could not go back into Iran without understanding better who this so-called Islamic messiah was and why people at the highest levels of the Iranian government seemed so focused on his appearance. Something was happening. Something dramatic and historic. Zalinsky didn't get it. But David's instincts told him this was real.

He went hunting for every scholarly work and serious analysis he could possibly find on the Internet, since his search of the database at Langley had turned up little of value. On the third day, David found himself poring over a study published by a Washington think tank in January 2008. It was a bit out-of-date, but it gave him an important context he certainly wasn't getting from anyone at Langley.

> Apocalyptic politics in Iran originates from the failure
> of the Islamic Republic's initial vision. The 1979 Islamic
> Revolution began with a utopian promise to create

heaven on earth through Islamic law and a theocratic
government, but in the past decade, these promises
ceased to attract the masses. Faced with this failure,
the Islamic government has turned to an apocalyptic
vision that brings hope to the oppressed and portrays
itself as an antidote to immoral and irreligious behavior.
This vision, which is regarded as a cure for individual
and social disintegration, appears in a period when the
Islamic Republic does not satisfy any strata of society,
whether religious or secular.

David was intrigued by the notion that "when the Iranian government failed to deliver its promises, many Iranians looked for alterna-
tives and found the cult of the Mahdi—the Messiah or the Hidden
Imam—and its promise to establish a world government." The number of people who claimed to be in direct connection to the Twelfth
Imam or even to be the Mahdi himself, the author noted, had increased
remarkably in recent years in both urban and rural regions.

That certainly rang true to David. His parents had spoken for years
about how desperate Iranians were for a rescue from the failure of the
Islamic Revolution of '79. His father had always stressed the medical
angle. Suicides in Iran, he said, were at an all-time high, not just among
the young but among people of all ages. Drug abuse was a national
epidemic, as was alcoholism. Prostitution and sex trafficking were also
skyrocketing, even among the religious clerics.

Given that David's mother was an educator at heart, she found it
both terribly sad and deeply ironic that Iran's high literacy rates and
increasing access to satellite television and the Internet seemed to exac-
erbate people's despair. Why? Because now, for the first time in fourteen
centuries—and certainly for the first time since Khomeini had come
to power—Iranians could see and hear and practically taste the intellectual, economic, and spiritual freedom and opportunity that people
elsewhere in the world were experiencing. Starved, Iranians were desperately seeking such freedom and opportunity for themselves. Indeed,
they were so desperate for hope that they were opening themselves up

to the deception of thinking it might come from a bottle or a pill or a needle. Was believing in a false messiah just another coping mechanism? David wondered.

The monograph was written by an exiled Iranian journalist by the name of Mehdi Khalaji, a visiting fellow at the Washington Institute for Near East Policy. As David continued reading, he was intrigued by Khalaji's assertion that "the return of the Hidden Imam means the end of the clerical establishment, because the clerics consider themselves as the representatives of the Imam in his absence. Hence, they do not propagate the idea that the Hidden Imam will come soon."

By contrast, Khalaji wrote, "in the military forces . . . apocalypticism has a very strong following." He wrote that an influential group within the Islamic Revolutionary Guard Corps with responsibility over Iran's nuclear program seemed particularly drawn to this fervor for the coming messiah.

That was what worried David most—not that everyone in Iran believed the Twelfth Imam was coming but that the country's top political and military leaders, including those running the country's nuclear weapons program, did.

That said, there was something in Khalaji's assessment that did not ring true. Implicit in the article was the notion that Iran's Supreme Leader was not a true believer in the soon coming of the Twelfth Imam but rather a shrewd political operator seeking to manipulate public opinion. Yet this certainly didn't square with Daryush Rashidi's or Abdol Esfahani's description of the Supreme Leader. Perhaps Hosseini had once been a skeptic, but no longer. As far as David could tell, Hosseini and his inner circle now seemed to see their role as preparing the hearts and minds of the people—and the military—for the coming of the Twelfth Imam.

These beliefs seemed to be driving Iran's nuclear weapons development to a feverish pace, and David wondered how he could persuade Zalinsky they weren't a sideshow. Washington's entire approach toward Iran thus far had been built on trying to engage Ayatollah Hosseini and President Darazi and their regime in direct negotiations while applying escalating economic sanctions and international isolation. It had worked with the Soviets, the Jackson administration argued. Ronald Reagan had engaged Gorbachev in direct negotiations, and the Cold War had ended without a nuclear war, indeed without a shot being fired between the United States and the Soviet Union. Now the administration wanted to take the same approach with the regime in Tehran. But they were wrong. Dead wrong. They were following the wrong historical model, and the results could be disastrous.

David opened a new document on his laptop and began drafting a memo to Zalinsky. He noted that Gorbachev—like all Soviet leaders of his time—was an atheist. Atheists, by definition, believed neither in God nor in an afterlife. So Reagan sought to persuade Gorbachev that any nuclear attack on the U.S. would result in the Gorbachev family's personal annihilation—that Mikhail, his wife, Raisa, and their daughter, Irina, would personally die a horrible, grisly death, that they would be snuffed out like a candle and cease to exist, unable to take their power and money and toys with them. Reagan's theory was that if he could convince Gorbachev that the U.S. policy of "mutual assured destruction" was real and viable, then he could persuade Gorbachev and the Soviet politburo to back off of their nuclear ambitions and truly negotiate for peace. It worked. Realizing there was no way the USSR could win a nuclear war with the technologically advanced West, Gorbachev launched a policy of *glasnost* (openness and transparency) and *perestroika* (restructuring). Eventually the Berlin Wall fell, Eastern Europe was liberated, and the Soviet Union itself unraveled and disintegrated.

By contrast, Hamid Hosseini was not Mikhail Gorbachev, David noted, typing furiously. Hosseini was not a Communist. He was not an atheist. He was a Shia Muslim. He believed in an afterlife. He believed that when he died, he was going to wind up in the arms of seventy-two virgins—not exactly a disincentive for death. Moreover, Hosseini was a Twelver. He was a member of an apocalyptic cult. The man wanted the Mahdi to come. He believed he had been chosen to help usher in the era of the Islamic messiah. He was convinced he needed to build nuclear weapons either to destroy Judeo-Christian civilization himself or to be able to give the Twelfth Imam the capacity to do it. How could the

U.S. successfully negotiate with such a man? How could the West successfully deter or contain him? What could the president of the United States possibly offer or threaten that would persuade Hosseini to give up his feverish pursuit of nuclear weapons? For the Supreme Leader to negotiate with the U.S. would, in his mind, be tantamount to disobeying his messiah and being sentenced to an eternity in the lake of fire. Why didn't Washington understand that? Why were they so consumed and distracted by other issues? Didn't they understand the stakes?

David finished the memo, tagged Eva with a blind copy, hit Send, and immediately wondered if he had done the right thing.

★ ★ ★ ★ ★

HAMADAN, IRAN

Najjar needed to see Dr. Saddaji's files.

He was drained and exhausted from the funeral. He was also still quite ill. He took Sheyda, Farah, and the baby back to the apartment and got them settled in for the night. His mother-in-law was still nearly inconsolable, and Sheyda didn't want her to be all alone that night. But Najjar explained that he could not stay. He had to get back to the office, where Dr. Saddaji's papers and personal effects had to be attended to and secured.

"Can't all that be done tomorrow, Najjar?" Sheyda asked, imploring him to stay with his family.

No, it could not wait, he told her. But the truth was also that he did not want to be home just then. He did not feel remorse for his father-in-law's death, and he didn't have the capacity to fake it for much longer, certainly not in front of two women he truly loved. More importantly, he knew he had to get to Dr. Saddaji's computer, break into it, and find out as much as he could. But Najjar said none of these things to his fragile wife. He simply kissed her and promised to drive safely and get home as quickly as he could.

Reluctantly she let him go, though not without more tears.

To his shock, however, when he got all the way to Dr. Saddaji's office, he found it already heavily guarded by plant security. Boxes full of files were being removed by armed guards. Dr. Saddaji's desktop computer had already been removed, along with his external hard drive. Najjar insisted that he be allowed to review his father-in-law's files and possessions to ensure that the family got what was theirs, but he was quickly introduced to the deputy director of Iranian internal security and told he would simply have to wait.

"Dr. Malik, as you know, your father-in-law was a very powerful, very influential man," said the intelligence official, who explained he had come from Tehran on direct orders from Defense Minister Faridzadeh. "He held many state secrets that the Zionists, the Americans, the British, and frankly all of our enemies would love to get their hands upon. I know you and your family are grieving. But please, give us a few days, and we will send to you everything that is rightfully yours."

Najjar was offended and angry, but he lacked the energy and the will to argue with anyone. Not there. Not then. He was still reeling from the day's events and weak from a fever he hadn't shaken. He had eaten nothing all day. He had barely been able to keep down water; the doctor had had to give him shots because he kept vomiting up the antibiotics he was on.

He excused himself from the intelligence official, went to the men's room, washed the perspiration off his face, and tried to figure out what to do next. He needed to know what Dr. Saddaji had been up to—not in theory but in fact. He needed proof. But he had none, and whatever shred of motivation he'd had to make it through the day was now gone.

63

For more than an hour, Najjar had been suffering dry heaves.

Now, physically and emotionally spent, he exited the building, cleared security, got in his car, and began the forty-five-minute drive home.

Hamadan is a city of concentric circles. At the center is a one-way street running counterclockwise that encircles Imam Khomeini Square. Connecting to this street are six boulevards radiating outward like spokes of a wheel. Each connects to a road that rings the heart of the business and cultural district. Eventually, they connect to a highway that surrounds the entire city, much like the *Boulevard Périphérique* that encircles Paris or the Beltway around Washington, D.C.

Hamadan's airport lies just beyond this outer highway, along the plains to the northeast. To the west lie the foothills of the Zagros mountain range, the largest and most rugged peaks in all of Iran.

Facility 278, the purposefully bland and unassuming name of the nuclear research center that Dr. Saddaji had run for so many years, was located about forty kilometers west of the city center. It was not in the foothills but rather deep in the mountains. Constructed in the early 1990s, the facility was built into the side of an 11,000-foot mountain known as Alvand Peak.

Najjar had always loved the remote location. He loved the long drive to and from work every day. It gave him time to himself, time to think, time to pray, time to enjoy the gorgeous views of the mountains and the valley below. Now, however, as he came down the snowy, ice-clogged service road and felt the winds picking up and a new snow squall beginning to descend on the mountain, he felt trapped. He had no friends, no family to whom he could turn and talk about the situation in which he now found himself. He needed wisdom. He needed someone to tell him what to do and how to do it.

Suddenly, as he came around a hairpin turn, he was practically blinded. It was as if a large truck with its high beams on were coming straight for him, yet something about the light did not seem normal. Najjar slammed on the brakes. His rear wheels began fishtailing. Turning the steering wheel furiously and pumping the brakes rather than locking them down, he tried desperately to regain control. Instead, his car slammed into the mountainside, then skidded toward the embankment and finally came to a halt by thudding hard into the guardrail.

Najjar's heart pounded. He could barely breathe. The light was intense. He squinted behind him and then ahead, hoping there were no other vehicles coming or going. Cautiously, he stepped out of the car to assess the damage and gain his balance.

But just as his feet hit the icy pavement, he saw him. Someone was standing on the road ahead.

As his eyes began to adjust, Najjar saw the man more clearly.

Rather than winter clothes, the man was wearing a robe reaching to his feet. Across his chest was a gold sash. His hair was as white as the snow that surrounded them. His eyes were fiery. His face shone.

Najjar fell at his feet like a dead man, but the figure said, "Do not be afraid."

"Who are you?" Najjar asked shakily.

But the reply shook Najjar even more.

"I am Jesus the Nazarene."

★ ★ ★ ★ ★

MUNICH, GERMANY

David was startled by the knock on the door.

He rubbed his eyes and checked his watch. It was almost 9 p.m. He wasn't expecting anyone. He hardly even knew anyone in the city. Grabbing his Beretta from the drawer of the nightstand by his bed, he disengaged the slide-mounted safety with his thumb and moved cautiously and quietly down the hallway, through the dining room, and to the front door.

Aside from cleaning it, weeks had passed since he had held the pistol in his hands, and his palms were perspiring. He pressed himself against the wall by the door and quickly looked out the peephole. A moment later, he reengaged the safety, though more confused than relieved.

What in the world is Eva doing in Munich?

He opened the door a crack.

"Delivery girl." She smiled.

"I wasn't expecting to see you," he replied.

"I couldn't resist," she said. "May I come in?"

"Of course."

She was toting several large boxes. He hoped they were satellite phones. The first box she handed him upon entering, however, was already open. It was from Amazon and contained Dr. Birjandi's book. Fully awake now, he flipped through it quickly and noticed it was already heavily marked up with yellow highlighter and notes in pen in the margins.

"I stole your book for a few hours," Eva confessed. "It's fascinating. You should read it."

David laughed. "I was hoping to."

"I'm doing some research on Birjandi, working up a profile on him," Eva said. "He's an interesting guy. Noted professor, scholar, and author. He's widely described in the Iranian media as a spiritual mentor or advisor to several of the top leaders in the Iranian regime, including Ayatollah Hosseini. They have dinner once a month. But at eighty-three, the guy is pretty reclusive; he's rarely heard from in public anymore. Until that conference a couple weeks ago, he hadn't given a sermon or speech in years."

"Why the reemergence?" David asked.

"Turn to page 237," Eva replied.

David did and began to read aloud the underlined passage.

"The Mahdi will return when the last pages of history are being written in blood and fire. It will be a time of chaos, carnage, and confusion, a time when Muslims need to have faith and courage like never before. Some say all the infidels—especially the Christians and the Jews—must be converted or destroyed before he is revealed and ushers in a reign characterized by righteousness, justice, and peace. Others say Muslims must prepare the conditions for the destruction of the Christians and the Jews but that the Mahdi will finish the job himself."

David looked up, his heart pounding. "Birjandi thinks he's here."

"That's my guess."

"We need to get this to Zalinsky."

"It's not enough," Eva said. "We need more."

"You said it yourself—Birjandi is Hosseini's advisor. If this is what Birjandi believes, it's got to be what Hosseini believes. Darazi, too."

"I agree," Eva said. "This is what's driving them to get the Bomb. But that's just us guessing. We need proof."

"What kind of proof?"

"I don't know," she conceded. "But more than this."

David sighed. She was right. He looked at the boxes.

"Tell me those are satellite phones," he said.

"They are. Twenty. Government-issue. Military-grade."

"And our friends back at Langley have toyed with them all a bit?"

"Actually, no. Jack was worried the Iranians would find any chip we put into the phones. These particular satphones are the product of a joint venture between Nokia and Thuraya."

"Thuraya—the Arab consortium?"

"Based in Abu Dhabi, right. Long story short, I have people on the inside at Thuraya. They gave me the encryption codes and all the satellite data. I gave them a boatload of money."

"And you're sure the phones all work?"

"My team and I personally tested them this afternoon," she said. "Langley heard everything, loud and clear. We're good to go."

"You're amazing."

"That's true," Eva said, smiling, "but that's not all. I have another gift for you."

"What's that?"

"I booked you on the next flight back to Tehran," she said. "I just e-mailed the itinerary to your phone. It's time to pack, my friend. You're going back in."

64

"I am Jesus the Nazarene," came the man's deep voice.

Najjar felt the sound of it rattle in his chest, as though the words went through him.

"You have come?" Najjar cried. "The lieutenant to the Twelfth Imam has actually revealed himself to me?"

But at these words, the ground below Najjar shook so violently that he feared it would open and swallow him. Rocks skittered across the road from ledges above. The wind picked up strength. Najjar flattened himself on the ground, covering his head with his hands.

"*I AM* first and last and the living One," Jesus said. "I am the Alpha and the Omega, who is and who was and who is to come, the Almighty. I was dead, and see, I am alive forever after, and I have the keys of death and of hades. Come and follow me."

The first sentences were uttered with authority such as Najjar had never heard before, not from any mullah or cleric or political leader in his entire life. Yet the last four words were spoken with such gentleness, such tenderness, that he could not imagine refusing the request.

Shaking, Najjar cautiously looked up. Though he was wrapped in a thick parka over his blue jeans and sweater, he felt completely naked, as if all of his private sins were exposed to the light and the elements. For as long as he could remember, he'd had a deep reverence for Jesus. Like his father and his grandfather and his great-grandfather before him, going back fourteen centuries, Najjar believed Jesus was born

327

of a virgin. He believed Jesus was a doer of miracles and a speaker of great wisdom and thus a prophet. But not God Himself. Never. And yet . . .

Jesus stretched out His hands and motioned for Najjar to come closer. Part of him wanted to run and hide, but before he knew it, he was taking several steps forward.

As he drew closer, Najjar was astonished to see holes where spikes had been driven through Jesus' hands. He looked away for a moment, but then, unable to keep his head turned, he looked back and stared at those hands. As a devout Muslim, Najjar had never for a moment in his life even considered the possibility that Jesus had been crucified at all, much less to pay the penalty for all human sins, as the Christians taught. He had never believed that Jesus had actually died on a cross. No Muslim believed that. It was sacrilege. To the contrary, Najjar (and everyone he had ever known) believed that at the very last moment, Allah had supernaturally replaced Jesus with Judas Iscariot, and Judas had been hung on the cross and crucified instead.

Questions flooded his mind.

How could Jesus be appearing to him as a crucified Messiah?

If the Qur'an were true, wouldn't it be impossible for Jesus to have nail-scarred hands?

If the ancient Islamic writings about the Twelfth Imam were true, then how could Jesus, who was supposed to be the Mahdi's lieutenant, have hands scarred by the nails of crucifixion?

Najjar kept staring at those hands. It didn't make sense. Then he looked into Jesus' eyes. They were not filled with anger and condemnation. They spoke of love in a way Najjar couldn't even comprehend, much less express. And Jesus' words echoed in his heart. He wasn't claiming to be the second-in-command to the Mahdi. He claimed to be God Almighty.

"Forgive me; please forgive me," Najjar said, bowing low. "But how can I know the difference between Muhammad and You?"

"You have been told, 'Love your neighbor and hate your enemy,'" Jesus replied. "But I tell you, love your enemies and pray for those who persecute you."

The words cut into Najjar's heart like a knife. This was an enormous difference between the two.

"Don't be angry with me, O Lord," Najjar stammered, "but I am so confused. All my life I was raised a Muslim. How can I know which way to go?"

"I am the Way. And the Truth and the Life," Jesus said. "No one can come to the Father except through Me."

"But my heart is full of sin," Najjar said. "My eyes are full of darkness. How could I ever follow You?"

"I am the Light of the World," Jesus replied. "Whoever follows Me will not walk in darkness. That person will have the light of life."

Najjar knew he was experiencing something extraordinary. At the same time, he was genuinely in agony. Was Jesus telling him that everything he had ever been taught was wrong? that his life had been on the wrong path up to this very moment? that it had been completely worthless? It was too much to bear. He began to formulate sentences but could not find a way to finish them.

Yet as Najjar looked into the eyes of Jesus, he sensed deep in his spirit that Jesus knew every thought he had, every fear, every question, and loved him anyway. He wanted to move toward Jesus but could not. Yet at that moment, Jesus walked toward him.

"God loved the world so much that He gave His only begotten Son," Jesus said. "Whoever believes in Him will never die but instead have eternal life. For God did not send His Son into the world to judge it, but that the world might be saved through Him. Whoever believes in Him is not judged; but whoever doesn't believe has been judged already, because he has not believed in the name of the only begotten Son of God."

Najjar just stood there in the snow. He had never read any of this in the Qur'an. But he knew it was true. And suddenly, irresistibly, Najjar fell to the ground and kissed the scarred feet of Jesus.

"*O Lord, open my eyes!*" Najjar sobbed. "*Help me! I am a wicked and sinful man, and I am undone—lost in the darkness, lost and alone. Open my eyes that I may see.*"

"Do you believe I am able to do this?" Jesus asked.

"Yes, Lord."

"Then follow Me," Jesus said.

At that, something inside Najjar broke. He wept with remorse for all the sins he had committed. He wept with indescribable relief that came from knowing beyond the shadow of a doubt that God really did love him and had sent Jesus to die on the cross and rise from the dead, thus proving that He really was the truth and the life and the only way to the Father in heaven. He wept with gratitude that because of Jesus' promise, he could *know* that he was going to spend eternity with Jesus.

He bowed before his Savior and Lord, weeping and rejoicing all at once for what seemed to be hours. How long it really was, he had no idea. But then he heard Jesus speaking to him again.

"If you love Me, you will keep My commandments. I have many more things to say to you, but you cannot bear them now. Remember, I am coming quickly!"

And with that, He was gone.

Suddenly, all was as it had been before—dark and windy and cold. Yet not all was the same. In that moment, Najjar Malik realized that he was not the same man he had been when he woke up that morning. Mysteriously, miraculously, something inside him had changed. How he would explain it to Sheyda or to his mother-in-law, he had no idea. But he felt a peace emanating from so deep within him it made no logical sense.

Najjar got back in his car, turned on the engine, and carefully headed down the mountain in the snow and ice. Only then did he realize that his fever was gone.

His mobile phone rang. It was Sheyda. She was up to feed the baby. She was asking him if he was okay, asking if he could stop by her parents' apartment to pick up some things for her mother. Najjar was so happy to hear Sheyda's voice, he would have said yes to almost anything she asked him.

But then a thought occurred to him. He wondered if Dr. Saddaji's laptop was still in his home office and if it contained any of the information he was hoping to find. What's more, he wondered if the authorities had been to his father-in-law's home yet.

Najjar hit the accelerator and prayed for the first time in his life to a nail-scarred Messiah.

65

Najjar struck oil.

Sitting on the desk in his father-in-law's home office was Saddaji's Sony VAIO laptop. Right next to it was a one-hundred-gigabyte external hard drive. Beside that was a stack of DVD-ROMs that Dr. Saddaji apparently used to back up his computer.

Najjar quickly gathered his mother-in-law's toothbrush, makeup, and the other assorted toiletries she had requested, along with all of her husband's electronics, and headed for his car. He didn't dare sift through it all now, for he fully expected plant security and intelligence officials to descend on the apartment at any moment.

Just before he turned the ignition, Najjar remembered what the police had told him about how Dr. Saddaji had died. Then he recalled the words of the mysterious caller: *You're next.* He was suddenly frightened again. Was he being followed? by his own security forces? by the Israelis? or even the Americans? Had they just planted a bomb in his car? He began trembling again.

But then he heard a voice and recognized it immediately.

"Do not fear them. There is nothing covered up that will not be revealed, nothing hidden that will not be known. What I tell you in the darkness, speak in the light; and what you hear whispered in your ear, proclaim upon the housetops."

Najjar wasn't sure whether he had heard an audible voice or whether the Lord had simply spoken to him in his spirit. But once again a peace he couldn't explain immediately came over him, and Najjar was no longer afraid. He turned the ignition without hesitation. The car started without a problem.

As he drove, Najjar again heard the voice of the Lord. *"Now you must leave this city. The Lord will rescue you. He will redeem you from the grip of your enemies."*

Racing toward home, Najjar was troubled by this message. *Leave this city? Why? To where?* He had been a follower of Jesus for less than an hour, but he knew his Shepherd's voice, and he was determined to follow Him wherever He led. Clearly Jesus wanted him to take his family and leave Hamadan. But how in the world would he explain all this to Sheyda and Farah? He had no idea, but Najjar clung passionately to the command of Jesus. He was not to succumb to fear. He was to live by faith in the One who had conquered the grave and who held the keys to death and hades in His own hands. *It will be okay,* he told himself. *Somehow it will be okay.*

It was nearly four in the morning when Najjar finally got home. He decided he would take his family to Tehran—as good a destination as any, he supposed. They could find a hotel there easily enough. He knew that the distance from Hamadan to Tehran was about three hundred and fifty kilometers—a five-hour drive. He had driven it a thousand times. They could be there for breakfast if they left quickly. That was the easy part. The hard part would be persuading the women to go.

Najjar entered the apartment as quietly as he could. He expected the lights to be off, but they were on. He expected his wife and mother-in-law to be sound asleep, but to his shock, they were lying prostrate on the floor of the living room.

Upon hearing the door open, Sheyda jumped up, ran to him, and hugged him as she never had before. Her eyes were red. Her makeup was running. She had obviously been crying, but that was to be expected. What wasn't expected were the words she spoke next.

"He appeared to us, too, Najjar," she whispered in his ear. "We're packed and ready to go. I'll get the baby. Meet us in the car."

★ ★ ★ ★ ★

It was 7 a.m., and Esfahani cursed Mina under his breath.

As his hired driver snaked the Mercedes through the streets of Hamadan, crowded with shopkeepers beginning their day, Esfahani wondered why in the world she had made these travel arrangements. Didn't she ever think about the difficulty of heading to the airport in the thick of morning traffic? Didn't he pay her to anticipate these details and make his life as comfortable as possible?

If she'd been smart and booked a later flight, he could have slept longer and waited until the roads cleared. Instead, the driver had picked him up at his family home southeast of Bu-Ali Sina University at 6:30 and was now winding along the edges of Lona Park and onto the ring road heading north and then east toward the airport. He wished he'd paid attention to the itinerary yesterday and demanded she change the ticket. *Foolish woman!* Perhaps it was time to fire her.

The previous day had been consumed with his large extended family and the business of Dr. Saddaji's funeral. Saddaji was the brother-in-law of his friend and boss, Daryush Rashidi, and their families had known each other for generations. And given the man's prominence in the world of science and energy, it was a fairly elaborate funeral, despite the fact that there was no body to speak of to bury. Esfahani went to the funeral in deference to Rashidi, but now he was anxious to return to Tehran and his work. He would not stay for *hafteh*, the seventh-day visitation of the grave. He wasn't that close to the man, tragic though his death was.

The car came to a stop as it approached the northern edge of the city, and Esfahani looked out the window to see why.

"There's a problem ahead, sir," the driver explained. "Maybe an accident. It will take me just a few minutes to get to the turnoff, but then we'll take an alternate route. Please forgive me, sir; I heard no warning about this delay."

Ten minutes later they turned onto a side road and headed toward the center of the city. Esfahani hoped the driver knew what he was doing.

As if reading his mind, the man explained, "I'm going to the inner ring road and then will try to circle around to the north. The traffic should ease up, sir. I beg your forgiveness."

"I don't care how you get there," Esfahani snapped. "I just don't want to miss this flight." He wasn't fully awake, and the last thing he needed was a detailed description of their route.

He looked outside and sighed heavily. He was proud of his birthplace, the most ancient of Iran's cities and a cradle of poetry, philosophy, and science. But right now, he wished he were asleep. It had been a busy few days, and time spent with his family was never peaceful. He longed for the solitude of his apartment in Tehran, far away from the domestic drama of his mother and her many siblings.

He closed his eyes and tried to remember the poetry he'd memorized as a youth. The great scientist and poet Ibn Sina, whose tomb was one of the proudest possessions of their city, had written, "Up from Earth's Centre through the Seventh Gate, I rose, and on the Throne of Saturn sate, and many Knots unravel'd by the Road, but not the Master-knot of Human Fate."

He had just begun to drift off when he felt a deep shudder beneath him and the car rising up and lurching forward. His eyes now wide open, Esfahani saw the earth outside his window moving like the waves of the sea. He saw an apartment building to his left rock and sway and then collapse before him.

"Hold on, sir! I don't know what is happening! Oh, save us, Allah!" the driver cried, calling out to heaven and trying to reassure his wealthy passenger at the same time.

The Mercedes pitched and heaved on the writhing pavement and then slammed down violently, crashing headlong into a telephone pole. As if in slow motion, Esfahani saw the pole snap in two and start falling back toward the car. There was no time to run and nowhere to hide. Esfahani covered his head and face with his arms, and an instant later, the pole slammed down across the front of their car, crushing his driver and sending glass and blood everywhere.

Terrified, Esfahani scrambled out of the backseat of the car, only to hear the rumbling of the massive earthquake intensifying. The road shook violently. People were running and screaming everywhere. Esfahani searched for a place to take cover but found none. He looked to his left and saw more houses and office buildings collapsing. To his right he saw a long cement wall, roughly two meters high, gyrating wildly as if alive. And then, as he watched in horror, helpless to do anything, he saw the wall collapse atop a woman and her baby.

Finally, after what seemed like several minutes, the ground stopped shaking. But the screaming from all sides of him grew louder and wilder. The air was rapidly filling with debris and clouds of dust. People were running through the streets, crazed with panic. They looked like ghosts, covered in white powder. Esfahani pulled out his cell phone, but there was no signal. What was he supposed to do?

He felt dizzy as he walked slowly toward the side of the road and the fallen wall, choking on dust. He slumped to the ground and closed his eyes tightly to shut out the chaos around him.

"Save me, Allah, most merciful!" he cried. "Show me what to do, where to go!"

When he opened his eyes again, he saw several men from a nearby construction site trying desperately to move massive slabs of concrete off the woman and her screaming child. They were calling for help to anyone who could hear them, calling for people to help move the rubble and try to save these people's lives.

At that moment, Esfahani felt a strong hand on his shoulder. He prayed it was a medical worker, a policeman, someone of use to him, but as he looked up, he met the eyes of a young mullah. The man had an urgency in his expression, but not fear, not confusion.

"I am here," he said.

The mullah quickly joined the workers heaving pieces of cement and rebar from the sidewalk, and as they did, they were able to pull the baby out first and then her mother. Remarkably, the child was relatively unscathed, but Esfahani turned away in disgust when he saw the woman's legs twisted gruesomely behind her and covered in blood. Yet the young holy man did not turn away. Rather, Esfahani watched in shock as the mullah knelt next to the woman while she wept with despair.

"You are a righteous daughter," he said.

"Help me!" she cried. "I can't move! I can't feel anything below my waist!"

The mullah began to speak in what sounded to Esfahani's ears like an ancient language, in a mesmerizing tone that seemed almost like poetry. Then the mullah took the woman's hands in his and lifted her gently to her feet. A crowd had formed, but now—stunned—people began to back away.

"She's walking!" someone exclaimed.

"He healed her!" another yelled.

Realizing it was true, that her crushed legs had suddenly been restored to normal and that even the bleeding had stopped and the ugly gashes had disappeared, the woman began crying all the more. Then she fell at the man's feet, praising him and thanking him for saving her.

"Walk in righteousness, daughter," the young man said, kissing her baby on the head and giving the child back to the woman. "And tell everyone you know that I am come, the long-awaited One, the Miraculous."

"Praise to the Prince of Mercy!" the woman cried out in ecstasy. *"It is our Imam! The Twelfth Imam! The Mahdi has come, blessed be he!"*

Esfahani stared at the scene in awe. He *had* come. He was standing right before them. Esfahani began to shout praises as well, and then the Mahdi unexpectedly turned to him, smiled, and placed his hand upon Esfahani's head, causing him to bow low in prayer. But when Esfahani lifted his eyes again, the Twelfth Imam was gone.

66

Just before dawn, David's mobile phone rang.

He was still awake, reading Dr. Birjandi's book cover to cover. He took the call and found Eva on the line asking him if he'd heard about the massive earthquake that had just hit northwestern Iran. David hadn't but immediately turned on his TV.

The epicenter of the quake, he soon learned, was not far from the city of Hamadan in the north of the country. Already, officials for Iran's Red Crescent emergency relief services were estimating at least three thousand people were dead and more than twenty thousand wounded. Yet just by watching the devastation in the early video images being beamed out of the ancient city, it was clear to David that the casualty figures were going to climb throughout the day. Eva said she was already in touch with the MDS technical crew in Tehran. None of them had been affected, and her team at the MDS operations center in Dubai was in the process of contacting their families to reassure them that they were all right.

"I have an idea," David said.

"What's that?"

"Find out if the muckety-mucks upstairs would be willing to set up a relief fund to care for families of the survivors in Hamadan. Maybe if Iran Telecom does something, we could provide matching funds."

"That's a great idea," Eva said.

But David wasn't done. "What if we let Rashidi and Esfahani know that if they'd be willing to run the fund—set it up, decide who gets

337

the money, that kind of thing—that they can keep 10 percent as an administrative fee?"

"That could be hundreds of thousands of dollars," Eva said.

"Exactly."

"Can they be bought that easily?"

"I think they can, as long as they don't think that they're being bought," David said. "They have to think it's simply money they're due for a job well done. What do you think?"

"It's brilliant," Eva said and hung up.

An hour later, she was back on the phone. She had reached the CEO of Munich Digital Systems at a conference in Singapore. He loved the idea and had already committed to put five million euros into the account. David was impressed with her persuasiveness.

Then it was David's turn. It took several attempts, but after a few hours he reached Esfahani on his cell phone. The man seemed out of breath with what David perceived as excitement rather than the stress he had anticipated.

"Most systems are down," Esfahani explained. "We've got crews working on things already, but I'm still amazed you got through. You must come to Hamadan immediately. I have seen him—he is here!"

"Who is here?" David asked cautiously.

"The Mahdi, of course! Who else? Reza, I tell you I saw him with my own eyes. He touched me; he spoke to me. I saw him do a miracle! Where are you right now?"

David explained that he was leaving Germany for Iran that afternoon. He also explained that MDS had established a fund to help the survivors of the earthquake in Hamadan.

Esfahani was deeply moved and was astonished when David suggested the generous offer of compensation. He agreed immediately, but with one condition.

"What's that?" David asked.

"Mr. Rashidi need not be burdened with this project, as honorable as it is," Esfahani said. "I don't think we should ask him to administer the fund. It would be too much. It would be a great honor to handle it myself."

It never ceased to amaze David how well hard, cold cash worked in the world of intelligence. "That's fine with me," he said.

"I'll have a bank account in Tehran set up by the end of the day," Esfahani offered, "then get you the SWIFT code so you can wire the money."

"Great," David said. "As for the gifts you asked me to pick up, where do you want me to bring them, and how do I get them into the country without drawing attention to myself?"

"You have twenty already?" Esfahani asked in surprise.

"You said it was important."

"Listen, you mustn't wait to come," Esfahani said. "Mina will meet you at baggage claim in Tehran. She'll clear you through customs and take you to the person who should receive the gifts. I'll call her right now."

★ ★ ★ ★ ★

EN ROUTE TO TEHRAN

Najjar knew nothing about the earthquake.

To let the baby sleep, he and Sheyda didn't have the radio on as they drove east along Route 48 toward Tehran. Instead, Sheyda talked nonstop about what had happened to her mother and her while Najjar had been out that night.

She began by explaining they had forced themselves to do their evening prayers, even though they were just going through the motions. With everything that had happened, she said, they had lost all faith in Allah and all faith in Islam. Then Jesus appeared to them in the living room, scaring them half to death. They compared notes with Najjar on how Jesus looked, what He sounded like, and what He told them, and it was amazing how similar their experiences had been.

"The first thing He said was, 'Fear not, little children,'" Sheyda recalled. "Then he said, 'I have loved you with an everlasting love. Therefore, I have drawn you with lovingkindness. I know the plans I have for you—plans for good, not for evil; plans to give you a future and a hope. Come and follow Me.'"

"What did you say?" Najjar asked.

"What could I say?" Sheyda replied. "I said yes!"

"Weren't you scared?"

"Jesus told me not to be."

"Weren't you worried about what I would say?"

"A little, but what could I do? I suddenly had a mere glimpse of just how much Jesus loved me, and I couldn't resist."

Najjar turned to his mother-in-law. "What about you? Your husband was awaiting the Mahdi."

"So was I," Farah replied.

"Then what did you say to Jesus?"

"I said yes!"

"But why?"

"Why did you?" she asked.

Najjar thought about that. "I knew He was telling me the truth."

"So did I," Farah said. "I knew it in my soul."

"Why do you think He came to us, of all people?"

"I don't know," Sheyda said. "But Jesus did say, 'You did not choose Me, but I chose you and appointed you to go and bear fruit, and that your fruit would remain, so that whatever you ask of the Father in My name He may give to you.'"

"I asked, 'What should we do?'" Farah said, smiling at the memory and savoring each precious word. "He said, 'Be strong and very courageous. Be careful to do all that I command you. My words shall not depart from your mouth, but you shall meditate on them day and night, so that you may carefully follow them; for then you will make your way prosperous, and then you will have success. Do not tremble or be dismayed, for the Lord your God is with you wherever you go.'"

For the next half hour, they discussed the meaning of these words. Was Jesus asking them to speak publicly about what they had seen and heard? They knew all too well the risks involved. Telling anyone in Iran that they had left Islam and become followers of Jesus Christ as the One True God—the *only* way to heaven—would lead to their arrest, torture, and possibly execution. Of this they had no doubt. Yet Farah reminded them that Jesus had told them not to be afraid but to follow His words carefully.

"We need a Bible," Sheyda said.

Najjar agreed but wondered aloud where they were likely to find one—in Tehran of all places. The two women had no idea, but they immediately bowed their heads and asked the Lord to give them a Bible, in Farsi if possible. Then they concluded by saying, "We ask these things, O Father, in the name of Jesus Christ, our Savior and our great God and King." They half expected a Bible—or Jesus Himself—to appear immediately, but nothing happened. Still, they all had peace that He would provide for them soon.

For now, however, Najjar had a somewhat-vexing question.

"What are we to believe about the Twelfth Imam?" he asked. "I have seen him myself. I have met him at least twice. He told me the future. He told me that I would marry you, Sheyda, when there was absolutely no prospect of that happening. He told me other things that have come true. How could the Mahdi tell the future if he is not the messiah? How could the Mahdi do miracles if he is not from God? I'm not saying I don't believe Jesus. I do. But I admit I'm confused, and if we were ever to say any of this publicly . . ."

"You mean, *when* we speak of this publicly," Sheyda gently corrected him.

Najjar was amazed by how deep his wife's faith had grown so quickly. "Right—*when* we speak of this publicly, people will ask me about the Twelfth Imam, and I don't know how to respond."

"Jesus told us something about that," Sheyda said.

"What do you mean?" Najjar asked.

"He said something about that," Sheyda repeated. "What was that, Mother? You wrote it down, right?"

"I did," Farah said, pulling a small notepad out of her pocketbook and passing it from the backseat, where she was sitting beside the baby, to her daughter, who was sitting in the front beside Najjar. "There, on the third page."

Sheyda scanned her mother's scribblings to find the line she was thinking of. "That's right. Jesus told us to read Exodus chapter 7 and Deuteronomy chapter 13."

"What are those?" Najjar asked.

"We're not sure yet," Sheyda admitted. "We're guessing they're in the Bible."

The three continued talking about their encounters with Jesus until they reached the outskirts of Tehran. Unsure where the Lord wanted them to go, how long they were supposed to be there, or what they were supposed to do, they prayed for wisdom, then pulled into a small motel near the Mehrabad Airport. Sheyda needed to nurse the baby. Najjar decided to use the time to shower. Farah needed to rest a bit.

But no sooner had Najjar stepped into the hot shower and begun thanking the Lord for His kindness and His mercies than he heard Sheyda cry out. He scrambled to turn off the water, wrapped himself in a towel, and bolted out of the washroom. He found his wife sitting in a chair, feeding the baby, and properly covered, but she had turned on the television to discover news of an earthquake that had struck their city not long after they had left. The images were shocking. Entire buildings and neighborhoods had been flattened. Major bridges and highways had crumbled and collapsed like sand castles. Newscasters said the death toll had now risen past six thousand. Countless other people were wounded, and emergency workers were responding from all over northwestern Iran.

This was why Jesus had commanded them to leave the city immediately, Najjar knew. He was leading them as a family, just as He had promised.

Sheyda picked up her cell phone and called their next-door neighbor at their apartment building, but there was no answer. She called another neighbor. Again, no answer. She called six more neighbors. None of them answered.

Farah called Dr. Saddaji's secretary, who lived in an apartment building around the corner from them. It took many rings, but the woman finally came to the phone. Farah put the phone on speaker so Najjar and Sheyda could hear the woman's news. She was safe but weeping for those less fortunate. And now she rejoiced to know that Farah was still alive. She'd known Farah had decided to spend the night at Najjar and Sheyda's, and she told Farah that the Maliks' apartment building had completely collapsed during the quake. Not a single resident who had been in the building was thought to have survived.

"Why weren't you asleep in your beds like everyone else when the quake struck?" the secretary asked.

Farah explained that the family had gone to Tehran for a few days to grieve in private. It wasn't a lie, though it wasn't the whole truth, either.

"Did you have a premonition?" the secretary asked.

Farah clearly wasn't sure what to say to that. "We just wanted to be alone," she finally said.

"Allah was truly looking out for you. You and your family should all be dead right now."

★　★　★　★　★

MUNICH, GERMANY

David paced in the waiting area of the Munich airport.

He had checked his luggage and cleared through security and passport control; now he watched continuing coverage of the earthquake in Hamadan as he waited for his flight to Tehran. As boarding began, he pulled out his phone and decided to check one more time to see if there were any messages on the phone back in his apartment. There was nothing. But when he checked his AOL account, there was an e-mail from Marseille.

Hi, David,

Thanks so much for your voice mail and your kind words about my father. I thought I might not hear from you at all, so I have to say I was relieved to know that you simply hadn't received my letter until recently. I was worried you were mad at me for not being in touch with you and your family for all these years. It must have seemed like we ceased to exist. In some ways, we did.

I've never been quite sure how to apologize, but I've come to the conclusion face-to-face would be better than e-mail or a note or a phone call. So thanks for being willing to get together with me.

I feel like this wedding being in Syracuse and my friend's insistence that I be there are part of God's plan for you and me to meet again.

Do you ever think about those days in Canada, before the world spun out of control? Sometimes I think they were just a wonderful dream I had, but then I am reminded that they were very much real. In fact, I think they were some of the most real days of my life. How did so much time pass so quickly? Who have you become?

Well, I guess you've become a successful international business-man, for one. Congratulations. Even as a girl, I think I always knew you were going to be very successful at whatever you did. Thanks for taking time to call me from overseas. I know you must be very busy, but it meant so much to me that you called. It has given me a bit more courage.

Write to me, if you'd like. I miss your friendship, and I know it's my fault. I'll be there in Syracuse. I'll be the one who's shaking in her boots a bit. :)

Your friend,
Marseille

P.S. Unless you'd like to go somewhere else, let's meet at the downtown Starbucks on M Street. I'll be there by 8 p.m. that Thursday. See you then.

67

David landed in Tehran shortly after 6 a.m.

He had spent far too much time on the flight thinking about Marseille's e-mail. He had wanted a diversion, any diversion, from the enormous stresses upon him. But this was more than a diversion. It was a reconnection, and it stirred deep emotions long held back.

He was glad to hear from her again, of course. He wasn't sure what to make of her idea that God had "a plan" for the two of them to meet again, but he liked the warm and even, at times, awkward tone of her e-mail. He liked that she missed their friendship and was willing to say so, and he was surprised but pleased by how much she wanted to see him again. Most of all, though, he deeply appreciated her apology and the hint that more was coming when they met in person. That meant more to him than anything else. The smiley face at the end made him chuckle; it seemed so childlike, as if the teenage Marseille were writing to him from the past.

For whatever reason, and at the most unexpected time, the ice was melting between them. And it turned out she did think about their time together in Canada. They had made a terrible mistake, he knew. They should never have gone as far as they did. He had always hoped she didn't hold it against him. But until now, he'd never had a shred of evidence that she had cherished all their time together as he had. To the contrary, the years of silence had sown years of doubt in his mind and heart. How could he not assume that she regretted their friendship? How could he not assume she was embarrassed for having ever liked him, even for such a brief time, and had chosen to put him out of her mind and move on with her life? Why else would she have become so cold so fast? He had been certain of such things for a long time. But he'd been wrong. In the blink of an eye, he had learned that she had never regretted their friendship but had actually valued it for all these years.

David tried to gather his emotions as the plane taxied to the gate. He wished he were back in Munich and could call her again. But it was not to be—not yet, anyway. And he had no idea when the opportunity would come.

As much as he wanted to meet Marseille in Syracuse, the truth was he was having a hard time imagining a scenario that would allow that to happen. He had given his life to the Central Intelligence Agency. They had sent him to Iran. The stakes for his country and for the world couldn't be higher. There was no guarantee he would live through today, much less until the first weekend in March. And even if he did, how exactly was he supposed to tell Jack Zalinsky and Eva Fischer he needed to take off a long weekend to see his first love?

Once again, he told himself he had to shift gears. His life depended on it. He could no longer afford to think like David Shirazi, or he would put at risk everything he had worked so long and so hard to achieve. And so, hard as it was, he forced himself to stop thinking about Marseille and instead to think about her mother. Radical Islamic mujahideen had murdered Claire Harper and 2,973 other people while the CIA slept.

He put on his game face.

68

Mina met him at baggage claim, as promised.

After David cleared customs, Mina introduced him to their driver, a bored young man who took David's bag and carried it to the car.

"Have you heard from Mr. Esfahani?" David asked as they headed for the parking garage. "He and his team must have their hands full trying to get mobile service up and running again."

"It's been a nightmare; that's true," Mina said. "At least he was there when it happened."

"Who?" David asked.

"Mr. Esfahani."

"He was already in Hamadan?"

"Yes."

"He went there before it happened?"

"Strange, huh?"

"It is," David said. "Why did he go?"

"He was there to attend a funeral for Mr. Rashidi's brother in-law."

"He could have been killed himself."

"Actually, several members of the funeral party were killed when their hotel partially collapsed."

"But Mr. Rashidi is okay?"

"Yes, praise Allah, he's fine," she said. "But everyone is devastated. It's just too much to take in all at once."

Mina got in the backseat, motioning for David to sit in the front with the driver, then explained that they were going to meet a young man named Javad Nouri, who would be given fifteen of the phones. When David asked who Nouri was, however, and where the remaining five phones would go, Mina became noticeably uncomfortable.

"I really can't say," she apologized.

Forty minutes later, they pulled up to a coffee shop.

"Park here on the side street," David directed the driver. "I'll bring him out to get the phones."

"Shouldn't I go with you?" Mina asked.

"Why? Do you know what this Nouri guy looks like?" he asked.

"Well, no, but—"

David cut her off. "Just wait here. I'll only be a few minutes."

He got out of the car empty-handed, entered the café, and went to the back by the restrooms. There he found a young man in his mid-twenties, smoking a cigarette and pacing nervously. That was Nouri, David thought, but he decided not to rush into things. He took a seat in a booth, his back to the wall. Behind the counter a television was on, showing coverage of the crisis in Hamadan.

"Rescue workers continue to struggle to clear rubble and bodies from the streets of Hamadan, where a government official said the death toll from this 8.7-magnitude earthquake may exceed ten thousand, with more than thirty-five thousand wounded," an Iranian newscaster reported from the epicenter of the flattened city. "Thousands of injured people are still waiting for care outside badly damaged hospitals, while an unknown number remain trapped inside collapsed buildings. Basic services like water and electricity are out, and the mayor says his government needs help clearing streets so rescuers can reach some of the hardest-hit areas."

"*Help us!*" one woman shrieked, holding her dead baby. "*We have no water! We have no food! Help us! Someone, please help us!*"

"Rescuers are digging though the rubble of leveled buildings with their hands, looking for survivors or bodies," the reporter continued. "But I must tell you, I have never seen devastation like this. Whole blocks of collapsed buildings. Bodies in the streets. And officials say they fully expect the death toll to soar throughout the coming days. International expressions of sympathy are pouring in."

The Iranian newscast cut to a clip of the White House press secretary.

"President Jackson and the First Family have been deeply moved by the images of suffering coming out of the Iranian city of Hamadan, as have many Americans and people of goodwill," the spokeswoman said. "The Jackson administration would like to extend its hand of friendship to the Iranian people. We currently have two U.S. planes filled with food, winter clothing, blankets, and other aid on the tarmac in Incirlik, Turkey. With the permission of the Iranian government, we can have those aircraft on the ground in Hamadan in a matter of hours."

The young man with the cigarette cursed the U.S. offer. "Our people are martyrs," he said to no one in particular. "They are martyrs for the cause. Allah will have mercy on their souls. We don't need the Great Satan's help. Curse Jackson. Curse them all."

David recoiled, but he wasn't about to defend the American government in a coffee shop in downtown Tehran. "Well, I don't know about martyrs," he said to the young man, "but you're right about the Great Satan. Let the Americans all burn in hell."

"But they *are* martyrs," the young man said.

"Not everyone who dies tragically is a martyr," David said.

"But these are. They died preparing the way for the Lord of the Age, peace be upon him."

David stood and approached the young man. The Kolbeh Café was popular and beginning to fill up with the breakfast crowd.

"Are you Javad Nouri?"

"Are you Reza Tabrizi?"

"I am."

"Do you have the gifts our friend asked for?"

"I do."

"Where are they?"

"In the car, in the alley."

"Lead the way," Nouri said.

David complied, leading the man out to the car. He instructed the driver to pop the trunk and stay in the car.

"Are they clean?" Nouri asked.

David assured him that they were bug-free.

"Good. That will be all," Nouri said.

A moment later a car pulled up behind them. Two men got out, took the boxes of satphones, put them in their own trunk, and departed, Javad Nouri with them. David memorized the license plate. He got back into his car, turned to Mina, and asked, "Now what?"

Mina explained that Esfahani had left a large envelope of cash for the phones in his safe and directed their driver to take them back to the Iran Telecom offices.

Once there, they headed into Esfahani's office, and David waited for Mina to open the safe.

"Here you go," she said, finally handing him a zippered cloth bag with a manila envelope stuffed inside. "You can count it if you'd like."

"That's okay," he said, smiling. "I trust you."

Mina adjusted her headscarf and looked away.

The phones were ringing off the hook, not just in Esfahani's office but throughout the technical support department. Everyone was abuzz with the earthquake in Hamadan and with the Herculean efforts the company was expending to get wireless service for the northwest quadrant of the country back up and running.

Mina's cell phone rang.

"Yes?" she said. "Yes, but . . . Yes, I will. . . . Do you want to speak to him? He's right . . . Okay, I will. . . . Bye."

"The boss?" David asked.

Mina nodded. "He wants you to come to him in Hamadan right away and bring the other five phones to him in person."

"Sure, whatever he wants."

"I'll book you a flight and a rental car," Mina said, heading back to her desk. "I don't know if there are any hotels operating right now, but I'll figure out something."

David suddenly found himself alone in Esfahani's office. He quickly glanced at the safe, but Mina had already closed and locked it. He checked the hallway—clear. He looked at Mina, already on the phone with the travel department. Then he noticed Esfahani's desktop computer was still on.

David recalled the transcript he'd read from the intercepted call made by his driver the day of David and Eva's disastrous first meeting with Esfahani. The driver had referred to Esfahani as the "nephew of the boss." Wondering just who it was Esfahani was related to, David quickly pulled up Esfahani's phone directory and scrolled through it. He began by searching for the name Ibrahim Asgari, commander of VEVAK, the secret police, but came up empty. Next he looked up Supreme Leader Hosseini. It was a long shot, he figured, but worth a try. Again, he came up empty. He tried President Ahmed Darazi. This, too, was a dry hole. Defense Minister Ali Faridzadeh was his next search. Yet again, the search came up blank.

Still, Esfahani had 837 contacts. There had to be someone useful in there, David figured. He glanced at Mina again. She was still on the phone and typing on her computer. Knowing he had only a few moments before she came back in, he pulled a memory stick from his pocket, inserted it into the USB port of Esfahani's hard drive, and downloaded the entire directory, as well as Esfahani's calendar.

"Okay," Mina called out, getting up from her seat and coming back into Esfahani's office, "I got you the last seat on the next flight to Hamadan."

Then she saw David sitting at her boss's desk.

First she was stunned, but she quickly grew angry. "What are you doing?" she snapped. "Get away from there."

As she marched over to see what he was doing on the computer, David's pulse quickened. But when she got there, she found him staring at a news site in Farsi and a stunning headline that read, "Twelfth Imam Appears in Hamadan, Heals Woman with Crushed Legs."

Mina gasped, David's offense forgotten.

69

David arrived at the airport with less than half an hour before his flight.

He checked in, cleared security, found a quiet corner near his gate, and powered up his laptop. With so many contacts in Esfahani's directory, he was hesitant to transfer them all onto his mobile phone. The NSA would be overwhelmed, and most of the numbers wouldn't produce anything of value. So with only a few minutes before departure, he began looking for specific names.

He began with Javad Nouri. Who was this guy, and how in the world was he connected to the Twelfth Imam? Unfortunately, he found only the young man's mobile number and no other information. Still, he entered the number into his Nokia and kept hunting.

Next David looked up Daryush Rashidi and found his various phone numbers, his private e-mail address, his birthday, and his children's names. He also found contact information for the man's wife, Navaz Birjandi Rashidi.

Birjandi? It had to be a coincidence, he thought. She couldn't possibly be related to . . .

David quickly searched the phone directory and hit pay dirt. Not only was Birjandi's home phone number there, so was his home address. The man was Daryush Rashidi's father-in-law.

Before David could fully absorb this development, however, a flight attendant suddenly announced the last call for passengers to board flight 224 to Hamadan. David realized he'd been so focused he'd lost all track of time. It was time to pack up his laptop and board immediately. Still,

he had one more thing to check. He was determined to find the identity of the "boss" to whom Esfahani was related. He had already ruled
out more than a dozen senior Iranian officials, including the Supreme
Leader and the head of state security. But David wasn't ready to give
up. He began scrolling through Esfahani's contacts but glanced up and
noticed the flight attendant preparing to close the door and seal the
flight for takeoff. He called to her and asked her to wait two more
minutes.

"No, sir," she snapped. "You have to board now or take the next
flight."

Pleading her patience for just another moment, David closed
Esfahani's phone directory and opened the file containing the man's
calendar. He did a search for the word *birthday* and came up with
twenty-seven hits. He glanced back at the flight attendant, who was
growing more annoyed by the second. He had to go. He was out of
time. But his instincts pushed him forward. He scanned through each
birthday. Esfahani's mother. His father. His wife. His daughters. His
in-laws. His grandparents. A cousin. Another cousin. A dozen more
cousins. And then: *Uncle Mohsen, birthday, November 5.*

David's heart rate accelerated. It couldn't be that simple, could it?
Why hadn't he thought of it before? He closed the calendar file and
reopened the phone directory.

"Sir, really," the flight attendant said, standing over him now. "I
must insist."

"I know, I know," he said. "Just one more minute, please."

She was not amused. "No, sir. *Now.*"

David hit the Search function and typed in *Mohsen*. A fraction of a
second later, the name Mohsen Jazini popped up on the screen, along
with all of his personal contact information. David did a double take.
Esfahani's uncle was the commander of the Iranian Revolutionary
Guard Corps?

He copied Jazini's information—along with Birjandi's—into his Nokia
and hoped the NSA would get it and be able to use it quickly. Then he
shut down his laptop and boarded the commuter flight, just before the
flight attendant slammed and locked the aircraft door behind him.

Yet as intrigued as he was by these two developments, his thoughts shifted as he buckled himself into the last seat in the last row. He found himself thinking about the headline he'd seen in Esfahani's office: *"Twelfth Imam Appears in Hamadan, Heals Woman with Crushed Legs."* How was that possible? If Islam was false, which he was increasingly convinced it was, how could their so-called messiah be appearing in visions and healing people? Didn't only God have the power to do great signs and wonders such as these?

70

TEHRAN, IRAN

The news broke at midday on February 22.

Supreme Leader Hosseini delivered the live address on Iranian television. It took only six minutes, but it was a shot heard around the world. In his speech, he announced the news for which the Shia world had longed for centuries and which the Sunni world had feared nearly as long.

"It is my great joy to announce to you that the Twelfth Imam—the Lord of the Age, peace be upon him—has come at last," the Grand Ayatollah declared, reading from a prepared text. "This is not rumor or speculation. I have been blessed with the honor of meeting with him and speaking with him in person several times. My security cabinet has met with him as well. Soon, all the world will see him and be astonished. Imam al-Mahdi has a powerful message to share with humanity. He is preparing to establish his kingdom of justice and peace. He has commanded me to inform you that he will make his first official appearance to the world in Mecca a week from Thursday. He invites all who seek peace to come and be with him for this inaugural sermon."

★ ★ ★ ★ ★

Not surprisingly, the evidence pointed to the Israelis.

The Twelfth Imam and his inner circle listened carefully to Defense Minister Faridzadeh's briefing. The assassination of Dr. Saddaji, the nation's top nuclear scientist, represented a serious blow to Iran's pursuit of nuclear weapons. Everyone was furious. But the Mahdi counseled patience.

"We all know the Zionists are descendants of apes and pigs," he began. "They got lucky this time, but let us all remember—they are destined to be wiped off the face of the earth once and for all, and it is our destiny to make this happen. But let us not be distracted from our higher calling. The Zionists would have no power against the Muslims if it were not for the American whores and lepers. It is time for the wave of jihad to crash upon them both. The day of the Judeo-Christian empire is over. The kingdom of Allah and his servant has come. Tell me, then, how soon will we be ready to launch the War of Annihilation?"

"Soon, my Lord," Minister Faridzadeh assured him. "But we need to replace Dr. Saddaji, and that won't be easy to do."

"Saddaji was the deputy director of your nuclear program," the Mahdi said. "Why not replace him with the director?"

"The director is a political appointee, my Lord," Faridzadeh said, choosing his words carefully. "He is a fine man, and we are deeply grateful for his service, but . . ."

"But he does not have the technical skills we need to run the weapons program," the Mahdi said.

"No, my Lord. I'm afraid he does not. He is really the face of the civilian program, working with the IAEA and other international bodies."

"But you obviously know how to move forward without Saddaji."

"That's true, my Lord," the defense minister agreed. "But that's because all the pieces were already put in place by Saddaji before he died and because the Supreme Leader wanted to send a message to his killers that they could not stop our plans."

"Who was Saddaji's right-hand man?" the Mahdi finally asked.

"Dr. Najjar Malik."

"Najjar Malik from Iraq?"

"Yes, my Lord."

"From Samarra?"

"Yes, yes, that is the one."

The Mahdi smiled. "I know Najjar; he is a faithful servant. He is married to Saddaji's daughter, Sheyda, is he not?"

"He is indeed, my Lord."

"Does he know all the details of the weapons program?"

"Unfortunately, no," the defense minister said. "He is a very able physicist, my Lord. He's also a first-rate manager, and he was personally recruited and trained by Dr. Saddaji. But for security purposes, and at my command, Dr. Saddaji kept everything compartmentalized. Dr. Malik knows the rest of Iran's civilian nuclear program better than anyone in the country, but we kept him in the dark about the weapons program. We operated that on a separate track."

"Could he learn it?" the Mahdi said.

"I think he could. He is definitely someone we could trust. He would need time to get briefed. But I think he would be ideal. And of course, he would have all the scientists and staff on the weapons team who reported directly to Saddaji to help him."

The Twelfth Imam smiled again. "Bring him to me at once."

71

On the way to the car rentals, David tried to call Mina.

With so much of the network in the region down, however, getting a signal proved impossible. So he called from a pay phone and finally tracked her down. Mina provided him with directions on where to find Esfahani but apologized that she still hadn't found him a functioning hotel. She asked him to be patient and promised to have something in the next few hours.

"No problem," David said, figuring he could always fly right back to Tehran if she couldn't find him any accommodations. "But I have a question to ask you."

"What is it?"

"I'm just wondering, would it be appropriate if I called Mr. Rashidi and offered my condolences for the death of his brother-in-law?"

"Of course," Mina said. "I think that would be very kind. Let me get you that number."

As he waited, David asked if Mr. Rashidi's brother-in-law was elderly or ill.

"Neither," Mina said.

"He wasn't killed in an accident, was he?"

"Not exactly," Mina answered.

"Then how?"

"He was killed in a car bombing."

"*What?*" David asked, not believing he had just heard her correctly. "In Hamadan? When?"

"Just a few days ago," Mina said. "And the odd thing is that you'd think something like that would make the news. But it didn't."

That was strange, David thought. If his mobile phone service had been working, he'd have immediately done a search for the story on the Internet. Instead he asked for the man's name.

"You mean Mr. Rashidi's brother-in-law?"

"Yes, who was he?"

"His name was Mohammed," Mina said. "Mohammed Saddaji."

David was stunned, though he tried not to let his voice betray that fact. "You mean Dr. Mohammed Saddaji? the deputy director of Iran's nuclear agency?"

"Yes. He was a brilliant scientist, and he and Mr. Rashidi were close. It's very sad."

"It certainly is. Why was Dr. Saddaji visiting Hamadan?"

"He wasn't visiting," Mina said innocently. "He lived there."

David had many more questions, but he didn't want to risk arousing suspicion. So he thanked Mina and promised to check back with her in a few hours about the hotel. Then he hung up the phone and proceeded to pick up his rental car while trying to process this new piece of information. There were no Iranian nuclear facilities in Hamadan—none that he had been briefed about, anyway. So why did such a high-ranking official in the Iranian nuclear program live there? Was Mina mistaken? Or was it possible there was a major facility in the area of which U.S. intelligence was unaware?

David found his car, pulled out of the airport grounds, and began driving south on Route 5 toward the city center. For the first ten minutes or so, he saw no serious signs of damage, confirming the news reports, which indicated the most severe impact had occurred downtown and to the west. He soon passed Payam Noor University on his right, then came through a roundabout onto the main beltway around the city, named after Ayatollah Khomeini. When he approached the neighborhood of the Besat Medical Center on the city's south side, he began to see the full effects of the devastation.

Ambulances passed every few moments with flashing lights and sirens. Army helicopters were landing on the hospital's roof, bringing in more casualties. All around, David could see single-family homes split in two and high-rise apartments lying toppled on their sides or crumpled into heaps of smoldering ruins.

He turned on the radio, and the news got worse. The confirmed death toll now topped 35,000 dead, with more than 110,000 wounded. Jumbo jets from the Red Crescent would be arriving soon, one reporter said, bringing tens of thousands of blankets and tents, along with desperately needed water and food. But movement on severely damaged roads was slow, the reporter explained, and rescue efforts were being hampered by the lack of reliable communications.

"It's not just that the cell towers are down," the newscaster reported. "Technicians from Iran Telecom are scrambling to restore wireless service, in particular, to help emergency crews of first responders rescue the wounded and care for the suffering. But thousands of landlines are down, fiber-optic lines have been severed, and even regular two-way radio service is being hampered by levels of static and blackout zones for which officials say they have no immediate explanation."

David turned down a one-way street, then another, and then a third. He looped around in a school parking lot, then zigzagged through another residential neighborhood, trying to determine if anyone was following him. Satisfied that he was not being tailed, he pulled over to the side of the road and fired up his laptop. He opened the file with all of Esfahani's contacts and searched for Dr. Mohammed Saddaji.

The search came up blank. Saddaji's information wasn't there.

Still, he knew he had to get that information back to Zalinsky as fast as possible. This wasn't Baghdad or Mosul or Kabul. Car bombings didn't happen every day in Iran. Certainly not in Hamadan. The Israelis were here, David concluded. They had to be. Which meant they knew more about what was going on with Iran's nuclear program than Langley did. They wouldn't have taken out Saddaji unless they had reason to believe that he was at the heart of Iran's weaponization effort and that the weaponization effort was about to bear fruit.

David checked his phone. The good news was that he now had some coverage. The bad news was that he had only one bar. That was too much of a risk. He couldn't take the chance and make an international call when so many cell towers were down. Even if he got through, a call to Dubai would likely get noticed by Iranian intelligence since call volume in the area had to be so low at the moment. Then again, David figured, he did have five secure satellite phones on the seat beside him.

He opened one, called Zalinsky, and coded in as Zephyr.

The conversation didn't go as David hoped.

"Your memo was inappropriate," Zalinsky began.

"Why?"

"Because your job is to gather and send us actionable information about the Iranian government, not political analysis about our own. Also because I told you not to get sidetracked by all this Shia End Times stuff. That's not the story. The weapons are the story. And even if all the analysis in your memo was right—and I highly doubt that it is, but even if it was—you provided no hard facts to back up all those dubious assertions. It's an op-ed piece for the *Post*, and not a particularly good one at that."

David gritted his teeth but didn't back down. He insisted he was sending back every scrap of intel he could. But he was equally adamant that he would be derelict in his duty not to report his impressions of the religious and political dynamic he was seeing inside Iran, and his sense that the U.S. was not doing nearly enough to stop the Iranians in time. Only having got all that off his chest did he tell Zalinsky that the deputy director of Iran's nuclear program had recently been killed by a car bomb, and that he suspected the Israelis were doing what the U.S. wasn't—fighting fire with fire.

Zalinsky was stunned that Saddaji was dead. Stunned, too, that Saddaji had been living for several years in Hamadan. He hadn't known that. No one in the Agency had. And David was probably right: it had to have been the Israelis who had taken Saddaji out. It certainly hadn't been anyone from Langley.

"The Mossad is treating this like a real war," David argued.

"We are too," Zalinsky said.

"No, we're not," David pushed back. "The Israelis have been sabotaging Iranian facilities and kidnapping or assassinating key scientists and military officials for the last several years. What have we been doing?

begging Hosseini and Darazi to sit down and negotiate with us? threatening 'crippling' economic consequences but imposing lame, toothless sanctions instead? No wonder the Israelis are losing confidence in us. *I'm* losing confidence in us."

"That's enough," Zalinsky said. "You just do your job and let me do mine."

"I'm doing my job, but it's not enough," David replied, trying to control himself but growing more frustrated and angry by the minute. "I'm sending you everything I have, but where is it getting us? Nowhere."

"You have to be patient," Zalinsky counseled.

"Why?"

"These things take time."

"We don't have any more time," David insisted. "The Israelis just ran the largest war game in their history. They just took out the highest-ranking nuclear scientist in the country. Prime Minister Naphtali is warning President Jackson and the world that if we don't act, Israel will. What are we doing? Seriously, what are we *really* doing to stop Iran from getting the Bomb? Because from my perspective on the ground, sir, things are spinning out of control."

"Believe me, I understand," Zalinsky said, "but we have to build our case with facts, not guesses, not speculation, not hearsay. We blew it in Iraq. I told you that. Not completely, but when it came to weapons of mass destruction, we didn't have the facts—not enough of them, anyway. We didn't have the 'slam dunk' case we said we did. So we'd sure better have one this time. We need to be able to carefully document the answers to every question the president or his advisors ask us. The stakes are too high for anything less. So give me a target. Give me something actionable, and we'll take action."

"What kind of action?" David asked. "You think the president is going to order someone assassinated? You think we're really going to blow up some facility? We already know of a dozen or more nuclear facilities here. Have we hit one yet?"

"First of all, that's not your call," Zalinsky said. "Your job is to get us information we don't have. What happens next is my job. But don't forget the president's executive order. We are authorized to use 'all means necessary' to stop or slow down Iran's nuclear weapons program. When the time is right, we'll do just that. But we can't afford any screwups. You got that?"

David wanted to believe Zalinsky. But he secretly admired the courage the Israelis had to defend the Jewish people from another Holocaust, and he worried his own government had either lost its nerve or become resigned to the prospect of a nuclear-armed Iran.

Shifting gears, David asked if Zalinsky and Fischer had gotten anything useful out of Rashidi's or Esfahani's phone calls. Unfortunately, the answer was no.

"We learned that Rashidi's brother-in-law had died tragically," Zalinsky replied. "We learned his name was Mohammed and that the funeral was going to be in Hamadan. None of the calls ever mentioned a car bomb or his last name. So this is good work, son. I'll get the rest of the team right on this, verifying all this. But this is exactly what I want you to be doing—giving me information I can use. I'm not saying you can't have your own opinion. But I'm not asking you for your analysis. I've got twenty guys doing analysis. What we need are facts no one else in the world has. Stuff like this. Just get me more."

David promised he would. He coded out, hung up the phone, and cleared the satellite phone's memory of any trace of the call. But his frustration was growing. It was one thing for the White House not to get what was truly happening on the ground inside Iran. But David feared his mentor might not fully get it either.

72

David pulled into an Iran Telecom switching station on the edge of the city.

The facility itself and the equipment inside had been heavily damaged by the earthquake, and the parking lot was filled with the trucks of Iran Telecom staff and contractors who had come to get the place back in working condition.

David found Esfahani on the second floor, wearing a hard hat and assessing the extent of the damage with a group of repairmen. He caught the executive's eye and held up his right hand, indicating he had the five remaining satellite phones with him. Esfahani excused himself from his colleagues and took David aside.

"Where are they?" Esfahani asked.

"They're in my trunk."

"How quickly can you get all the rest of them here?"

"All 313?"

"Exactly."

"I really don't know if that's possible."

"Look, Reza, we don't have a lot of time," Esfahani said. "Things are moving very rapidly now. I will go to the Chinese if I have to, but I want to work with you, so long as you understand we have to move fast."

"I completely understand," David said. "I know you're under a huge time constraint. I'm just saying we have to be careful. Do you know how hard it was to get these twenty without drawing suspicion from within my company, much less from all the international intelligence agencies who are watching everything that comes in and out of this country like hawks?"

"The Chinese couldn't care less about international intelligence agencies," Esfahani said.

"But you have to," David said, taking a risk. "Look, these phones aren't for just anyone. They're for the Lord of the Age, correct? Shouldn't he have the very best?"

"Of course."

"Then I'll be blunt. The Chinese phones stink. I mean, they'll do if you're a business guy trying to sell steel or cars or toys or whatever. But you told me you needed state-of-the-art, top-of-the-line, didn't you?"

"I did."

"Then you need me, not the Chinese," David assured him. "We just have to make sure we do it the right way so you don't invite scrutiny that you don't need and I don't get caught by my company. We have to do it in a way that provides Imam al-Mahdi and his team with exactly what they need so they can talk without Beijing or the Russians or, Allah forbid, the Americans or the Zionists listening in."

"You're right," Esfahani said. "We need to be careful."

"You're trying to help the Mahdi—peace be upon him—build an army," David continued. "I want to help you. I want to be part of changing history. Just tell me what I need to do, and I'll get you whatever you need. You have my word."

"I appreciate that. Now let me see what you brought me," Esfahani said.

David took him to the car, opened the trunk, and gave him the five boxes.

Esfahani opened one and smiled. "These are nice."

"Best in the world."

"My people back in Tehran scrubbed the ones you gave them this morning," Esfahani said, leafing through one of the instruction manuals. "They said they're all clean."

"They are. I checked them all myself before I brought them from Munich. This is the very same phone the chancellor of Germany uses, and the president of France, and the prime minister of Italy, and all of their top staff. And believe me, the Europeans don't want the Americans or Israelis intercepting their calls either."

"You've done well, Reza. I am very grateful."

"It's an honor to help my country," David said. "I want only the best for my people."

"I believe that's true," Esfahani said, taking the five boxes to his own car and locking them in the trunk. "Which is why I want to tell you something."

Then Esfahani quietly explained what the Group of 313 was and why he and Rashidi were searching for devout Shia Muslims who possessed strong administrative and technical skills and would be completely loyal to the Mahdi.

"We are recruiting an army of ten thousand *mujahideen* ready to give their lives to annihilate Tel Aviv, Washington, New York, and Los Angeles and usher in the reign of the Promised One."

David didn't dare say anything that might get Esfahani suspicious. "How can I join?" he asked after a few moments.

"No one joins," Esfahani said. "You must be chosen."

"But you could recommend me."

"We are considering you. Mr. Rashidi will decide. But if you can deliver all these phones quickly, I think you will win his confidence and his recommendation."

David couldn't believe what he was hearing, and he wondered what Zalinsky would say.

"I will do my best to earn that honor."

"I know you will. In the meantime, I want you to learn from a master. He is one of our greatest scholars and he lives close to here. You will spend the evening there; there are no hotels available anyway. Tomorrow, I expect you to start working on the rest of the phones we require. But for tonight, you will sit at a master's feet and learn about our beloved Imam."

"Who is he?"

"He is a great teacher. He also happens to be related to Daryush."

David immediately knew whom he meant, but he said nothing.

"Have you ever heard of Dr. Alireza Birjandi?" Esfahani asked.

"Of course," David said. "I recently read one of his books. But isn't he living in seclusion?"

"I think he would like to meet you. He is a professor at heart, and he loves bright, young, eager minds."

"I couldn't impose on him."

"It is all arranged. You should bring the man some food. It is never acceptable to visit empty-handed."

"That is very gracious," David said. "May Allah bless you and your family. May I ask one more question before I leave?"

"Of course," Esfahani said. "What is it?"

"Did Imam al-Mahdi actually reveal himself here in Hamadan?"

"Yes, he did," Esfahani said. "It was astounding!"

"Did he really heal a woman who had her legs crushed in the earthquake?"

"Yes, he did. Everyone has been talking about it."

"But how do you know it's really true?" David asked. "I'm always a little skeptical about what I hear on the news."

"You are a very wise and thoughtful young man," Esfahani answered. "But I didn't hear it on the news."

"How then?"

"I was there."

73

An hour later, David arrived at Alireza Birjandi's house.

It was a modest, single-story, two-bedroom home that might be called a bungalow back in the States. Built of concrete and wood on the outskirts of the city, it appeared to David as if it dated back to the 1940s or 50s and hadn't seen many updates since.

Carrying a bag of bread and cheese, a sack of potatoes, and a case of bottled water that Esfahani had given him from the Iran Telecom regional substation's supplies, David went up to the front door and knocked several times. It took a few minutes, but the elderly cleric finally came to the door carrying a white cane and wearing dark glasses.

Esfahani had failed to mention that the man was blind.

"Is that you, Mr. Tabrizi?" the old man said, his voice sad, his body frail and gaunt. "I've been expecting you."

"It is, but please, call me Reza."

"Is that what they're calling you these days? Very well; please come in."

David was a bit startled by that response and was glad Birjandi couldn't see his reaction. What did the man mean by that? What else would people be calling him?

"Forgive me for being late," David said. "I got a bit lost."

"That is quite all right," Birjandi said. "I can't imagine driving out there at all right now. Of course, I've never driven, but still . . ."

His voice trailed off, and David felt sorry for the old man. "Mr. Esfahani speaks very highly of you," he said. "It is a great honor to meet you. Thank you for making time to see me on such short notice."

"It is nothing," Birjandi sighed. "Daryush and Abdol speak very highly of you, as well. You seem to have made quite an impression."

"Well, they have been very kind to me. Oh, and Mr. Esfahani asked me to bring you these groceries and said he would send more supplies over soon."

"He's a good boy," Birjandi said. "I've known him since he was eight years old. He and Daryush were the best of friends growing up. Did he tell you that?"

"No, sir," David said, noting this new clue. "He never mentioned it."

"Well, they were very competitive boys," Birjandi said with a touch more animation in his voice. "I'm sure Abdol can't stand the fact that Daryush is the boss. It was always the reverse when they were kids. Abdol was smarter, faster, stronger—learned the entire Qur'an by the time he was ten. Not Daryush. I don't think he ever memorized it. But Daryush . . . Well, let's just say he was more diplomatic, had more savvy than Abdol. It's made all the difference. Now come, let's put the food away; then we'll go into my study and talk."

As they entered Birjandi's home, David was immediately struck by the sheer number of books that were in the living room alone. Every wall was lined with bookshelves, and every shelf was stacked with so many tomes the shelves themselves were sagging and looked like they might collapse at any moment. Books were piled on the floors and on chairs, together with boxes of scholarly journals and other publications, and David couldn't help but wonder what a blind man living alone did with them all. Nothing looked dusty or filthy, so he wondered if someone came and cleaned on a regular basis. He certainly couldn't imagine this poor old man taking care of this home himself. Fortunately, aside from a cracked front window and some noticeable cracks in his walls and ceiling, the house had sustained remarkably little damage from the earthquake.

David took the supplies into the kitchen, which was cramped but clean. There were no dirty dishes in the sink. No garbage in the trash bin. Nor was there any food in the pantry or much of any in the refrigerator. It was no wonder the old man was so thin.

After instructing David where to put the groceries, Birjandi padded down the hall, and David followed. They ended up in the old man's study—actually a retrofitted dining room. It, too, had bookshelves lining the walls, sagging with the weight of books, many of which looked fifty or a hundred years old or more. In one corner was a desk stacked with books on tape, along with a large tape player from the 1980s, a set of giant headphones, and an assortment of unopened mail. In another corner stood a television that was on but whose screen was full of snow and static that hissed so loudly it actually hurt David's ears. Seemingly not bothered by the noise, Birjandi found a well-worn armchair that was clearly his favorite and plopped down in it. Then, much to David's relief, the old man found the remote on an end table and turned off the TV.

"Please have a seat."

"Thank you, sir," David said, carefully removing a stack of yellowed newspapers from the 1990s from another armchair. "I have many questions, and Mr. Esfahani said you would be the best man to ask."

There was a long, uncomfortable silence, so long that David wasn't sure the old man had heard him.

"We are living in extraordinary times, wouldn't you say?" David finally offered, searching for a way to begin the conversation.

"I see days of great mourning," Birjandi said with a heavy sigh.

"But at least Imam al-Mahdi has come, right?" David said, his voice upbeat and hopeful. "I'm sure you've heard all the reports."

"I have no joy in my heart," Birjandi said.

"None?"

"Young man, a very dark day has dawned upon the earth."

David was taken aback. Wasn't this man's life's work studying and teaching about the coming of the Twelfth Imam? Why wouldn't he allow himself a bit of joy? Yes, the day had come with death and destruction. But hadn't all that been prophesied anyway? Didn't the old man believe all this suffering was Allah's will?

"He who knows not, and knows not that he knows not, is a fool; shun him," Birjandi said, seemingly out of the blue. "He who knows not, and knows that he knows not, is a child; teach him. He who knows, and knows not that he knows, is asleep; wake him. He who knows, and knows that he knows, is wise; follow him."

"Is that from the Qur'an?" David asked.

Birjandi smiled a little and shook his head.

"From the hadiths?"

Again the old man shook his head.

"Something Zoroaster said?"

"No, it is an ancient Persian proverb."

"Well, it sounds very wise."

"Which one are you?"

"Me?"

"Yes."

"I don't know."

"Think."

David pondered that for a moment, silently reciting the proverb several times to understand its meaning.

"I suppose I am the child," he said finally.

"Why?"

"Because I know not, and I know that I know not. That's why I am here, because I believe you know."

"Very good," Birjandi said. "Then start with this. What Hamadan just experienced was not a natural earthquake."

"What do you mean?" David asked.

"The size. The scope. The timing. Think, Mr. Tabrizi. What triggered all this? Do you really think it was the arrival of Imam al-Mahdi?"

What was the man talking about? David's confusion grew still more when Birjandi suddenly rose, excused himself, and said it was time for him to pray.

"We can talk some more in six hours," Birjandi explained simply, without apology.

Six hours? David looked at his watch. It was only three in the afternoon. What was he going to do for the next six hours?

"Thank you for the groceries," Birjandi said before he left for his room. "Feel free to have anything you would like. I am not hungry. I don't have a guest room, but I hope you are comfortable on the couch. There are more blankets in the closet. Take a nap, Mr. Tabrizi. You need the rest. You seem tired. And, I suspect, you could use some prayer time as well."

Then he turned and walked away. His bedroom door closed softly behind him. David was startled and a little annoyed. He didn't want to nap. He didn't want to pray. He had questions. He had come for answers. But he wasn't getting any. At least not for the next six hours.

74

As the hours passed, there was one bit of good news.

Wireless service had now been restored for sections near the airport, which meant David's phone worked and he could use it to get on the Internet. He grabbed his laptop and waited for it to boot up.

As he did, he kept thinking about Birjandi's words. What did he mean that the earthquake wasn't a natural event? There were only two other possibilities. One was a *supernatural* event, perhaps connected to the arrival of the Twelfth Imam. But Birjandi had seemed to dismiss that notion, which was odd, given the man's specialty. The only other possibility was that it was a man-made event. But the only way for man to trigger an earthquake was . . .

No, David thought, surely that wasn't possible. Birjandi wasn't suggesting the earthquake had been triggered by an underground nuclear test, was he?

Once connected to the Internet, David did a quick search. What he found unnerved him.

On May 28, 1998, Pakistan conducted five nuclear weapons tests, triggering an earthquake that measured 5.0 on the Richter scale.

On October 9, 2006, North Korea conducted a nuclear test in the North Hamgyong province, resulting in a 4.3 seismic event.

On May 25, 2009, North Korea conducted another nuclear test, resulting in an earthquake with a magnitude of 4.7.

David was no physicist or geologist. He had no way of knowing for certain. But on its face, it did seem possible that an earthquake could be triggered by a nuclear test or a series of tests. Was that what had just happened? If so, how huge must the nuke have been to trigger an earthquake measuring 8.6 on the Richter scale?

Barred from accessing Langley's database from inside a hostile country, David continued scouring the open-source articles on previous nuclear tests, looking for similarities and differences. The article that worried him most was an October 2006 piece by David Sanger in the *New York Times.*

> North Korea said Sunday night that it had set off its first nuclear test, becoming the eighth country in history, and arguably the most unstable and most dangerous, to proclaim that it has joined the club of nuclear weapons states.
> The test came just two days after the country was warned by the United Nations Security Council that the action could lead to severe consequences.

Since when has a U.N. Security Council warning ever stopped a country from building the Bomb? David wondered.

The White House and State Department were kidding themselves. The president and the secretary of state and all their muckety-mucks could huff and puff all they wanted, but in the end, negotiations and diplomacy and high-level talks and Security Council meetings were all just words, and words weren't going to blow the Big Bad Wolf's nuclear house down.

David continued reading.

> North Korea's decision to conduct the test demonstrated what the world has suspected for years: the country has joined India, Pakistan, and Israel as one of the world's "undeclared" nuclear powers. India and Pakistan conducted tests in 1998; Israel has never acknowledged conducting a test or possessing a weapon. But by actually setting off a weapon, if that is proven, the North has chosen to end years of carefully crafted and diplomatically useful ambiguity about its abilities.

"I think they just had their military plan to demonstrate that no one could mess with them, and they weren't going to be deterred, not even by the Chinese," a senior American official who deals with the North Koreans said. "In the end, there was just no stopping them."

Was there any stopping Iran? Not like this, David thought. The CIA was learning too little. They were doing too little. And too much time was going by.

He did a quick search of the headlines in the last twenty-four hours. Had there been any indication by the Iranians that they were testing a bomb? He found none. If they had just tested, that may have been a key lesson they learned from the North Koreans: Why announce the test? Why confirm it? Why let the world know they had the Bomb? In this case, why let the Israelis know? Then again, David thought, maybe the Iranians were still going to announce it. Maybe they were just buying time, reviewing the technical data, making sure they really had an operational weapon—or several of them—before telling the world the apocalyptic news.

David did some more poking around the Internet to double-check his memory on the Comprehensive Nuclear Test Ban Treaty. Sure enough, Iran was one of the 182 signatories to the pact. By signing, it had agreed with all the other signatory states to two central provisions.

First, "Each State Party undertakes not to carry out any nuclear weapon test explosion or any other nuclear explosion, and to prohibit and prevent any such nuclear explosion at any place under its jurisdiction or control."

Second, "Each State Party undertakes, furthermore, to refrain from causing, encouraging, or in any way participating in the carrying out of any nuclear weapon test explosion or any other nuclear explosion."

By way of enforcement, David knew, the International Monitoring System (IMS) and International Data Center (IDC) had been established. These networks included over three hundred primary and auxiliary seismic monitoring stations worldwide specifically tracking all seismic events and determining whether they were natural or triggered by a nuclear explosion. The difference was fairly simple for experts to discern. In an earthquake, seismic activity was slow at first and then steadily intensified as tectonic plates scraped against one another. But when a nuclear blast occurred, the seismic activity would be incredibly intense at first and then would slow down over a few minutes.

Which one had just happened at Hamadan? David didn't know, but he had to get Langley checking. Taking a risk, he decided to use his Nokia to send an encrypted message back to Zalinsky and Fischer. There was a slight chance that the encrypted message would be picked up—not read but noticed—by Iranian intelligence, since it was being sent from an area so close to the epicenter of the quake. But it was a risk he had to take. He typed quickly.

> FLASH TRAFFIC—PRIORITY ALPHA: Request immediate focus on Hamadan earthquake. Stop. Possible nuclear test. Stop. Check IMS/IDC data. Stop. Request immediate CP pass. Stop. Possible link to death of Saddaji. Stop. Also: indications that TTI recruiting army of 10,000 mujahideen. Stop. Source close to TTI says plan is to "annihilate" Tel Aviv, DC, New York, and LA. Stop. Working to get more details. Stop. Will call secure when I can. Stop. Out.

★ ★ ★ ★ ★

DUBAI, UNITED ARAB EMIRATES

Zalinsky was getting frustrated again.

The Saddaji news had been useful. But was David Shirazi actually suggesting the Iranians had just conducted a nuclear test—the first in the country's history—in Hamadan, of all places? The notion was ridiculous. The Iranians had their Shahrokhi Air Base about thirty miles north of the city. But they certainly didn't have nuclear facilities in or around Hamadan.

Then came the audacity of Zephyr's suggestion that the United

States Air Force dispatch its high-tech WC-135 "nuclear test–sniffing plane"—code-named CP for Constant Phoenix—over Iran. Did he really think the secretary of defense and the joint chiefs of staff were going to authorize an expensive flyover of a hostile country amid such a delicate diplomatic dance with the Iranians? Based on what? speculation? guesses? gut instincts? Zalinsky could just imagine the dressing-down he'd receive from the higher-ups within the CIA, at the Pentagon, and at the White House when the air sample data sent from Constant Phoenix to the Air Force Technical Applications Center at Patrick Air Force Base in Florida came back negative. No radiation. No evidence of a nuclear test whatsoever. He'd be a laughingstock.

What's more, "Reza Tabrizi's" interest in TTI, presumably the Twelfth Imam, was a distraction. It worried Zalinsky, and it disrupted the controlled and careful tone with which he wanted this operation to be carried out. The kid seemed to think this religious fervor was going to boil over into drastic events any minute, but Zalinsky wasn't convinced anything new was happening in the hearts of these madmen. They were on a steady course to develop nuclear weapons, and his team needed to remain on a steady course to stop them, not to act rashly.

75

It was almost 10 p.m. when Birjandi's door finally opened.

David, devouring his third book on Shia eschatology from the old man's shelves, watched him make his way slowly to the kitchen.

"Would you like some help?" he asked, setting a hefty tome aside.

"Yes, son, that would be very kind."

Together, they made a pot of tea and set out a plate of naan, Iranian bread that was a favorite of David's. He was anxious to ask his host about the Twelfth Imam, the earthquake, Iran's weapons program, and a thousand other things. But as David carried the tray to the study and the two sat down together, he sensed the man was not quite ready to talk about such things. He had to be patient, he reminded himself. He had to pace himself. This was a source and a potentially high-value one at that. He needed to build a relationship, some camaraderie, some trust. Above all, he had to be careful not to offend the man. Birjandi had been described by many as a recluse. David needed to find a way to open him up.

He smiled as Dr. Birjandi popped a sugar cube in his mouth and then began sipping his tea. It was just the way his father used to drink tea. He hadn't seen his father do it in many years, but somehow watching Birjandi made David feel homesick. He missed his father, worried for his mother, and felt a sudden hunger for home that surprised him. He looked out the window at the quiet suburban street and saw a young family walking past, the man a few strides ahead of the woman and several children running around them. They sat in silence for a while, and Birjandi seemed to enjoy the quiet. And then, as David took a piece of bread and began to chew it slowly, he had an idea.

"May I ask you a question, sir?" he began.

"Of course," the old man said. "What's on your mind?"

"Were you ever in love?"

Dr. Birjandi cleared his throat in surprise. "That was not a question I was expecting when Abdol said you wanted to come over to meet me."

"I'm sorry. It's just that—"

"No, no, it's a good question," Birjandi interrupted, "and an honest one. I appreciate a young man who is not all business."

David had been taught at the Farm not to throw fastballs straight down the center of the plate. Curveballs and the occasional slider tended to work better, throwing the batter off a bit. It didn't always work. But this time, he sensed it just might.

"I will tell you the truth, son," the old man said between sips of tea. "I was in love with the same girl for sixty-seven years, and I'm still in love with her. She passed away six months ago, but I think about her every moment of every day. I have an ache in my heart that will not leave."

"I'm so sorry," David said.

"It's okay," Birjandi responded. "It hurts now, but soon enough we will walk hand in hand in paradise, reunited forever. I cannot wait."

David was moved by the man's devotion to his bride. "What was her name?"

"Souri."

"A red rose," David said. "That's a beautiful name."

"As was she," Birjandi said. "Her heart, anyway. Her voice. The touch of her hands. The smell of the flowers she would pick in the morning. I never had the joy of seeing her. But then again, I didn't need to see her to know her. All I could do was listen to her speak, but the more I listened, the more I knew her, and the more I knew her, the more I loved her. Someday, when we meet in paradise, I will finally get to see just how beautiful she really is. That will be something, won't it?"

"It will indeed," David said. "May I ask how old you were when you met?"

"I was sixteen; she was seventeen. My mother hired her to tutor me in Arabic, because her family was originally from Najaf, in Iraq. We married the following year."

"It was an arranged marriage?"

"Of course, though we did our best not to seem happy about it."

"Why's that?"

"We were afraid if our parents knew how in love we were, they would force us to marry someone else!"

David began to laugh but quickly covered his mouth.

"It's okay, son. I still laugh about it myself. I still savor each and every memory with that woman. I can remember our entire first conversation, the day we met. And I can remember our last. I can tell you how her hand felt as I held it at the hospital, sitting beside her cancer-ravaged body. I can tell you what it felt like the moment she breathed her last breath and slipped into eternity, leaving me all by myself. I'm not going to, but I could." The old man's voice had grown thick as he was overcome with emotion.

Moments passed slowly in silence. Then Dr. Birjandi asked an unexpected question. "Her name is Marseille, right?"

David's heart stopped. "Pardon?" he said, hoping he hadn't heard the man right.

"The girl that you love," the old man continued, "her name is Marseille; am I right?"

In shock, David didn't know what to say.

"Your real name is David," Birjandi added. "David Shirazi."

"I'm afraid I don't know what you're talking about," David stammered. "You must have mistaken me for someone else."

"So you're not the David Shirazi who fell in love with Marseille Harper on a fishing trip in Canada, who was arrested for beating up a boy who thought you were an Arab? You weren't recruited by a Mr. Zalinsky to be an agent for the Central Intelligence Agency?"

Stunned, David rose to his feet without thinking. *"Who are you?"* he demanded. *"Why are you accusing me of such lies?"*

"You know they're not lies," Birjandi said gently. "And I'm not accusing you of anything. I'm just telling you what God told me to tell you."

David's mind was reeling. "The Twelfth Imam told you all this?"

"No."

"Then I don't understand."

"I don't follow the Twelfth Imam," the old man said.

David was more confused than ever. "What are you talking about? No one knows him better than you."

"That's why I don't follow him."

David scanned the empty room, looking from side to side and listening carefully for any sign that they were not alone. What was going on? His mind scrambled to think how best to handle such a bizarre and dangerous breach of identity. What options did he have? If he'd been compromised at levels this high up and was about to be seized by Iranian intelligence, there wasn't much he could do. He had no weapon, and the old man didn't seem like a promising hostage. It was unlikely he could successfully run. In the absence of another viable alternative, maybe he should find out as much as he could and try to control his emotions. He needed to think clearly for whatever came next.

"Now, just sit down," Birjandi said. "Take a deep breath. Be patient. You are in no danger from me. And I'll explain everything. It will take some time, but it is vitally important that you listen until the end. I will give you the information you seek and point you in the right direction. But first I need to tell you a story."

76

"I have been blind from birth," Birjandi began. "But I was always a devout Muslim. My father was a mullah. So were most of my fore-fathers, going back several centuries. So I was raised in a very devout environment. But my parents didn't force me to believe. I *wanted* to. Growing up, I loved to hear my parents teach me the Qur'an, especially my mother. She would read to me for hours, and when she stopped, I would beg her to read more and to answer all of my questions. She insisted I study Arabic because she wanted me to hear and understand and memorize the Qur'an as my heart language.

"By the time I was nine or ten, I would often go to the mosque by myself, praying and meditating for hours. I couldn't see the trees and the flowers and the colors of the world. All I had was my own inner world. But I knew Allah was there, and I wanted to know him and make him happy.

"Souri, my wife, was even more devout than I. She memorized the Qur'an faster. She prayed longer. She was smarter. By the time we graduated from high school, she was fluent in five languages. I knew only three.

"We got married right after high school. I went to college and then to seminary. I was going to be a mullah, of course. It was not anything forced on me. I wanted to spend my days and nights learning about God, teaching about God. And Souri was at my side every step of the way. She read my textbooks to me. I dictated my homework to her. She typed my papers. She walked me to class. We did everything together.

"With her help, I always got high marks on my exams and papers. When I graduated from seminary, I was first in my class."

David's heartbeat was slowly returning to just above normal. He tried to sound calm. "Was eschatology your main focus?"

"It was, and with Souri's assistance I wrote a thesis that was later published in 1978 as my first book, *The Imams of History and the Coming of the Messiah*."

"It became a huge best seller."

"No, no, not initially."

"Really?" David asked, perplexed. "On the cover of my copy, it says, 'Over one million copies in print.'"

"You've read it?"

"Absolutely—it was riveting."

"Well, that's very kind," Birjandi said. "Yes, the book did become popular in Iran and around the world, but that happened much later. The first printing was only about five thousand copies in Tehran and another few thousand copies in Iraq because there were a lot of Shias there. But you have to understand that Khomeini rose to power in 1979, just a year after the book was published. And from that point forward, it was illegal to discuss the Twelfth Imam. Well, not against the law per se, but severely frowned upon, especially in Qom and especially in academia."

"Why?" David asked.

"Very simple. Khomeini was threatened by it. He wanted people to believe that *he* was the Twelfth Imam. He never claimed to be, mind you—not directly—but he certainly didn't discourage people from thinking it. That's why he insisted that everyone call him Imam Khomeini. Before him, no one ever dared call a religious man *imam*. Among Shias, that title was reserved for the first eleven special descendants of Muhammad and, of course, for the twelfth and last. Religious leaders were called clerics, mullahs, sayyids, ayatollahs—but *never* imams."

Because of Khomeini's effective prohibition on speaking or teaching about the coming of the Islamic messiah, Birjandi explained, his book had been banned in Iran in 1981. Nevertheless, during that time, he and his wife had developed an even greater fascination with—and love for—Shia eschatology. The more forbidden it was, he said, the more intriguing it became.

"We were determined to understand how and when the end would come, what would be the signs of the End Times, and how a devout Muslim should live in the end of days. Most of all, we wanted to understand what would happen on Judgment Day and how to be saved from the flames. After Khomeini died, an entirely new era of intellectual and religious freedom began to dawn. Not for Jews or Christians or Zoroastrians or other religious minorities, mind you. But certainly for Shia scholars and clerics. Certainly for Souri and me. That's when we began to openly and aggressively accelerate our studies about all things related to the Twelfth Imam."

"So when was the ban lifted?"

"In 1996. And that's when the thing took off—over the next year or so. I honestly never thought of it as a book for the general public. I originally wrote it to serve as a textbook for a seminary class I hoped to teach. But somehow it became hugely popular, almost overnight, and soon I was speaking and teaching all over Iran."

"And interest in the Twelfth Imam skyrocketed as a result."

"Well, interest in the subject definitely grew exponentially, but not because of my book," Birjandi humbly insisted. "My book just happened to be rereleased at the perfect time. One millennium was ending. Another was beginning. Talk of the End Times was in the air. Suddenly, it seemed as if everyone was writing and speaking about the coming of the Mahdi. Then Hamid Hosseini read my book. He gave it to President Darazi to read. Then the two of them invited me to begin meeting with them once a month to discuss my findings and talk about these and other spiritual and political matters. When the public learned of our meetings through the national press, interest grew in a way that shocked us."

"It vaulted you into the status of the world's leading expert on Shia eschatology and a close advisor to the nation's leaders," David said.

"Strange but true," Birjandi conceded, shaking his head. "But along the way, something changed for me."

"What?"

"Well, first of all, you have to understand that during this time my elderly parents died. Then our only child, a daughter, was killed in a car accident in 2007. Souri was devastated. I was devastated. I couldn't work. I couldn't teach. My fellow professors were very understanding. They gave me a sabbatical to grieve and rest and recover. But I kept sinking. I was sure that I would be next, or Souri. I thought about death constantly. I became a slave to fear. What really happens when one stops breathing? Does that heart beat again in paradise? I was sure such a place existed, but I doubted the certainty of my ever arriving there. After a lifetime of study, I realized I had no answers. And the joy of life was gone. I had no will to teach, no will to be a good husband. I barely desired to get up in the morning."

"What did you do?" David asked.

"I made a decision not to give up on Allah," Birjandi said. "Many people do in similar situations, and I understand why. They're hurt. They're depressed. They blame God. But let me be honest with you, son—and I am not being pious when I say this—I just knew in my heart that somehow Allah was the only answer. I knew he was there, even though I felt so far from him. Despite all my religious training, all my family's history, all my knowledge of the Qur'an, I felt cut off from God, and it haunted me."

David said nothing, waiting for the old man to continue at his own pace.

"I thought about it for a long time," Birjandi continued after a moment, "and I concluded that the problem was that I only knew Allah intellectually, and that wasn't enough. What I really needed was to experience him. Now, Shia Islam, as you know, is a very mystical religion. We teach students that there are higher and higher levels of spiritual consciousness they need to discover and help others discover. But as you probably also know, Shia doctrine teaches that God's love is not available for everyone. It's only for those who go through a very specific spiritual journey. So in my classes, I would teach my students to meditate until they entered a trance. In that trance, if they were truly devout, they would eventually see visions of ancient imams and the various prophets and other historical figures. The goal is to go higher, deeper, closer to Allah. But truthfully I had never taken this so seriously for myself. I loved learning *about* Allah, but I had never really tried to *know* him personally.

"Then one day I went for a long walk through our neighborhood, alone with my cane. I knew I was sinking deeper and deeper into despair. I thought about ending my life, but I was not ready to die. I believed that committing suicide would condemn me to hell for sure. I was lost. Yet so many looked to me as if I had all the answers. Finally I came home and went to my room. I begged Allah to reveal himself to me. I pleaded that he show himself to me. I told him that I had done everything he had asked me, but it wasn't enough. I was ready to do more, but first I asked him to come and speak to me directly. But nothing happened. Months went by and nothing happened."

David listened, entranced.

"I became even more despondent. I wouldn't talk to my wife. I would stay up all night, unable to sleep. I would turn on satellite TV and mindlessly scan through the channels, listening to whatever was on. And one day I came across a program that caught my attention. It was an Iranian man who had been on the streets of Tehran during the Revolution in '79, shouting, 'Death to America!' For some reason, he and his wife applied to graduate school in California; they were accepted, and they went. But then their marriage started failing and their lives started falling apart, and they questioned Islam. It promised peace, but he said it gave them no peace.

"And that's when I started to listen more carefully. Until the man said he did a careful study of the Qur'an and the Bible and concluded that the Bible was true and that the Qur'an was false and that Jesus was the One True God. Then I cursed the television and turned it off, as furious as I had ever been.

"But after a few nights, when my wife was out doing errands, I couldn't help myself. I became curious and found that show again and kept listening. And the next time she went out in the evening, I listened again. I wanted to be able to prove that this man was insane. I wanted to be able to write an article or a book refuting everything he said.

"Then something very strange happened."

77

"What?" David asked.

"I simply knew."

"Knew what?"

"I knew that this man on television was the Creator's answer to my hunger. That I could not refute him. Through this man, God was telling me the simple truth about Himself. About His Son, Jesus. The anger in my heart for this man had displaced the despondency. Now that anger was suddenly gone, and only peace remained. Peace and the most solid, unmistakable knowledge that it was Jesus I should follow for the rest of my days."

David felt as though he had been struck mute. He heard Birjandi's words, but he could not believe they were coming from the mouth of such a revered Islamic scholar and counselor. Was this all a trick? But the man seemed to be filled with an energy that was growing as he told the story.

"Then I had this intense hunger and thirst—not for food and water but to know more about Jesus."

"What did you do?" David finally asked.

"What could I do?" Birjandi responded. "I already knew the Qur'an held no real answers about Jesus. Some tidbits, to be sure, but nothing solid. So one weekend when my wife went to Qom to visit her sister, I left the house and took a bus to Tehran. I must have asked a dozen people for directions, and finally someone helped me find my way to an Armenian church. I went there and I begged them for a Bible. They wouldn't give me one. They feared I might be a spy. I said, 'Don't be ridiculous. Look at me. I'm an old man, not a spy.' I pleaded with them to read to me about Jesus just for an hour, even just for a few minutes. They asked me if I was a Christian. I told them the truth—that I was a Muslim. But they said they could only give Bibles to Christians, never to Muslims. I told them I wanted to know more about Jesus. But they sent me away, and I was very aggrieved.

"It took me eight months to find a Bible. I went to every bookstore I could find, asking for one. I went to every library. Finally, to my surprise, I reconnected with a retired colleague of mine from the seminary. I learned that he had been given a Bible in a comparative religion class in college in England during the days of the Shah. I told him I needed it for a research project I was doing, and he told me I could have it; he had no use for it."

Dr. Birjandi leaned forward in his chair, drawing David in closer as well. "David," he continued, "I had never been more excited in my life. My hands trembled as my colleague set that book in them, and I came back to my home and realized I had a problem. I obviously couldn't read the Bible myself, not being able to see it. And I was scared to death to tell my wife what was happening with me. So I lied a little."

"You lied?"

"Yes, and I still feel terrible about it. But I didn't know what else to do."

"What did you say?"

"I told Souri that the seminary wanted me to consider writing a chapter for a book they were going to publish about the fallacies in Jewish and Christian eschatology, and that this intrigued me," Birjandi said. "To my relief, it intrigued her, too. So we locked ourselves in this study for several weeks and read and studied the Bible for ourselves from morning to night, from the first verse of Genesis—the first book of the Bible—to the last chapter of the last book, Revelation. We studied it. We discussed it. We filled up whole books with notes, and when our notebooks were full, Souri went out to get more, and we filled those up too. And as we did, I have to say, I was amazed by the life and teachings of Jesus. I fell in love with the Sermon on the Mount, for example. Have you ever read it?"

"No, I haven't," David admitted. None of this was clearing up his questions. He wondered how much more of this, no matter how interesting it was, he would need to listen to before he got the information he'd come for.

The old man leaned back in his chair, tilted his head against the faded cushion, and smiled. A look of restful delight crossed his face. He pressed his hands together at his chest and recited in a steady, melodic voice, "'Blessed are the poor in spirit, for theirs is the kingdom of heaven. Blessed are those who mourn, for they shall be comforted. Blessed are the meek, for they shall inherit the earth. Blessed are those who hunger and thirst for righteousness, for they shall be satisfied. Blessed are the merciful, for they shall receive mercy. Blessed are the pure in heart, for they shall see God. Blessed are the peacemakers, for they shall be called sons of God.'

"In all my life, I had never read more powerful words. I knew they were not the words of men. They were the words of God. And then we began to study Jesus' warnings."

"Warnings?" David asked.

"Throughout the New Testament, Jesus warned again and again of false teachers and false messiahs who would come to deceive the world after His death and resurrection. 'Beware of the false prophets, who come to you in sheep's clothing, but inwardly are ravenous wolves,' Jesus warned His disciples in Matthew chapter 7. 'You will know them by their fruits,' He said. 'Grapes are not gathered from thorn bushes nor figs from thistles, are they? So every good tree bears good fruit, but the bad tree bears bad fruit.'

"I thought long and hard about such verses and many others like them. And I thought about the fruit of Muhammad's life, about the violence. Muhammad lived by the sword and taught others to, while Jesus taught the exact opposite."

Birjandi then asked David to go to the bookshelf to his left and pull out the first and second books on the right-hand side of the top shelf; behind them he would find a copy of the *Injil*—the New Testament—in Farsi. David did as he was told and found it immediately.

"Turn to the Gospel according to Matthew, chapter 24," Birjandi said. "Matthew is the first book in the *Injil*, so it won't be difficult to find."

David did so.

"Okay, let's begin in verse 3," Birjandi said, beginning to recite the Scriptures aloud from memory as David followed along silently in the text. "'As He'—Jesus—'was sitting on the Mount of Olives'—that's near Jerusalem—'the disciples came to Him privately, saying, "Tell us, when will these things happen, and what will be the sign of Your coming, and of the end of the age?"' You see, Jesus' disciples wanted to understand when their Lord was coming back to earth to set up His kingdom and reign upon the earth. They wanted one sign, just one, that would indicate when His return was close at hand. But Jesus didn't give them just one sign. He gave them many. Earthquakes. Famines. Natural disasters. Wars. Rumors of wars. Apostasy. Persecution of the believers. The spread of the Christian gospel message all over the world. All that will happen in the last days, Jesus warned, just before He returns."

"That's all happening right now," David said.

"That's true," Birjandi said. "But look at the first sign Jesus warned His disciples about, beginning in verse 4. 'And Jesus answered and said to them, "See to it that no one misleads you. For many will come in My name saying, 'I am the Messiah,' and will mislead many."'"

David read the verse for himself. Birjandi was right.

"Now look at verse 11," Birjandi said. "What does it say?"

"'Many false prophets will arise and will mislead many,'" David read, curious at why Jesus was repeating Himself.

"Did Jesus say false messiahs and false prophets *might* arise in the last days?" Birjandi asked.

"No," David said. "He said they *will* arise."

"Did He say they *might* mislead many?" Birjandi pressed.

"No, He said they *will* mislead many."

"Okay, now read verses 23 through 27."

David turned the page and continued reading. "'Then if anyone says to you, "Behold, here is the Messiah," or "There He is," do not believe him. For false messiahs and false prophets will arise and will show great signs and wonders, so as to mislead, if possible, even the elect. Behold, I have told you in advance. So if they say to you, "Behold, He is in the wilderness," do not go out, or, "Behold, He is in the inner rooms," do not believe them. For just as the lightning comes from the east and flashes even to the west, so will the coming of the Son of Man be.'

"That's the third time in the same chapter that Jesus is warning about false prophets and false messiahs," David observed.

"That's right," Birjandi said. "And the more I thought about it, the more I realized that my life's work was built on lies."

78

"So let me get this straight," David said. "You're not a Muslim anymore?"

"No, I'm not."

"What are you, then?"

"I am a follower of Jesus."

"You don't believe that Muhammad is a prophet?"

"No."

"You don't believe the Twelfth Imam is the messiah?"

"No."

"How long ago did this happen?" David asked, dumbfounded.

"About eighteen months ago."

"Did you tell your wife?"

"I was going to," Birjandi said.

"What happened?"

"When we learned she had cancer, I started praying for her eyes to be opened to the truth about Jesus. I didn't pray five times a day for her. I prayed *twenty-five* times a day for her. And one day, as she slept, she dreamed of Jesus. He said, 'Souri, do not let your heart be troubled. Believe in God; believe also in Me. In My Father's house are many dwelling places; if it were not so, I would have told you; for I go to prepare a place for you. If I go and prepare a place for you, I will come again and receive you to Myself, that where I am, there you may be also. And you know the way where I am going.' And in her dream, Souri said to Him, 'Lord, I don't know where You are going, so how can I know the way?' And Jesus said to her, 'I am the Way, and the Truth, and the Life; no one comes to the Father but through Me.'

"Then she woke up, and right there and then, Souri realized that what she had been taught all her life, even by me, was wrong. She wasn't angry with Islam. She wasn't angry with me. She just knew in that moment that Jesus was the One True God, and she renounced Islam and became a follower of Jesus."

"How did you find out?" David asked.

"She told me right away," Birjandi said.

"Really?"

"Yes."

"She wasn't scared?"

"She was scared," Birjandi said. "But she told me that she loved me too much not to tell me the truth."

"You must have been very happy," David said.

"Actually," Birjandi said, "I felt ashamed."

"Why?"

"Because up to that moment, I had been too much of a coward to tell my own beloved wife that Jesus had saved me. When she told me her story, I broke down and cried, asking her to forgive me for not saying anything sooner. I could have lost her. She could have died and gone to hell, and it would have been my fault for not telling her the good news of Christ's love. But you know what?"

"What?" David asked.

"Souri forgave me immediately," Birjandi said. "It has taken me a long time to forgive myself, but my Souri forgave me immediately. That's the kind of woman she was."

There was another long pause while David tried to absorb all of this and make sense of it. "So to be clear, you don't believe the Twelfth Imam is real?" he finally asked.

"Oh no; he's real, all right. He's just not from God. He's from Satan."

"But you believe he exists?" David asked.

"Of course," Birjandi said. "He's here now. He was right here in Hamadan. Haven't you heard the news?"

"I've heard the rumors, but I—"

"They're not rumors, son. He's really here, and he's doing miracles to attract attention and a following. But as Jesus said—and you read it yourself just now—they are signs and wonders designed to deceive people, not to save people. Which brings us to you."

"Me?"

"Yes, you," Birjandi said. "You see, a week ago, the Lord told me you would be coming to see me."

"A week ago?"

"Yes. He told me all about you, and he instructed me to tell you things I'm not supposed to tell anyone. Things about Iran's nuclear weapons."

David could hardly breathe. He had come to Birjandi expecting to be taught about Shia eschatology and the Twelfth Imam. Instead he had gotten a crazy story about Jesus. And now the old man was about to tell him about Iran's nuclear program? None of it seemed possible. Yet Birjandi continued to speak.

"Hosseini and Darazi built nine nuclear warheads. One was just tested. That's what caused the earthquake. There are eight left. And they are large bombs. Each one of them could destroy Tel Aviv, New York, Washington, Los Angeles, London, you name it. But Iran doesn't yet know how to attach them to a long-range delivery system, so they cannot fire ballistic missiles with nuclear warheads on them. Not yet. When they use them, they will have to transport them by ship or truck and detonate them on site or by remote control."

David was trembling. In his head, he was still a skeptic. But in his heart, he believed it all. "How do you know this?"

"Hosseini told me last week at our monthly lunch together."

"Why would Hosseini tell you all this?"

"I am his closest personal advisor, an old and trusted friend. He's excited because he believes what I always taught him. That once we had the ability to wipe out the Jews and Christians, then the Mahdi would come. But he also asked me to pray that Allah would give him wisdom to know how best to proceed. He had not confided this to me before last week, guarding his secrets carefully, as usual."

"Do you know where these warheads are?" David asked.

"They were all in Hamadan last week, but now they have been dispersed around the country," Birjandi said. "The last chance to take them all out at once would have been to hit Saddaji's research center in Hamadan. But no one did. The Israelis took out Saddaji, but that was the wrong move. They needed to hit the research center. Now it's too late."

"Do you have proof of all this?" David asked.

"I'm not sure it matters," Birjandi said.

"What do you mean?"

"I mean we are in the last days," the old man said with a sigh. "The arrival of the Twelfth Imam means that an apocalyptic war between Iran, the U.S., and Israel is imminent. I honestly don't know why God has brought you here, but His ways are not our ways. His thoughts are higher than our thoughts."

"I want this nuclear program stopped," David answered. "These men are madmen, and I believe they are hell-bent on killing millions."

"I don't know if it can be stopped," Birjandi said. "You certainly can't stop all of the wars and devastation and death. They are foretold. The same is true of the rise of false messiahs and false prophets and false teachers. It is written they will come. Now they are here. Such things are determined by God, and nothing can thwart or change His will."

"But does the Bible say these deceivers win?" David pressed. Clearly Birjandi chose the Bible for his motivation, just as Hosseini and Iran's leaders chose the Qur'an. He would have to appeal to this internal compass of the old man, no matter how crazy it seemed.

"No," Birjandi said. "They do great damage, but ultimately they don't win."

"Then maybe God will use mere mortals like you and me to stop them," David said.

"I don't know that. But I hope so."

David wasn't sure what to think about Birjandi's story of converting to Christianity. Maybe the man was crazy. He clearly hadn't told this story to the leaders of this country during their monthly meetings. If they were sharing state secrets with him, they must believe he was still loyal to Islam. Birjandi was wise to keep his experiences to himself and try to live out the last few of his years in peace.

David didn't think the man was trying to trick him. Maybe Birjandi would be a key, game-changing source for him, but he'd have to tread carefully. "I need to verify the things you've told me. Is there a trail I can follow, a person who might also want this nuclear program stopped, maybe someone on the inside?"

Birjandi paused. "Before you worry about the world, son, you should be sure your own soul is secure in God. He knit you together in your mother's womb. He loves you. But you must choose without delay. The forces of evil are gathering, rising, and believe me, David, you will never be able to stand against the tempest unless you have been forgiven, washed by the blood of Christ, filled with His Holy Spirit, and suited up in His full and mighty armor."

That wasn't what David wanted to hear. "I appreciate that very much, Dr. Birjandi," he replied. "But I'm not worried about myself."

"You should be."

"What about the souls of the innocent? What about the millions of people who will die if the Twelfth Imam orders Iran to detonate nuclear weapons in my country or in Israel?"

"You need to think of yourself first."

"That's selfish."

"No, that's wisdom," Birjandi said. "You don't know what you're going up against. Satan is not to be taken lightly. That's who is giving power to the Twelfth Imam—Lucifer himself. You can't possibly thwart him on your own."

"I'm not on my own," David said. "I am an agent of the United States of America. We are the wealthiest and most powerful nation on the face of the planet—in the history of mankind. If anyone can stop the Twelfth Imam—if there is anyone who can stop Iran—it's the United States. We have this country surrounded. We've got forces in Iraq and the Gulf states. We're in Afghanistan. We're in Turkey. We've got submarines and aircraft carriers parked off your coastlines. We've got Predator drones and spy satellites hovering overhead. But we need proof. We need specific targets. And we need them now."

Several minutes went by. Birjandi said nothing. David looked at his watch.

"Najjar Malik," Birjandi finally said.

"Who is that?"

"He lives in Hamadan. He's the son-in-law of Saddaji and the next in line to lead the nuclear program. I'm told that he and his young family have disappeared since Saddaji's murder and that there are many people looking for him."

"Would he talk to me?"

"I don't know."

"Where can I find him?"

"I don't know that either. But let me be clear, David—you'd better find him before the Mahdi does."

79

Every Muslim was commanded to make *hajj*.

As David had thoroughly studied during his college years in Munich, *hajj* was the fifth of the five pillars to which every follower of Islam must submit.

The first pillar was saying the *shahada*, the basic profession of faith in Allah and Muhammad as his prophet. The second was performing *salat*, praying five times a day at the prescribed times. The third was *zakat*, the giving of alms to the poor. The fourth was *sawm*, fasting from food, drink, and sexual relations during the daylight hours of the month of Ramadan and at other times in the Islamic calendar. But it was the *hajj* that was the most difficult and thus the most honored act of the five.

David had never done it, but every year, despite enormous poverty and deprivation throughout the Islamic world, more than 1.5 million foreign Muslims joined roughly an equal number of Saudi Muslims to make their pilgrimage to the city of Mecca. Considered a holy city, Mecca was the epicenter of Islam, the city where Muhammad was born in AD 570, the city where he claimed he first began receiving revelations from Allah, a city whose people tried to resist and crush Islam in its infancy after Muhammad moved his base camp to nearby Medina, and the city that was ultimately conquered by Muhammad and his army of ten thousand *mujahideen* in AD 630.

After the conquest, Muhammad declared that no infidel could ever enter Mecca, but every year Muslims entered in wave after wave, fully doubling the normal population of the city that once had little, if any, historical significance. Some came by train. Some came by bus or automobile. Others trekked across the desert. When the hotels filled up, they camped out in the thousands upon thousands of white tents erected by the Saudi government. When the tents filled up, they slept on floors or out under the stars. Most saved their entire lives for one opportunity to pray at the Kaaba, the black, granite, cube-shaped building that stood in the heart of Al-Masjid Al-Haram, the Sacred Mosque, also known as the Grand Mosque.

But every Muslim knew the *hajj* took place in the fall. This was late February, and no one had ever seen anything like this.

The Islamic world had been electrified by the announcement that the Twelfth Imam had returned and would soon appear publicly. With rumors spreading of the great signs and wonders he was doing, Muslims were converging on Mecca in a way that threatened to overwhelm all of the normal systems.

It was still the middle of the night, but David decided to use his rental car and drive rather than fly from Hamadan back to Tehran. Rather than get cut off from the flow of news and information in airports and on a plane, he wanted to be able to listen to the continuing coverage from Mecca on the radio. He also wanted to be able to transport the Farsi Bible that Dr. Birjandi had given him without some security guard at the airport finding it in his luggage and making a big deal of it.

One report that caught his attention on the way came from the official Saudi news agency. Every seat on every flight coming into the kingdom in the next seventy-two hours was full. A spokesman for Saudi Arabian Airlines said they were doing everything they possibly could to add charter flights, but he pleaded for patience and understanding.

So far, David noticed, the palace in Riyadh had not put out any official statement, either positive or negative, commenting on the Twelfth Imam's coming to Mecca. But he interpreted the efforts of the Saudi government to move so quickly to truck in hundreds of thousands of tons of food, millions of gallons of water, and tens of thousands of additional tents as a sign of the Sunni kingdom's acceptance, however reluctant, that the Shia leader's imminent journey to Mecca was a *fait accompli.*

The question was, why?

It didn't make sense that Saudi Arabia's Sunni leaders were countenancing this visit by the Twelfth Imam to their country at all, much less enabling it. Why was the king essentially rolling out the red carpet for a religious figure in whom he did not believe, a political leader who could in a single sermon steal his kingdom right out from under the House of Saud? Was someone forcing their hand? Were they being blackmailed?

★ ★ ★ ★ ★

TEHRAN, IRAN

"What do you mean you can't find him?"

Defense Minister Faridzadeh had been up all night, and he was apoplectic. It had been hours since he had ordered his staff to track down Najjar Malik. Since issuing the orders, Faridzadeh had been locked away in his office, consumed with poring over the final results of the nuclear warhead test. It had never dawned on him that his aides were so inept as to be unable to find the man who was now the most important figure in the Iranian nuclear program.

"We don't even know if he is alive," Faridzadeh's chief of staff explained, standing in the center of his boss's spacious corner office in the Ministry of Defense.

"Why not?"

"Hamadan is still chaos, sir. There's not enough food or water. The roads are a disaster. The phone system is only now coming back online. Tens of thousands are dead. Over a hundred thousand have been wounded, and many of those getting medical treatment don't have identification with them."

"Has anyone personally gone to Dr. Malik's apartment and knocked on the door?"

"We tried, but the apartment was completely destroyed by the earthquake."

"No survivors?"

"None, sir."

"So he could be at the bottom of all that rubble?"

"It's possible, sir."

"What about the staff at Facility 278? Have any of them heard from Dr. Malik?"

"He was at the plant the night of Dr. Saddaji's funeral, but no one we've talked to has seen or heard from him since."

Faridzadeh stared at his chief of staff and delivered his ultimatum. "You've got six hours to find him and bring him to me. Don't ask for a minute more."

★ ★ ★ ★ ★

DUBAI, UNITED ARAB EMIRATES

Zalinsky checked his caller ID and tensed.

"Zalinsky," he said, picking up the phone on the third ring.

"Jack, it's Tom Murray. I'm calling from Langley."

"Hey, Tom."

"We've got a problem," the deputy director for operations said.

"What's that?"

"I received a very uncomfortable call from the director."

"What about?"

"Apparently President Jackson just got off the phone with Prime Minister Naphtali. Naphtali won't say whether the Israelis took out Mohammed Saddaji or not. But he did say Israeli intelligence is detecting significant radiation emanating from a mountain west of Hamadan. What do you know about this?"

"Nothing concrete, sir," Zalinsky answered, not exactly lying but not quite telling the whole truth either.

"You have a man in Hamadan right now, don't you?"

"Yes, sir."

"Does he have indications that the Iranians may have just conducted a nuclear test there?"

"He's hearing rumors, sir, but nothing solid."

"Rumors?"

"Speculation," Zalinsky said. "Hearsay. But there's nothing to back it up."

"The Israelis are requesting a Constant Phoenix pass over the city," Murray said. "The president was blindsided by the request. He's furious that no one gave him a heads-up that there was even a possibility that the earthquake could have been triggered by a nuclear weapons test. Not us, not DIA, not the Pentagon."

"We're working on it, sir," Zalinsky assured the DDO.

"It's not enough," Murray fumed. "You need to do better, Jack. The president is ordering Constant Phoenix to head to Iran, but we won't have data for another twenty-four hours. You need to get me something more, and fast."

"We're on it, sir."

But Murray wasn't finished. "What's all this commotion about the coming of the Twelfth Imam?" he demanded to know. "Naphtali said the arrival of the Twelfth Imam could mean the Iranians are close to launching a strike against Israel. The Saudi ambassador was just at the White House and told the president the Iranians say the Twelfth Imam is going to give a major address in Mecca, and the king is afraid the Iranians are planning to overthrow his regime by flooding the country with Shias from Iran. Quite frankly, until today, neither the president nor I had even heard of the Twelfth Imam except as some vague Muslim concept."

"My people are working on all that, too, sir," Zalinsky said. "But we need more time."

At that, Murray lost it. "We don't have more time. You're supposed to keep me ahead of the game. I needed something yesterday. I gave you all the money you requested—black box, no congressional oversight—and what have you given me in return? Nothing, Jack. Nothing I can use."

Murray was right, and it made Zalinsky ill. He was failing his boss and his country at a critical moment, something that had never happened in his life. He tried to stay calm. All he had new on the Twelfth Imam was Zephyr's memo. He cringed at the thought of sending that up the chain of command but wasn't sure what else to do.

"I'll get you something soon," Zalinsky promised.

"You've got six hours," Murray said. "I want a backgrounder on the Twelfth Imam and hard new intel on what's happening in Hamadan on my desk. And I want an update every six hours after that. You need to squeeze your people, Jack. All of them. The director said he's never seen the president so livid. He's afraid the Israelis are going to launch any minute. You have got to get ahead of this, or there will be hell to pay."

80

Zalinsky called Eva into his office.

"What's wrong?" she asked, startled by his ashen face.

"Tell me we have something new—*anything*—on the Iranian weapons program and the Twelfth Imam," he demanded.

"We do, Jack," Eva said. "I was about to bring all this in, but you were on the phone."

"What do you have?"

"The data is starting to come in from the international monitoring sites near Iran."

"And?"

"It looks like Zephyr was right. The seismic activity around Hamadan is consistent with a nuclear weapons test, not a natural earthquake—unbelievably intense at first but then slowing down rather than building."

If only I'd had that information an hour earlier. "Anything else?" Zalinsky asked, steeling himself for more "good news."

"Actually, there is, though I'm not exactly sure what yet," Eva said, showing Zalinsky the latest transcripts of intercepted calls from the NSA. "Zephyr has delivered the satellite phones, and the phones, in turn, have been delivered to senior Iranian officials. They've apparently already been scrubbed for bugs and given the *Good Housekeeping* seal of approval, because they're starting to crackle."

"Are we getting anything on Hamadan?" Zalinsky asked.

"Indirectly," Eva said. "No one's talking about a nuclear test, per se.

They seem quite cautious about what they say on the phones, even if there aren't any bugs that they can detect. But there is a firestorm of interest in some guy named Najjar Malik. The Twelfth Imam is asking for him personally, but they can't seem to find him."

"This Twelfth Imam is a real person, not a fable or a myth of some kind?"

"They're talking about him like he's flesh and blood, boss."

"Unbelievable."

"I know."

"Do you have any background on who the religious scholars say this guy is and what he's supposed to do when he appears?"

"Actually, I do."

"Fine—I need you to write a fast backgrounder on all that for the president," Zalinsky said.

"Sure. By when?"

"I need it in four hours. Murray needs it in six."

"Done."

"Good. Now, who is Najjar Malik?"

"We don't know," Eva conceded. "We're running the name through all of our databases and haven't come up with anything yet. But the search is being directed out of the defense minister's office. Look at these transcripts."

Zalinsky scanned the documents she handed him.

"Both mention Malik in context with Saddaji," Eva noted. "And see, in both he's referred to as *Dr.* Malik. My best guess at this point is that he's a nuclear scientist. He probably worked for Saddaji on the weapons program, very likely as a deputy or at some other senior level. What's curious is that when you look at all the calls, it becomes clear that they're looking for Dr. Malik in Hamadan. They're afraid he might be dead because his apartment was destroyed in the earthquake and no one in the building survived."

There it was again, Zalinsky thought—the city of Hamadan.

There was no question about it now, he realized. Zephyr *was* right. There was a secret nuclear facility in Hamadan, and the CIA had totally missed it. What's more, Zephyr and the Israelis were also right that the earthquake to the west of the city had been triggered by an underground nuclear blast. Which meant Eva had to be right, as well. Dr. Najjar Malik had to be a nuclear scientist, probably a big shot in the program if he worked for Saddaji. Iran's defense minister wanted to see him urgently. The Twelfth Imam, whoever he was, was asking for him. The evidence was circumstantial, but for Zalinsky, the next step was clear. If Najjar Malik was still alive, he was now a high-priority target. The Agency needed to pull out all the stops to hunt him down and capture him before the Iranians or the Israelis got to him.

Zalinsky looked up from the transcripts. "Get Zephyr on the phone; I need to talk to him—*now.*"

★ ★ ★ ★ ★

TEHRAN, IRAN

There was a knock at the door.

"Come in," Defense Minister Faridzadeh said, exhausted and growing more anxious by the hour.

"We found his secretary," an aide said.

"Whose?"

"Dr. Saddaji's."

"Where's she been all this time?"

"She's been going from hospital to hospital and to the morgue, trying to identify Facility 278 employees."

"Does she know anything about Dr. Malik?"

"Yes, she knows he's alive, sir. She spoke to Mrs. Saddaji by phone. She says they went as a family to Tehran to mourn in solitude."

"Fine," the minister said. "Get him here so he can see Imam al-Mahdi."

"Well, that's just it, sir. She doesn't know exactly where he is."

"What?"

"She only knows he's somewhere here in the capital."

"Can't she call him?"

"She has, sir, numerous times. But he's not picking up. Like I said, he's in mourning with his family. He probably turned his phone off."

The defense minister cursed and slammed his fist on the desk. "I don't care," he shouted. "Just find him!"

★ ★ ★ ★ ★

David was entering the outskirts of Tehran when his phone rang.

He glanced at the caller ID and recognized the number as one used by Eva Fischer in Dubai.

"Hello?"

"Hey, Reza, it's me," she said. "The boss needs you to call him."

"I'm kind of busy at the moment, Eva. Can it wait?"

"I'm afraid it can't," Eva said. "It's about the expense reports for your team. They're racking up quite a bill over there already."

David sighed. "Expense reports" was Eva's code. Whenever she mentioned them on an unencrypted call, he knew he was supposed to call Zalinsky immediately on a secure line.

"No problem; I'll call him as soon as I get back to the hotel," he said for the benefit of Iranian intelligence, sure to be taping this like all other international calls.

"I'll let him know."

"Thanks," David said. "How's business?"

"It's picking up," she said cryptically. "We're going to have a good quarter so long as you and the boys there don't spend us into oblivion."

"We'll try to be more careful."

"I know you will," Eva said. "Now get some sleep. Bye."

David hung up the phone and checked his rearview mirror as he turned off the Saidi Highway and headed north through the city's western neighborhoods. He hadn't seen anyone following him at any point during the trip from Dr. Birjandi's, but now that he was back in Tehran, he took special care. He joined the hundreds of cars that clogged Azadi Square, circling the iconic Azadi Tower, also called Freedom Tower, built in 1971 to celebrate the 2,500th anniversary of the founding of the Persian Empire. David took the exit onto Meraj Avenue, past the National Cartographic Center and the Iranian Meteorological Organization, before taking a left on Forudgah, just beyond the airport grounds. Satisfied that he was alone, he pulled into a quiet little neighborhood of single-family homes and parked on Hasanpur Street. There he pulled out his phone again, switched to the encrypted system, and dialed Zalinsky's private line from memory.

This must be big, he thought. He was taking a risk making this call from inside the capital. It was impossible for Iran's intelligence services to hear what he was about to say or what was being said to him. But if they were watching him closely, he was bound to trigger suspicion.

Zalinsky picked up on the first ring. "Have you ever heard of a Dr. Najjar Malik?" he asked immediately.

And hello to you, too, Jack. "Why do you ask?" David said, startled by the request.

"I've just decided he's the highest-value target in the country at the moment," Zalinsky said. He explained the intercepted calls and the enormous and growing urgency inside the Defense Ministry and the Twelfth Imam's inner circle to find Malik. "We know he's a wanted man, but we know almost nothing about him."

"I do," David said. "He may be the key in helping us unlock the entire Iranian nuclear weapons program."

"Talk to me," Zalinsky insisted.

"Malik was born February 1, 1979," David said, drawing on the profile Birjandi had sketched out for him just hours before. "He's Persian but was raised in Samarra, Iraq. Speaks Arabic, Farsi, and English fluently. Did his doctoral work in nuclear physics at the University of Baghdad. Dr. Saddaji recruited him to come to Iran soon after 9/11, though I'm not sure exactly when. Malik married Saddaji's daughter and became Saddaji's right-hand man. They worked out of a place called Facility 278, which I'm told is the headquarters for the nuclear weapons development team. Saddaji oversaw Iran's entire civilian nuclear power program. But that was his cover. Most of the day-to-day work on the civilian side was run by Malik. Saddaji himself focused primarily on building weapons. But he used very few Iranians. Most of his team is comprised of Pakistanis whom Saddaji hired from A. Q. Khan. Apparently, Saddaji also recruited a senior Iraqi nuclear scientist. Bottom line: Najjar Malik wasn't just on the inside; he was family. As far as I can tell, he knows everything about the program, and he knows where the bodies are buried. I'm guessing that's why the Twelfth Imam wants to meet with him so badly. They need someone new to run the weapons program now that Saddaji is dead."

"Who's your source?"

David explained who Alireza Birjandi was, his relationship with the leaders of the regime, and the time they had just spent together.

"You're saying this Birjandi is a senior advisor to the Supreme Leader?" Zalinsky asked.

"He's not on the payroll, but from all that I have gathered, few people are closer to Hosseini or Darazi. You should ask Eva for more. She's the one who first told me about him and has been working up a profile on the guy."

"And you believe him?" Zalinsky pressed.

"I do."

"Even the conversion story?"

"It's strange, I know, but I think he honestly believes it."

"Why?"

"Why else would he tell me? I mean, it's a capital offense here to convert to Christianity. Especially if you're a spiritual advisor to the Supreme Leader. Why tell a complete stranger? It's a statement against interest."

"Why *is* he talking to you?"

It was a good question, one David had been contemplating since the moment he left the man's house. "Birjandi strikes me as a classic dissident," he told Zalinsky. "No one knows more about Islam than him, but Islam has failed him. The regime has failed him. And now he's rejected both. What's more, he's deeply worried the leadership is going to bring ruin upon his country."

"How?"

"By trying to bring about the end of the world. And Birjandi believes they now have the means to do it."

"Meaning what?"

"Birjandi says the regime now has eight nuclear warheads ready to go."

"He said that?"

"Yes."

"How does he know?"

"Hosseini told him."

"When?"

"The last time they met for lunch, about a week ago."

Zalinsky was silent for so long that David finally asked if he was still on the line.

"Yeah, I'm still here," Zalinsky replied.

"Why aren't you asking me if I have any proof?"

"Do you?"

"No," David said, "but it's strange you're not asking."

"I'm not asking because I already believe you."

"Why?"

"The president ordered the Constant Phoenix pass over Iran."

"Really?"

"Yep."

"And?"

"And we got the seismic report. You were right. There was a nuclear explosion in a mountain range just west of Hamadan. That's what triggered the earthquake. So that's it. Iran has the Bomb. The Israelis are about to launch a preemptive strike. And we're out of time."

David was silent for a few moments. The magnitude of what was unfolding was almost more than he could bear.

"Does this Birjandi guy know where those warheads are at the moment?" Zalinsky asked. "They can't possibly still be in Hamadan?"

"No, you're right," David said. "He says they've been scattered all over the country. But he says our best shot is finding Najjar Malik before the Iranians do."

"Malik knows?"

"We'll see, but he's our best shot."

"So how do we find him?"

"At the moment, I have no idea," David admitted. "Do you?"

"No," Zalinsky said. "But I'm going to put a special ops force on standby. If you can find him, we need him alive. Get him to a private airstrip; use any means necessary. We'll get him out. I promise."

"Any means?" David asked, just to be clear.

Zalinsky wasn't taking any chances. "*Any* means necessary," he repeated, and the line went dead.

81

Najjar was worried as he entered the tiny motel room.

He put down the bag of groceries he was holding, then quickly locked the door behind him and pulled the drapes shut. He kept telling himself he was supposed to be "strong and courageous," but the truth was that fear was getting the better of him. If the Israelis could get to Dr. Saddaji, they could certainly get to him. The Americans couldn't be far behind. And how soon until Iranian intelligence began suspecting he was on the run? Maybe they knew already.

Four days had gone by since they'd arrived in Tehran. Najjar had been crisscrossing the city looking for a Bible for him to read with his wife and mother-in-law. Everywhere he went, he heard footsteps behind him. He feared someone was waiting for him around every corner. At any moment, he imagined a car would come screeching to a halt, and men with guns and masks would jump out, seizing him and putting a bullet through his skull or forcing him into the trunk to be taken somewhere and beheaded. He'd seen it happen to others. He had no doubt they could do it to him. Every time he came back to the motel room, he feared Sheyda and Farah and the baby would either be dead on the floor with their killers waiting for him or bound and waiting to be killed in front of his eyes.

Najjar was haunted by the sober, bitter truth that he was a target, and thus so was his family. And the two women he loved were still haunted by the sudden and horrific death of Dr. Saddaji, a man they practically regarded as a saint. At some point, Najjar would have to tell them the truth, but he couldn't do so now. Sheyda and Farah were grieving. It was natural. He didn't blame them for it. It could hardly be otherwise. But Najjar worried it was only a matter of time before they were going to ask why he wasn't shedding tears over the loss.

Sheyda still had no idea her father had been the head of Iran's nuclear weapons program. Farah hadn't the foggiest notion her husband had been planning a second holocaust while working for a regime that denied the first had ever even happened. Neither of the women had any idea that Dr. Saddaji's laptop—the one Najjar had stolen out of his home office and now had hidden in the motel closet—contained details about Iranian weapons. Was he actually going to tell them? He couldn't imagine how.

"Did you find a charger for your phone?" Sheyda asked as Najjar unpacked fresh-baked bread, cheese, pomegranates, and some bottles of water.

"Yes," he told her, coming over to kiss her on the forehead. "But that's not all—look."

He pulled out a copy of the Bible in Farsi, and his wife lit up instantly.

She immediately took the Bible from his hands, kissed it, and examined it with great reverence. After a moment, she looked at Najjar. "Where did you get this?"

He grinned. "You'll never believe me."

"Tell us," Sheyda said, her face filled with joy.

"I was coming back to the motel after visiting five different bookstores. No one admitted to having a Bible, and I was becoming convinced I'd never find one. I was praying and asking Jesus to help me, but I kept getting more and more discouraged. But then I stopped by an electronics shop to pick up a charger for the phone. The owner took one look at me and said, 'I have what you want.' I said, 'What do you mean?' and he said, 'I have what you're looking for.' I told him I was looking for a cell phone charger, and he said, 'Yes, yes, but I have your other item as well.' By now I was totally confused. He left me standing there and disappeared into the back somewhere, and when he returned, he was holding this Bible. I tell you, I almost turned around and ran out of the shop! He told me his family had been followers of Jesus for several years but had never had a Bible of their own until just a few weeks ago, when he received a shipment of electronics supplies for the store. Hidden in the bottom of the box were two Bibles. He took one home and had been praying about what to do with the other one, when just before I came into the store, he felt the Lord speaking to his heart that the next customer would be looking for a Bible. And a second later, I walked in."

"Thank You, Jesus!" Sheyda said, tears in her eyes. "I can hardly believe it!"

"I said you wouldn't," Najjar said.

"Would you read to us, Mother?" Sheyda asked as the baby began to cry. Sheyda picked her up from the bed to nurse her again.

"Yes, of course," Farah said. "Let me find those passages Jesus told us to read. Deuteronomy 14 was one of them, right?"

"Actually, it was chapter 13," Sheyda said.

Najjar was eager to hear the words from the Bible, but he took a moment to plug in his phone, thinking he should check his voice messages. Then he sliced open several pomegranates in their little kitchenette and shared them with Sheyda and Farah. None of them had had much of an appetite for the past few days. But the fruit tasted wonderful and picked up their spirits.

Farah, meanwhile, turned to the table of contents. She had never seen a Bible in her life and had certainly never held one. None of them had. But after a few minutes of fumbling through the pages, Farah found the chapter and began reading.

> "If a prophet or a dreamer of dreams arises among you
> and gives you a sign or a wonder, and the sign or the
> wonder comes true, concerning which he spoke to you,
> saying, 'Let us go after other gods (whom you have not
> known) and let us serve them,' you shall not listen to
> the words of that prophet or that dreamer of dreams; for
> the Lord your God is testing you to find out if you love
> the Lord your God with all your heart and with all your
> soul. You shall follow the Lord your God and fear Him;

and you shall keep His commandments, listen to His
voice, serve Him, and cling to Him."

Sheyda listened to the words and turned to her husband. "Those
verses are speaking to you, don't you think?"

"They could be," he replied.

"Of course they are. When the Twelfth Imam appeared to you those
times as a boy, he was predicting your future, right?"

Najjar nodded.

"And those predictions came true."

Najjar nodded again.

"But that doesn't mean the Twelfth Imam was speaking for God,
right?" Sheyda continued. "Just the opposite—the Twelfth Imam was
trying to take you away from the Bible, away from the One True God.
But Jesus was merciful to you. He appeared to you to counter the
Twelfth Imam, and now He's explaining to you that He was testing
you back then."

"But I failed the test," Najjar said. "I followed Islam all those years.
I believed in the Twelfth Imam all those years."

"But you don't now, my love," Sheyda said, comforting him. "Now you
know the Twelfth Imam is a false prophet, because God has opened your
eyes. And I think He is calling you for something very important."

"What's that?"

"I think you're supposed to help people understand what's true and
what isn't so they have the chance to be set free as well."

Najjar wasn't sure about that. He hoped she was right. But at the
moment he was so filled with regret for the life he had lived for so
many years—so many wasted, lost years—that it was hard to think of
anything else.

Farah suggested they read the next passage listed in their notebook.
She handed the Bible to Najjar, who found the book of Exodus and
turned to chapter 7.

"Then the Lord said to Moses, 'See, I make you as
God to Pharaoh, and your brother Aaron shall be your

prophet. You shall speak all that I command you, and your brother Aaron shall speak to Pharaoh that he let the sons of Israel go out of his land. But I will harden Pharaoh's heart that I may multiply My signs and My wonders in the land of Egypt. When Pharaoh does not listen to you, then I will lay My hand on Egypt and bring out My hosts, My people the sons of Israel, from the land of Egypt by great judgments. The Egyptians shall know that I am the Lord, when I stretch out My hand on Egypt and bring out the sons of Israel from their midst.'

"So Moses and Aaron did it; as the Lord commanded them, thus they did. Moses was eighty years old and Aaron eighty-three, when they spoke to Pharaoh.

"Now the Lord spoke to Moses and Aaron, saying, 'When Pharaoh speaks to you, saying, "Work a miracle," then you shall say to Aaron, "Take your staff and throw it down before Pharaoh, that it may become a serpent."'

"So Moses and Aaron came to Pharaoh, and thus they did just as the Lord had commanded; and Aaron threw his staff down before Pharaoh and his servants, and it became a serpent.

"Then Pharaoh also called for the wise men and the sorcerers, and they also, the magicians of Egypt, did the same with their secret arts. For each one threw down his staff and they turned into serpents. But Aaron's staff swallowed up their staffs. Yet Pharaoh's heart was hardened, and he did not listen to them, as the Lord had said."

"It's a pattern," Sheyda said softly when Najjar had finished reading.

"What do you mean?" Najjar asked.

"Sometimes false prophets and ungodly rulers can do signs and wonders. Sometimes they can do tricks that look like miracles of God, but they are really tapping the power of the devil. But we should not fear because God is greater, and in due time, He will swallow the enemy and thwart the enemy's plans."

"That makes sense," Farah said. "But do you think the Lord is saying the Twelfth Imam is like Pharaoh?"

"Maybe so," Sheyda said, "but let's keep reading."

Taking turns reading a chapter at a time, they backed up to chapter 1 of Exodus, read all forty chapters, and discussed them for hours. Was the Lord going to raise up a Moses to lead the Iranian people out of Islam?

It was almost two in the morning when they finally turned out the lights. But as Najjar lay his head on the pillow next to his wife and heard her begin to snore softly almost immediately, he found he could not sleep. His mind swirled with new thoughts and ideas he'd never even heard of before, much less considered seriously.

He was completely captivated by the person of Moses. In Islam, Moses was certainly considered a prophet, but Najjar was enthralled by the richness of the biblical details of Moses' life and interaction with the One True God. Moses had been chosen by God from birth. He had been taken from his home as an infant but by God's grace given a great education. His character had been shaped in the halls of power of the mightiest empire of the day, until one day the Lord God called him out. It didn't make sense at first. God required Moses to give up all that he had, all that was important to him. But God had a plan for the man of God, Najjar realized, and that captured his thoughts.

As the clock kept ticking into the wee hours of the morning, Najjar began wondering what plan God had for him. He loved Sheyda's new passion and her conviction that perhaps God was calling Najjar, of all people, to speak for Him, to reach Iran with the message of Christ's love and forgiveness. He was by no means convinced she was right. It seemed too lofty a role. But there was a more immediate question: What were they supposed to do next? They couldn't stay in a motel on the edge of Tehran for too many more days. They couldn't go back to Hamadan.

Where, then? Was the Lord going to take Najjar and his family out of Iran, the way He took Moses out of Egypt to prepare him for his future role? He hoped so. He couldn't imagine staying and living under this bloodthirsty regime and now under a false messiah. But the only thing more difficult to imagine than staying in Iran was getting out alive. Millions of Iranians were heading to Mecca. The traffic jams all around them, so close to the airport, were proof of that, as were the constant reports on radio and television. Maybe they should join them? Maybe they should head to Saudi Arabia under the pretense of going to Mecca, then find a way to slip into Jordan or even Egypt.

Najjar suddenly felt thirsty and got up to get a glass of water in the kitchenette. As he did, he noticed his phone and realized he had forgotten to check his messages earlier. Powering up the phone, he was shocked to see twenty-three voice messages, all from Dr. Saddaji's secretary.

The first message instantly sent terror into his heart. The defense minister was looking for him? Why would Faridzadeh want to see him immediately? It was a trap, Najjar thought. What else could it be? Yet what could he do? Each message proved progressively more ominous than the last, but the final voice mail was the most terrifying of all. Najjar was supposed to have reported to the defense minister's office several days before. From there, he was to have been taken to a private meeting at the palace with the Twelfth Imam. Najjar had been instructed to tell no one about the invitation and bring no one else and nothing but his ID. No briefcase. No camera. No notebook. Nothing. The Mahdi and the minister were looking forward to seeing him, Saddaji's secretary said, and they were eager to give him some "good news" that they promised would "cheer him and his family." Najjar had no idea what that meant, nor did he want to find out. He quickly powered down the phone and set it back on the table.

What was he supposed to do? Moses had gone back to Egypt and confronted Pharaoh and his magicians directly, hadn't he? Then again, hadn't Jesus specifically said that when a false messiah comes—especially one who performs "great signs and wonders, so as to mislead, if possible, even the elect"—and someone says to you, "Behold, He is in the inner rooms," that you should *not* go?

Najjar was chilled with fear. Sheyda and the baby were asleep. So was Farah. He had no friends he could call. He had no family to whom he could reach out. So he did the only thing he knew. He got down on his knees and begged the Lord for mercy.

82

David paced his tiny hotel room.

He stared out the window at the traffic beginning to build up and tried not to panic. It was Tuesday, March 1. He'd spent most of the last several days searching for Najjar Malik on the Internet, in Iranian phone directories, through real-estate transaction records, and on Iranian newspaper and magazine databases, all to no avail. He had dozens of analysts back at Langley searching every intelligence database they could and data-mining all other materials toward the same end, but with no results. He had the NSA feverishly translating and transcribing intercepted calls, whose frequency were growing exponentially and beyond the Agency's capacity to keep up.

None of the transcripts indicated Faridzadeh or his men had found Najjar yet, but they were definitely closing in. According to the tidbits Eva had relayed, the Iranians now knew Najjar was in Tehran. They'd even gotten a momentary ping from his cell phone in the middle of the night somewhere on the west side of the city.

In desperation, David thought about calling Mina and saying he had urgent business at Iran Telecom. Could he persuade her to let him in the building this early in the morning? Even if the answer were yes, could he persuade her to let him break into the company databases and search Malik's phone records to see whom he had called in the last twenty-four to forty-eight hours? Maybe there was someone in Tehran, someone with an address, someplace David could focus his attention? But he quickly dismissed the notion. Faridzadeh and the chief of VEVAK certainly already had that information, and there would be agents at any of those locations. David's showing up at any one of them would only raise suspicions he couldn't afford. And he wasn't sure Mina would help him anyway. She was no fan of her boss, Esfahani, but she seemed loyal to the company. David believed he could eventually turn her into an asset. But he hadn't yet, and he concluded she'd be no help now.

He considered calling the head of the MDS tech team in Tehran. Maybe he could help David break into Iran Telecom's database and at least get Najjar Malik's cell phone number. Without it, Langley and the NSA couldn't listen in on Najjar's calls in real time once he turned his phone back on. But once the man turned his phone on, how much time would he have before VEVAK triangulated his position and swooped in to take him down? Ten minutes? Fifteen, tops? Even if the NSA was listening in, there wouldn't be enough time to find him before the Iranian authorities did.

David rubbed his eyes and stared in the mirror. He wondered if he should call Dr. Birjandi. The man had been extraordinarily helpful in so many ways. But to talk on an open line was too much of a risk. And what exactly would he ask? The old man didn't have a crystal ball, though David desperately wished that he did.

He glanced at his watch. It was now almost quarter past six. The call of the muezzin would begin soon, and dawn prayers would start before the sun rose. He still had no desire to pray, certainly not to the god of Islam. But once again, he had no choice. He had to maintain his cover, however worthless it seemed at the moment.

Thousands of men were already on their knees, bowing toward Mecca, by the time David arrived by taxi at the Imam Khomeini Mosque. He paid the driver, ran in, performed his ritual washing, and found a spot in the back. He knelt down, bowed toward Mecca, and picked up the morning prayers in progress.

"Glory to my Lord, the Most High," David began, chanting in unison with the others. *"Glory to my Lord, the Most High. Glory to my Lord, the Most High. Allah is great. All good, whether rendered by speech, by prayer, by deed, or by worship, is for Allah only. Peace be unto you, O Prophet, and the mercy and blessings of Allah. Peace be unto us and the righteous servants of Allah."*

At the next line, however, he froze. He knew what was coming. But he couldn't say it.

"I bear witness that there is no God except Allah, and Muhammad is His slave and Messenger."

Everyone else chanted the words, but David did not. He had said them thousands of times. But this time he could not. He continued going through the motions, hoping no one would notice he had stopped speaking.

Someone did.

"What happened?" the man beside him to his right whispered as the room continued chanting.

"What do you mean?" David whispered back.

"You stopped praying," the man said, bowing in unison with David and the others.

"I didn't," David lied, his heart racing. "I just had . . . to clear my throat."

David bowed again and finished this particular prayer more loudly than usual, making certain all those around could hear him clearly.

"As you praised and venerated Abraham and the followers of Abraham, in the worlds, surely You are praised and magnified," he chanted. *"Amen. Peace be unto you and the mercy of Allah. Peace be unto you and the mercy of Allah."*

But the stranger on his right would not let it go. As they moved on to a different prayer, he began asking David questions.

"Are you new here? I've never seen you here before."

David grew more concerned. "I'm from Dubai," he whispered between chants. "Germany, actually, but—"

The man cut him off. "Munich?"

David was silent.

"Is your name Reza?" the man asked.

David was stunned but tried to keep his cool and continued praying. Maybe this was one of Esfahani's men. He had met Esfahani here before. Or maybe it was one of Rashidi's men. Maybe Javad Nouri had sent a colleague to summon him, though for what he couldn't imagine.

"Why do you ask?"

There was a long pause while the two men continued praying in synchronization with the thousands of others in the great mosque.

"Because my name is Najjar Malik," the stranger said. "As soon as this prayer is over, get up and follow me."

83

The baby's cries woke Sheyda just before dawn.

And the call to prayer from a nearby minaret wasn't far behind.

Sheyda rubbed her eyes and forced herself to get up, surprised to find that Najjar was not at her side. Assuming he was in the bathroom, she rolled over, picked up the baby, and tried to nurse her. Only then did she see the note Najjar had left on the bedside table saying that he had gone out and would be back soon. Something about that troubled her, but she was not sure what.

Eager to find out if he was okay, Sheyda asked her mother, just waking up as well, if she would get her cell phone out of her pocketbook and bring it to her so she could call Najjar without moving the baby. Farah was still groggy, but she happily got up and found Sheyda's cell phone and turned it on.

"Not that it's going to do you any good, dear," she said.

"Why not?"

"Look," Farah replied, pointing to the counter by the kitchenette.

Najjar had forgotten to take his cell phone. Sheyda sighed with disappointment, her anxiety growing. She asked her mother to turn it on and check for new messages. There were none, Farah reported as she set the phone back on the counter and went to wash for prayer.

The baby was fussing. She didn't want to eat, so Sheyda got up and walked her around the room, patting her lightly on the back and swinging her gently in her arms. Farah finished washing and bowed down on the carpet, but not toward Mecca. After much discussion over the past few days, the three of them had decided as a family to pray toward

Jerusalem instead, and to do so in the name of Jesus. Farah prayed for a few minutes, but the baby wasn't calming down. In fact, she seemed to be crying louder.

"I'm sorry, Mom," Sheyda said. "Let me take her for a walk, and I'll come back when you're done."

"Don't be silly, dear," Farah said. "I'll go with you. We could all use a little fresh air. She'll fall asleep, and then we can both come back, put her down for a nap, and pray together."

★ ★ ★ ★ ★

David's head was filling with questions.

But his only hope for answers was about ten paces ahead of him and moving rapidly toward the east gate.

David worked his way quickly through the thick crowd, trying not to lose sight of the man claiming to be Najjar Malik. Was this a setup? How could it not be? How could this really be Najjar Malik? If it was, why would Najjar have come to him? And why here? The mosque was crawling with undercover policemen and intelligence operatives.

An elderly man hobbled into his path, and David almost knocked the poor man over in his bid to keep up with the stranger. For a moment, he lost visual contact. He turned to the right but saw nothing. He turned to the left and noticed the man turning a corner. He made sure the old man was okay, then elbowed his way through the crowd, walking as fast as he could to catch up but not daring to run lest he draw too much attention—which meant any attention at all.

A moment later, David caught up to the stranger, who was getting into a car parked along a side street. The man motioned for David to get in quickly. David looked up one end of the street and down the other. There were plenty of people still pouring out of the mosque and walking through the surrounding neighborhoods, but no one looked particularly worrisome. Besides, even if someone had looked threatening, David was too intrigued not to get in the car and find out who this was.

The instant David closed the door, the stranger hit the accelerator and pulled out onto Panzdah e-Khordad boulevard.

"Who are you really?" David asked.

"My name is Dr. Najjar Malik," the man said, pulling his Iranian passport from his trouser pocket and handing it over.

David carefully looked over the document. If it was a fake, it was an awfully good one, and he wondered why anyone would go through the trouble. He had never seen Najjar Malik before. He had no idea what the man would look like. Anyone could say they were Najjar and catch his attention. But why would they, and why now?

"What do you want with me?" David asked.

"I want to leave Iran."

"What?"

"You heard me," the man continued. "I have information your government wants. I will give it to you in exchange for political asylum."

"You've got the wrong guy," David said cautiously. "I'm just a businessman. I don't know what you're talking about."

"No," the man said, "you've been looking for me, and now here I am. I'm offering you my help, but you must also help me."

"You're crazy," David said. "Pull over the car."

"Why?"

"Because you're a lunatic. I'm a businessman. I sell phones. Now pull over and let me out."

David didn't know whom he was dealing with, but if this was some test by Esfahani or Rashidi or someone else, he was determined to pass it. Yet he could see the stranger turning white. The man was perspiring and gripping the steering wheel for dear life. If he was acting, he was good. David wondered for a moment if this could be the real deal, but he quickly banished the thought from his mind. It was impossible. There was no way that—

"I have a laptop," the stranger blurted out.

"You need to pull over now," David insisted.

"I have a laptop you will want," the stranger said again. "It was Dr. Saddaji's laptop. I am sure you know who he was."

If this was a trap, David thought, it was becoming irresistible.

"The Israelis killed him," the man continued. "Or maybe you did. I don't know. Either way, I don't regret it. The man was . . . Anyway, I have his laptop."

There was a long silence as the man kept driving through increasingly congested city streets. David said nothing. He didn't dare say anything. What the man was offering was the crime of treason.

"I haven't had time to review all of the material on his hard drive," the stranger said, "but some of it I have. Your government needs to see it immediately."

"I don't work for the German government," David said. "I told you, I'm a businessman. I work for Munich Digital Systems. We sell—"

"Mr. Tabrizi, please," the stranger said. "I'm not interested in talking to the German government. I want this laptop and the information I have to go to the Americans, to *your* government. I know you work for the Americans, and I know you want what I'm offering. So please, I don't have time to play these games. I'm risking my life here. I'm risking my family's life. I was told that you could help me. Can you?"

The man suddenly took a hard right on a Vahdat e-Islami Street, and then another right into Shahr Park, a quiet, wooded oasis in the middle of Tehran's concrete jungle. When he found a parking space with no one else around, he stopped the car but kept it running.

"Let me be perfectly clear, Mr. Tabrizi," the stranger continued, obviously trying to keep his emotions in check. "I have studied the reports on my father-in-law's computer. Iran now has eight nuclear warheads in its possession. By the end of March, they will have fourteen. By the end of April, they will have twenty. The weapons work. Our scientists don't yet know how to deliver them via a missile, but that's not going to stop this regime from using them soon. Ayatollah Hosseini ordered my father-in-law, Dr. Saddaji, to write a detailed plan for how one of these warheads could be shipped to Egypt, smuggled across the Sinai desert, into Gaza through the Hamas tunnels, and then into Israel to be detonated in Tel Aviv. I have the memo. It's on the laptop, along with dozens of e-mails to and from Hosseini's top aides—mainly General Jazini—refining the plan and improving it significantly. But that's not all, Mr. Tabrizi."

David finally bit. "What else do you have?"

"I have dozens of e-mails between Jazini and my father-in-law discussing the technical challenges of transporting several of these warheads first to Venezuela, then to Cuba and Mexico, and finally into the United States. Like I said, I haven't had time to review everything that's on the laptop, but I can tell you there are detailed discussions on how to ship the warheads safely, how to evade international detection, how to maintain operational control over the trigger mechanisms, and so forth. I'm willing to turn it all over to your government. But my family and I want asylum and protection."

★ ★ ★ ★ ★

DUBAI, UNITED ARAB EMIRATES

Eva burst into Zalinsky's office.

"We've got a problem," she said.

"What's wrong?"

"We're getting all kinds of chatter on the satphones. The Iranians just found Najjar Malik. They're sending agents to pick him up as we speak."

84

They sat in the park with the car still running.

"Why are you telling me all this?" David asked.

He was increasingly convinced he was really speaking to the actual son-in-law of Dr. Mohammed Saddaji. But to be sure he wasn't being set up, he needed to better understand the man's motive.

"I don't want innocent people to die," Najjar explained.

"All of a sudden you have a conscience?" David countered. "You've been working with your father-in-law on building nuclear weapons for years."

"No, that's not true," Najjar said. "He hired me to help him develop civilian nuclear power plants, not to build the Bomb."

"That's easy for you to say now."

"It's the truth," Najjar insisted. "I never even suspected what my father-in-law was up to until recently. But even then I had no proof."

David was still skeptical. "What changed?"

"Everything has changed," Najjar replied. "Dr. Saddaji was killed by a car bomb. I read what was on his laptop. Then there was the earthquake, which you must know was not a natural event. It was triggered by a nuclear test. There are scores of e-mails in which my father-in-law was scheduling the test and assigning tasks for the final details. It's all on the laptop."

David listened carefully. It was all adding up. Everything Najjar was saying was consistent with the evidence he and his team had collected so far, but far more detailed and far more dangerous. If it was all true, it certainly explained why the Iranian regime was working so hard to hunt this man down.

"Why me?" David asked.

"What do you mean?"

"Of all people, why did you come to me? And how did you know who I am or what I look like?"

David could see the hesitation in the man's eyes.

"I'd rather not say."

"Then no deal," David said.

"What do you mean?"

"You heard me. I'm not making you a deal unless you explain how you found me and why."

"What does it matter?"

David ignored the question. "How could you have even known I would be at the mosque this morning?" he demanded. "I wasn't even sure I was going to come until just before the prayer service began."

It was clear Najjar didn't want to answer his question, but David wasn't going to give up. He had to call this in to Zalinsky, but not unless he was sure, and at that moment, he still had doubts.

"We should go," Najjar said, glancing at his watch. "We're not safe here anymore."

But David pulled out his phone. "I can help you, Najjar," he said calmly. "One phone call, and I can get you and your family out of this country forever. I can get you set up in America with a new life, safe from your enemies here. But first you need to answer all of my questions."

"I'm telling you what I know. I'll tell you more. But not here."

"Najjar, you came to me," David reminded him. "You obviously believe I will help you, and I will. But I need to know—who sent you to me?"

"Please, Mr. Tabrizi," Najjar implored. "My family is not safe. I must get back to them."

"We will pay you. More money than you've ever seen."

"I'm not doing this for money! I'm doing this for my family."

"Then just tell me. Who sent you? It's a simple question. Give me a name."

"It's not that simple," Najjar said.

"The name, Najjar; just give me the name."

★ ★ ★ ★ ★

DUBAI, UNITED ARAB EMIRATES

Zalinsky's phone rang.

It was Tom Murray from the CIA's Global Operations Center.

"Talk to me, Jack. What have you got?"

"It's not good," Zalinsky said. "Best we can tell, the Iranians have tracked down Najjar Malik. They've dispatched about a dozen police and intelligence units to pick him up. They should be there any moment."

"So what do we do now?"

"I'm working on it, sir."

"What about your man in Tehran?" Murray asked.

"He's been working on this nonstop," Zalinsky explained. "But at this point, I don't think there's anything more he can do."

"Call him," Murray ordered. "We can't let this guy slip away. The Israelis are on edge. They're 100 percent sure now the Hamadan earthquake was triggered by a nuclear test, and the president is afraid Naphtali is going to launch a preemptive strike. If the Iranians get Malik . . ."

Murray didn't finish his sentence, but he didn't have to. Zalinsky promised to get back to Murray in a few minutes, then hung up and speed-dialed Eva.

"Get me Zephyr."

★ ★ ★ ★ ★

TEHRAN, IRAN

David wasn't sure how to respond.

He'd asked for a name, and Najjar had given him a name. It just wasn't one he could possibly have expected. In any other country, at any other time, the whole notion would have been ludicrous. But with all that had been happening in recent weeks . . .

"Let me make sure I have this straight," David said. "You were a

Twelver. But you've converted to Christianity because you saw a vision of Jesus. And now you're saying that Jesus told you to come here and meet me? That doesn't strike you as strange?"

"Not that strange. It happened in the New Testament all the time," Najjar said.

"What's that supposed to mean?"

"Jesus told people things were going to happen, and they happened."

"Really."

"Jesus sent people to certain places and they went. Jesus told Ananias to go to Straight Street in Damascus and heal a blind man named Saul of Tarsus at the house of Judas, and Ananias did it. He didn't know Saul. He'd never seen Saul. The Lord just led him, and he obeyed."

"And I'm supposed to believe that Jesus sent you to me?" David asked.

"Believe it or don't believe it; I'm sitting here, aren't I?"

He certainly was, and David realized he had entered an entirely different dimension. He had come to Iran to engage in a clandestine geopolitical war but had come face-to-face with something else entirely. There was a spiritual battle going on for this country unlike anything he had ever heard of or imagined, and he wasn't prepared for any of it. People were talking about visions of the Twelfth Imam and visions of Jesus as if such events were commonplace. What's more, it was becoming clear that the people of Iran were being asked to choose sides between the two.

It occurred to David that he wouldn't have even known the name Najjar Malik or his importance to the Iranian nuclear program if it hadn't been for Dr. Birjandi—a brilliant octogenarian former Shia Muslim scholar who sometime in the past few years had secretly renounced Islam and become a follower of Jesus. What's more, according to Birjandi, more than a million Shia Muslims in Iran had converted to Christianity in the past three decades. Many of them had converted after seeing dreams and visions, he said, and more were converting every day. In a strange sort of way, while Najjar Malik's story was far outside of anything David had ever experienced, it did have a certain logic to it.

The ultimate proof, perhaps, was in the laptop, and David was eager to see it. Just then, his phone rang. It was not a welcome call. Not at the moment.

"Hey, I really can't talk right now," he told Eva. "I'll call you back."

"Actually, this can't wait," Eva said.

"This really isn't a good time."

"Too bad."

"Why? What's the problem?"

"It's your expense reports, Reza. They're still not in order. The boss wants to talk to you about them before he heads into a budget meeting."

"Fine," he said. "Tell him I'll call in a few minutes."

He hung up the phone and turned to watch a jogger running through the park. He followed the man for a moment and scanned the woods to see if there was anyone else around. For now, they were still alone. But Najjar was right; they couldn't stay much longer. They had to keep moving or be questioned by the next patrol car that came through the park. But there was something he had to do first.

"Where is the laptop now?" David asked.

"In the trunk," Najjar said.

"Can I see it?"

"Do we have a deal?"

"If you have what you say you have, then yes, we have a deal."

They got out of the car, and Najjar opened the trunk. Sure enough, there, wrapped in a motel blanket, were a Sony VAIO laptop, an external hard drive, and a plastic bag filled with DVDs. Najjar powered up the laptop and briefly showed David some of the files and e-mails he'd been describing.

Thunderstruck by what was in front of him, David told Najjar to gather it all and bring it up to the front passenger seat.

"I'm going to drive," he said. "You're going to read to me."

"Where are we going?" Najjar asked.

"Where's your family?"

"In a motel near the airport."

"We need to get them, and fast."

85

DUBAI, UNITED ARAB EMIRATES

For Eva's taste, information wasn't flowing fast enough.

It was taking too long for the NSA to transcribe and interpret the intercepted calls and get them to her and Zalinsky. So Eva called her NSA counterpart and insisted she and Jack be able to listen in to any of the intercepted calls in real time, only to be told that such a request couldn't be made by someone at her level but had to come from at least the CIA's deputy director for operations.

Furious, Eva slammed down the phone and drafted a memo to Tom Murray to that effect. She e-mailed it to Zalinsky for his approval, then walked over to his office to follow up, wondering as she walked how exactly they were supposed to fight and win the war on terror with such insane bureaucratic constraints. She knocked on the door and popped her head in as Zalinsky was picking up the phone.

"Code in," he said.

"Is that Zephyr?" she whispered.

Zalinsky motioned for her to come in quickly and shut the door behind her. But rather than answer the question, he put the call on speakerphone. Zalinsky confirmed Zephyr's passcode, then cut to the chase.

"We've got a problem," he told David. "The Iranians have Malik."

"No, sir; I've got him!"

"What do you mean you've got him?"

"He's with me right now."

"That's impossible," Zalinsky said. "VEVAK forces just stormed Malik's motel room near the airport."

"No, sir," David said. "I'm telling you, he's sitting right beside me. We're driving to the motel now."

Zalinsky paused. "Son, can he hear what I'm saying?" he asked quietly.

"No, sir."

"You're sure?"

"I'm sure," David confirmed.

"Then listen to me very carefully," Zalinsky said, getting to his feet. "You've got the wrong guy. The VEVAK team tracked Najjar Malik's cell phone to a motel near the airport. They raided the place a few minutes ago."

There was a pause. "Hold on."

Eva could hear David asking the person sitting next to him if he had his cell phone with him.

"No," they heard the man reply, "I left it at the motel."

"Sir," David said, "we may have a problem."

"You've got the wrong guy," Zalinsky said.

"No, I've got Dr. Najjar Malik, all right. I've got his passport. I've got his father-in-law's laptop. I've got Saddaji's external hard drive. I've got Saddaji's memos, his e-mails. I've even got his backup discs. It's real, sir. It's all that we've been looking for. But Dr. Malik left his cell phone at the motel. Iranian intelligence must have triangulated the signal and tracked it down. If they just stormed his motel room, then we have another problem."

"What's that?"

"They now hold his wife, his daughter, and his mother-in-law."

★ ★ ★ ★ ★

Ayatollah Hosseini picked up the phone.

He found the Twelfth Imam on the other end of the line.

"Do you have Malik yet?" the Mahdi demanded to know.

"No, my Lord," Hosseini said. "Not yet."

"I thought you had him at a motel."

"We thought we did, too, my Lord. His cell phone was there, but he was not. We think . . ." Hosseini hesitated.

"What?"

"I hesitate to say because we're still—"

"It's okay, Hamid," the Mahdi said calmly. "Just tell me what you know."

"My people think he has defected, my Lord."

"What makes you say this?"

"General Jazini says Dr. Saddaji's laptop is missing from his apartment. We know that Dr. Malik went to Dr. Saddaji's office the other night, ostensibly to get his personal effects. But the general thinks Malik might really have gone there to gather evidence of the nuclear program. He may now have what he needs."

"To do what?"

"We don't know, my Lord. We would just be guessing at this point."

"Then guess."

"Worst-case scenario?" Hosseini asked. "He could be trying to sell it to the Americans or perhaps the Israelis. We may have to accelerate our attack plans before either can launch a preemptive strike. But for the moment, there is a more urgent matter. We must stop Dr. Malik from getting out of the country."

"What do you recommend?"

"For starters, we need to close the airports, the bus stations, the train stations. We'll also set up police checkpoints on all the major highways leading in and out of Tehran."

"No, that's a mistake," the Mahdi said, catching Hosseini off guard. "All that would stop the flow of Iranian pilgrims heading to Mecca to see me revealed to the world. And it would create a negative news story right at the moment when I am receiving excellent worldwide coverage about my imminent arrival. No, you must keep all this quiet. Don't let the media catch wind of the manhunt or report it in any way."

Startled, Hosseini said nothing for a moment.

But then the Twelfth Imam said one more thing. "Make no mistake: I want you to find Najjar Malik. I want you to find him, and I want you to bring him to me that I may separate the head of this infidel from his neck and rip his heart out of his body."

★　★　★　★　★

Najjar Malik was rattled.

"Mr. Tabrizi, those monsters have my family. We have to find them," he insisted.

"We're doing everything we can," David promised as he drove. "We're putting our best people at the CIA on it right now."

"I can't leave without them. You understand that, right? I'm not leaving this country without my family."

Najjar didn't seem to be panicking, but there was no question in David's mind that his new asset had the weight of the world on his shoulders.

"I understand," David assured him, "but for the moment we need to focus. We need to get you someplace safe. You're no good to your family if you get captured or killed. Do you understand me?"

Najjar nodded and grew quiet.

"You guys are on Azadi Road, heading west, correct?" Eva said.

David was startled to hear her voice. For a moment, he had forgotten that he still had Fischer and Zalinsky on the line and that they were following him via the GPS tracker in his phone.

"Affirmative," David said. "We just passed the metro station and should be at Azadi Square in a few minutes."

"How's traffic?" Zalinsky asked.

"Not good, and getting worse," David said. "We're on an eight-lane boulevard. I'm doing ten to twenty kilometers an hour at the moment, but half a klick ahead it's all brake lights."

"We need a plan to get you guys out of there," Eva said.

David already had one. "Once I clear through this mess, I'm heading for Safe House Six," he said, referring to a basement apartment the CIA owned on the outskirts of the city of Karaj, about twenty kilometers west of Tehran, in the foothills of the Alborz Mountains. "We should be there in about an hour."

"That's good," Zalinsky said. "What then?"

"If the regime shuts down all the airports, we'll hunker down at the safe house, upload all the contents of the laptop to you, and wait until things quiet down a bit. But let's assume for a moment that they keep the airports open."

"Why would they do that?" Eva asked.

"They might not want to stop all these Iranians from being able to get to Mecca to see the Twelfth Imam. That's a huge deal for this regime."

"I think you're wrong about that," Eva said.

"Maybe," David conceded. "But if by some chance I'm not, I say we use this mass pilgrimage to our advantage."

"How?" Zalinsky asked.

"Send a private plane to Karaj under the guise of a charter flight," David said. "Report the flight as a group of wealthy pilgrims heading to Mecca to see Imam al-Mahdi. With any luck, we'll get lost in the exodus. They can't possibly keep tabs on everybody. State-run radio says they're expecting another half-million Iranians to leave for Saudi Arabia in the next twenty-four hours."

"I don't have a private plane to send," Zalinsky said. "I have a CIA special ops team on standby in Bahrain to extract you guys out of a site in the desert."

"No, I don't want to take Dr. Malik into the desert; it's too risky," David said. "We need to hire a plane out of Dubai and try to get it to Karaj by tonight before they think twice and really do shut down the airports. It's our best shot, Jack. It may be our only shot."

86

Suddenly David wondered if they'd even make it to Karaj.

As they inched toward Azadi Square in the stop-and-go traffic, they saw the flashing lights of police cars ahead of them. More seemed to be coming from every direction, and despite the roar of jumbo jets and cargo planes landing at Mehrabad International Airport, the two men could hear the sirens approaching.

"We're only a few blocks from the motel," Najjar said. "Look, over there, to the left—it's just a few blocks."

"That explains it," David said.

"What do you mean?"

"All the police."

"That's just because of the traffic, all the people trying to go to Mecca, right?"

"No," David said, "they're setting up a roadblock."

Najjar stiffened. "Then we need to get off this road."

David agreed. They did need to get off the main thoroughfare and avoid the roadblock. The problem was that every side street from here to the square was clogged with hundreds of other drivers trying to find their way around the logjam as well.

"Is this your car?" David asked.

"What do you mean?"

"I mean, do you own it? Is it registered in your name?"

"Yes, yes, it's mine."

"We're going to have to get rid of it."

"Why? What for?"

"The moment a police officer runs these license plates, it's going to come up with your name. We don't want to be in the car when that happens."

"What do you recommend?"

"Hold on," David replied.

Then, without any more warning, David pulled the steering wheel hard to the right. He darted across two lanes of traffic, triggering a wave of angry drivers honking their horns before he got off Azadi onto a street called Nurshahr and began to head north. Unfortunately, it, too, was practically a parking lot. It wasn't totally stopped. They were moving, but progress was slow, and David was getting edgy.

He needed to get Najjar out of Tehran. He was too exposed. They both were. At any moment, David knew, the Iranian police would in all likelihood be issuing an all-points bulletin. Every police station in the city was about to be faxed a wanted poster with Najjar's face and details, which would be bad enough. But David had other concerns to worry about as well. Under no circumstances could he allow himself to get caught or implicated in Najjar's extraction from the country. To do either would blow his cover and compromise all the work he'd done. The Twelfth Imam's inner circle would stop using their new satellite phones. The MDS technical teams would be thrown out of the country. The CIA's multimillion-dollar effort to penetrate the Iranian regime's command and control would be ruined. And given that Iran already had the Bomb and a war now seemed both inevitable and imminent, the CIA needed every advantage it could possibly get.

Suddenly they heard a siren behind them. David cursed as he glanced in the rearview mirror and saw the flashing lights about ten cars back. He guessed that a police cruiser had spotted his rapid and reckless exit from Azadi Road and gotten suspicious.

Najjar, cooler than David would have expected under the circumstances, bowed his head and began to pray. David admired the man's courage. He was trying to do the right thing for himself, his family, and his country. But already he was paying an enormous price. David couldn't imagine the grief he and his family were suffering. His wife had almost certainly been captured by his enemies, as had her mother and their baby daughter. Who knew where they were right now? Who knew what kinds of torture they were now being subjected to? Yet Najjar's initial anxiety seemed to be fading, and the worse things got, the more calm the man became.

The siren and flashing lights were getting closer. David knew what he had to do. He turned the wheel, jumped the curb, pulled Najjar's car off the congested street and onto the sidewalk, and hit the accelerator. Najjar's eyes popped open as he was thrust back against his seat. Pedestrians started screaming and diving out of the way as David plowed through trash cans and mowed over fire hydrants. Every driver on the street was cursing at him. Every horn was honking, but the police cruiser was left in the dust, and David let himself smile. He hadn't had such fun in a car since training at the Farm.

The escape, however, was momentary. By the time David reached Qalani Street and took a hard left, another police cruiser was waiting for him and began pursuit.

David wove in and out of traffic, blowing through one light after another. The traffic on Qalani was not nearly as bad as the other streets they'd been on, but David was steadily losing ground. Najjar was not praying anymore. He was craning his neck to see what was happening behind them and urging David simultaneously to go faster and be more careful.

One block passed. Two. Three. The police car was hot on their tail and gaining. But the road ahead was coming to an end. They were coming up to a T. David suggested Najjar grab the door handle and brace for impact.

"Why?" Najjar asked at the last moment. "What are you going to do?"

David didn't answer the question. It was clear he wasn't going to be able to successfully turn right or left without rolling the car. Instead, he slammed on the brakes and turned the steering wheel hard to the right, sending the car screeching and spinning across four lanes of traffic.

They were hit twice. The first was by the police cruiser itself since it was too close behind them and the officer hadn't expected David to slam on the brakes. The second was by a southbound delivery truck that never saw them coming. The air bags inside Najjar's car exploded upon impact, saving their lives but filling the car with smoke and fumes. But theirs was not the only collision. In less than six seconds, David had triggered a seventeen-car pileup on Azizi Boulevard, shutting down traffic in all directions. Up and down the boulevard David and Najjar could hear the clash of twisted, tangled metal and smell burning rubber and burning engines.

David quickly unfastened his seat belt. "You okay?" he asked.

"Are we still alive?"

"Yeah," David said, checking his new friend for any signs of serious injuries. "We made it."

"Are you insane?"

"We needed a diversion."

"That was a diversion?"

"It was," David said. "Now listen, are you okay?"

"My arms are burning."

"That's from the air bags. You'll live. Any broken bones?"

"I don't think so."

"Check yourself. Check the computer, and stay here. I'll be right back."

David couldn't get out the driver's-side door. It had been too badly mangled from the force of being hit by the delivery truck. So he climbed into the backseat, which was littered with shards of broken glass, and kicked out the back passenger-side door. His hands were covered with blood, he felt blood on his face, and his arms were badly burned by the air bags as well. Other than that, he was fine. He jumped out of the car and surveyed the scene. It was a terrible mess in both directions, but he saw what he needed—the police cruiser—and made his way to it as quickly as he could.

The car was a smoldering pile of wreckage. Gasoline was leaking everywhere. David feared a single spark could blow the whole thing sky-high. Inside, the solitary officer was unconscious. He couldn't have had any time to react to David's slamming on the brakes, and that had been the point. David had needed the element of surprise, and he'd gotten just that.

Using all his strength, David pried the driver's door open and checked the man's pulse. Fortunately, he was still alive, but he had an ugly gash on his forehead, his face was covered in blood, and David realized to his regret that no air bag had deployed. But he saw what he needed and pocketed the officer's .38-caliber service revolver and portable radio. Then he pulled the officer from the wreckage, carried him a good distance from the glass and gasoline, and laid him on the sidewalk.

David hobbled back to Najjar's car, suddenly realizing his right knee had gotten banged up worse than he'd first realized. He looked down and noticed his pants were ripped and that blood was oozing out of the knee. But he had no time to worry about it. They needed to get out of there before the place was swarming with more police.

"You ready to move?" David asked, coming over to the passenger side.

"I think so," Najjar said, his arms filled with the laptop and accessories.

"Is that everything?"

"Yes."

"Good. Follow me."

"Where are we going?" Najjar asked.

"You'll see."

They walked north about a hundred meters before David turned, pulled out the .38, aimed at the gas tank of Najjar's crumpled Fiat, and pulled the trigger. The car erupted in a massive ball of fire that not only obliterated the vehicle but all traces of their fingerprints and DNA as well. The force of the blast threw Najjar onto his back. David, still standing, gave him a hand and helped him back to his feet.

"What was that for?" a stunned Najjar asked, shielding his eyes from the intense heat of the flames.

David smiled. "Insurance."

87

David walked north down the center of Azizi Boulevard.

With Najjar close behind, he limped his way past wrecked cars and distraught motorists fixated on all the fire and smoke. He clipped the police radio to his belt, put in the earphone, and made sure it was plugged into the radio so the transmissions couldn't be overheard by anyone else.

His phone vibrated. It was a text message from Eva, telling him to call Zalinsky in the secure mode. He did so right away and coded in, but it was Eva who actually picked up.

"What in the world just happened down there?" she asked, her voice betraying her distress.

"We had a little accident."

"A *little* accident? Have you gone insane? The entire Global Operations Center—and everyone in our safe house—is watching you via a Keyhole satellite. What are you doing?"

The chatter on the police radio suddenly intensified. Reports of the accident and explosion were coming in from concerned citizens and drivers on their cell phones. Police units, ambulances, and fire trucks were being dispatched. David knew they had only a few minutes before the first units arrived on the scene.

"I can't really talk now," he said. "I need to boost a car that's still running. Do you need something, or are you just interfering in my operation?"

"I found you a plane," she said, not taking the bait. "It'll be in Karaj tonight. And we've got more intercepts about the motel. I thought Dr. Malik would want to know."

"And?"

"There was no one there."

"What do you mean?"

"I'm saying, when the Iranians stormed the room, no one was in there," Eva said. "Just Dr. Malik's phone, some clothes, and a few overnight bags."

"Where's his family?"

"That's the thing," Eva said. "We have no idea."

David turned to tell Najjar the good news, but just then shots rang out, shattering a windshield beside them. Instinctively David hit the ground and pulled Najjar down with him between a Peugeot and a Chevy, dropping his phone as he did so. People started screaming and running for cover. He could hear Eva yelling, *What is that? What's going on?* but he had no time to respond. He grabbed the phone and jammed it into his pocket. Ordering Najjar to stay on the ground, he pulled the revolver and tried to get an angle on whoever was shooting at them. Was it one officer or two? Did they know who he was? Had they ID'd him and Najjar? He couldn't take that chance.

Two more shots rang out, blowing out the front windshield of the Peugeot. David again flattened himself to the ground and covered his head to protect himself from the flying glass. His knee was killing him as bits of glass ground into the already-injured joint. But there was nothing he could do about it now. As he opened his eyes again, he could see under the cars that someone was moving toward him. He got up into a crouch and took a peek. Another shot whizzed by him and ripped into the door of the Chevy.

Dead ahead, maybe ten yards away, was a garbage truck. David double-checked to make sure Najjar was okay, then made a break for the rear of the truck. With his wounded knee, he was slower than usual. His movement also drew more fire. But it also gave him a chance to see who was doing the shooting. The blue jacket and cap were the giveaway. This was a Tehran city police officer and he didn't look much older than himself, David thought.

Then the officer's voice crackled over the radio.

"Base, this is Unit 116. I'm at the crash site. One officer is down. I repeat,

one officer is down with multiple injuries. Witnesses say they saw someone steal the officer's service revolver. I'm currently pursuing two suspects on foot. Shots fired. Requesting immediate backup and helicopter support."

"Unit 116, this is Base—roger that. Backup en route. Stand by."

This was not good. David had to defend himself and his asset, which meant he had to move fast. He crept along the side of the garbage truck, hoping to outflank the officer from the right, then stopped when he heard the sounds of crunching glass just a few yards ahead.

David was confused. How could this guy be so close so quickly? It didn't make sense. A moment before, he'd been at least four cars over. Quickly wiping the sweat from one hand, then the other, David tried to steady his breathing and carefully choose his next move as the footsteps got closer and closer. Should he wait for the officer to come around the corner or seize the initiative and take the first shot?

Moving first was risky. He had seen only one officer, but there could be more. He could hear more sirens rapidly approaching. He couldn't wait. He was out of time. He took three steps and pivoted around the front of the truck, aimed the .38, and prepared to pull the trigger. But it was not the officer. It was a little girl, no more than six, shivering and scared. David, a millisecond away from firing, was horrified by how close he had come to killing a child.

How did she get here? Where is her mother?

Three more shots suddenly rang out. At least one round ricocheted off the grille of the truck. David dropped to the ground and covered the girl with his body. The pain in his knee was now excruciating, but his first priority had to be the girl. He quickly checked her over to make sure she hadn't been hit. She hadn't been, but she was definitely slipping into shock. Her eyes were dilated and she looked vacant. Her skin was clammy and cold. David took off his jacket and wrapped her in it, then got back in a crouch and tried to reacquire the officer in his sights.

But now there were two.

David had a clean shot at one of them, but he didn't dare fire from right over the child. So he broke right, hobbling as best he could for a blue sedan just ahead. Once again, gunfire erupted all around him, as did the screams of terrified motorists who had no idea what was going on or why. David barely got himself safely behind the sedan. He gritted his teeth and caught his breath, then popped his head up again to assess the situation.

To his shock, one of the officers had decided to ambush him. He was running straight toward David, while the other started running toward Najjar. David didn't hesitate. He raised the revolver and squeezed off two rounds. One shot hit the officer coming toward him in the stomach. The other hit him in the face. The man collapsed to the ground no more than six yards from David's position. David quickly pivoted to his left and fired twice more, missing the second officer but sending him sprawling for cover behind the garbage truck.

David could hear a helicopter approaching from the southeast. He had no time to lose. Adrenaline coursing through his system, he made his way to the first officer, grabbed the revolver from his hand, and sprinted toward the second officer. Racing through the maze of cars, he approached the garbage truck, stopped quickly, and glanced around the side. The second officer was waiting for him and got a shot off. David pulled back, waited a beat, then looked again and fired.

The round hit the officer in the shoulder. Screaming in pain, the man spun around but didn't drop. Instead, he began firing wildly at David, stumbling backward as he did.

David's first .38 was now out of bullets. Using his shirt, he wiped it clean of his fingerprints and tossed it aside. Then, with the second .38 in hand, he circled back to the other side of the garbage truck. Using the truck as his shield, he made a dash for where he had left Najjar.

But to his shock, Najjar wasn't there. The second officer was.

The man fired three more times. David could hear the bullets whizzing past his head. He dove left behind the Chevy, then flattened himself against the ground and fired under the car at the officer's feet. One of the shots was a direct hit. The man fell to the ground but refused to quit. David could hear him radioing for help and giving his superiors David's physical description. Then, before David realized what was happening, the officer crawled around the front of the Chevy, took aim at David's chest, and fired again.

David instinctively leaned right, but the shot grazed his left arm.

Still, with all the adrenaline in his system, he didn't feel a thing. Not yet, anyway. Instead, he righted himself, took aim, and squeezed off two more rounds at the officer's head, killing the man instantly.

David's mobile phone rang, but he ignored it. Blood was every-where. More sirens were approaching, as was the helicopter. They had to get out of there. They couldn't let themselves be caught. But Najjar was nowhere to be found.

Again his phone rang, but still David ignored it. Frantic, he looked for Najjar in, behind, and around car after car. Up and down the block he searched, to no avail. Now his phone vibrated. Furious, he checked the text message. It was from Eva.

EF: 3rd bldg on rt.

David suddenly got it. He glanced at the sky, thankful for Eva and her team watching his back from two hundred miles up. He made his way up the street to the third apartment building on the right, a four-story walk-up that had seen better days. A few bright orange geraniums in ceramic pots gave the place a look of pride and even some cheer, despite its faded glory. Why was Najjar in there? Who had taken him? There wasn't anyone standing outside the building.

David was out of time. How could he search every apartment before the whole area was flooded with police? But what other choice did he have? He pressed himself close to the dirty windows, thankful that the caked dirt from the city streets obscured any view from inside. His gun drawn, he slowly edged his way toward the entrance, wondering what had happened to the doorman. There was one at every apartment build-ing in this city; they were there supposedly for security but in reality spent their time smoking cigarettes and minding everyone's business. But there was no doorman here, only an empty chair on the front steps.

David did a quick peek into the lobby, fearing the worst.

Najjar was there, but he was not alone. On the marble floor next to him were the laptop and accessories. And in Najjar's arms was the six-year-old girl from the street. He was trying to keep her warm and telling her everything would be all right.

David began to breathe again. "Didn't I tell you not to move?"

"I didn't want her to get hit," Najjar said.

David wiped blood from his mouth. "We need to go."

"There's a Renault out front, and it's running," Najjar said.

"Where's the owner?"

"She jumped out to help me with the girl. I asked her to find a blanket, and she went upstairs to knock on doors."

David nodded. "Then we'd better move now, before she gets back."

88

It was beautiful—and theirs for the taking.

Not seeing anyone looking their way, David and Najjar bolted across the street and got in the platinum Renault coupe. David did a K-turn and swung the Renault around, and the two men were on their way.

With the exception of emergency vehicles approaching them, the northbound side of Azizi Boulevard was fairly clear. The disaster behind them prevented any vehicles from heading north and had no doubt backed up traffic for many kilometers. David turned west on Salehi, then took a right on the Jenah Highway. Their route to Karaj was going to be a bit circuitous and would take longer than he'd hoped, but at least they were finally on their way as Eva—using live imagery from a KH-12 Keyhole satellite—helped them navigate around police checkpoints, roadblocks, and further traffic.

David felt no sense of relief, however. They were far from safe, and he was under no illusions. His diversion hadn't worked as intended. He'd hoped to create a wreck that would shake the police car following them, lock up traffic behind him, allow him to steal a car that still worked, and let him slip away with Najjar unnoticed. He hadn't planned on becoming a cop killer in the process, and the notion haunted him. Everything had spiraled out of control. He'd had no other choice. He'd only fired in self-defense. But his mission was now in jeopardy.

If anyone could give an accurate description of him to the Tehran police . . .

David couldn't bear the implications of where that sentence led, and he dreaded his next conversation with Zalinsky, who, of course, had watched it all play out in real time. He needed to focus on something else. So as they left the city limits of Tehran, David turned to his passenger, who was sitting silently, his head down in prayer.

"Najjar, I actually have some good news."

Najjar looked up.

"I was about to tell you this earlier, but then everything started going crazy."

"What?"

"My team tells me your family wasn't in the motel room when the police got there."

Najjar sat up straight. "You're sure?"

"Absolutely. We've intercepted phone messages from the local police saying the place was empty when they raided it."

"Thank God," Najjar said. "Where are they?"

"We don't know," David said. "But I told you my people would do everything they can to find them, and they are."

"Thank you." Najjar's face brightened in an instant. "Thank you so much, Mr. Tabrizi. How can I ever repay you?"

"Your information is more than enough."

"But you're risking your life to help me, to protect me. I am very grateful."

"You're risking your life, too, Najjar." David kept driving for a few moments. "But you're welcome," he added quietly.

Najjar looked out the window, then suddenly turned back to David. "Could I have your phone?" he said. "I just had an idea. I want to try to call my wife."

"How?"

"She has a mobile phone."

"She does? You never said that."

"We thought she'd been captured," Najjar said. "There was no point. But now . . ."

David wasn't authorized to let a foreign national use his Agency phone. But there was a mobile phone plugged into the cigarette lighter right in front of them. "Here, use this one," he said.

Najjar punched the number and hit Send, and ten seconds later, he was talking to his wife, telling her how much he loved her, asking where she was, and relaying David's cryptic instructions on how they should get to Karaj and where they should meet.

David thought he had never seen a man so happy.

★ ★ ★ ★ ★

KARAJ, IRAN

At the safe house, David dressed Najjar's wounds.

Only then did he tend to his own and find some clothes for them to change into that reasonably approximated their sizes.

Najjar ate a little and fell fast asleep. David unlocked a vault stacked with communications gear and uploaded everything on Dr. Saddaji's laptop, external hard drive, and DVD-ROMs to Langley, with encrypted copies cc'd to Zalinsky and Fischer in Dubai. Then he typed up his report of all that had happened so far and e-mailed that encrypted file to Zalinsky and Fischer as well.

At six the next morning, word came that the plane had arrived. David woke Najjar, loaded the computer equipment into a duffel bag, and took the bag and Najjar to the garage downstairs, where he had parked the Renault. Ten minutes later, they arrived at the edge of the private airfield.

David pointed to the Falcon 200 business jet on the tarmac. "There's your ride," he said.

"You're kidding me," Najjar said.

"Have you ever flown on a private jet?" David asked.

"No, never."

"Well, it's about time. Your family is already onboard. My people are taking care of them as we speak. They're all waiting for you. You'd better hurry."

"What about you?" Najjar asked. "You're coming too, aren't you?"

"No."

"Why? You can't stay here."

"It's my job, and there's more to be done," David said.

"But if they find out you were connected to me, they will kill you."

"That is why I have to stay."

"I don't understand."

"Najjar, I could tell you, but then *I* would have to kill you," David said, smiling. "The things you don't know about me will have to remain unknown. But believe me, you and your family will be very happy in the U.S."

Najjar was quiet for a moment. "Sheyda would have liked to have met you," he said finally.

"I would have liked that too."

"Someday?" Najjar asked.

"Perhaps."

Najjar shook David's hand and held it for a moment, then got out of the car, duffel bag in hand, and ran for the plane.

David watched him go. He wished he could stay and watch the plane take off as the sun rose brilliantly in the east. But he couldn't afford the risk. He had to dispose of the Renault, steal another car, and get back to Tehran before Esfahani, Rashidi, or his team realized he was missing.

89

David's phone rang as he approached the outskirts of Tehran.

It was Esfahani, finally. "It's been a nightmare here. Have you heard about the manhunt for this traitor Malik?"

"I've been glued to the coverage. I just hope they catch him."

"And the man who was with him," Esfahani added. "They both deserve to be hanged."

David winced but played along. "Exactly."

"It's despicable what they've done. But that is not why I called. Things are moving very rapidly right now, as you can see. The Twelfth Imam's plane just took off for Riyadh a few minutes ago."

"I thought he was going to Mecca."

"He is, but I'm told he's going to meet with the king first. Then the two of them will go to the holy city tomorrow morning for the Mahdi's address to the world."

"I wish I could be there," David said.

"Me, too," Esfahani agreed. "But there's much work to be done. That's why I'm calling."

"What do you need?"

"The Mahdi wants an update on the satellite phones. Rashidi said he asked about them just before his flight took off. They want to know how quickly you can get them."

David hesitated. Again he knew Zalinsky and Eva could have the phones for him in a few days, but he couldn't let it seem too easy, or it might raise suspicion. "Mr. Esfahani, I'll do my best," he said, "but I can't make any promises. It was hard enough to get twenty, but you're asking for almost three hundred more."

"It's not me who is asking," Esfahani reminded him.

"I know, I know, and I promise you, I will do my best. But I'm going to need some time. And it's going to cost a lot of money."

"Don't let the cost be your concern, young man. Just get the phones, and I will make sure you get the money, plus a generous bonus for your troubles."

David knew the CIA wasn't going to let him keep any money, but he saw an opportunity, and he seized it. "No, I cannot take any more," he said. "You were too generous before, and I shouldn't have taken the money then."

"Don't be ridiculous. You earned it."

"But I don't want it," he insisted. "Please, I want this to be a pure act of worship for the Promised One, peace be upon him. Nothing else."

Esfahani paused, clearly taken aback by David's declining what would amount to a payoff north of a quarter of a million dollars.

"Allah will reward you, my friend."

"He already has."

With that, Esfahani explained that Mina had already booked David on a 6:45 Emirates flight that night to Dubai and then a 7:45 direct flight to Munich the following morning on Lufthansa.

"It was the best she could do on short notice," Esfahani apologized. "Everything else was booked. But at least we put you in first class."

"That's really not necessary. And I could have made my own arrangements."

"Believe me, I know," Esfahani said. "But it was Mr. Rashidi's idea. In fact, he insisted."

David thanked Esfahani and asked him to thank Rashidi. Then he hung up the phone and found a safe place to ditch the stolen car he was driving. He walked a few blocks to distance himself from the car, then caught a cab back to the Simorgh Hotel to pack. He didn't seem to be under any suspicion from Esfahani.

Meanwhile, he knew Eva and her team were tracking the satellite phones as well as the police radio traffic in Tehran. They weren't picking up any indications he was in danger either. If all continued to go as planned, he'd be sitting with Zalinsky and Fischer and briefing them by ten that night.

That was the good news. The bad news was that it was now Wednesday, March 2. It was becoming painfully obvious to David that there was no way he was going to make it back to Syracuse to see Marseille that weekend, much less by the following night. Even if he could physically make it there before the wedding was over, Zalinsky would never let him go. There was too much at stake. He had to be in Germany to get the phones and then head straight back to Tehran. There was no way around it. It was his job. It's what he had dedicated his life to doing.

But something in him grieved.

★ ★ ★ ★ ★

DUBAI, UNITED ARAB EMIRATES

The moment he landed in Dubai, David found a pay phone.

It was a depressing thought that he would have to call and let Marseille know he wouldn't be there. But it would be unforgivable to just stand her up, so he determined to contact her now before it became impossible.

Unfortunately, he got her voice mail. He wanted to talk to her, to hear her voice, to let her know how truly sorry he was. But she was probably teaching, and he didn't know when he'd get another chance to call. He had no choice. He left a message.

"Marseille? Hey, it's David. Look, I've only got a moment, but I'm calling to apologize. I feel terrible about this, but I'm not going to get back to Syracuse in time to see you. I'm very sorry. I'm in Budapest, working on a deal that's critical to my company, and let's just say, it's not going well. The client's asking for extensive revisions to the contract. We've been over it a million times. But my boss is pressing me to get this thing done. My company desperately needs the business, so, anyway, all that to say, I'm going to have to stay until it's done. I feel terrible—I really do. I've been looking forward to seeing you again and catching up with you and just telling you in person how sorry I am for all you've been going through. But I'm afraid it's not going to happen this weekend. I've got to go right now, but I promise to call you again the moment I can. I hope you're well. Bye."

David hung up the phone, wincing at all the lies he had just told. But at the moment, he honestly had no idea how to do it better. As he got his luggage, he checked his phone for e-mails. The first one he opened was from his father. His mother was going downhill fast.

Twenty minutes later, David stepped out of a cab at the regional office of Munich Digital Systems. The place was dark. All the staff had gone home for the day. But in a back office, Zalinsky and Fischer were waiting for him. Eva welcomed him back with a hug. To his surprise, Zalinsky did as well. They had a long night of debriefing ahead of them, but Zalinsky made it clear they were proud of him and were glad he was once again out of Iran safe and sound.

"Are Najjar and his family okay?" David asked as Eva poured each of them a cup of coffee.

"They're all fine," Zalinsky said, glancing at his watch. "In fact, they should be touching down in the U.S. in just a few minutes."

"Did you get all the files off Saddaji's laptop?"

"Absolutely," Eva said, taking her first sip. "It was a gold mine. We'll go over all that in a few minutes."

David sighed and slumped in a chair. His eyes felt gritty, and he'd definitely lost some weight.

"You must be exhausted," Zalinsky said.

"No—well, yeah, but it's not that," David said. "It's just . . ."

"What?"

"Nothing."

"Spit it out," Zalinsky ordered.

"No, it's nothing; let's just get started. We've got a lot to cover."

"David, what's the matter?"

So David took a deep breath and confessed, "It's my mom."

"Nasreen?" Zalinsky asked. "Why? What's wrong?"

"She has cancer. It's pretty serious. She's had it for a while."

Zalinsky and Fischer were quiet. David never talked about his personal life. They'd had no idea. But Zalinsky's relationship with the Shirazis went back more than thirty years.

"I'm so sorry," he said. "How long have you known?"

"Just a few weeks," David said. "They decided to tell me when I went back there to visit. But I just got an e-mail from my dad. He says she's taken a turn for the worse, and they don't know how long she'll be able to hang on."

Eva reached for David's hand.

"You need to get home," Zalinsky said.

"Yeah, right."

"No, you have to, David."

"Jack, how can I? Look at what's happening."

"It's your mother, David. You only get one. Go. It's okay."

90

David landed in Munich around noon on Thursday.

He was booked on a flight to Newark with a connection to Syracuse later that afternoon. But for now he sat in the Lufthansa business lounge, sending e-mails to his father and to Marseille and watching live coverage of the Twelfth Imam's address in Mecca.

The imagery was overwhelming. Saudi police estimated more than 14 million pilgrims had descended upon a city whose normal population was fewer than 2 million. Commentators were describing the event as the largest gathering of Muslims in history, larger even than the funeral of Ayatollah Khomeini, which had drawn nearly 12 million to Tehran in June 1989. To maintain order, a quarter of a million Saudi soldiers and police officers were present, and an estimated five thousand journalists and producers were there to capture the moment and transmit it to the world.

The Saudi king arrived first, cloaked in his standard white robes but with none of the pomp and circumstance that typically accompanied the monarch. To David's eyes, the man looked ashen. His hands trembled slightly as he read from a prepared text off a single sheet of paper.

The introduction was short and unmemorable. What would be remembered and discussed for quite some time, David was certain, was the image of the king of the House of Saud finishing his remarks, backing away from the microphone, and then bowing down to the point of lying prostrate, together with two dozen other Sunni and Shia emirs, clerics, and mullahs.

Then the Twelfth Imam emerged and took center stage. He was younger than David had expected—he looked to be around forty—and in contrast with the other men on the stage, he wore a black robe and a black turban, denoting that he was a descendant of Muhammad.

The crowd in Mecca erupted with an intensity David had never witnessed in any public event. The roar of the applause and cheering and the unabashed weeping was surprisingly intense, even coming through the TV speakers. He could only imagine what it sounded like in person.

And it went on and on. Sky News cut away after several minutes to a roundtable of three commentators in their London studio discussing the significance of the Mahdi's reemergence. But even then it was another ten or twelve minutes until the crowd calmed enough for the Mahdi to speak, and when he did, the people seemed transfixed.

"It is time," the Twelfth Imam said with a strong, booming voice that instantly seemed to command both reverence and respect. "The age of arrogance and corruption and greed is over. A new age of justice and peace and brotherhood has come. It is time for Islam to unite."

Again the crowd went wild.

"No longer do Muslims have the luxury of petty infighting and division. Sunnis and Shias must come together. It is time to create one Islamic people, one Islamic nation, one Islamic government. It is time to show the world that Islam is ready to rule. We will not be confined to geographical borders, ethnic groups, and nations. Ours is a universal message that will lead the world to the unity and peace the nations have thus far found elusive."

David pulled a pad and pen out of his briefcase and made notes. The Mahdi was calling for the re-creation of the caliphate, an Islamic empire ruled by one man, stretching from Pakistan in the east to Morocco in the west. It would never happen, but it made good theater.

"Cynics and skeptics abound," the Mahdi said. "But to them I say, it is time. Time for you to open your eyes and open your ears and open your hearts. It is time for you to see and hear and understand the power of Islam, the glory of Islam. And today, let this process of education begin. I have come to usher in a new kingdom, and today I announce to you that the governments of Iran, Saudi Arabia, and the Gulf States are joining together as one nation. This will form the core of the caliphate. My agents are in peaceful, respectful discussions with all the other governments of the region, and in short order we will be announcing our expansion."

David was stunned. The Saudis and the emirates both hated and feared the Iranians. But just as he wondered how they could possibly join forces, the Twelfth Imam explained.

"To those who would oppose us, I would simply say this: The caliphate will control half the world's supply of oil and natural gas, as well as the Gulf and the shipping lanes through the Strait of Hormuz. The caliphate will have the world's most powerful military, led by the hand of Allah. Furthermore, the caliphate will be covered by a nuclear umbrella that will protect the people from all evil. The Islamic Republic of Iran has successfully conducted a nuclear weapons test. Their weapons are now operational. They have just handed over command and control of these weapons to me. We seek only peace. We wish no harm against any nation. But make no mistake: any attack by any state on any portion of the caliphate will unleash the fury of Allah and trigger a War of Annihilation."

91

David needed to walk a little to clear his head.

He had spent Friday and Saturday with his parents in the hospital and had promised his father that he'd be back when visiting hours began at noon. But now, to his amazement, he was actually about to meet Marseille face-to-face. The thought both excited and terrified him at the same time.

Anxious to be on time, he got up early and drove his rental car to the hill where Syracuse University perched, finding the campus largely still asleep on this cold, quiet Sunday morning. He found a parking space on Crouse Avenue right away, got out, and began a brisk stroll through streets whose memories echoed from his past. Marseille would meet him in about forty-five minutes for an 8 a.m. breakfast at the University Sheraton, where she was staying. Then she'd be leaving to meet up with some friends from the wedding party for a 9:30 church service in the eastern suburb of Manlius. Her flight back to the West Coast left at one that afternoon. That gave them about an hour to talk.

It had been a long time since David had been on an American college campus. Marshall Street, the students' main drag, wasn't exactly charming, but somehow it had a worn-in feeling that seemed rather comforting to him at this moment. It was a slice of the familiar world he'd left long ago, though it wasn't really one that belonged to him anymore.

As he stepped over a break in the sidewalk and around a pile of trash—beer bottles and fast-food wrappers apparently left over from the night before—he flashed back to scenes of the delirious chaos in Syracuse whenever S.U.'s basketball team won a key game. He remembered once or twice when the school made it to the Final Four and his brothers took him to eat pizza with them at the Varsity and buy sweatshirts at one of the many shops on M Street. He used to love hanging out there with Azad and Saeed. It made him feel older, cooler, than he was.

As he walked the few short blocks toward the Sheraton, he tried to savor these memories, in part because he didn't want to think about a world on the edge of war. He wished he could dial back the clock to a time that was simpler and happier. Maybe that's why he was headed to breakfast with a woman whose memory had such a strong hold on him, a woman with whom he had longed to reconnect since he was only an adolescent.

David still had another fifteen minutes before breakfast, so he stepped into the Starbucks on the corner. The place was quiet but for the Wynton Marsalis jazz music playing in the background. He ordered a triple-shot latte and sat at a table in the corner, thankful it was too early for the place to be filled with students. He found himself wishing he'd brought a book, something to occupy him as he waited. He certainly didn't want to be early.

Finally it was time. He took a deep breath, crossed the street, entered the lobby of the Sheraton, and was soon sitting by himself at a table in Rachel's Restaurant with a new cup of coffee. He was starting to worry that he might get a little too jumpy with all this caffeine.

And suddenly, there she was, carrying a red scarf and black wool coat and sporting a turtleneck sweater to ward off the late-winter chill. Wearing faded jeans with a leather backpack thrown over her shoulder, she could have been a graduate student herself. She was even more beautiful than he remembered, especially those large green eyes.

She walked in, spotted him, and gave him a shy smile. He stood to greet her and was grateful when she gave him a quick hug.

"David, it's really you!"

"Hello, Marseille," he replied with a warm smile.

In another few minutes they had ordered—eggs Benedict for him, blueberry pancakes for her. She had settled in across from him with her own cup of coffee and was looking suddenly hesitant. He glanced around the warmly lit room, noticed the waitstaff beginning to set up the tables for Sunday brunch, and was glad they were in a quiet corner, away from the preparations.

He spoke first. "It's really good to see you, Marseille. I was sorry to hear about your father."

"It's been a difficult year. But you know, things have been difficult for a long time. How's your mom doing?"

"She's a fighter, but I'm not sure how much longer she has. Thanks for sending her flowers, by the way. It meant a lot to her—and my dad, too."

Neither of them spoke for several moments. Then David said, "It must have been hard on you, losing your dad. What happened?"

She smiled sadly and looked away for a moment before meeting David's eyes again. "I guess he never really recovered from my mom's death. You know we moved to Oregon right away. He believed he'd never be able to raise me alone. He wanted me to have at least a grandmother in my life, and he was wise in that. A girl needs a woman's touch as she goes through life. My grandma helped me through a lot. . . ."

She trailed off, and David remembered reading that her grandmother was suffering from Alzheimer's and living in a nursing home.

He shifted back to her father. "Did your dad end up teaching out there? He was so brilliant. He'd been a professor at Princeton, right?"

"He was, but no, he never taught in Portland. He tried to write articles for some newspapers and Middle Eastern journals. But he couldn't ever keep up with the deadlines. He'd spend months researching and then quit after writing half an article. He seemed haunted. He'd tell me he was a cursed man, that everyone was against him somehow. In the last few years, he lived in another world. He'd mutter things in Farsi even, and he'd look at me as though he was wondering who I was."

"That must have been awful for you."

"It was sometimes. But on other days, my dad seemed his old self, and we'd go for long walks or bicycle rides. Those were wonderful, but he was unpredictable. Lots of days he'd simply stay in his room. But I didn't want to talk about my dad right away. I wanted to apologize first and try to explain."

"You don't need to apologize, Marseille. It's been a long time. We were just kids."

"I know, but we had a real connection; I've always believed that."

She paused and looked at him as if hoping he wouldn't contradict her. He didn't, and when she spoke again, she seemed to have a bit more strength in her voice. "I wanted to reach out to you. You have no idea how much I wanted to talk with you and see you again. But my father absolutely forbade it. He was furious with you, David."

"Why?"

"Because of what happened between you and me in Canada. He would rant against the Iranians—all Iranians—that they'd caused him nothing but heartbreak all his life. What you and I did . . . we shouldn't have let ourselves go so far. I don't blame you, but my father did. He blamed you for ruining my life."

"Why did you tell him? I mean, I agree, it was wrong. But wouldn't that be hard for a father to hear?"

Marseille looked down at her hands resting on the table. She seemed to be gathering courage again. "I didn't tell him about us, David. Not at first. I didn't have to. After a few months, it became kind of obvious."

92

"I was pregnant."

David couldn't believe what he was hearing. "You have a child?"

She shook her head. "The pregnancy was difficult from the beginning. I was so young. . . . Anyway, I lost the baby when I was three months along."

David was silent.

"I know this must be shocking for you. And I know that saying I'm sorry now for not telling you—for not being in touch at all—can't make up for it. It's just that my world fell apart, you know? I was living on the other side of the country with a dad who was spinning out of control. I had lost my mom, and I had lost you, and then I was sick all the time. Then when I lost the baby, too . . . These are all just excuses, I know. But by then so much time had gone by, I was afraid to reach out to you. I told myself it wasn't as important as it was."

David didn't move as the words poured out from Marseille. He wasn't sure what to say. He noticed she had tears in her eyes and her face showed a hint of fear. He didn't want that.

"I'm not upset with you, Marseille. I just . . . I can't believe you've gone through all this alone. I wish I could have helped you somehow."

"Thank you. That means a lot. But I don't expect you to forgive me so easily. It wasn't right to keep you in the dark. You must have been hurting too, wondering why I wouldn't respond. But you are very kind."

Some light seemed to return to her eyes. He was still puzzled by a lot, but at least he could understand now why she had cut off all contact.

She had to because her father had lumped him and his family into the growing list of Iranians who had supposedly poisoned his life. But he wondered what Marseille wanted from him now. Just to reconnect? to be forgiven?

The food arrived, but he couldn't eat, and neither could she.

"Is there any way I can help you now, Marseille? Is there anything you need?"

She was quiet for a while, picking at her food. "When Dad died, it took me a while to go through his things," she said at last. "His office was a disaster, and I was tempted to just gather it all up and take it to the trash heap. But I knew somehow that I should go through everything slowly and read carefully. There was so much about my parents that I didn't know. Dad never spoke about my mom after 9/11, and I never even got the chance to tell him what I'd learned from you about their escape from Iran with your parents."

David noticed she still hadn't told him how her father had died, though he certainly didn't blame her.

Marseille reached into her bag and pulled out an envelope, unwrapping the string around it and setting it on the table. "My dad kept journals—did I ever tell you that? He wrote a lot of journals over the years. Even though there were large gaps over time, I learned a lot. My parents were pack rats, and their files went back into the sixties. Look, this is a medical record from their time in Iran. See, it's issued from the Canadian Embassy. My mom miscarried their first child during the Revolution."

"I never knew that," David said.

"The records are incomplete, but I think she was badly injured before they escaped. It doesn't seem like it was a normal miscarriage. I think that's why they never wanted to tell me about Iran. It was too painful for them."

David remembered the quiet, normal home on the Jersey Shore that he had visited so long ago. What a difference it must have seemed to the Harpers from the craziness of Tehran.

"It makes sense now," she continued. "That's why they stayed at the Canadian Embassy so long. It wasn't just to come up with an escape plan. My mom had to heal enough to travel. I wish I could have talked to them about it all. I wish I could hug my mother. I feel like, in some ways, I never really knew them. You know?"

Marseille looked so wistful and seemed so fragile; David wanted to hold her, to protect her. But he had no right to do it. And anyway, he couldn't go back to those days when life was normal. Things weren't normal anymore. Not for him. And soon, maybe not for anyone. Right now, here in this place with Marseille, he could almost forget what his task really was. Then she interrupted his thoughts, and he realized he'd been silent for too long.

"David? Are you okay? This is strange, isn't it? My just showing up and dumping all this information on you. I'm sorry. It's just that my friend insisted I come here to be in her wedding. It's so . . . I don't know, random that she grew up near Syracuse. I couldn't imagine coming to your home-town without looking for you. And with my father's death and everything I've been reading in his files . . . I just . . . needed to see you."

"I'm glad," he said. "I've thought about you often, even when I didn't want to. I always wished things had turned out differently between us. But I thought it was all gone. Those few days were so amazing, and then everything just caved in. I went home, back here, back to high school, and you were gone, and the world was a different place. It's never been the same again."

"I know," she answered quietly. Now it was her turn to seem lost in her thoughts, lost in old memories.

David wasn't sure what else to say or where to go from here. Their food was cold, and it was almost time for her to go. But he didn't want her to leave. He wanted to find a way to ask her to stay longer in Syracuse. He wanted to pick up where they had left off and pretend everything that had happened in between hadn't happened at all. He wanted to forget Iran, forget MDS, forget Eva Fischer and Jack Zalinsky, forget Esfahani and the Twelfth Imam and the threat of world war. He wanted to call his mother and tell her he was ready to settle down, stay in central New York, marry Marseille, and give her some grandchildren. She'd be thrilled. Maybe it would give her a new reason to fight for life and survive. Was it all so impossible?

Suddenly Marseille came back from her daydream and interrupted his. "David?"

"Yes?"

"There's one other thing I wanted to tell you about my father. I guess it's okay to tell you. I haven't said anything to anyone about it yet, and somehow it seems like you're the only one in the world who might care."

"What is it?" David asked. He was half-listening and half desperately scrambling to come up with a way to run off with her. Would she go with him if he asked?

"I always thought my dad worked for the State Department—you know, a political analyst or whatever. He spoke Farsi, and I thought he translated and analyzed news reports for our government. But I found something in his papers that makes me believe he never worked for the State Department at all. I don't even think my mom knew. David, he was in the CIA all along. Look at this."

She moved her chair next to his and showed him a document on CIA stationery. It was a letter of commendation for Charles Harper for valor under fire in Iran. It mentioned the crisis of 1979 and thanked him for his crucial work for the Agency. And it was signed, *Tom Murray, Director of the Near East Division.*

"Wow, this is really something," David said.

"It is, isn't it?" Marseille said. "It's been so long, and now that he's gone, I suppose it's okay for people to know. Nobody back in Oregon ever really knew my dad. There's no one to share this with. But you knew him. Your family was part of our past—a crucial part—which is why I wanted to tell you. I don't know if he continued with the CIA when he came to the States. I find myself trying to remember long trips he took when I was growing up. 'Research trips,' he called them. I thought they were for his books and lectures at the college. I just wonder what my dad's life was really like."

David wondered too, intrigued by this striking new connection between the two of them and feeling terrible that he couldn't tell her what he was doing and why. But at that moment, his phone buzzed in his pocket. He pulled it out and recognized Zalinsky's number on the caller ID.

"Sorry; it's my boss," he said and took the call. "Hey, it's me. Can I call you right back? I'm in the middle of something."

Zalinsky's voice was somber. "David, you need to get somewhere private and call me in the next five minutes. Do you understand?"

"Absolutely. I will."

David clicked the phone off and glanced apologetically at Marseille. He hated to lie to her, but he had no choice. "That was my boss; things are not good. I'm afraid I have to go."

"Seems like a very stressful job." She smiled. "I think I'll stick to my first graders."

"Yeah, well, it's not always like this. It's just a particularly urgent moment for us. I can't believe the timing of all this." David ran his fingers through his hair in frustration. "Marseille, I'm going to take a risk here. I want you to know that I'd like nothing more than to sit here with you for hours, take a long walk with you, even fly back to Oregon with you, for that matter. I don't want to be cut off from you again. I'm not sure how to even put it into the right words. But believe me, I'm going to wrap up this business in Europe and then, if it's okay with you, I'd like to come to wherever you are. There's so much more to talk about, wouldn't you say?"

"I would," Marseille said, clearly moved by his earnest words. She reached out and touched his hand, and his fingers closed around hers.

"I've hardly even asked anything about you," she said. "I've been just talking nonstop, I'm afraid. There are so many questions I have about you and your work and your family."

He held her hand tightly for a moment, then gave her a slight squeeze and let go. He stood, and she did too. "I have to go."

"I know. It's okay."

He slid some cash under his water glass to pay for the meals, and she thanked him for breakfast.

"I'm not sure how long I'll need to be over there. It's going to be a bit all-consuming for a while. But I'll be in touch as soon as I can. I promise."

"I look forward to it."

And then he gave her a long hug and walked away from Marseille

Harper, out of the restaurant, through the lobby, and into the crisp morning air.

★ ★ ★ ★ ★

Zalinsky got right to the point.

"I just got back to Washington. We need you back in the game. The Israelis want to talk, and I want you in that meeting. Plus, Najjar Malik has given us some critical leads that someone needs to follow up on quickly. How is your mother?"

"Jack, my mother is dying right now. I need to sit with her, at least for a few more days, and then there may be a funeral. I owe her that. You said so yourself."

"Listen, you can probably get back there in a day or two. But right now, you are needed here for some things."

"What things?"

"I can't talk about it on the phone. You need to be in Washington by noon tomorrow."

"Jack, please, don't make this harder than it is."

"David, this isn't a request. It's an order."

"From who? Tom Murray?"

"No."

"The director?"

"No."

"Then who?"

"The president."

A NOTE FROM THE AUTHOR

In an effort to create a realistic setting for this story, I have borrowed from multiple real-world sources so that the people, places, and events my fictional characters experience could be as close to reality as possible. Following is a list of some of these sources.

The dialogue in chapter 2 between an announcer for Radio Tehran and a spokeswoman for the Iranian students who seized the U.S. Embassy in Tehran is based on the actual dialogue of this nature on November 4, 1979, the day of the seizure. The student communiqués to the world used in this chapter are excerpts of the actual communiqués issued that day. See Massoumeh Ebtekar (as told to Fred A. Reed), *Takeover in Tehran: The Inside Story of the 1979 U.S. Embassy Capture*, pages 69-71.

The *U.S. News & World Report* article quoted in chapter 25 is real. It was written by David E. Kaplan and entitled "Not Your Father's CIA." The article appeared in the November 20, 2006, issue of the magazine, though I have used it as though it appeared in a January 2002 issue.

In Chapter 32, I mention an actual *Wall Street Journal* story, "Iran's Web Spying Aided by Western Technology," written by Christopher Rhoades and Loretta Chao. The story ran June 22, 2009.

In the same chapter, I cite an actual *New York Times* story, "Revolutionary Guard Buys Stake in Iran Telecom," published in the "Deal Book" section, edited by Andrew Ross Sorkin. The story ran in the September 28, 2009, edition.

The story from the *Times* of London entitled "Discovery of UD3 Raises Fears over Iran's Nuclear Intentions" mentioned in chapter 41 was written by Catherine Philip and ran on December 14, 2009.

In Chapter 43, I quote from an actual book, *The Awaited Savior,* by Baqir al-Sadr and Murtada Mutahhari. It is published by Islamic Seminary Publications in Karachi, Pakistan, and can be found online at http://www.al-islam.org/awaited/index.htm.

The physical descriptions of the Twelfth Imam and the depictions of the signs that are said to precede his arrival are taken from various traditions and hadiths. Numerous sources describe these signs, including the Web site www.awaitedmahdi.com.

In Chapter 62, I excerpt a monograph written by Mehdi Khalaji and published by the Washington Institute for Near East Policy. It is entitled *Apocalyptic Politics: On the Rationality of Iranian Policy.* You can find it at http://www.washingtoninstitute.org/pubPDFs/PolicyFocus79Final.pdf.

The Thuraya satellite phones mentioned in chapters 54 and 63 are real; the details and specifications were drawn directly from the company's Web site, http://www.ts2.pl/en/News/1/24.

The TV news report on the Hamadan earthquake in chapter 68 was adapted from an actual CNN report during the Haiti earthquake. See "Haiti appeals for aid; official fears 100,000 dead after earthquake," January 13, 2010, http://www.cnn.com/2010/WORLD/americas/01/13/haiti.earthquake/index.html.

The words the Twelfth Imam uses when describing Jews as the descendants of "apes and pigs" (chapter 70) and when giving instructions about decapitation and ripping his enemies' hearts from their chests (chapter 84) are based on an actual communiqué issued by a radical Islamic jihadist group based in Gaza known as Jama'at Al-Tawhid wa'l-Jihad. The message was issued on March 20, 2010. It was picked up, translated, and reported by the Jerusalem-based Middle East Media Research Institute. See http://www.memri.org/report/en/0/0/0/0/0/0/4060.htm.

In Chapter 74, I cite an actual *New York Times* article, "North Koreans Say They Tested a Nuclear Device," written by David Sanger. The story ran on October 9, 2006.

Readers who are familiar with the geographic layout and landmarks in Tehran may notice that I've taken a few liberties with the locations of certain buildings such as the Imam Khomeini Grand Mosala Mosque. All other physical descriptions of buildings, street layout, and the surrounding areas are based on research and are as factual as possible.

ACKNOWLEDGMENTS

Thank You, Lord, for letting me live and write, and thanks for all the people You have given me as friends and allies in life and in publishing. I do not deserve them, but I am deeply grateful for each and every one of them. Please bless them beyond anything they can hope for, dream of, or imagine.

Thank you, Lynn, for being my amazing and wonderful wife of twenty years and my best friend for even longer. Thank you so, so much for loving me and encouraging me and praying for me and doing life with me all these years. I don't deserve you, but I'm so grateful for you! I love you so much.

Thank you, Caleb, Jacob, Jonah, and Noah, for your humor, insight, encouragement, and strength, and for all the joy you bring to your mom and me with your individual personalities.

Thank you to our wonderful families—my mom and dad, Len and Mary Jo Rosenberg; June "Bubbe" Meyers; the Rebeiz family; the Scoma family; the Meyers family; and the Urbanski family—for all your love and prayers.

Thank you to Edward and Kailea Hunt, Tim and Carolyn Lugbill, Steve and Barb Klemke, Fred and Sue Schwien, Tom and Sue Yancy, John and Cheryl Moser, Jeremy and Angie Grafman, Nancy Pierce, Dave and Barb Olsson, Jeff and Naomi Cuozzo, Lance and Angie Emma, Lucas and Erin Edwards, Chung and Farah Woo, Dr. T. E. Koshy and family, and all our other friends and allies with The Joshua Fund and November Communications, Inc., for all your wise counsel, hard work, and faithful friendship.

Thank you to General Boykin, Hormoz Shariat, and Tom Doyle for all the research, experience, and advice you have provided for this and other books.

Thank you to Mark Taylor, Jeff Johnson, Ron Beers, Karen Watson, Jeremy Taylor, Jan Stob, Cheryl Kerwin, Dean Renninger, Beverly Rykerd, and all the amazing and talented people on the Tyndale House Publishing team for helping launch this new series.

Thank you to Scott Miller, my trusted agent at Trident Media Group, for your continued great advice and valued friendship.

ABOUT THE AUTHOR

Joel C. Rosenberg is the *New York Times* best-selling author of five novels—*The Last Jihad, The Last Days, The Ezekiel Option, The Copper Scroll,* and *Dead Heat*—and two nonfiction books, *Epicenter* and *Inside the Revolution,* with some 2 million total copies in print. *The Ezekiel Option* received the Gold Medallion award as the "Best Novel of 2006" from the Evangelical Christian Publishers Association. Joel is the producer of two documentary films based on his nonfiction books. He is also the founder of The Joshua Fund, a nonprofit educational and charitable organization to mobilize Christians to "bless Israel and her neighbors in the name of Jesus" with food, clothing, medical supplies, and other humanitarian relief.

As a communications advisor, Joel has worked with a number of U.S. and Israeli leaders, including Steve Forbes, Rush Limbaugh, Natan Sharansky, and Benjamin Netanyahu. As an author, he has been interviewed on hundreds of radio and TV programs, including ABC's *Nightline, CNN Headline News,* FOX News Channel, The History Channel, MSNBC, *The Rush Limbaugh Show, The Sean Hannity Show,* and *Glenn Beck.* He has been profiled by the *New York Times,* the *Washington Times,* the *Jerusalem Post,* and *World* magazine. He has addressed audiences all over the world, including those in Israel, Iraq,

Jordan, Egypt, Turkey, Russia, and the Philippines. He has also spoken at the White House, the Pentagon, and to members of Congress.

In 2008, Joel designed and hosted the first Epicenter Conference in Jerusalem. The event drew two thousand Christians who wanted to "learn, pray, give, and go" to the Lord's work in Israel and the Middle East. Subsequent Epicenter Conferences have been held in San Diego (2009); Manila, Philippines (2010); and Philadelphia (2010). The live webcast of the Philadelphia conference drew some thirty-four thousand people from more than ninety countries to listen to speakers such as Israeli Vice Prime Minister Moshe Yaalon; pastors from the U.S., Israel, and Iran; Lt. General (ret.) Jerry Boykin; Kay Arthur; Janet Parshall; Tony Perkins; and Mosab Hassan Yousef, the son of one of the founders of Hamas who has renounced Islam and terrorism and become a follower of Jesus Christ and a friend of both Israelis and Palestinians.

The son of a Jewish father and a Gentile mother, Joel is an evangelical Christian with a passion to make disciples of all nations and teach Bible prophecy. A graduate of Syracuse University with a BFA in filmmaking, he is married, has four sons, and lives near Washington, D.C.

To visit Joel's weblog—or sign up for his free weekly "Flash Traffic" e-mails—please visit www.joelrosenberg.com.

Please also visit these other Web sites:

www.joshuafund.net
www.epicenterconference.com

and Joel's "Epicenter Team" and the Joel C. Rosenberg public profile page on Facebook.

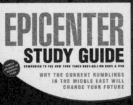

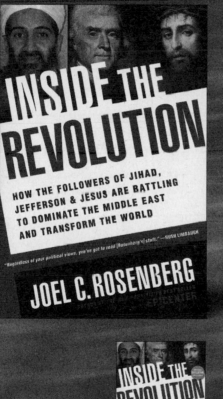
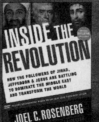
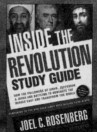

have you visited
tyndalefiction.com
lately?

Only there can you find:

→ books hot off the press

→ first chapter excerpts

→ inside scoops on your
favorite authors

→ author interviews

→ contests

→ fun facts

→ and much more!

*Sign up
for your **free**
newsletter!*

Visit us today at: tyndalefiction.com

Tyndale fiction does more than entertain.

→ *It touches the heart.*

→ *It stirs the soul.*

→ *It changes lives.*

That's why Tyndale is so committed to being first in fiction!

TYNDALE
FICTION